Everyone told Chloe

not to trust a man like Ben.

But one touch is all it takes

to open her mind—

and her heart....

continued . . .

Praise for the contemporary novels of Catherine Anderson

Always in My Heart
"Intense emotion and deeply felt relationships."
—Jayne Ann Krentz

Sweet Nothings
"Catherine Anderson is an author with an amazing expertise with words." —*Romantic Times*

Phantom Waltz
"Anderson departs from traditional romantic stereotypes in this poignant, contemporary tale of love that transcends all boundaries . . . romantic through and through." —*Publishers Weekly*

Seventh Heaven
"No one writes riveting emotion quite like Catherine Anderson. Her talent for delving into rich, emotional depths is unmatched." —*Romantic Times* (4½ stars)

Baby Love
"Her stories are consistently magical and filled with deep emotion." —*Romantic Times* (4½ stars)

Forever After
"Literary magic . . . heartwarming humor, beautifully handled sexual tension, and exceptionally well-developed characters add to this poignant, compelling story of wounded protagonists and their ultimate healing through the power of love." —*Library Journal*

Only by
Your Touch

Only by
Your Touch

Catherine Anderson

A SIGNET BOOK

SIGNET
Published by New American Library, a division of
Penguin Putnam Inc., 375 Hudson Street,
New York, New York 10014, U.S.A.
Penguin Books Ltd, 80 Strand,
London WC2R 0RL, England
Penguin Books Australia Ltd, 250 Camberwell Road,
Camberwell, Victoria 3124, Australia
Penguin Books Canada Ltd, 10 Alcorn Avenue,
Toronto, Ontario, Canada M4V 3B2
Penguin Books (N.Z.) Ltd, Cnr Rosedale and Airborne Roads,
Albany, Auckland 1310, New Zealand

Penguin Books Ltd, Registered Offices:
Harmondsworth, Middlesex, England

First published by Signet, an imprint of New American Library,
a division of Penguin Putnam Inc.

First Printing, April 2003
10 9 8 7 6 5 4 3 2 1

 REGISTERED TRADEMARK—MARCA REGISTRADA

Printed in the United States of America

PUBLISHER'S NOTE
This is a work of fiction. Names, characters, places, and incidents either are
the product of the author's imagination or are used fictitiously, and any resem-
blance to actual persons, living or dead, business establishments, events, or
locales is entirely coincidental.

This book is dedicated to my Shoshone ancestors who once ranged the forests and high deserts of Central Oregon. Some would say, "Suvate," it is finished, but for those of us who remember in our hearts, the story will never end. The People whisper in the wind to us of beautiful things, and the land they so loved is a legacy always to be treasured.

ACKNOWLEDGMENTS

I wish to thank our local veterinarian, Gordon Pickering, for sharing a bit of his knowledge with me about parvovirus and its prevention and treatment. He is greatly concerned because many people don't realize that their puppies are not automatically immune to disease after receiving their first shots. If you have a puppy, please get a full round of immunizations for your pet and consult with your veterinarian before you begin his or her social training.

Chapter One

In the three weeks since Chloe Evans had moved to the mountain resort community of Jack Pine, Oregon, she'd lost count of the times she'd driven by the feed store to let her son, Jeremy, watch the animated scarecrow pitch hay and the old farmer milk his cow. Like all the buildings in the business district, the barnlike structure was quaint and charming. Flanked by towering Ponderosa pines, the store had weathered cedar siding complemented by forest-green trim.

Jeremy grinned as Chloe jockeyed the Honda into a parking space. His sherry-brown eyes danced with excitement. "Are we *really* going in there, Mom?"

"We sure are." Chloe pushed ineffectually at the wispy auburn curls that had escaped her French braid. "Sue says this store has the best selection of puppy food." She narrowed an eye at her son. "You *do* still have our list, I hope."

Jeremy waved a crumpled piece of paper. "Hurry, Mom!" He threw open his door. "Rowdy's home all alone. After being 'bandoned, he might think he got left again."

"Whoa!" Relieved to see her son acting like a normal little boy for a change, Chloe leaned over to unfasten his belt. "You can't go anywhere still strapped in. And no crossing the parking lot without holding my hand."

"Aw, Mom."

"Aw, Jeremy."

"I'm not a baby anymore. I won't get hit by a car."

Chloe grabbed her purse as she climbed out on her side. "As of yesterday, I officially became an old lady, remember? Maybe I need you to hold *my* hand."

"You're not that old."

Chloe felt old. She'd never expected to be divorced and starting over at thirty. Taking Jeremy's hand, she swung her arm and forced a jaunty bounce into her step. That chapter of her life was closed, she reminded herself. She and her son were making a brand-new start. That was what she needed to think about, this delightful little town and the wonderful future it offered them.

With so many wealthy tourists flocking to the area all year long, there was a lot of money to be made in Jack Pine, and if Chloe's father had his way, she would have a piece of the action someday. In three years, her folks planned to pull up stakes in Washington and join her, using the proceeds from the sale of their home to buy a business. He claimed he needed something to keep him busy after he retired, but Chloe wasn't fooled. Once the business was purchased, he would inform her that he was unable to handle the workload, and he'd plead with her to save him from financial ruin by taking over.

My dad. Just thinking about him made Chloe smile. In many ways, Mike Pritchard had been all that had kept her sane during the difficult times with Roger, a living reminder that there were a lot of good men left in the world. Too often over the last year, Chloe had found it difficult to remember that.

Breathing deeply of the mountain breeze, Chloe focused on the whimsical, fairy-tale feeling of Jack Pine. At the edge of the parking lot, a red sleigh parked under a tree bore a dusty sign on one its runners that read, SLEIGH RIDES, $15. Chloe could almost see the small town blanketed with snow, with all the rustic buildings sporting icicles along their eaves.

Across the road was the Christmas Village, a darling little log structure with a shake roof and frosting-pink gingerbread trim, its twin bay windows chock-full of twinkling lights and holiday decorations. Christmas being her favorite season, Chloe couldn't wait to browse for at least an hour in there.

That was for later, though. Today she had to make this shopping expedition special. It wasn't every day that a small boy got a new puppy, after all.

Jeremy beamed. "Thank you, Mom," he said for at least the twentieth time. "I know we can't 'ford a puppy right now."

"Sure we can. Remember all those pop bottles and cans we've been picking up off the side of the road? Tomorrow night while I'm at work, you can put them in plastic bags, and we'll go redeem them on Friday."

"Will we make a lot of money?"

Not by a long shot, Chloe thought dismally, but she wasn't about to tell Jeremy that. "Enough to afford puppy chow and chew toys." She bent over to plant a kiss on his forehead. "No worries. Okay?"

" 'Kay." Jeremy suddenly braked to a stop, his gaze fixed on something high and to Chloe's right. In a faint, tremulous voice, he asked, "What's that?"

Chloe's heart kicked hard against her ribs. Perched atop the cab of a dusty green pickup, a silver-and-black wolf stared at them with feral yellow eyes. Instinctively, Chloe moved her son behind her and retreated a step. It was only a dog, she assured herself. Malamute huskies had a wolfish look. This animal was probably a malamute mix.

"Nice doggy," Chloe said. Normally she got along well with canines, but the ones she'd encountered had never stared at her with a hungry look in their eyes or been sitting on top of pickup trucks, poised to leap. "Good boy," she trilled as she shoved Jeremy back another step.

The dog growled low in its throat. Getting a tight grip on her purse in case she had to use it as a weapon, Chloe continued backing away. *One step, two.* Jeremy clung to her leg, the clutch of his hands conveying his terror.

"It's just a dog, sweetie. Don't be afraid."

"He's *big,* Mom, and he looks mean."

When Chloe had put some distance between them and the dog, she walked calmly to the boardwalk, where she felt marginally safer, and hurried toward the front doors. An overhead bell jangled as they pushed inside.

Still clinging to her slacks, Jeremy, his eyes as round as quarters, went up on his tiptoes to peek out the door window. The wolf stared through the glass at them with its eerie yellow gaze.

"Big bully," Chloe muttered.

She wanted to find the dog's owners and give them a piece of her mind for allowing such a vicious animal off its leash in a public place.

"He's scary." Jeremy finally let go of Chloe's leg.

"I know." Mustering a smile, Chloe swatted at the wrinkles in her slacks, where Jeremy's damp fingers had bunched the twill. "I doubt he would bite anyone, though. Mean dogs aren't usually left loose like that."

Jeremy's eyes went wide. "Uh-oh." He held out his hands. "I dropped our list."

Chloe looked out the window and saw the crumpled piece of paper fluttering across the parking lot. Ruffling Jeremy's hair, she said, "I think I can remember what we need."

"Puppy chow," he reminded her.

"Oh, yes, definitely."

"And dishes, Mom. We can't forget those."

"And puppy biscuits."

"And a chew toy so he doesn't eat our shoes."

Taking her son's hand, Chloe headed for the merchandise area of the feed store. Open wooden barrels lined both walls of the foyer. Being from Seattle, she found the earthy scents strange and unfamiliar, but placards on the barrels identified the commodities as barley, oats, and alfalfa pellets.

As they moved up the center aisle, Chloe saw an older woman with sandy hair working behind the counter. Wiping her hands on her green bib apron, the woman asked, "Can I help you folks find somethin'?"

"We're looking for the puppy food," Jeremy informed her.

"Puppy food, huh? Sounds to me like somebody just got a dog."

"Yup," Jeremy said proudly. "A golden 'triever."

"Ah." The clerk nodded. "That's a very popular breed."

"Do you have any chew toys?" Jeremy asked.

"Aisle five." To Chloe, the clerk added, "You'll find the dog food there as well. The carts are by the front windows."

"Thanks."

Tugging Jeremy along beside her, Chloe set off for the dog-food section. With her gaze lifted to read the overhead signs, she wasn't watching where she was going as she rounded the end of an aisle, and she ran face-first into what felt like a cement wall. She lost her grip on her son and her purse. Lipsticks, pens, car keys, and loose coins spilled over the floor as she staggered to catch her balance.

Large, capable hands clamped over her shoulders to keep her from falling. "Are you all right?" a deep voice asked.

"I'm fine." Chloe was so jarred by the impact that she couldn't focus for a moment. She couldn't believe she'd barreled into someone. "I'm so sorry." She realized she was apologizing to a shirt button, broke off, and located the face that went with the chest and shoulders. "I should have been paying attention."

"That makes two of us. I didn't mean to mow you down like that."

His voice was a rich, vibrant baritone with a raspy edge. Even with the brim of a brown Stetson dipping low to shadow his face, she could see that his features were striking. High, sharp cheekbones underscored eyes so clear and intense a blue, they were startling in contrast to his dark skin and jet-black brows. Deep creases slashed his lean cheeks, bracketing a perfectly shaped mouth that might have looked hard if not for the sensual fullness of the lower lip. He had a strong, angular jaw, and his cheek muscle bunched and rippled, giving him the look of a man with turbulent emotions roiling just beneath the surface.

"Are you sure you're not hurt?"

"No, no, I'm—fine."

The collar of his blue shirt lay open at the throat, revealing a circlet of cobalt beads, from which was suspended a crude stone medallion with a star burst etched on the face. Chloe had never seen anything quite like it. Slipping free of his grasp, she bent to collect her things.

When he crouched to help, she said, "Oh, no, please. I can manage."

Ignoring her protest, he began picking up stuff, a blur of blue shirt and sun-bronzed skin as he shoved items in her bag. He had the hands of a man who labored outdoors, callused at the palm, with rough ridges capping his knuckles. The sleeves of his shirt were folded back to reveal thick, sinewy forearms with only a sparse dusting of dark hair.

Low in her abdomen, Chloe felt a quickening. It had been so long since she had experienced the sensation that it took her a moment to realize it was sexual attraction. Surprised at herself and more than a little unsettled, she forced her attention back to the task at hand.

As the mother of a small boy, she had developed a bad habit of carrying a little of everything in her purse, not to mention all the little treasures that Jeremy had given her—pretty rocks, a wilted violet, a ring he'd made from braided pine needles. The collection was a junky-looking mess.

When the stranger picked up an unwrapped peppermint candy with more hair on it than stripes, Chloe wished the floor planks would separate and swallow her. His hard mouth twitched as he dropped the candy back in her purse along with an emergency tampon whose wrapper had nearly disintegrated.

"Thank you," she said when the mess was finally cleared away.

"No problem." Still hunkered at her eye level, he nudged up the brim of his hat to regard her with unsmiling intensity. "I just hope I didn't hurt you."

Chloe waved a hand as she pushed to her feet. "I'm fine. Next time maybe I'll watch where I'm going." Smiling at Jeremy, who'd backed away to stare, she added, "My little boy just got a new puppy, and we were searching for the dog-food section."

"Ah." He glanced at the child. Then he tipped his hat to Chloe and said, "I'll leave you to it, then."

As he walked away, Chloe turned to get a better look at him. His chambray shirt and snug denim jeans were common garments for a man in Jack Pine, but nothing else about him was ordinary. Hooked behind his ears, his jet-black hair fell to his shoulders, the gleaming strands as straight as a bullet on a windless day. In place of a standard leather belt, he wore a woven sash decorated with intricate beadwork. The band encircling the dusty crown of his Stetson bore a similar design, as did his knee-high moccasins of heavy canvas.

"He's wearing a necklace!" Jeremy blurted loudly.

"Shh!" Chloe herded her son down aisle five.

"Well, he *is!*"

"I know. Lots of men wear jewelry."

"Not that kind."

"I think he's a Native American, sweetie."

"What's a native 'merican?"

Chloe wished her son would speak softly. "An Indian," she whispered.

"Oh." Jeremy glanced worriedly behind them. "Does he scalp people?"

"No, of course not. Native Americans don't scalp people anymore. That happened more than a century ago when they were fighting to keep their land."

"What land?"

Chloe searched her son's upturned face. "This land," she finally found the presence of mind to say. "That's why they're called Native Americans, because they lived here first. We came along much later and took everything from them."

Leaning closer, Jeremy asked, "Do you think he's still mad about it?"

"No, I don't think so."

"He looked kind of mad to me."

Chloe struggled not to smile. If the stranger was overhearing this, she could only hope he liked kids and had a sense of humor. "I'm sure he's not mad, sweetie."

"He didn't smile."

"Just because people don't smile doesn't mean they're mad."

"What's it mean then?"

Jeremy had a knack for asking dozens of questions at the most inopportune moments. "I don't know. I guess maybe it means he doesn't feel like smiling. You don't always feel like smiling, do you?"

They reached the pet-food section. Chloe tapped a sack of puppy kibble. "Down to business, big guy. You have a hungry puppy waiting for you at home."

Chloe bent over the stacks of dog food, struggling to shift the forty-pound bags so she could read the ingredients on the sides. Jeremy homed in on a bag with a picture of a golden retriever on the front. "Here's a good one!"

"That's six dollars more than anything else, Jeremy. How about this kind here?" Chloe strained to shift a bag with a picture of a black Lab on the front.

"But Rowdy's a golden 'triever! He needs golden 'triever food, Mom!"

"Sweetheart, the pictures don't mean anything."

Her son's bottom lip started to quiver. A year ago, Chloe would have stood firm, but recently, she had fallen into the habit of giving in whenever possible. Jeremy had an asthmatic condition that, according to his doctor, was caused by emotional stress. The breathing attacks frightened Chloe, and whether it was wise or not, she would go to almost any lengths to ensure he didn't have one.

"Jeremy, I—"

"Please, Mom!" His eyes filled with tears. *"Please?"*

Chloe was about to give in when a deep voice said, "Excuse me."

The raspy baritone, coming from so close behind her, made Chloe jump. She wasn't surprised when she turned to find the beaded stranger standing almost on top of her. Her heart kicked hard against her ribs. "Oh, hello again," she managed to say with a semblance of calm.

This time, one corner of his hard mouth actually turned up, not exactly a smile but close. He extended a ballpoint pen. "I think we missed this when we were picking up. I spotted it lying under the edge of a shelf."

"Oh, thank you." Chloe took the pen and slipped it in her purse.

He glanced at the sacks behind her. "I couldn't help overhearing the puppy-food debate. I happen to be something of an expert, if you'd like some advice."

"You are?"

His half-smile deepened into a grin that softened his stern countenance. "You could say that, yes." He turned to Jeremy. "Your mom's absolutely right about the pictures, son. They mean nothing." With impressive strength, he flipped over a bag to reveal the list of ingredients. Tapping the print with a long finger, he said, "This is the number to check, percentage of protein. Too much is bad for a pup's skin and may cause hot spots."

Jeremy ducked behind Chloe to peer around her hip at the stranger. Under the best of circumstances, the child was timid around men, and given their recent discussion about Native Americans, he was warier than usual.

The stranger's smile blinked out. After studying the boy for a long moment, he directed a burning look at Chloe. All warmth gone from his voice, he said, "You can take the advice for what it's worth. No skin off my nose, either way."

She stared bewilderedly after him as he strode off. She didn't know what had upset him, but his gruff tone had frightened Jeremy and set him to trembling.

She smoothed a hand over Jeremy's curly hair. "It's okay, sweetheart."

The child clung more tightly to her leg. "See? He doesn't like us."

Chloe could think of no better explanation. "I guess maybe not."

Twenty minutes later, when Chloe pushed a brimming cart to the checkout counter, the dark stranger had already left. Still upset over the way he'd frightened Jeremy, Chloe was glad to find him gone.

The clerk greeted them with a friendly smile. An older woman, she had a wiry, no-nonsense look well suited to someone working in a feed store. Propping her elbows on the counter, she took in the cart of merchandise, her blue eyes dancing with amusement. "Looks like you found everything."

Chloe nodded. "And then some. I'm afraid we went a little overboard."

"You must be the new gal over at the sheriff's department."

Chloe was momentarily taken aback. "Why, yes. How did you know?"

"I've seen your car parked over there—or one like it, anyway. You could have been a tourist, but when you mentioned the puppy, I figured you had to be the new gal. You'll get used to our grapevine. Jack Pine isn't very big. Gossip travels fast, and a new hire at the sheriff's office is hot news." She thrust out a hand. "Lucy Gant."

Returning the handshake, Chloe said, "Chloe Evans and my son, Jeremy."

"Hi, Jeremy." Lucy grabbed a jar of individually wrapped candy from a nearby shelf and unscrewed the lid. "Help yourself, young man." Jeremy politely selected one piece. "No, no, take a handful," Lucy urged.

Jeremy helped himself to several candies. "Thank you."

"You're quite welcome," Lucy said. "I got a soft spot for boys. Have two of my own." She watched Jeremy wander away to look at the animated displays in the front windows. "Handsome boy."

"Thank you. I think so."

"I heard your last name is Owens."

"That's amazingly close. I guess there really is a grapevine."

"Anytime you want to know anything about anybody, honey, just come see me. How do you like the new job?"

"I love it. The people I work with are really nice, it pays pretty decent, and the health insurance is great."

"With the cost of insurance nowadays, that's a plus. You get weekends off?"

"Unfortunately, no. I work the three-to-eleven with Wednesdays and Fridays off. But I lucked out on a sitter. Deputy Bower's daughter, Tracy, stays with Jeremy. He absolutely adores her."

Lucy nodded. "Nice girl, Tracy. Spittin' image of her mama, that one." Lucy leaned across the counter to pass a scanner over the bag of dog food. "Sheriff Lang's a decent fellow. A little too laid back to be a good lawman, but nice. We graduated the same year. He went off to college." She tapped her chest. "I got married to a good-for-nothing, gave him two sons, and then got left to raise them alone."

Chloe knew how hard that was. She laid a red puppy collar on the counter. "I'm sorry to hear that. It must have been very difficult for you."

"I managed. All things considered, I was better off. He was a mean-tempered man and quick to rile."

Chloe's throat tightened. She and Lucy Gant had a great deal in common, it seemed.

The older woman shook open a sack and glanced after Jeremy again as she began bagging items. "So what did you think of Crazy Ben?"

"Pardon?"

"Ben Longtree, the fellow who about knocked you down."

"Oh! I really couldn't say. I spoke with him only briefly."

Lucy's mouth thinned. "I'm not your mama, but I'll give you a piece of advice anyway. Watch your step with that one."

Chloe lifted a rubber chew bone from the cart. "No worries. I'll probably never see him again."

"Trust me, honey, you'll see him again. When a man gets that look in his eye, he always comes back around for another sniff."

A cold sensation moved through Chloe. "Oh, I don't—"

"Cash or charge?" Lucy interrupted.

Thanks to her ex-husband, Roger, Chloe's credit cards were all maxed out. "Cash—or rather a check. You do take checks, I hope?"

"Sure. If it bounces, I know where to find you. That's forty-two dollars and ninety-three cents. The advice is free." While Chloe fished through the jumbled contents of the purse for her checkbook, Lucy rattled on about Ben Longtree. "I always did say he'd come to no good. Wasn't no surprise to me when he up and killed a man a few years back."

Chloe gave the clerk a startled look.

"Figured that'd get your attention. One blow of his fist—next stop, the funeral parlor. Happened down in Riverview. I figure Ben was probably drunk. Quarter-breed Shoshone, you know. Mix Injuns with booze, and you get trouble every time. Not that I'm racist or anything."

Chloe glanced over her shoulder to make sure Jeremy was still out of earshot. "He actually killed someone?"

"Deader than a doornail. Highfalutin lawyer got him off. Self-defense and lack of malice, they said. Ha. Money talks. That's the truth of it. A cold-blooded killer's walking our streets, all because he could buy himself an innocent verdict."

Recalling the burning anger that had flashed in Ben Longtree's eyes, Chloe had no trouble believing he had a hot temper. "How terrible."

"He's a mean one—make no mistake," Lucy continued. "His father beat on his mama every day of their marriage. The apple never falls far from the tree. I could tell you some stories that'd curl your hair."

"I'd better pass. My little boy is sensitive."

Lucy went on as if Chloe hadn't spoken. "There's some real strange happenings up on that ridge."

"What ridge?"

"Cinnamon Ridge, where Longtree lives. You don't know nothin' about nothin', do you? I take it you've never driven out that way. Beautiful place. A quarter section of Ponderosa pines, bordered on three sides by forestland. From the house, you can see clear into next week. Isolated, too. Not many people venture up that way, but those that have can tell you some mighty spooky stories. Wild animals milling around everywhere. And rumor has it that Ben has been seen walking a grown cougar on a leash.''

"A grown *what?*"

"A mountain lion. We got a lot of them in these parts, but most folks don't make pets of them.''

"I don't imagine so.''

"There's something strange going on up there— mark my words.'' Lucy rubbed her sleeves and shivered. "Take that wolf of his, for instance. Who in his right mind would have a dangerous critter like that for a pet? Claims it's a hybrid, but no one believes it. Looks like a real wolf, don't it?''

Chloe recalled the creature that she and Jeremy had encountered in the parking lot. She wasn't surprised to learn that Ben Longtree was its owner.

"What if the thing attacks someone?'' Well into gossip mode, Lucy ignored the check Chloe laid by the register. "Mandy Prince over at the Clip and Curl thinks Ben is dabbling in witchcraft. She got into all that hocus-pocus stuff at college, and she thinks that cougar could be his familiar.''

Chloe struggled not to smile. Granted, Ben Longtree had been surly, but it struck her as being a little outrageous to accuse him of practicing witchcraft.

"He's a big man,'' Lucy went on. "If he's a witch, maybe a regular-size house cat isn't big enough to suit him.''

Chloe nudged the check closer.

"Something is attracting those animals to his place. Maybe he casts some kind of spell over them. Even as a boy, he was a strange one.'' She arched her eyebrows. "You heard about the two young fellows that vanished up that way?''

"No, I don't believe I have.''

"Went out bow hunting last summer and never came back. There's a number of folks who think Ben killed them and let his critters eat the evidence."

Chloe's stomach lurched. She shot a pointed glance at Jeremy, but Lucy just kept talking. "Ben gets fighting mad if anyone pesters his critters. Those boys were out hunting. What's to say they didn't accidentally wander onto Longtree land and shoot one of the deer?"

"I suppose that's possible."

"More than just possible. Then they up and vanish? Ben Longtree had a hand in it—mark my words."

"I'm sure Sheriff Lang would take action if he thought that were the case."

"No evidence," Lucy volleyed back. "You gotta have a body—or bloodstains or something. You can't arrest a man on supposition."

Exactly, Chloe thought. And so far, Lucy had spouted nothing but supposition.

"You know what I think?" Lucy asked in a stage whisper. "I think something more dangerous than witchcraft is happening on that ridge. When Ben came home after that murder trial, he was flat broke. Now he's rolling in it." She pointed to a poster on the bulletin board. "How can a man without a job offer that kind of a reward?"

Chloe turned to regard the poster in question. It read

$10,000 REWARD FOR INFORMATION LEADING TO THE ARREST AND CONVICTION OF THE PERSON/PERSONS RESPONSIBLE FOR WOUNDING WILD ANIMALS NEAR CINNAMON RIDGE.

Below the large block print were particulars, namely that the weapon being used was a .22-caliber rifle, and that the intent of the shooter was to maim the animals, not kill them.

"Why would anyone want to wound helpless animals?" Chloe mused.

"The thing that bothers me is, where did Ben Longtree get ten thousand dollars to give away?"

Chloe had no idea, and suddenly she wanted to get out of there. She glanced at her watch. "My goodness! Look at the time. It's almost four."

The clerk barely paused to draw breath. "No more'n a year after he came back to town, he started building that big, fancy house he lives in now. You can bet he didn't foot the bill with his mama's social security checks."

"This is very interesting, Lucy, but we've got a hungry puppy waiting at home. I really need to be going."

Lucy held up a finger. "The way I see it, honey, I'm doin' you a favor. If, by chance, Ben does come sniffing around, you'll know to run the other way."

Chloe had no intention of allowing Ben Longtree or any other man within sniffing distance.

"He's doing something illegal up there. I'd bet my retirement on it. Nan—that's his mother—never worked a day. She must be drawing on Hap's social security, and God rest his soul, he was always too busy drinking and fornicating to hold down a steady job. She can't be getting very much per month."

"Maybe Mr. Longtree got some kind of inheritance."

"Nah. His daddy frittered away every cent they had on booze. When he plowed his truck into that Ponderosa pine on Dead Man's Curve a few years back, he died drunk and flat broke."

Chloe didn't care to hear any more of this. "I need to—"

"I think Ben has a drug lab up on that ridge—that's

what I think. Big money to be made in drugs, and being a vet, he's got the education to know about chemistry and such. That would explain why he runs folks off his land with a shotgun. A man doesn't behave that way unless he has something to hide. Now, does he?"

Jeremy returned to the check stand just then. Chloe flashed Lucy a warning look. The older woman fell silent and reached across the counter to pat the child's auburn curls. "Well, now, young man, I can assure you of one thing. You got yourself the best puppy food in the store."

"I did? Mostly, we got it 'cause it's cheap."

Lucy laughed. "Cheap or not, it's good puppy chow. People can say what they want about Ben Longtree, but he knows animals. He's a vet. It's a shame he lost his practice after that spot of trouble with the law. Healing critters is the only useful thing he ever did in his life."

Chloe piled her purchases back into the cart. Left with no choice, Lucy finished the transaction. Handing over the receipt, she said, "It's been a pleasure talking to you, Chloe."

Chloe wished she could say the same.

Though it was her day off, Chloe felt as if she had worked a full shift by the time she parked her Honda in the dirt driveway in front of their rental. Eager to check on his puppy, Jeremy was out of the car like a shot. Chloe almost called after him not to run, but she gulped back the warning. According to the doctor, Jeremy was fine physically. A sprint to the house wouldn't hurt him, and she had to stop being so paranoid.

The child never broke stride as he raced up the rickety steps. Chloe stared after him, feeling oddly disoriented. This was their home now, she reminded herself as she studied the ramshackle house. She spent a moment taking inventory of the needed repairs, all of which would be at her own expense. The landlord had just shaken his head when Chloe asked him to fix things.

"As is!" he'd shouted, fumbling with his hearing aid. "You think this is New York City or somethin'?"

Chloe merely felt seven hundred dollars a month entitled her to a kitchen faucet that didn't drip, a back door that locked each time she turned the key, and a living room floor that didn't sag under her weight.

Ah, well, I'll manage, she assured herself. Some paint and elbow grease would work wonders on the house, inside and out.

The screen door slapped back open just then, and Jeremy spilled onto the porch. One look at her son's face, and Chloe knew something was wrong.

Bolting from the car, she cried, "What is it, sweetheart?"

As pale as milk, Jeremy worked his mouth, but no words came out. Chloe broke into a run. When she reached the front steps, Jeremy wheeled and dashed back into the house.

"He's *sick*!" the boy shrieked. "He's really, *really* sick, Mom."

The smell almost took Chloe's breath. She raced to the bathroom, where they'd left Rowdy while they were shopping. At the doorway, she careened to a stop. Never had she smelled anything quite so foul. Puppies made messes on the floor. That went with the territory. But Rowdy had messed and vomited everywhere. Blood was mixed in with the watery excrement.

Chloe's heart plummeted to her knees. The puppy had seemed a little listless that afternoon, but she had blamed it on weakness due to starvation. One of a litter, he had been abandoned in an old barn at the edge of town, and he'd nearly died before someone found him. Chloe had hoped good care and plenty of food would turn him around.

Stupid, so stupid. She inched into the bathroom. For a moment, she didn't see Rowdy anywhere. Then she spotted him slumped against the chipped tub, his front paws spread, his muzzle flattened on the floor.

"Oh, dear." She crouched by the motionless puppy. That he was still alive was the best that could be said for him. "Oh, you poor baby."

"He's so sick," Jeremy said shakily. "We need to take him to the doctor, Mom."

Chloe couldn't afford a vet bill. She had just under a hundred dollars to last until she got paid. Granted, the situation was heartbreaking, but she had other, equally pressing concerns, like keeping food on the table. Only how could she tell Jeremy that? He had already been through so much. This puppy was the first really wonderful thing that had happened to him in a very long time.

Surely veterinarians carried balances for services rendered. Maybe she could get Rowdy treatment now and pay for it later. It was worth a shot, wasn't it? She just hoped the puppy wasn't beyond help.

She opened the cupboard under the sink and plucked out a towel. "We'll just bundle him up and take him to the vet, sweetie."

When Chloe lifted Rowdy into her arms, his head hung limply over her arm. His furry little body felt hot even through the towel.

Jeremy started to keen—an awful wailing sound that nearly broke Chloe's heart. Wrapping his thin arms around himself, he swayed on his feet. "He's gonna die, isn't he?"

"Oh, Jeremy, I don't know." Without loosening her

hold on the puppy, she twisted her arm to look at her watch. It was 4:40, which left only twenty minutes to find a vet.

Thirty minutes later, Chloe stood at one side of a stainless steel examining table, staring stupidly at the veterinarian across from her. The half-dead puppy lay stretched out between them.

"Can't you make an exception? I'll have the money here in the morning."

The balding doctor stared at Chloe over the rims of his glasses. "No payment, no service, that's our policy. We accept credit cards."

Chloe wanted to reach across the table, grab him by his smock front, and give him a hard shake. "I don't have any credit cards."

His eyebrows lifted. "May I ask why?"

It was none of his business. "My husband fell ill. All my cards are limited out."

"I see." He sniffed. "That's unfortunate. Treating parvovirus is very expensive. I won't demand payment in full, of course, but I need three hundred down."

Chloe thought of her child sitting in the waiting room. For all intents and purposes, he'd lost his father a year and a half ago. And three weeks ago, she'd taken him away from everything familiar, including his doting grandparents. He'd been so thrilled to get this puppy, and now, only a few hours later, he was about to lose it. She couldn't let that happen. No matter what, she absolutely couldn't let it happen.

"My little boy isn't well," she tried. "It'll half kill him if this puppy dies. Please. I have a ruby brooch— a family heirloom. I can get at least three hundred for it. I'll be back with the money before noon to-morrow."

"The dog will probably make it through the night,

Mrs. Evans. Bring him back when you have the cash."
He gave her an apologetic look. "I'm sorry. Everyone
is long on promises when a pet's life is at stake. It's
a different story when the crisis has passed."

He turned and left the examining room. Chloe
stared at the closing door. This couldn't be happening.
Shaking with impotent anger, she gently gathered the
puppy back into her arms.

Jeremy leaped up off the bench when Chloe reentered the waiting room. His small face was pale, his
eyes huge. "Can't the doctor make him well?"

Chloe was so furious she could barely speak. "I'll
tell you about it outside, sweetie."

Once in the car, Chloe carefully transferred Rowdy
into her son's waiting arms. Jeremy pressed his face
against the puppy's matted fur. "Please, Mom, don't
let him die."

Chloe clamped her hands over the steering wheel
and stared balefully at the clinic building. "The doctor
says Rowdy has a disease called parvo," she said carefully. "The vet wants three hundred dollars down."

"Three hundred is a lot, isn't it?"

"All we have right now is ninety-eight." She forced
a smile. "But, hey, all isn't lost. The vet thinks Rowdy
will be okay until morning, and I've got an idea how
to get the money then."

"But, Mommy, he's so sick." Jeremy's breathing became ragged. "What if he—?" The child gulped and
dragged in a laborious breath. "What if he dies tonight?"

Searching her little boy's face, Chloe thought, *A
child his age should still believe in miracles.* All she
saw in her son's eyes was shattered hope.

The wheezy whine of his breathing filled the car.
Chloe's heart clutched with fear. "We'll pray really,
really hard that that doesn't happen," she tried.

Jeremy bent his head over the puppy. "Praying didn't help Daddy."

Chloe looked away. "No," she conceded hollowly, "praying didn't work for Daddy."

"It prob'ly won't work for Rowdy, either."

Tears sprang to Chloe's eyes. What could she say? A dozen lies came to mind, but Jeremy had already heard them all.

Once they'd sponged Rowdy off and Chloe got her son tucked into bed that night, she collected the sick puppy and sat on the sofa with him cradled in her arms. As deathly ill as Rowdy was, he emitted that sweet puppy smell that Chloe could remember so clearly from childhood. Through the bath towel and her clothing, she felt the heat of his fever. He was so very sick. She feared only a miracle would save him.

The thought nearly broke Chloe's heart. Running a fingertip up the bridge of the puppy's nose, she huddled there in the shadows, too exhausted to weep. Why was it that she so often failed at even the simplest things? Other people got puppies for their children, and those dogs didn't die. Recently Chloe had begun to feel as if life and its many problems were bigger than she was—that no matter how hard she tried, nothing went right.

God, she was tired, an awful, bone-melting weariness that made her limbs feel leaden. If Rowdy died during the night, how would she tell Jeremy?

Moonlight slanted through the living room windows, feeble fingers of illumination that spilled over the floor like puddles of silver. Chloe gathered the puppy closer and pressed her cheek to his head. Exhausted though she was, she was afraid to put him in his box and go to bed. He might die while she slept.

And so she sat there in the darkness, rocking him

as she might a sick child, holding on to the fragile thread of life for him because he was too weak to hang on himself. The clock ticked loudly in the silence. The night wind puffed against the exterior walls of the house, and bushes scratched the siding. The sounds made her nerves jump, and she kept looking over her shoulder. Not so very long ago, she'd heard similar noises outside her Lynnwood apartment, and it hadn't been bushes making the sounds.

The memories filled Chloe's mouth with the metallic taste of fear. She tried to tell herself she was being silly, that Roger couldn't find her now that she was living in another state. But somehow that didn't make her feel better.

The minutes dragged by, small eternities that mounted, one by one, into an hour, and then two. Occasionally, Rowdy's small body would convulse with heaves. He brought up only bile. Each time, Chloe wiped his face and wrapped him in a clean towel. Keeping vigil, she lost track of time. Her eyes grew dry and started to ache, and her arms cramped from the weight they cradled.

When the first faint rays of dawn lightened the windows, she stirred from the sofa, carefully laid the puppy in his box, and staggered to the kitchen. Her joints throbbed like those of an old woman as she filled the coffeemaker with water and scooped grounds into the basket. She punched the BREW button and went to the window to watch the sunrise.

The sky turned a gorgeous pink, long, wispy streaks of rose and burgundy threading through clouds as soft and fluffy as cotton candy. Watching the glorious transformation, Chloe felt a resurgence of hope. The puppy had made it through the night.

Chapter Two

Morning sunlight filtered down through the branches of the pine trees to bathe the lawn and woodland floor with dancing patterns of shimmering yellow. The warmth worked on Ben's knotted shoulder muscles like the clever fingers of a masseuse. This was one of his favorite times of day, a stolen moment solely for him, when he could sit and listen and sort his thoughts while he watched the deer enjoy their breakfast.

In the treetops, black-capped chickadees, robins, and sparrows raised their voices in joyful song, thankful for the sunshine, the tasty bugs under the bark, and the water in the birdbath. The necessities of life and a few simple pleasures were all they needed or wanted.

Ben envied them that. Over the last several weeks, his schedule had been nightmarish, without enough minutes in the day to get everything done. Sometimes he yearned for rest like a starving man did food. Unfortunately, a malevolent presence had invaded his forest, and the wounded animals continued to seek him out in an unending stream. He got at least one new patient a day, sometimes more.

He had seven furry convalescents at the cave a mile

and a quarter northwest of his land. Counting the quarter-mile walk to his property line, the twice-daily commute was three miles round trip. Normally Ben would have enjoyed the exercise. But he also had recovering creatures inside the house. Providing all the critters under his care with medical treatment kept him on the run from dawn until dark, leaving little time for his writing, which paid the household expenses and bought much-needed veterinary supplies.

Ben could have reduced the travel time to and from the cave by riding his Arctic Cat, a four-wheel ATV that sailed over rough terrain, but he was afraid the noise and tire tracks might give away the cave's location. He couldn't take that chance. Whoever was wounding the animals stalked the surrounding hills practically every day. If the bastard found that cave, he wouldn't hesitate to enter and open fire on the cages. At all costs, Ben had to protect his patients from further harm.

A hummingbird buzzed Ben's head. He ducked and then chuckled, amused by the tiny creature's audacity. He stood six feet five inches tall in his stocking feet and weighed 243 pounds. Feathers and all, the hummingbird would tip a postal scale at about an ounce, yet the little bugger still dared to take him on. *My fault,* Ben decided. He never should have hung the nectar feeder so close to the steps where he liked to sit. Hummingbirds were territorial about their feeders, and a loitering human being posed a threat to their existence.

One of the browsing bucks suddenly lifted its head to sniff the air. Preoccupied with the antics of the hummingbird, Ben might have ignored the deer's odd behavior if it hadn't snorted and tapped the earth with a sharp front hoof.

Ben pushed up from the steps and cocked his head

to listen. He heard nothing out of the ordinary. Turning back to the group of deer at the edge of the lawn, he saw a doe break off from enjoying its grain to stare at the west end of the house.

Something was up. Not really alarmed because the deer seemed more inquisitive than frightened, Ben went to investigate. He'd taken only two steps when he heard a faint but shrill tooting sound.

As he circled the west end of the house and stepped into the carport area, he glimpsed a small boy. Bold as polished brass, the kid was standing astride a bicycle out in the driveway. Sunlight glanced off his curly auburn hair, tipping the ends with glinting copper. He wore a blue Winnie-the-Pooh T-shirt, faded jeans mended at the knees, and scuffed white leather sneakers, one of which had come untied. Something about the child seemed vaguely familiar, but Ben couldn't recall where he'd seen him.

Every few seconds, the boy squeezed the rubber bulb of the bike horn. Ben had NO TRESPASSING signs posted all along his fence line at twenty-foot intervals. Nobody could accidentally wander onto his property—unless, of course, the interloper happened to be a little squirt who couldn't read.

On the rare occasion that intrepid souls ventured up to the house, Ben always ordered them off his land, sometimes cradling a shotgun in the crook of one arm to emphasize the point. This was just a kid, though. As Ben moved closer, he noted the child's pallor, his feverish brown eyes, and the way his narrow chest heaved with exertion. Ben guessed he'd ridden his bike up the driveway, which was a quarter mile long and very steep.

Slowing to a stop at the front end of the breezeway, Ben treated the child to his most intimidating glare. That alone was usually enough to send people running. Not this kid. He swung off his bike and lowered the kickstand.

Looking scared half out of his wits, the boy gulped and said, "My name's Jeremy. I need your help."

The silent-glare treatment wasn't working. Ben spread his feet and planted his hands at his hips. "If you're selling magazines, forget it. I can't read."

"I'm not selling nothing."

The kid's lips looked a little blue. Ben told himself it was a trick of the light. "I don't like people trespassing on my property. Turn that bike of yours around, and get off my ridge."

Damn it. With 160 fenced acres, a man was entitled to some privacy. Ben didn't want any locals up here. Every blasted time, they saw something they shouldn't and carried tales back to town.

"Go on!" he barked. "Get off my land, I said."

The tremors that racked the child's body gained force to become a violent quaking. Ben's throat thickened with shame. He could scare off adults and teenagers without a qualm, but a small child was different. He felt like a first-class jerk.

As frightened as the boy clearly was, he still didn't run. He had more backbone than a lake trout, Ben decided with reluctant admiration.

"I rode my bike a long ways. If you're still mad 'cause we stole your land, I'm real sorry, but I'm not leaving until I talk to you."

"Fine, then. Spit it out, and then make tracks."

"My puppy Rowdy's dying. I brung him to you 'cause the lady at the feed store said you know a lot about curing animals."

Ben's studied the child's freckled face. He placed him now. It was the kid he'd seen at the store yesterday. A picture spun through his mind of the mother. She was a looker with a wealth of auburn hair, big, wary brown eyes, and a tidy figure. Since his divorce, Ben didn't often notice women, but he'd given her a second look, much to his self-disgust a few minutes later.

This child had cowered behind her when Ben had approached them in the dog-food section. Since returning to Jack Pine, he'd grown used to the gossip. Oh, yes, he'd heard the stories—about witchcraft and random murders, with him feeding the human remains to his critters. The stories were so preposterous and sick that he had long since decided not let them bother him. It carried a harder punch when a child cringed from him, though.

What kind of mother allowed her child's head to be filled with such tripe?

To hell with it. Like he gave a rat's ass?

And yet, deep down, he actually did care a great deal, especially when he saw how deep-rooted the distrust of him really was. The boy had eyes like his mother's—big splashes of liquid brown fringed with dark lashes. Something about her had appealed to him in a way no other woman had in years. Several times that morning, he'd caught himself thinking of her— and how good she had looked in khaki slacks and a form-fitting green knit top that showcased her sweetly rounded breasts.

Ben shifted his attention to the pup that lay so still in the towel-lined handlebar basket. He hated to see the kid lose his dog. But, hey, it wasn't his problem. If he helped this child, he'd be signing the death warrant of almost twenty other animals, his cougar, Methuselah, included.

Three months ago, a power company employee had driven up to Ben's place to read the electric meter and seen Ben walking the cougar on a leash. Less than a week later, Deputy Bobby Lee Schuck had paid a visit to Cinnamon Ridge with two game wardens in tow. Caught off guard, Ben hadn't had time to hide the animals in his outdoor hospital, which had been behind the house at the time. Several convalescents in cages had been confiscated. The only reason Methuselah hadn't met with the same fate was because Bobby Lee hadn't thought to search the house.

It was against Oregon law to keep wild animals in captivity without a special permit. Ben had received a hefty fine for his infraction and been told he would go to jail if he broke the law again. None too thrilled at the prospect, he had tried the legal route, applying to the state for a special permit, but his application had been turned down, a result, he felt sure, of Bobby Lee's blackballing him. For Ben, the choice of either abiding by the law or breaking it was no choice at all. He couldn't condemn Methuselah to a slow death by starvation out in the wild, and he couldn't turn his back on the other animals that came to him for help, either.

Eventually his illegal veterinary practice would land him in jail. He understood that and was willing to pay the price. He just hoped to postpone the inevitable for as long as possible, and that meant keeping people off the ridge, including small boys who came to him with sick puppies.

"I'm not a vet anymore," Ben said firmly. "And I don't like being pestered."

"Don't you still know vet stuff?" Those big brown eyes welled with tears. "Please? He's gonna die, Mr. Longtree. He needs your help."

The child's body suddenly snapped taut, and what little color remained in his face drained away. Ben realized he was gaping at something behind him. *Not Methuselah,* he thought. *Please, God, don't let it be Methuselah.*

But, of course, it was. Just as Ben turned to look, the cougar stumbled over a six-pack cooler in the carport and sent it flying. The resultant clatter might have startled a less stalwart feline, but Methusaleh was accustomed to bumping into things.

Ben was tempted to let loose with a string of curses to turn the air blue. Only what good would it do? The cat was out of the bag now. The kid would race home to tell his mother. She'd grab up the phone to tell a friend. By this time tomorrow, everyone in Jack Pine, including Bobby Lee Schuck, would have heard the story. Ben didn't kid himself. If the deputy saw an opportunity to cause him more grief, he'd jump at it, and the old cougar's fate would be sealed.

To Ben's surprise and even greater dismay, the boy suddenly started wheezing—an awful whining sound that rattled up from his narrow chest. Clutching his throat with one hand, he began fumbling in the pocket of his jeans. Ben realized he was groping for an inhaler and hurried over to help.

"Easy, son, easy." Ben plucked the canister from the child's pocket and pressed the orange mouthpiece to his lips. "The cougar won't hurt you, I promise." He depressed the cap to release a blast of medication. The boy tried to breathe it in but the inhalant didn't help. Growing truly alarmed, Ben dropped to one knee to get a better angle and released more medicine. "What is it, asthma? Calm down, son. Try to relax."

Easy to say, but not so easily done. The boy dragged in a whistling breath of the mist, gulped, and grabbed frantically for more. A small eternity and several doses later, his wind passages finally cleared. Whether that was due to the medicine or simply because he began to calm down, Ben didn't know.

Exhausted by the ordeal, Jeremy leaned his weight against the circle of Ben's arm as the last of the spasms abated. His wide, wary gaze remained fixed on the cougar.

"Does that happen to you often?" Ben asked.

The boy nodded. "I got asthma," he said, his voice gone hoarse from wheezing. "The doctor says it'll go 'way someday."

In most cases, asthma was an allergic disorder, but Jeremy's attack had clearly been brought on by panic. "Not being able to breathe can't be much fun."

"Nope."

The cougar, intrigued by Jeremy's high-pitched voice, moved closer. Almost blind from a slight stroke, the cat had a perpetually bewildered look on his face. "This old fellow is Methuselah, Jeremy. I know he looks scary, but he's a friend of mine."

"Will he eat me?"

Ben figured a dash of humor couldn't hurt. "Not until he goes in the house and gets his dentures." Reaching out to coax the cougar closer, Ben peeled back one of the cat's lips. "See? Hardly any teeth."

Jeremy smiled faintly. Apparently still shaky in the legs, he let Ben support more of his weight. "Is he a real cougar?"

What had worked once might work twice. "Nah," Ben said, "he's stuffed. There's a winder behind his right ear. When I want him to move, I crank him up."

Jeremy rewarded him with a grin that dimpled his cheek. "That's silly."

"Got you to smile, didn't it?"

Jeremy shrugged. Taking stock of his small face, Ben noted that some color had returned to his cheeks and that his lips no longer looked blue.

"He isn't stuffed," the child observed. "I see him breathing."

"No, he isn't stuffed." Ben gave Methuselah a scratch behind the ear, which earned him a wet nuzzle on the wrist. "He's just a poor old toothless cougar who's missing a front foot and almost blind."

"I've never seen a real cougar before. Only on TV, and they were scary."

In that moment, Ben knew he was a goner. Something about this child touched his heart. Maybe it was the unlikely mixture of timidity and courage that had so quickly melted his resistance. Or maybe it was just those big brown eyes that appealed to him in a way that defied explanation.

"Most cougars are pretty scary animals," Ben said. "And they're dangerous, as a rule. But Methuselah is an exception." He allowed the cougar to sniff the child's shirt. "He's just saying hello. Can you say hello back?"

"Hi, 'Thuselah." Jeremy touched a fingertip to the cat's nose, then jerked his hand away. "What happened to his foot?"

"He got it caught in a trap." Judging by the confusion in the child's expression, Ben decided that he'd never heard of an animal trap. "A trap's a gadget made of steel that resembles the jaws of an animal with very large teeth."

Withdrawing his arm from around Jeremy, he lifted his hands to approximate the size. Startled by his sudden movement, Jeremy hunched his shoulders and threw up a frail arm to shield his face.

Ben felt as if a horse had kicked him in the guts. A child didn't flinch that way without good reason, and he had a very bad feeling he knew what it was. He remained stock-still, a dozen different reassurances circling through his mind—first and foremost being that he would never hit a child—but the words wouldn't come. Not that it mattered. Words were pitifully inadequate weapons against fear.

Jeremy slowly inched down his hand to peek at Ben

over his wrist. When he finally determined that it was safe, he lowered his arm. The high color that flagged his cheeks told Ben that he was embarrassed. Ben remembered how he'd felt thirty years ago in a similar situation.

His voice grated like a rusty hinge as he continued his spiel, explaining how a trap worked. He watched Jeremy closely as he talked about springs and releases, and described how the jaws of a trap snapped closed.

Jeremy slowly relaxed. Ben doubted the boy was registering much of what he said, but again, it wasn't words that mattered.

"The trapper lays the trap on a well-traveled path and hides it with brush and grass. When an animal happens along and steps on it, the spring mechanism snaps the jaws closed."

"What happens then?" Jeremy asked.

"The teeth bite into the animal's foot, sometimes to the bone, and it can't get away because the trap is anchored."

"Does it hurt?" Jeremy asked solemnly.

Ben looked deeply into Jeremy's eyes, and he knew this child had experienced pain. "Yes," he replied, his voice going thick. "It hurts a lot."

The boy glanced at Methuselah. "How come do people set traps, then?"

"People just do it because—actually I have no idea why. They just do, is all."

"What happens to the animals?"

"All they can do is lie there until the trapper comes or they die of thirst. Sadly, most trappers don't check their lines daily, so it's often a long, painful death for the animal."

"That's *mean*."

"Yes, it is mean. That's why traps like that have

been outlawed in Oregon. Unfortunately, some people ignore the law and set traps anyway, and poor old Methuselah stepped in one."

"How did he get away?"

Ben reached over to stroke the cougar's fur. "Well, now, I wasn't there, and Methuselah's not talking, but judging by the damage to his paw, I think he fought his way free." In truth, it had appeared to Ben that the cat had chewed off his foot to escape, but that wasn't something to share with a child. "By the time he made it into my yard, he was half-dead with infection. I gave him a shot to make him sleep, amputated what was left of his foot, and got him on antibiotics to clear up the infection. By the time he was well, we'd become good friends. It took several weeks for him to heal."

"So now he lives with you?"

Ben nodded. "Being blind, lame, and toothless, he can't hunt anymore. Out in the forest, he'd starve. Here on the ridge, he gets fed." He grinned as he ran a hand over the cougar's well-padded ribs. "More than he needs, truth told. He's getting a little fat. I guess he figures it's pretty fine pickings."

The child moved away from Ben to stand by the bicycle. Placing a protective hand over his puppy, he asked, "Does 'Thuselah eat little dogs?"

Ben smiled. "He has to have his meat cut up for him. The pup is safe."

"No, not safe," Jeremy said, his voice still hoarse from wheezing. "He's dying. The vet in town says he's got parvo. It costs a lot to cure. My mom went to Pineville to hock her grandma's brooch, but it's so old and ugly, I don't think the pawnshop man will give her three hundred dollars for it."

"Three hundred?"

"That's how much we gotta pay before the vet'll give Rowdy medicine. It'll cost lots more to make him all the way well."

Ben could scarcely believe his ears. "The vet in Jack Pine refused to treat your puppy until your mother came up with three hundred bucks?"

Jeremy nodded. "We only got ninety-eight."

Neil Fenderbottom, the vet, always had been a mercenary bastard. Ben's impression of the kid's mother underwent a favorable change. Not many people would consider hocking a family heirloom to save a mixed-breed pup.

Ben pushed erect and moseyed closer. Once again, the child acted nervous. Ben recalled the gossip in town, the most obvious explanation for the child's distrust of him. Yesterday at the store, he'd looked no deeper than that. Now, he wondered if he hadn't jumped to the wrong conclusion. In his experience, flinching that way was a learned behavior. He would have wagered his last dollar that someone had been knocking the boy around.

The thought made Ben angry. He couldn't figure the child's mother as the culprit. She'd had a wary look in her eyes like Jeremy's. Yesterday Ben had figured she was merely shy with strangers. But what if there was more to it than that?

Ben knew firsthand what it was like to live in terror of your dad. Home became a prison, and there was no escape until you turned eighteen. Jeremy had a long way to go.

He made fast work of giving the puppy a preliminary examination. The poor little mite was burning up with fever, and a pinch test told Ben that he was dangerously dehydrated. He needed to get the dog on intravenous fluids and antibiotics immediately, or he'd be a goner.

"Okay, here's the deal. There's only one thing I'll accept in payment for treating your puppy. Silence." Ben hooked a thumb at the old cougar. "If anyone, including your mom, finds out about Methuselah, I'll go to jail, and he'll be taken away. Considering all his physical problems, it's unlikely the state will relocate him. They'll probably just put him down. You know what that means?"

Jeremy nodded. "That they'll put him to sleep?"

"Exactly. His life depends on you keeping your mouth shut."

"How come they couldn't just put him in a zoo?"

"Most times, people want to see healthy animals at a zoo. There are people trained to care for cougars, and if Methuselah got lucky, someone like that might take him. But what if he didn't get lucky?"

Jeremy rubbed his hands on his jeans. "It's just—" He broke off and swallowed. "I'm not s'posed to keep secrets from my mom."

"And I don't like encouraging you to."

"My mom wouldn't tell anyone."

"All it would take is one slip. If anyone in town finds out for certain I've got a cougar, the sheriff's department will be on me like bears after honey."

Jeremy's eyes went huge. "The sheriff's 'part-ment?"

"What?" Ben asked. He had a bad feeling, a *really* bad feeling, that Lady Luck had just thrown him another curveball. "Your mom's not a deputy, is she?"

"Nope."

"What, then?"

"She's a 'patcher."

"A what?"

"A 'patcher. She answers phones and calls deputies on the radio to tell them where they gotta go."

"Well, damn it to hell." Ben pinched the bridge of

his nose. A dispatcher? It couldn't get much worse than that. She probably saw Bobby Lee Schuck on a daily basis. "If that's not a fine how-do-you-do."

Jeremy cast a worried look at his puppy. "If you'll give Rowdy medicine, I won't tell. Not my mom or anybody. 'Thuselah won't get put to sleep, I promise."

Ben doubted the boy would keep his mouth shut. That was a worry for later, though. The damage was done, the puppy desperately needed attention, and Ben had struck a bargain.

It was strange how life turned out, he thought as he lifted the pup from the basket. At eighteen, he'd set out to change the world, determined to get through college and make his mark as a veterinarian. Now, nineteen years later, here he was, back on Cinnamon Ridge, tickled pink because he was about to provide medical treatment for a mixed-breed pup.

So much for setting the world on fire. Why, then, had he never felt more content? Ben guessed it was because he knew things now that he hadn't then. In the end, when the scores were tallied, all that counted was the knowledge that he'd made a difference. When he released a deer from its cage and watched it walk again, he knew he'd made a difference. When he set a raccoon free and watched it shinny up a tree, he knew he had made a difference. There was suffering and pain everywhere. He'd never needed to leave Cinnamon Ridge to find it. At the ripe old age of thirty-seven, he'd finally come to understand that the most important place to make things happen was right here in his own backyard.

It reminded Ben of something his Shoshone grandfather had been fond of saying, that a young man could travel a great distance and never go anywhere. As a child, Ben hadn't understood what Grandfather meant. Now he did.

Diablo joined them in the driveway. Ben immediately tensed, for the wolf was a formidable-looking critter. He shifted the puppy to the crook of one arm and grabbed hold of Diablo's collar.

"This is another friend of mine. Jeremy, meet Diablo." To the wolf, Ben said, "He's a friend, you ornery cuss. Mind your manners and shake hands."

Diablo sat back on his haunches and extended his right front paw, much to Jeremy's delight. In truth, Ben was pleasantly surprised as well. From one time to the next, he never knew if Diablo would cooperate. The wolf was loyal, and he had a pack mentality, but Ben's status as the alpha male afforded only certain privileges, which didn't include absolute obedience.

Fortunately, Diablo was keenly intelligent and perceptive. He seemed to understand that this particular situation called for diplomacy.

"Go ahead, Jeremy. Diablo would like to shake hands with you."

Jeremy scrunched his shirt in his small fist. "He growled at us yesterday."

Ben leaned down to give the wolf a scolding look. "Have you been acting cantankerous? He doesn't mean anything by it. Mostly it's when people talk to him using baby talk. Diablo finds it insulting."

"Yup. My mom talked baby talk. She called him a nice doggy."

"Ah. You see? If you were a big, tough fellow like Diablo, would you want to be called a nice doggy?"

"She didn't mean to 'sult him. We just didn't want him to bite us."

"Diablo doesn't bite."

Jeremy turned loose of his T-shirt and gingerly grasped the wolf's toes. Not much handshaking occurred, but contact was made. Ben promised Jeremy that he'd show him more of Diablo's tricks later and led his entourage to the back door. Before entering the house, he paused. "What's your last name, Jeremy?"

"Evans."

"Well, Jeremy Evans, here's the story. My mother, Nan, has Alzheimer's, an illness that makes people confused and forgetful. Sometimes she gets things turned around inside her head. If she comes out of her bedroom while you're here and says funny things, you shouldn't feel afraid."

The child nodded. "My dad gets stuff all turned around inside his head, too. That's how come me and my mom got a 'vorce."

Ben was glad to hear that. Suspecting as he did that the child's father had a mean streak, Ben figured it was better for Jeremy with the man out of the picture. Once again, Ben's estimation of the child's mother went up a notch. It wasn't easy for a woman to leave a marriage and strike out on her own when there was a child to rear. It was even more difficult when that woman had possibly been battered.

Now Ben knew where the kid had gotten his backbone.

Chloe knew something awful had happened the instant she parked in her driveway. Before she could pull the keys from the ignition, Tracy flew out the front door and raced down the rickety porch steps. Her eyes were red and swollen from weeping, and she trembled with agitation.

"What is it?" Chloe got out of the Honda, prepared to hear the worst. "Is the puppy dead?"

"He's *gone,* Chloe, gone. His little friend from across the street came and told me just a couple of minutes ago. I was about to call Daddy when you pulled in. I thought he was out playing. But he took off."

"Took off?"

"I'm so sorry. I was watching him. Truly I was. You said he could go pretty much wherever he wanted in the neighborhood because there isn't much traffic. He said he wanted to play in Boober's tree fort, and I believed him!"

Chloe grasped the girl's slender shoulders. "Calm down, sweetie."

Tracy nodded and gulped. Her eyes welled with fresh tears. "I never thought he'd fib to me. He's always so good about being where he says he'll be. Boober says he put the puppy in his bicycle basket and went that way." She flung her arm to indicate the direction. "After you left this morning, he kept talking about Ben Longtree, that crazy guy up on the ridge. He told me Lucy Gant said he was a vet. I think he took Rowdy up there."

"Oh, God." Chloe spun to look up the road. Every awful thing that Lucy Gant had said yesterday about Ben Longtree came back to haunt her. "Oh, *God*."

Tracy made a mewling sound. "I really was keeping tabs on him, Chloe. I swear I was. You said it was okay for him to go play wherever he wanted in the general neighborhood, that I didn't have to have my eye on him every second."

Chloe tamped down her worry to give the girl a quick hug. In a rural area like this, it was safe for a child to run and play without constant supervision. That was one of the reasons she'd moved here, to give Jeremy that freedom. "Of course you were keeping tabs on him, Tracy. I'm not blaming you." A picture of the wolf flashed through Chloe's mind. If Longtree allowed the creature to run loose in a parking lot, he definitely wouldn't bother to restrain it at home. On a bike, Jeremy would be defenseless against an attack. "Do you know how to get to Longtree's house?"

The girl nodded. "He lives up on Cinnamon Ridge." She flung her arm again. "It's not far from here, a mile, maybe two, to his main gate. You just drive to the end of Ponderosa Lane and turn left on what looks like an old logging road. About a quarter mile farther, you'll see a big log arch on your right. That's the road going up to the house."

Chloe was already racing to her car.

Chapter Three

"So you divorced your dad, did you?" Ben mused aloud as he led the way through the laundry room to the hallway that ran the entire length of the house.

The child's sneakers made squeaky sounds on the terra-cotta tile as he scampered behind Ben. "Me and my mom—her name's Chloe—had to get a 'vorce. Then we had to move far away 'cause my dad wouldn't leave us alone."

"Ah." There was a story there, and Ben wanted to hear it. Unfortunately, he valued his own privacy too much not to appreciate the sanctity of someone else's. "So how do you like Jack Pine now that you're here?"

"Real good. We're gonna stay here for always, and when my pappy 'tires, he and my nana are gonna move here, too. I'll be real glad, 'cause I miss 'em lots, and so does my mom."

While passing his mother's bedroom door, Ben touched a finger to his lips. Nan Longtree lay down for a midmorning nap at about this time, and the closed door told Ben she was asleep.

"Wow!" Jeremy exclaimed when they reached the front of the house.

Ben wanted to believe the kid was impressed by

the layout of his home, which he'd designed himself. Unfortunately, he doubted a boy Jeremy's age would appreciate the open floor plan or the wealth of sky-lights and windows.

"Where'd you get 'em all?" Jeremy asked as they reached the kitchen.

Ben guessed the child was referring to the caged animals that had become an integral part of the kitchen decor. Nerves formed a knot just behind his solar plexus. Until now, no one from town had ever been inside his home and seen all his patients.

Not wishing to consider the possible consequences, Ben barely spared the cages a glance as he skirted the end of the kitchen desk, which housed a computer workstation and was backed by a six-foot-high book-shelf. The U-shaped kitchen, bordered on three sides by cabinetry, included a state-of-the-art work island and a rectangular oak dining table where Ben per-formed emergency surgery. The wall of windows in the sunroom beyond offered a panoramic view of Newton Crater, showcasing Shoshone Peak and Cinder Butte.

Ben laid the puppy on the table. "How strong is your stomach, Jeremy?"

The boy placed a hand over his tummy and kneaded with his fingers. "I dunno. I don't have very many muscles yet."

The child had a way of making Ben want to laugh when he least expected it. "Does it bother you to see people get shots?"

Jeremy shrugged. "I don't like it when I get one."

"Well, I have to put a needle in Rowdy's leg."

"What kind of shot do you gotta give him?"

Urgent as the situation was, Ben could see the fright in Jeremy's eyes. After grabbing some needed utensils from a nearby drawer, Ben began a preliminary exam-ination of the dog as he explained, "Actually, it's not really a shot. It's a long, tall glass of water, only we have to put it in Rowdy's vein."

"How come?"

"By giving him fluids in his vein, we can bypass his upset tummy." Ben checked the pup's gum color. "Dogs are just like us. Without water, they die. Right now, everything Rowdy drinks is coming back up—or out his opposite end. His little body is screaming for fluids."

Jeremy nodded. "He did the diarrhea all over our bathroom floor."

"Uh-oh." Grasping the pup's head, Ben flashed a light in his glazed eyes. "Your mom can't have been very happy about that."

"Nope. She was real sad. She wrapped Rowdy in a towel and hurried real fast to the vet."

While examining the pup's ears, Ben murmured a distracted "Ah."

"They were almost ready to close. My mom grabbed Rowdy and stuck her foot in the way before the lady could lock the door. At first they said we'd have to come back later, but my mom wouldn't leave."

Ben glanced up. "Your mom sounds like quite a lady."

"Yep. She doesn't have long fingernails, though."

Ben wondered how in blue blazes that related. Then he thought of the clawlike acrylic nails that so many women wore and almost grinned again. "It doesn't take long fingernails to make a lady."

"Nope. My mom says they're germ clackers."

Ben mentally circled that. "Collectors, you mean?"

Jeremy nodded.

"She's probably right about that." Jeremy's chatter was distracting, but Ben enjoyed it. His mother hadn't been long on conversation since the onset of her illness, and sometimes the only human voice Ben heard for days at a time was a disc jockey's when he played the radio. "As fancy as long fingernails look, they're bound to collect dirt."

"She grew some long ones once, but then she decided they were a big waste of time and cut 'em all off." A frown pleated Jeremy's brow. "We bought a thing to cut Rowdy's. But now he might never get to grow any."

Ben concentrated on his patient, checking gum color, reflexes, pupils, and pulse rate. It was quiet in the kitchen for a few seconds. Ben said, "I'm going to get the fluid pack now." He patted the table. "Can you stand right here and watch Rowdy while I go get the stuff I need?"

"What's a fluid pack?"

"A very special kind of water for sick puppies. It has really good stuff in it to make him feel better."

Ben went to the pantry off the hall, where he kept a freezer and an extra fridge for medicine. He quickly gathered a sack of saline solution, an IV pack, a drip stand, and a vial of hard-hitting antibiotic.

Veterinary medicine, by the seat of the pants. Ben had no lab, X-ray machine, or proper surgery. He had to go on gut instinct. On the other hand, he never had to ask himself if he was performing surgery merely to make a buck. Money had been removed from the equation.

Jeremy was stroking his puppy and looking glum when Ben returned to the kitchen. "Here it is," he said. "A long, tall glass of water."

Jeremy gave him a hopeful look. "Will giving him a drink make him well?"

Ben avoided the child's gaze as he positioned the drip stand. What was it about this kid that made him want to promise the impossible? He guessed the answer to that was simple enough. There was no love quite so innocent, no devotion quite so absolute as that of a boy for his dog. Jeremy would grieve terribly if the puppy died, but there was only so much he could do. The rest, he'd learned long ago, was best left up to God.

"I can't promise he'll get well, Jeremy." Ben bent back over the puppy. "All I can do is my best."

The child hung his head, his expression bereft.

"How old are you, son?"

"Six."

Ben set to work shaving Rowdy's leg. He'd been seven when he lost his grandfather. Even now, all these years later, Ben grieved for him. Isaiah Longtree had been one of a kind, a full-blooded Shoshone with a song in his heart. He'd seen beauty in things that others overlooked and shared that gift with those around him, making even a raindrop seem like a miracle. Ben had adored him. He would have given a great deal for some of his grandfather's wisdom right then.

"Rowdy's young," he offered. "At least he has that going for him."

In truth, Ben thought the puppy had been weak and unhealthy before contracting the virus. His ribs were visible. If no one had bothered to feed the poor little guy, it was unlikely that he had been wormed or inoculated against disease.

"Where'd you get Rowdy?"

"At the animal shelter." The child lightly stroked the puppy's fur. "My mom tried to get me to pick another dog, but Rowdy was the one I wanted."

Ben nodded. "He's a cute little guy," he settled for saying. "I can see why you chose him."

Ben had a soft spot for runts himself. There was nothing that tugged on the heartstrings like a sad-faced, skinny puppy—unless it was a sad-faced, skinny little boy with freckles and a curly cowlick poking up like a corkscrew from the crown of his head.

"The lady said she'd give my mom her money back if he got sick. They gave him puppy shots and stuff, but I guess not in time."

"Parvo's sneaky," Ben said, cleaning away the fur shavings. "The virus lingers in the soil under the snow. Come spring melt, the conditions are perfect for infectious contact. If a puppy isn't kept inside until he's been inoculated and had time to build up antibodies, he runs a risk of infection. Most people don't know it takes time for the shots to work. Puppies can get sick just by sniffing someone's shoes."

"Rowdy was 'bandoned in an old barn, and he only got found day before yesterday. Somebody left him and his sisters there to die."

It was a story Ben wished he'd never hear again. He tied a strip of rubber around Rowdy's front leg to distend the vein.

Glancing at the cages around the kitchen, Jeremy said, "I never knew anybody with a hospital in their kitchen before."

Ben sterilized Rowdy's leg with alcohol. "Before winter hits, I hope to add on to the house. The kitchen works for now. I've got drawers for my utensils, good lighting, a table, and water close at hand. It's kind of handy, being able to stir the stew and keep an eye on my patients at the same time."

"Do you find all the animals in the woods?"

"Sometimes. Other times they show up in the yard." He glanced up, uncertain if he should say more. The wondering look in Jeremy's eyes told him the child was too young to have preconceived notions of what should or shouldn't be. "It's always been that way for me with wild things. They just come."

"It's probably 'cause they know you won't hurt them."

That was as good an explanation as any. It was as much as Jeremy or anyone else could understand anyway. The animals came. They always had, and they always would. As a boy, Ben had prayed for them to leave. *Run,* he'd think. *Go away before my dad sees you.* Sometimes the animals had disappeared. Other times they hadn't, and Hap Longtree had shot them.

Ben's father was dead now, and there should be peace on the ridge again. But some trigger-happy jerk from town was invading the woods and using the animals for target practice.

Ben's only consolation was that no rifle fire greeted the critters at the house when they came to him for help. He also found peace in the fact that he could finally be who he really was, what he had been born to be, a throwback, more Shoshone than white, even though his blood belied the fact. He Who Walks with Mountain Lions, his grandfather had called him. It had been a big name for a little boy, but it had helped Ben feel like less of a freak, making sense of the undeniable, that he was different from other children.

As always, the memories depressed Ben, so he shook them off. The sun had set on those days, and he made the rules here now.

"The animals you see are very sick or badly injured. I have to keep them close at hand so I can watch over them until they get stronger."

The child studied him curiously. "How come you don't have a clinic?"

"My mom can't be left alone. If I had a place in town, I'd be gone all day. I checked into starting a practice up here, but zoning ordinances prohibit it."

"What are zoning ordances?"

"Rules."

Ben was quickly coming to realize that Jeremy was full of questions. Never having been around children, he was at once amused and baffled.

"What's the matter with the owl?"

Ben glanced at the bird. "He has an injured leg."

"How did it get injured?"

"Someone shot him with a .22 rifle."

"What's wrong with the rabbit?"

The rabbit had also been shot, and Ben suspected the bullet had come from the same gun. "He had a spot of bad luck and got his shoulder hurt."

Rowdy stirred. Ben checked the IV. The pup raised his head. Then his tummy rumbled. Ben guessed what was about to occur, but before he could grab any paper towels, Rowdy's bowels moved. The resultant mess went everywhere.

Jeremy cried, "Oh, no!"

Racing to the counter, the child grabbed paper towels and tried to mop up, *tried* being the operative word. He was too short, and his scoop-and-wipe technique needed work. Ben almost took over. Then he decided against it. Jeremy was upset, and clearing away the mess might make him feel better.

"I'm sorry. I'll clean it up, Mr. Longtree. I'm real sorry."

Ben grabbed a trash bag from under the sink. When he shook it out, the plastic gave a loud snap that made Jeremy jump. Not for the first time over the last hour, Ben burned with anger at the man responsible for the child's timidity. "Put the soiled ones in here."

Nose wrinkled with distaste, Jeremy put the towels in the sack, then tore off more to attack the table again. As he worked, he began to wheeze.

Ben grew more concerned by the moment. The breathing problem was a panic reaction of some kind, which explained why the inhalant hadn't seemed to help. "Don't get in a dither. No real harm's been done, and it's not the first time there's been a mess."

Looking unconvinced, Jeremy continued trying to clean up.

Ben addressed his next reassurances to the puppy. "Don't worry, little guy," he said as he administered an injection of antibiotics. "Accidents happen to all of us. We know you didn't mean to do it." Ben glanced up. "Maybe you should tell him yourself. Sick as he is, the last thing he needs is to get all upset."

Jeremy cast Ben a distrustful look, but dutifully stepped around the table to speak to his puppy. "It's okay, Rowdy," he said, stroking the dog's curly ears. "You're just real sick, is all. We know it was a accident."

Ben capped the syringe and stuck it into a hazardous waste receptacle under the sink. "There, you see? He just needed to hear it from you. He looks more relaxed already."

The boy looked more relaxed, too, and the wheezing had stopped. "How come you aren't mad?"

"It isn't that big a deal."

"But he went pooh on your table."

"It's not the first time. I always disinfect everything after treating a patient. The table will be perfectly clean before I eat on it again."

"I'm glad I don't have to eat supper here."

Ben laughed, and that felt good. "Disinfectant kills the germs." He helped Jeremy with the final wiping up, using towels and spray disinfectant. Then he sealed the plastic bag and went to open the sunroom doors. When he returned to the kitchen, he said, "This is where I performed surgery on Methuselah."

"It is?"

Ben nodded. "My most recent patient is in intensive care under the table."

Jeremy leaned down to look. "Wow!" he said when he saw the raccoon. "I didn't know he was there."

Ben was glad for the distraction. While he sterilized his tools and put them away, Jeremy carried on a monologue with the injured raccoon. Diablo, roused from his nap by Jeremy's singsong voice, pushed up to nuzzle the child for petting. Jeremy obliged, burying his nose in the wolf's thick fur. Watching the pair, Ben wondered if Jeremy wasn't a kindred spirit. Few people had Ben's extraordinary rapport with animals, but this child clearly loved them.

After disposing of the plastic bag, Ben decided the boy could stand some fluid intake, too.

"You up for some lemonade?"

Jeremy straightened and nodded eagerly. Ben fetched the pitcher from the refrigerator and poured them each a tall glass. Then he joined Jeremy at the table. The child was barely tall enough to sit on a chair and drink from his glass. Ben thought about making him a booster seat with books, then decided against it. He still remembered being six and thinking he was grown up. It stung a boy's pride 'to be reminded he was still just a sprout.

Beckoned by the sound of the refrigerator being opened, Methuselah limped into the kitchen and nudged Ben's leg. Ben rifled through the meat drawer. After finding two chunks of beef, he fed the wolf and cat their customary morning snack. The animals happily settled down to eat, Methuselah lying by the potted fig to make a mess on the floor.

Jeremy touched the puppy's fur. "Do you think he's gonna die?"

"He's very sick," Ben said carefully. "Sometimes, all we do isn't enough, and things we love just slip away. Let's hope that isn't how it goes this time."

Rejoining Jeremy at the table, Ben took a long

drink of lemonade, whistling as he came up for breath. Jeremy grinned and mimicked him, then wiped his mouth with the back of his hand. With Rowdy stretched between them and the coon scrabbling at their feet, a peaceful feeling settled over the kitchen.

Chapter Four

Ben had gotten up to put the glasses in the sink when Diablo growled. The wolf didn't raise false alarms. Before Ben could react, a crashing sound came from the front of the house. As he approached the foyer, Jeremy's mom appeared. Behind her, the entry door still swung on its hinges.

Ben's first reaction was anger. How dare she burst into his house without knocking? He was about to say as much when Diablo circled from behind him, gave a low snarl, and sprang for the woman's throat.

"Diablo, *ka*!" Reacting instinctively and with a speed that surprised even him, Ben snaked out a hand, caught the wolf's collar, and stopped the attack mid-leap. The wolf yelped and tried to twist free. "*Ka*, Diablo! *Toquet*. Sit!"

Growling, the wolf did as he was told, but Ben kept a hold on his collar.

Chest heaving, face pale, Chloe Evans cried, "Where's my son?"

Ben noticed she was trembling, whether for herself or her child, he wasn't sure. What impressed him was the way she stood her ground. She hadn't backed off an inch when the dog lunged.

"Where is my son?" she cried again, her voice rising to a shrill pitch.

Ben had faced more fearsome opponents, but never an angrier one. "He's in the kitchen."

She wore snug blue jeans and a camp shirt of ivory silk that hugged the small but perfectly shaped breasts he remembered so well from yesterday. In the sunlight that poured through a skylight, the wind-tossed curls that framed her oval face and fell over her slender shoulders gleamed like molten copper.

Methuselah chose that moment to lift his head. "Oh, dear God," she whispered. "Oh, dear *God*."

Ben had completely forgotten the cougar. He held up a hand. "He's harmless. Really." He saw that she was staring at the blood on the cougar's chin, recalled the horrendous stories circulating about him in town, and quickly added, "He just had his morning snack. Beef—from the market."

"It's not a dog," she said shakily. "I thought it was a big yellow dog."

"No. His name's Methuselah. He isn't dangerous. I know he looks—"

"Mom?" Jeremy stepped from the kitchen. "How come you're here?"

"Jeremy!" Chloe circled Ben and Diablo to grab her son up into her arms. "You scared me half to death. What were you thinking, coming up here all alone?" She cupped a fine-boned hand over the back of his head and hugged him fiercely. "Thank God you're all right!"

Still clutching her child, she turned to face Ben again. He knew she wanted to race from the house, but he and Diablo blocked her way. Ben almost stepped aside. Then he thought better of it. In her present frame of mind, she would drive straight to town and tell anyone who would listen about Methuselah.

"The cougar isn't dangerous," he said. "I know it's unusual, having a cougar as a pet."

"Unusual?"

"Okay, really strange. If you'll just let me explain, maybe—"

"Explanations aren't necessary. What you do in the privacy of your home is your business. I just don't want my child here."

Ben wasn't going to be put off that easily. "As a rule, cougars are dangerous. What most people don't know, however, is that they're easily tamed. Methuselah's circumstances have made him more adaptable than most."

Jeremy squirmed to get down. Chloe tightened her hold on him.

"The cougar got his paw caught in an illegal trap," Ben said, determined to continue.

Her eyes grew strangely blank as he talked, making him wonder if she was even hearing him.

"If you'll only look more closely, you'll see that he's almost blind," Ben added. "All totaled, he has only three teeth left in his head, and they're all decayed. He may knock you over with halitosis, but otherwise he's harmless."

Jeremy finally managed to wriggle free of her arms. When his feet touched the ground, he grabbed her hand and began tugging her toward the kitchen. Ben didn't want her in there. She'd see all the animals, and then his goose really would be cooked.

"Jeremy," he tried.

But it was no use. The child was talking a mile a minute. "Mr. Longtree is giving Rowdy a drink of water in his vein, Mom. You gotta come see!"

Ben had been born with a measure of fatalism, inherited, he felt sure, from his Shoshone grandfather. The invasion of his home spelled disaster, but it was done. All he could do was pray Chloe Evans didn't turn him in.

The last thing Chloe wanted was to go deeper into the house. That wolf had tried to rip her throat out, and no telling what the cougar was capable of. She just wanted to get her son to the car, lock the doors, and drive like a madwoman off this ridge.

Unfortunately, Jeremy was bent on taking her to see his puppy, and Chloe couldn't think how to gracefully refuse.

At a glance, the kitchen looked normal with its custom cabinetry and high-end appliances. The counters were clean, and the dark green porcelain of the sink shone in the sunlight that poured through the sunroom windows. Chloe saw no pots or residue spills on the range top to indicate illegal drugs had been produced there.

Then she saw the cages—big ones, small ones—taking up every available space. Atop the green granite breakfast bar, a cylindrical pen of wire mesh housed an owl with a bandaged leg. At each end of the U-shaped counter, other cages were stacked three and four deep with all manner of wild creatures confined in them.

"I hope you'll excuse the menagerie," Longtree said from behind her. "I no longer hang my shingle anywhere, but I'm still a vet. When I come across wounded critters in the woods, I can't bring myself to turn a blind eye. At present, the kitchen is the only place I have to treat them."

Chloe took a hasty inventory. In addition to the owl, she saw an opossum, a rabbit, two raccoons, a one-legged quail, a silver gray squirrel, a red fox, and what looked alarmingly like an ordinary rat.

Longtree moved past her to the table. He spent a moment fiddling with the IV taped to the puppy's leg. "I know it probably seems strange." His black brows drew together in a frown. "No *probably* to it, it *is* strange. But I'm a vet, and these animals needed my help."

Just that, nothing more? Given the fact that he was breaking the law nine ways to perdition, she thought he should offer more of an explanation. He knew she could turn him in and send him to jail. In Oregon, it was illegal to cage wild animals without a permit, and the state didn't mess around when it came to prosecuting offenders.

Just last week at work, a man had been hauled in for poaching. He'd not only lost his rifle and vehicle, but he'd also forfeited his hunting privileges for two years, been fined five thousand dollars, and would serve up to twenty-four months in jail. The arresting deputy had been sporting a black eye and a bloody lip, which he'd received while trying to cuff the offender. Criminals didn't happily surrender to arrest when they faced such stiff punishments.

Chloe hadn't lived here when Bobby Lee Schuck brought the game wardens to Cinnamon Ridge, but she'd heard stories. Half a dozen animals had been confiscated, and Longtree had received a hefty fine along with a warning that he would be arrested if he were caught breaking the law again.

He didn't strike her as being dim-witted, so why wasn't he concerned about her seeing all this? An awful thought occurred to her. Maybe he had no fear of her turning him in because he didn't intend to give her the chance.

Chloe tightened her grip on her son's hand. Behind her, a wolf and cougar blocked her escape. Yesterday,

Lucy Gant's allegations that this man had done murder and disposed of his victims' bodies had seemed outlandish. Now Chloe wasn't laughing. Normal people didn't let an adult cougar lounge around like an ordinary house cat.

"If you don't practice as a vet anymore, what do you do for a living?"

"This and that."

His reply did little to allay her concerns. This home had cost him a pretty penny. He had to be making money. The question was, doing what?

"I'm a dispatcher at the sheriff's department."

Chloe silently congratulated herself on slipping that into the conversation. Their chances of getting out of there would be much better if he realized she was on friendly terms with individuals who would search for her if she disappeared.

He flicked the IV tube with his finger and readjusted the clip. His lips thinned, deepening the slashes that bracketed each corner of his mouth. "Jeremy mentioned that you'd just moved here. How do you like the new job?"

His burning blue gaze started at her toes and traveled slowly upward. Chloe had sworn off men, and her sensual radar was definitely rusty, but she still recognized an appreciative once-over when she got one. She locked her knees to stop them from quaking.

Oh, God. He was a very large man. If he was bent on keeping them here, she was in big trouble. His arms and shoulders rippled with strength every time he moved, and she'd seen how fast he was with his hands when he collared the wolf. She had pitted her strength against Roger's more than once and always come out the loser. She still remembered how it felt to see stars and manage to stay on her feet by sheer force of will. Even worse, she knew that even will-power wouldn't keep her standing if a man like Longtree put his weight behind a blow.

His examination of her person ended at her face. Arching one eyebrow, he met her gaze with an insolent challenge. In that moment—which seemed inexorably long—Chloe had the eerie feeling he knew what she was thinking. Even worse, the twitch of his lips told her he found her fear of him amusing.

Today the Stetson was absent, giving her a better view of his face. Black eyebrows without a hint of an arch capped eyes as blue as the ocean on a summer day. His features had the hard, sharp edges of chipped granite polished to a high sheen. He wore his shoulder-length hair loose with a multicolored braided cord serving as a headband to keep the glossy strands out of his eyes.

For the life of her, Chloe couldn't remember what he'd asked her. Standing there, she felt numb yet excruciatingly nervous, trying to recall his last words. Her job, she finally remembered.

"So far, I love the work." She really, really wished her voice wouldn't squeak. "I've never worked in a place where everyone's so friendly." She swallowed to clear her throat. "Frank Bower—one of the deputies—has a daughter, Tracy, who's turned out to be the nicest sitter Jeremy's ever had."

"Frank's a good man."

"Oh, you know him, then?" That was good. Very good.

"We went to school together."

"Mr. Bower took me for a ride in his Bronco," Jeremy chimed in. "I got to make the lights flash and talk on the radio!"

Longtree winked at the child. "It pays to have connections."

"Yep."

Chloe glanced pointedly at her watch. "We should be going. I told Tracy to call her dad if I wasn't back in thirty minutes. I'd hate for Frank to drive all the way out here to find us."

As Longtree studied her with cool detachment, his cheek muscle started to tic. In that moment, Chloe knew how hapless settlers must have felt when they came face-to-face with a Shoshone warrior.

"Are you threatening me, Mrs. Evans?"

Chloe's stomach dropped. She *had* been threatening him, but she hadn't meant for him to realize it. "Good grief, no! What on earth makes you think so?"

"Now, there's a question."

Chloe tried to laugh. The result was a thin, quavering cackle that sounded half-hysterical. "We just need to get going. I was just trying to explain."

"What about Rowdy, Mommy?" Jeremy tugged his hand free from hers, ran to the table, and went up on his tiptoes to pet his puppy. "Will we come back later to see him?"

If she got her son out of here, she would never step foot on this property again.

Longtree turned to rest his narrow hips against the counter behind him. After crossing his ankles and folding his arms, he studied her for what seemed forever, staring first at her face and then taking another measure of her person with an insolent slowness that made her skin burn.

His eyes gave away nothing of his thoughts. "I have no intention of keeping you here. If you want to take Rowdy with you, that's fine, too. However, before you make that choice, understand the consequences. The pup is burning up with fever and dangerously—" He glanced at Jeremy, fell silent, then changed course. "He's dehydrated, and I felt mild cardiac fibrillation when I took his pulse. Neil Fenderbottom's a good vet, but he's got a heavy patient load. If you take Rowdy to the clinic, chances are they'll put him in a cage and get to him as quickly as they can." He lifted a black eyebrow. "Time is of the essence. If you'd like to chance it, that's your choice."

The word *choice* rattled around in her head. Her stomach, knotted with nerves, did a funny little bump and roll. He didn't mean to keep them here then?

Searching his eyes, Chloe saw that he didn't. She also realized that he was coldly furious because she'd thought he might.

"I see."

"I would hope. My business is healing, not harming irrational women and helpless little boys."

Chloe couldn't think of a single thing to say.

Longtree straightened, took a glass from the cupboard, and stepped to the refrigerator. "I'll pour you each some lemonade. You can powwow at the table. Decisions are always easier to make if you can sit somewhere and think things through." After refilling Jeremy's glass, he set one for Chloe beside it, then returned the pitcher to the fridge. "There's a pad on the counter with my number on it. If you decide to leave the pup, jot down your phone number and take mine so we can keep in touch. While you talk it over, I have work I need to be doing. The IV is easily removed. Just undo the tape, pull it out, and redo the bandage to apply pressure so he doesn't bleed." He smiled at Jeremy and thrust out his hand. "Jeremy, it's been a pleasure. With your mom's permission, I hope you'll come see me again."

Jeremy solemnly shook hands with the man. "Does this mean you aren't gonna make Rowdy well for me?"

Ben flicked a hard look at Chloe. "That's up to

your mother. If you decide to leave the pup, I'll do everything I can for him."

Chloe was beginning to feel like a worm. Oh, how she wished she'd never met Lucy Gant and listened to her stories. "If we leave the pup, I will expect to pay you, Mr. Longtree. Can you give me an idea of the cost?"

"You can't afford me," he said icily. "Fortunately, Jeremy can, and we've already agreed on the terms. Right, Jeremy?"

"Yup. It won't cost any money for medicine or anything, Mom."

Ben Longtree ruffled the child's hair and grinned. The smile transformed his face. "Good-bye, Jeremy." His voice turned chilly again when he addressed Chloe. "I wish I could say it's been a pleasure, Mrs. Evans."

As he left the kitchen, he snapped his fingers. The wolf and cougar rose from their respective positions to follow him to another part of the house. Chloe gazed after the unlikely trio. Never had she felt quite so ashamed of herself.

"Mom?" Jeremy leaned around to make her look at him. "Please, can't I leave Rowdy here? Mr. Longtree will take real, real good care of him. I know he will. And it won't cost us any money."

After the way she'd behaved, Chloe cringed at the thought of accepting the man's charity. On the other hand, she was in no position to refuse. She went to stand over the puppy. His breathing was rapid and shallow. She could tell just by looking that he was hanging on to life by a thread. If she removed the IV, how could she be sure he would make it to the clinic?

Decision made, Chloe jotted down her phone number. She signed off with two words, *I'm sorry*. As apologies went, it was inadequate. Maybe, as an olive

branch, she could bake Ben Longtree a cake or something. It was the least she could do. He'd even given
her son lemonade. God, she felt like such a witch.

She had just laid down the pen when a feminine
voice rang out behind her. "Well, I'll be! He actually
did it."

Chloe whirled. A slender woman in a floral dress entered the kitchen. Her short brown hair was threaded
with silver, and her blue eyes shone with warmth.

"Hello," Chloe found the presence of mind to say.

The woman smoothed her bodice and patted her
hair. "Isn't it just like a man not to mention someone's
coming? I would have prettied up if I had known."

Chloe thought she was lovely as she was. This must
be the demented Nan Longtree. Only she didn't seem
crazy. She looked sweet—and embarrassed to have been
caught with her dress wrinkled and her hair mussed.

"Actually, I dropped in unannounced."

"Oh. That explains it, then, and no matter. It's glad
I'll be to have some female company once a week."

Bewildered, Chloe just smiled.

"Has he shown you through the house?"

"Oh, no, we didn't get so far as that. I, um, think
we have our wires crossed, Mrs. Longtree. I just—"

"Why am I not surprised?" Nan flapped her hand.
"It's just as well that I do it. He'd never in the world
think to tell you all that needs done."

Even with the glass office doors closed, Ben heard
his mom's voice. He cocked his head. *Great.* Just what
the situation needed, a performance by his mother.

Pushing up from his caster chair, he left the office.
As he strode to the main part of the house, he heard
Nan ask, "Do you do windows?"

Chloe Evans laughed, the sound light and airy. "I've
scrubbed a few."

"No store-bought stuff. Vinegar and newspaper. It never leaves smears."

"That's how my mom cleans windows."

Nan replied, "It's the only way to do them properly."

Just as Ben reached the kitchen, his mother jerked open a drawer. "Will you look at this?" She clucked her tongue. "With all these critters, we've got hair everywhere. In my day, I kept a spotless house. I can't anymore."

"This is a large home," Chloe said sympathetically.

"Yes. I'm so glad Ben finally hired someone. To his credit, I have to say that he tries. But he's so busy, he only gives the house a hit and a miss. The drawers are driving me crazy." Nan opened another one. "Isn't this awful?"

Ben descended on his mother. "Mom?" Heat crawled up his neck. She might as well show off his soiled underwear. "What are you doing?"

Nan smiled up at him. "I'm walking Chloe through, dear. You run along and see to your business. I'll get her all lined out."

Chloe arched her russet brows. "There seems to be a bit of confusion."

"Mom, Mrs. Evans isn't a cleaning lady."

Nan kept talking. "It won't be necessary to clean drawers weekly. Just vacuum them out with the crevice attachment a couple of times a month."

"Mom?"

Nan waved him away and opened the silverware drawer. "He keeps this one wiped out, thank goodness." She dampened her finger and chased a lone raccoon hair. "Mostly, anyway." A speck of something on the front of a cupboard caught her attention, and just that quickly, her voice trailed away. The next instant, she was humming a lullaby.

Ben stared at the back of his mother's head. In the

beginning, it had broken his heart to see her like this, but now he just bled a little each time.

"I'm sorry about this," he told Chloe. "A few weeks ago, I said something about needing a housekeeper." He shrugged. "She has Alzheimer's."

Ben half expected Nan's dementia to send Chloe Evans running, but instead she turned a compassionate gaze on Nan. "It's fine. I understand."

If Ben lived to be a hundred, he would never get women. She was looking at him now as though he were almost human.

Touching a hand to Nan's shoulder, she leaned around to say, "Nan, I'm leaving now. It was lovely talking with you."

Nan turned, her expression vacuous. Still humming, she wandered from the kitchen, took up her usual station in the family room, and set her chair to rocking as she began to crochet. Chloe gazed after her, her bottom lip captured between her teeth.

"I really am sorry," Ben said again. "She drifts in and out. She probably felt embarrassed. Stress of any kind seems to trigger it."

Chloe nodded. "I realized something was—well, not wrong, exactly, but not exactly right." Her gaze clung to his. "Mr. Longtree, I want to apologize. My behavior has been deplorable, and I—"

Ben cut her off with a lift of his hand. "It's not necessary. I've heard the stories in town, too. Why don't we leave it at that?"

Her face flushed crimson, whether with anger or embarrassment he couldn't say. In that moment, he didn't really care. He just wanted her gone. His mother's illness was something private and painful that he shared with no one.

Chapter Five

Chloe's feet were dragging when she got to work. The security system chimed as she pushed open the front door. Sue Baxter, her coworker—a chubby brunette with laughing green eyes, a warm smile, a wonderful husband, and five little Baxters to keep her busy—waved as she ended a conversation on the phone.

Waving back, Chloe circled her desk to stuff her purse into its cubbyhole. "Oh, Sue, you're a saint!" she cried when she saw the take-out latte on her blotter. "I can't wait to lock my lips on that. I'm so exhausted, I can barely see."

Sue rocked back on her chair, keyed the mike, and said, "Dispatch, calling all deputies." She flashed Chloe an impish grin. "Old Sylvia Patterson is doing a striptease in front of her window again. Joe doesn't want her arrested, but he would like her to get a boob lift before she strips for him again. Over."

Chloe burst out laughing. "For a second, I thought you were serious."

"You looked a little down."

"*Down* isn't the word." Chloe uncapped the cup, breathed in, and sighed. Every evening, Sue went to the espresso stand and bought them each a latte.

Today she'd evidently stopped by on her way to work. "What do I owe you?"

"The next round is on you."

"You've saved my life. I didn't get a wink of sleep last night, and I've been on a dead run all day. Maybe this will perk me up."

"What on earth kept you up all night?"

Chloe was about to answer when one of her phone lights started to blink. By the time she slipped on her headphones, took the call, and radioed out, another line was blinking. Before she knew it, she was swamped.

Two hours later, she and Sue got their first lull. Chloe's latte was stone cold, but she took a grateful sip anyway. Sue propped her feet on her desk.

"Wednesdays. Don't you love them? I swear it's a middle-of-the-week syndrome. People cause trouble so they won't die of boredom."

"Full moon."

"That, too, I suppose." Sue rubbed her temples. Then she kicked up, lowered her feet to the floor, and fixed Chloe with a curious look. "So why didn't you get any sleep last night? You never got a chance to say."

Chloe launched into the story about her son's sick puppy. She had just described Jeremy's emergency bicycle ride to Cinnamon Ridge when Deputy Schuck entered by the front door. Every afternoon, shortly after five, he stopped in to do paperwork. There was a back entrance, but he never used it, preferring to pass through Chloe's work area to reach the glass cubicle behind her.

"Evening, ladies."

Chloe broke off and pasted on a smile. Bobby Lee seemed like a nice guy, but for reasons she couldn't pinpoint he made her uncomfortable. She guessed it was a chemical reaction of sorts—a wary, very *dis*interested female reacting to an interested male's pheromones. She had no intention of complicating her life with a sticky situation at work.

He drew his sunglasses low on the bridge of his nose to look at her over the rims. He had a high-voltage grin and gorgeous baby blues lined with thick, black lashes. The effect was wasted. The only man in Chloe's life was her son. Bobby Lee's khaki uniform shirt, worn a half-size small to showcase his muscular chest, didn't hold a candle to Jeremy's freckles and curly cowlick.

"Did I hear you say Cinnamon Ridge?"

Red alert. Chloe was relieved when her phone started to blink. She went to line three, hoping Bobby Lee would start doing paperwork and forget the question. Unfortunately, while she handled the call and dispatched out to a deputy, Bobby Lee cornered Sue. By the time Chloe got off the radio, he had heard about the sick puppy and Jeremy's mercy flight to Cinnamon Ridge.

Hooking his glasses over his shirt pocket, he turned a questioning look on Chloe. "So what did you see up there on the ridge?"

Because Jeremy had told her about his agreement with Ben Longtree to tell no one about Methuselah, and she had promised to keep the secret as well, Chloe couldn't possibly answer that question. A deplorably bad liar, she stuck as close to the truth as possible. "Mostly Ponderosa pines. No wonder the place is called Cinnamon Ridge."

"I know you saw trees, Chloe. I'm more interested in what else you saw."

She drew her eyebrows together in what she hoped was a bewildered frown. "The manzanita bushes are losing their blooms, and there's a great view of the mountains from up top. Not that I had time to appreciate it."

"You must have seen something more than trees and bushes."

"I saw Longtree's house."

Bobby Lee raked a hand through his hair, the very picture of a frustrated male. "Did you see any animals?"

"Oh, yes."

"Now we're getting somewhere. What kind?"

"A wolf." Chloe didn't have to fake a shudder. "Have you ever seen that thing? It has fangs an inch long. Yesterday at the feed store—"

The deputy cut her short. "A hybrid and perfectly legal. I'm more interested in any wild animals you saw, particularly any in cages."

"Why would anyone want to keep wild animals in cages?"

Bobby Lee settled a wondering gaze on her. His expression said more clearly than words that he thought she had a room temperature IQ. "Did you see any? That's the question."

"I didn't see a single cage." That wasn't precisely a lie. She'd seen several cages. "Lots of chipmunks everywhere. They're so darling."

Bobby Lee braced a hand on the edge of her desk and leaned down to look deeply into her eyes. She half expected him to say, "Is anyone home in there?" Instead he asked, "Did you by any chance see a cougar?"

"A *what*? My goodness!" Answering a question with a question was a strategy Jeremy used. Chloe wasn't proud, but at least she was still taking the high road and not lying through her teeth. "Are there a lot of cougars around here?"

"We've got a fair number."

"That's spooky."

"I've heard rumors that Longtree keeps one as a pet."

"You're not serious. A cougar? Oh, my. Does he have a death wish?"

"I'm not concerned with his motivations, only with the possibility he's breaking the law. I need a warrant to check it out, and they aren't easy to get. Butterworth is a picky bastard when it comes to that."

It sounded to Chloe as if the judge was merely observing the law. Citizens had a right to their privacy. "Mr. Longtree is a vet. If he's providing care for wild animals, isn't it safe to assume he's doing them no harm?"

Wrong thing to say. A flush crept up Bobby Lee's neck. "Any time *anyone* messes with wild animals, he's doing potential harm."

"Oh?"

"If he's doctoring animals up on that ridge, he could be saving the genetically inferior ones and weakening the gene pool."

He launched into an explanation about gene pools, and how the natural order culled out the weak. Chloe's eyes had glazed over by the time he wound down. "Save the weak, and they propagate. Pretty soon, the whole damned population has that weak set of genes. Along comes a virus, and bad news."

"I see." Chloe folded her hands on her lap. What Bobby Lee said was true—but genetic inferiority wasn't the issue. Unless one was speaking of the sadistic human being who was going around shooting animals. "I never really thought about it like that. I had no idea you were so knowledgeable."

His shoulders relaxed. "Yeah, well—in this country, we're surrounded by wilderness areas. A law enforcement official has to keep abreast of the game laws and understand the reasons for them in order to do his job effectively."

"I see what you mean. One thing, though. Wouldn't a vet know even more about gene pools and all that stuff than we do?"

The hard glint that entered Bobby Lee's eyes sent a chill up Chloe's spine.

"Ben Longtree is a fruitcake," he bit out. "He's on a mission to save the animals, never sparing a thought for the damage he may do." He pressed closer until they were nearly nose to nose. "Did you see a cougar? If you did, tell me. Your position here demands that of you."

Her duty as a mother took precedence. She wouldn't break a promise to her son, not over a job or for any other reason. "No, I'm sorry. I didn't see a cougar."

Sue left the room to use the copier. Bobby Lee gazed after her, then shoved things out of the way to prop a hip on Chloe's desk. She bit back a protest. Everything had a place, and Bobby Lee's rump wasn't in the lineup. She grabbed her paperweight before it toppled off the desk. The Japanese lantern had been a gift from her dad, a memento of a day they'd spent beachcombing in Brookings, Oregon. She'd treasured it ever since.

"You know, Chloe, it wouldn't be wise to let your boy hang around up on the ridge. If you need a loan to pay for a vet, I'll happily front you."

"I, um—thank you, Bobby Lee, but that wouldn't be appropriate. We work together. What if something happened, and I couldn't pay you back?"

"I'm sure we could work something out."

Chloe fiddled with her notepad. "Be that as it may, it's unwise to mix personal and professional. It's less complicated that way."

"And a lot less fun. Loosen up, Chloe. Live a little."

Here went nothing. "Please, try to understand. I'm still reeling from my divorce. I'm not ready to loosen up yet. You know what I'm saying?"

"That you're still hung up on your ex?"

"I'm just not ready yet. It's nothing personal. Please don't think that. I just need some time."

He touched a finger to her cheek, and his eyes went cloudy with concern. "You know how to cure that problem?" He winked at her. "It's high time you had a little fun occasionally. All work and no play. Take a chance on me."

Not in this lifetime. "I'll think about it. Some people just take longer to regroup and heal. I'm afraid I'm one of them. Right now, I only want to focus on my son and my job. The rest will come with time."

"In the interim, can I give you a piece of advice, one friend to another?"

"Sure. I'm always open to good advice."

"Don't accept favors from Longtree. The man's unstable."

"I've heard that about him."

"But you don't buy it?"

"I didn't say that." She picked up a stack of papers and moved them out of his way. "To be perfectly honest, though, he seemed sane enough to me."

The moment Chloe said that, she knew it was true. She'd entered Longtree's house, expecting to encounter a lunatic. Instead, she'd found her son safe and sound, happily polishing off a glass of lemonade. Ben Longtree was a little odd—okay, extremely odd—but that didn't mean he was nuts.

"Longtree killed a fellow a few years back. Have you heard that story?"

Chloe had almost forgotten. "Yes. Lucy Gant mentioned it."

"Imagine hitting a man with enough force to kill him with one blow."

For just an instant, in her mind's eye, Chloe glimpsed a fist coming at her face. Her skin went cold, and she felt a little sick. Bobby Lee didn't know what crazy was. Not really. "There must have been more to it than that."

"There wasn't," he assured her. "I read the police report myself."

"Why did you read the report? It didn't happen here, did it?"

"I like to keep tabs on the riffraff in my county. The man's a killer."

"Wasn't he found innocent?"

"High-priced attorney, rinky-dink court. Our judicial system is far from perfect. The man's over the edge. I'll feel better if you stay clear of him."

She straightened her pens. "I know this may sound bad, but even if Longtree is crazy, it's nothing to me. My son isn't going up there again."

"Good."

"As for accepting favors from the man, Ben seems willing to treat the puppy free of charge. I really can't afford to pass up a deal like that."

"Ben? Sounds to me like you've gotten pretty cozy with the guy. You don't have a thing for him, do you?"

Chloe almost laughed, but the look in Bobby Lee's eyes dampened her amusement. "Ben Longtree is a little too eccentric for my taste. In answer to your question, no, I don't have a thing for him."

"I'm glad to hear it. If you're going to let him doctor your dog, and I really wish you wouldn't, you need to keep your distance. All that stuff I just told you about genetic tendencies? Take it to heart with him."

"Meaning?"

"His father was a violent drunk. Like father, like son?"

Chill bumps rose at the nape of Chloe's neck.

Bobby Lee took Sue's return to her desk as his cue to proceed into his office. Chloe was relieved. Had she imagined that burning look in his eyes when he questioned her about Cinnamon Ridge? She didn't think so. She had a feeling there was bad blood between him and Ben Longtree.

Not my problem, she assured herself, and she intended to keep it that way. She'd moved here to build a new life for herself and her son. Getting involved in other people's feuds wasn't on her agenda. After this, she would make sure Bobby Lee was nowhere around when she mentioned Ben Longtree.

At twenty of eight, Bobby Lee left to go back out on patrol. Soon Chloe was swamped. When she got a break, she ate her supper while Sue chatted on a separate line with her husband, Jerry.

After finishing her sandwich and yogurt, Chloe dug some Tylenol out of her purse and took them with the cold dregs of her latte. Then she found the slip of paper with Ben Longtree's number on it. *Benjamin Isaiah Longtree* capped the heading. It was a lot of name, she thought, but he was a large man, and somehow it fit.

Stalling. Why didn't she just dial the number? *Because.* The man made her nervous. She was also embarrassed. Her behavior that morning had been inexcusable.

She finally worked up the courage to dial. When Longtree answered the phone, his voice was like a rasp of silk. She pictured his dark features and intense blue eyes. "Mr. Longtree? Chloe Evans."

Long silence. Then he said, "Hi."

She picked up her paperweight and turned the blue

glass to catch the light. "You have every right to hang up on me. I know I was rude this morning."

Another stretch of silence. Then he laughed. It was a rusty sound—as if he didn't do it often. "I'm not in the habit of hanging up on people."

"That's good. I got a break at work and thought I'd call to see how Rowdy's doing."

"I wish I could say he's improved."

Her heart sank. "He isn't going to make it, is he?"

"He's not responding to the fluids and antibiotics. Later this evening, I'll know more. The longer he hangs on, the better his chances."

"However it turns out, I want to thank you. The puppy means a lot to my little boy."

"I know."

Coming from someone else that might have been a polite response, but Chloe had a feeling he meant it. "In the grand scheme of things, a dog isn't all that important. But he's become very important to us in a short time."

She heard a tapping sound. "In the grand scheme, we're all insignificant."

Over the last year and a half, Chloe had come face-to-face with her own insignificance. One moment, she'd been sailing through life, everything going her way, and the next, a twist of fate had taken her to her knees. Before that, she'd been so confident, believing she was in control. Six months later, she'd been pacing a hospital corridor, bewildered, in shock, covered with Roger's blood, and unprepared for what lay ahead.

"My son's been through a lot. The puppy is a touch of magic in his life."

"I only wish I could do more."

It was easier to talk with him over the telephone. There was safety in distance. She could concentrate on his voice—and the sincerity in it. His raspy baritone soothed her in a way she couldn't define.

"Mr. Longtree—"

"Mrs. Evans," he said at precisely the same instant. "I just—"

"About this morning."

They both laughed. Then silence. She supposed it was only her imagination filling in the blanks, but she sensed that he was searching for words. She found herself holding her breath.

"I, um . . ." The tapping grew louder. She pictured him striking the counter with a pencil or pen. Then it stopped. "I acted like a jerk this morning."

Chloe grinned. He hadn't acted like a jerk. It had been her behavior that was deplorable. "I know Diablo scared the blazes out of you, and Methuselah, as well. I've heard the stories, and you don't know me from Adam. I shouldn't have taken such a hard line."

"I'm the one who should apologize. You were very nice to my little boy. I was—well, running on adrenaline, I guess. I'd heard rumors, and they all came rushing back when I saw—" She broke off, acutely aware of Sue sitting across the room. "Well, your three-legged sidekick threw me."

"He has a way of doing that."

"I panicked, not thinking, just reacting. Your place is a long way from—"

"Help?"

"I meant to say town."

"Same thing."

"You're not making this easy."

"I hate apologies. Goes against my grain to let anyone else off too easily."

"You're a real friend."

He chuckled. "Apology accepted. Now, it's my turn.

Confession time. I knew exactly what you were thinking. I, um . . . well, those looks I gave you? I did it
on purpose."

Chloe gave a startled laugh. "You frightened me
deliberately?"

"You were already frightened. I got pissed off. I'm
sorry about that. After a while, all the witchcraft and
lunatic stories get kind of old. You know?"

Chloe imagined they would. Bobby Lee swore up
and down this man was unstable and dangerous, and
Lucy Gant seconded that opinion. Chloe no longer
knew what to believe. "I know it can't be an easy
situation for you."

"Most of the time, I ignore it. Today—well, I don't
know what happened."

She ran a hand over the blotter. "I guess we both
did things we regret."

"Yeah. Can we just call it even?"

She grinned. "Well, you really stepped over the line
with that last look you gave me."

She could feel the warmth of his chuckle coming
over the wire. Recalling his burnished countenance,
she had to admit that she found him sexy in a dark,
dangerous way. That was okay. His dangerous edge
was all the motivation she needed to keep her
distance.

"That last look was a good one, wasn't it? If it's
any consolation, you got yours. When you threw the
door open, the knob knocked a hole in my wall."

Chloe gasped. "Oh, no. It did?"

He chuckled. "Not a big deal. I'm slick with mud
and tape."

"I feel terrible."

"Yeah, well, don't. It wasn't your fault. Methuselah
has knocked most of the doorstops off the mopboards.

He likes the twanging sound they make when he swats them, and he gets a little carried away."

Chloe pictured the half-blind, decrepit cougar swatting the doorstops. "How on earth does he find them?"

"He seems to know they're stock equipment for all doors. He's working on the one in my mom's room now. When he disappears, I follow the twangs."

A cougar, playing like a kitten. Ben Longtree definitely kept eccentric company.

"What time do you get off work?" he suddenly asked.

"Why do you ask?"

He gave another rusty laugh. "I have that coming, I guess. I was just thinking I could call with an update on the puppy, is all."

Chloe felt silly. "Oh, of course. I get off at eleven."

"I'll give you a ring about thirty past if that's not too late. Maybe there'll be a change in his condition by then."

Chloe dreaded receiving that phone call. She didn't expect the news to be good. "I'm always up until about one. Eleven-thirty isn't too late."

"Until then."

She let the receiver slip into its cradle. For several seconds, she just sat there, going back over the conversation. Neither of them had said very much, but it felt as if they'd said a great deal. Chloe was relieved. He hadn't sounded like a killer, and nothing she'd seen so far indicated that he was a raving lunatic, either. So why did so many people seem to distrust him?

She began putting things on her desk back in order. The task reminded her of the talk she'd had with Bobby Lee.

"Do you know Ben Longtree very well, Sue?"

"As well as anyone, I guess. He's not exactly a social butterfly."

"I get the impression that Bobby Lee dislikes him."

"They've never been what you'd call chummy. Even as far back as grade school, they had it in for each other." Sue rose from her desk to get a cup of water from the corner dispenser. "I was a year behind them, so I don't know what happened to cause the rift."

"How can two adults still be at odds over a childhood rift?"

"I hear you." Sue narrowed an eye, took careful aim, and threw the empty cup into the trash can by her desk. "Testosterone. Who can figure men?"

"Did you hear Bobby Lee grilling me about Cinnamon Ridge?"

"Yeah. Sorry. He's a nice enough guy, and a good deputy. He's just a little overzealous when it comes to Ben Longtree."

"That doesn't strike me as being very professional. I was under the impression that personal issues were taboo in law enforcement."

"Strictly speaking, personal issues shouldn't interfere with a police officer's performance, but this is not a perfect world. You should've been here right after Deputy Joe Samples caught his wife in bed with the preacher."

Chloe gulped back a horrified laugh. "You're kidding."

"That got *really* ugly. Joe kept his cool when he found them. Didn't do anything except kick the guy out of his house. It was only the next day, after Joe had packed his bags and left, that he really lost it. For the next six months, his wife couldn't drive anywhere without Joe pulling her over. I bet she could have wallpapered her living room with traffic citations."

"He's still a deputy. I guess that means he got over it?"

"With some coercive persuasion from the sheriff, he went to counseling. It helped that his wife and the preacher had a falling out, and she left town."

"The moral?"

Sue's green eyes danced with laughter. "That Bobby Lee may have a grudge against Longtree, but so far, he hasn't stepped over the line to get something on him. If Bobby Lee ever does, the sheriff will jerk him up short."

"So I wasn't imagining that Bobby Lee has it in for Ben."

"Definitely not."

Line one on Chloe's phone started blinking. The call was from the bar up the road. Two men in the billiard room were cracking each other's skulls with pool cues. After the call had been dispatched, Chloe filled out the customary report. By the time she had finished, Sue was busy. It was a few minutes later before either of them was free to resume their conversation.

"There has to be some reason why Bobby Lee and Ben dislike each other," Chloe mused aloud. "People don't hold lifelong grudges over nothing."

Sue tossed her report into a basket on her desk. "Maybe it's because Ben's better looking, and Bobby Lee doesn't like the competition. Who knows? Ben was a loner and marched to his own drumbeat. There were always stories circulating in school—off-the-wall stuff—that made him a favorite topic of gossip. It was negative attention, but I think Bobby Lee resented him because of it."

"What kind of off-the-wall stories?"

"My favorite was the cat story. It got hit by a car. A tire had supposedly run over its hips, and it was trying to drag itself off the road. Several kids were standing around wondering what to do when Ben

showed up. The story went that he laid his hands over
the poor thing's hindquarters, and the cat took off
running like it had never been hurt. My friend Sally
swore she saw it happen. Ben claimed the cat was just
stunned, not hurt, but the more popular version was
that he performed Shoshone magic and healed the
poor thing."

"Which story did you buy?"

"Which one do you think? Ben was born here. He's
what, a quarter Indian? I think the poor cat was just
stunned. Unfortunately, the truth's never as exciting
as fiction. Bobby Lee always craved the limelight. He
sweat blood to excel in school, pulling high grades,
campaigning for student body president, and becoming
a star quarterback. Compared with Ben's Shoshone
magic, all his accomplishments seemed pretty mun-
dane."

"So he grew to resent Ben."

"That's just my take."

"And your take on Ben? Do you like him?"

"The truth? I used to have the world's worst crush
on him. I can't remember what grade it was, but I was
a big-time pain in the neck, I'm sure. A lot of boys
would've told me to get lost, but Ben was kind to
me." A distant expression entered her eyes. "When
we were growing up, I felt sad for him."

"Why is that?"

"His father, Hap, was a drunk. A mean drunk, by
all accounts—the kind who liked to fight and always
picked on smaller men so he'd be sure to kick ass. A
guy like that doesn't turn into a pussycat when he
walks in the door at night. Ben's mother, Nan, rarely
came to town, but folks claim she always had bruises
when she did. I don't imagine Ben and his sister escaped the abuse entirely."

Chloe thought of Nan, with her sweet smile and

gentle manner. "How sad. If things were that bad, I wonder why she didn't leave him."

"Chances are she never went to college or even had a job before she got married."

"We've come a long way, I guess."

"Thank God. Even nowadays, though, it takes a lot of guts to strike out on your own when you've got kids to keep in shoes."

Chloe could testify to the truth of that.

"What was Ben like as a boy?"

"Gentle. Or maybe *kindhearted* would be a better word. He didn't have it in him to hurt anyone or anything—unless he got pushed into it."

"Pushed?"

"Yeah. For example, we had a retarded girl at our school named Mandy Jean. Her parents didn't make her bathe, so she was dirty, and the boys on the bus used to torment her. One day, they knocked her books out of her arms when we got off at the stop, and every time she tried to pick one up, someone would kick it farther up the sidewalk. Ben lived out of town, so he didn't get off there, but evidently he saw what was happening as the bus pulled away, got off at the next stop, and ran all the way back."

Chloe propped an elbow on her desk and rested her chin on her hand. "What happened?"

"He squared off and gave the boys a choice. They could push Mandy Jean's books back to the corner with their noses or have a knuckle sandwich for their after-school snack."

"And they did it?"

"You've seen Bobby Lee's grin. He's still got his teeth, doesn't he?"

"Bobby Lee was one of the boys tormenting her?"

Sue laughed. "He was a brat. He wasn't driving yet. Fourteen, maybe fifteen. Boys are ornery at that age."

Unless they were gentle souls. "Poor Mandy Jean."

"After that, they backed off, afraid Ben would re-arrange their faces."

"So he is capable of violence."

"Aren't we all? Ben wasn't a kid to go looking for trouble. He just couldn't tolerate cruelty of any kind. If he saw someone kick a dog, he went ballistic."

"Do you—?" Chloe paused, feeling almost guilty for asking the question. "Do you think he's dangerous, Sue? Bobby Lee seems to think he might harm me or Jeremy, that he's genetically predisposed to violence."

"Genetically?" Sue rolled her eyes. "If our genes control our behavior, God help us all."

"That's my feeling, too."

"That isn't to say you shouldn't be careful," Sue hastened to add. "He did kill a guy. I just don't think his genes had anything to do with it."

Chapter Six

The pup was losing ground fast. Ben sat at the table, listening to the rattle of the dog's breathing. It wouldn't be long, a few minutes, maybe an hour. He'd turned off the lights. It was more peaceful in the shadows. Having failed to save the little guy, Ben at least wanted to make him as comfortable as possible at the end.

It was always difficult when he lost a patient. Life was sacred, and every creature, large or small, mattered to him. But it was doubly hard to fail when he knew a child would grieve as a result.

"He's dying, isn't he?"

Lost in his thoughts, Ben hadn't heard his mother enter the kitchen. "Yeah, I'm afraid so. I've done all I can, and he just isn't responding."

"I'm sorry to hear it. That little boy loves him so."

His neck ached with tension. Even in the dimness, he could see the lucidity in her expression. It was strange, how she drifted in and out. The doctor said it was common with milder forms of Alzheimer's, especially at first, but Nan had had the disease for five years. On the one hand, Ben was glad her condition hadn't deteriorated, but it hurt when she came back to him this way, only to leave again.

"I remember another boy who loved his dog."

Ben nodded. "Yeah, me, too."

"For months afterwards, you'd go missing, and when I went searching, I'd find you outside, sitting under that old tree beside his grave. All that winter and the following summer, you kept vigil. At times I wondered if you'd ever get over it."

"In ways, I never have."

"I hope little Jeremy doesn't take it that hard. His heart was in his eyes today while he was petting that puppy."

"It's out of our hands now, Mom."

"No, never that. As long as there's life, there's hope."

Ben stared into the darkness.

"There's nothing quite so beautiful as a child and dog, running and playing together on a sunny day. Just imagine, being able to make that happen."

His throat felt so thick, he could barely reply. "You're tired, Mama. Why don't you go along to bed?"

"Yes, very, very tired." She moved closer to rest a hand on his shoulder. "I love you, Ben. Do you know how much?"

He stroked her frail wrist with his thumb. "I love you, too. Never doubt it."

"I don't. What breaks my heart is that you no longer love yourself." Ben could almost feel the sadness emanating from her. "As a mother, I've countless regrets, but the one that haunts me most is that I let him do this to you."

"You shouldn't blame yourself. You did all you could."

"Did I?" She let the question hang there a moment. "It's always easier to say we've done all we can, isn't it? But it's seldom true. We can always do more—if only we find the courage." She tightened her grip on his shoulder. "Seeing you like this would break your grandfather's heart. He was always so proud of you, and he tried so hard to teach you to be proud of yourself. Where has your pride gone, Ben? Why do you deny what you are?"

"I'm not denying anything. Look at me."

"You wear the trappings." She fingered the beaded thong around his neck. "I know you're trying. I see you touch the medallion sometimes—to remind yourself, I think. *'I am Shoshone.'* But those are only words, Ben, and the medallion is only a stone passed down to you by your grandfather. 'Wear it with pride,' he said. You were only seven years old the night he died, but he saw in you the man you'd one day become."

"And I've failed him. Is that what you're saying?"

"No, Ben. You're failing yourself. And that's the heartbreak of it, don't you see? You've closed the door to your soul."

She drew away from him then, becoming part of the shadows again. He could hear her slippers shuffling over the tile as she left the kitchen. Long after the sound of her footsteps faded away, he sat there with his head bent, listening to Rowdy's laborious breathing. He'd heard the death rattle too many times not to recognize it now.

With a trembling hand, Ben reached out to stroke the puppy's fur, thinking of Jeremy. In ten or twenty years, would the child look back and remember this time in his life with an ache in his heart? Even worse, would he eventually become like Ben, afraid to let himself love again?

. The thought made Ben ache with regret and myriad other emotions he couldn't sort out or analyze. He allowed the weight of his hand to rest on the puppy's

heaving rib cage. Images of Jeremy and the dog running and playing together drifted slowly through his
mind, like the turning pages of a picture book. His
mother was right; there was nothing more beautiful
than a child and dog romping together in the sunlight.
And what a joy it should be to have the power to
make that happen.

Just once, Ben thought. *How could it hurt if he did
it only once?* He closed his eyes, let the tension drain
from his body, and curled his fingers over the puppy's
wasted body.

When Chloe's shift was over, she decided to drive
home with her window down. Whispering Pines, the
subdivision where she lived, lay ten miles west of
town, a pocket of private land surrounded by national
forest and countless small lakes that attracted fish-
ermen. At this late hour there was never much traffic
out that way. Normally, Chloe enjoyed driving the
curvy, two-lane highway. But tonight, fearing she
might fall asleep, she needed the wind in her face.

As she nosed the Honda through town at a sluggish
twenty-five, she loosened her hair and sighed with delight at the breeze moving over her. The scent of pine
and manzanita from the woods made the air smell
fresh and clean.

As she turned left onto Shoshone Road, she acceler-
ated and set her speed at fifty, slowing only when she
passed one of the residential or business districts en
route to the subdivision. The little store where she
sometimes stopped to get Jeremy a treat was dimming
its lights. The owner, a grossly overweight man, stood
out by the gas island, balancing a clipboard on one
hand. Just as Chloe passed, he bent over to read a
pump meter. The waistband of his baggy jeans dipped

low in back, flashing a broad expanse of bare rump that gleamed in the moonlight like the underbelly of a dead fish.

She gulped back a startled laugh. *Country living.* Just last week, her brother Rob had asked if she missed the cultural diversity of Seattle. Heck, no. She had all the cultural diversity she could handle right here.

She sighed as she reached her favorite stretch of the road, bordered on both sides by trees. Some five miles long, it was intensely dark, with a windy ribbon of moon-silvered asphalt stretching ahead of her and a midnight-blue sky overhead, studded with thousands of stars. This was the Oregon she'd come to love as a girl when she'd vacationed here with her family, and it had been memories of this place that had drawn her back as an adult.

As she turned off onto Whispering Pines Lane, a two-mile stretch that led to the housing district, Chloe slowed her speed, ever watchful for deer. No deer leaped out in front of her, but she did come upon a porcupine waddling up the center of the road. *Jack Pine's version of a traffic jam.*

Ringed by towering pines that blocked the moonlight, her front yard was cloaked in darkness when she pulled into the driveway. Tracy hadn't turned on the porch light. The illumination inside the house, diffused by curtains at the windows, cast only a dim glow over the shrubs bordering the foundation. In the breeze, shadows shifted, creating sinister shapes.

Chloe hesitated before exiting the car. Then, scoffing at herself for being a goose, she wrenched open the door, got out, and forced herself to walk, not run, to the steps. This was a sleepy town, the crime running to domestic disturbances, traffic infractions, and poaching, with an occasional fight at the bar to keep things interesting. She had no reason to feel uneasy.

Foiled by darkness, she fished for her keys, which, like an idiot, she had dropped in her purse. *Oh, duh.* Sleep deprivation. Her brain was on autopilot. She fumbled to insert the key in the lock. When she pushed into the living room, Tracy, engaged in conversation on the kitchen phone, waved hello.

"Gotta go. Chloe just came home. Yeah. Me, too." She made kiss noises. "Bye." After hanging up, she said, "Ooh, bummer. You look totally wiped. Was it a busy night?"

"Not too." Chloe limply patted the girl's shoulder. "I'm just tired."

The supper dishes had been washed and stacked in the blue drainer. "You're an angel, Tracy. Thanks for cleaning up."

"No problem." Tracy's brown hair was secured in a twist with a big purple clip. Glitter gel made her sweet face sparkle like a showgirl's, and she'd slashed her skintight jeans in strategic places. "I put some clothes in the washer for you and ran the vac. Jer spilled his popcorn."

"When my ship comes in, I'm giving you a raise." Chloe moved past her to go check on her son.

The night-light in her son's bedroom cast a fanlike glow over the wall, illuminating his bookshelf and the posters above it, depictions of John Deere tractors, Winnie-the-Pooh, and monster-faced characters from his favorite movie, *Shrek.*

Chloe bent over to smooth his hair. Life was complicated as a single mother, but she had no regrets. Jeremy was the joy of her life. She kissed his forehead. "I'll be back in a blink, big guy." The Bower house was only one street over. Jeremy would be safe for the few minutes it took her to drive Tracy home.

After dropping Tracy off, Chloe drove home faster than usual.

She no sooner killed the car engine than she realized the yard was still dark. She hadn't thought to flip on the porch light. She muttered under her breath.

Stiff with tension, she struck off across the lawn. It was stupid to be so jumpy. Roger was an entire state away, and she had no reason to believe he might show up here. It was time to turn loose of her fear and get on with her life.

Just as she reached the rickety steps, a deep voice said, "Hi, there."

She braked to a halt so suddenly that she almost pitched forward on her face. Her heart gave a wild leap when a man emerged from the shadows on the porch. For a horrible instant, she thought it was Roger. Then her panic-stricken brain registered the fact that he was far taller, and darker as well.

Ben Longtree. Chloe clamped a hand over the center of her chest, where her heart was doing an erratic tap dance. "Oh," she said weakly.

"I'm sorry. I didn't mean to startle you."

She moved her hand to her throat. It was going on midnight. What reaction did he expect? "It's okay. I, um, just didn't anticipate company."

"I was going to telephone." He rubbed his jaw. "Then I got to thinking that I'd rather tell you in person. Are you all right?"

"In need of defibrillation to reestablish a normal heartbeat, but otherwise I'm fine."

He chuckled. "I'm sorry. I wasn't thinking. I should have parked in your drive or stayed in the truck until you reached the house."

He stepped into the moonlight. He looked so—well, big. He looked big. And masculine. Too masculine for her taste. She could almost feel the heat rolling off him.

"I suppose you're wondering how I found your place."

She made a noise that passed for an affirmative.

"Jeremy called this evening. He gave me the address. I hope you don't mind. I know it's late for guests."

Chloe's brain had stuck on one thought. "Rowdy— he's dead, isn't he?"

Even in the moonlight, she saw his mouth tip into a grin. "Actually, no. He's doing better. Right when I thought sure I'd lose him, he started to rally."

Chloe groped for the wobbly porch rail. "He started to rally?" she repeated incredulously.

"He isn't out of the woods yet," he added. "Judging by the look of him, I'd venture a guess he was weak from starvation before he got sick, and the virus has robbed him of what little strength he had. But with proper care—meaning rest and plenty of nourishment—I think I can pull him out of it. I wanted to tell Jeremy. You know that saying, 'Bad news can't wait.' In this case, it was good news that wouldn't keep."

Chloe imagined him working over the puppy half the night and then making a special trip over here to share the news. "Jeremy will be over the moon. I don't usually wake him so late, but this calls for an exception."

Ben's eyes shimmered in the moonglow. "You don't have to do that. The good news will wait till morning. I wasn't thinking in terms of a six-year-old's time schedule."

"Hey, you have no idea how I dreaded having to

tell him the puppy didn't make it. Now I won't have to." A smarting sensation washed over her eyes. "He had such grand plans. Then they all blew up in his face. I felt responsible, you know? When he was choosing a dog, I knew Rowdy wasn't the best choice, but I didn't put my foot down and—" She broke off and sighed. "I'm sorry. I'm blabbering, aren't I? It startled me out of ten years' growth when I saw you on the porch."

"I got the impression you thought I was someone else."

"For a second, yes."

He nodded. "It takes a while."

What took a while? She was tempted to ask, but she had a bad feeling she wouldn't like the answer. Jeremy was still too young to understand there were some things he shouldn't tell people. Apparently he'd been filling Ben in on her personal life.

"Now I've upset you. Kids aren't quite as reticent as they should be sometimes. If it's any consolation, I admire you for getting Jeremy out of it. I know that took a lot of guts."

With every word he said, Chloe felt more uncomfortable. "I, um—thank you for saving Rowdy, Mr. Longtree."

"Ben," he corrected.

"And for stopping by to deliver the news in person, too. It was thoughtful."

"My pleasure, and you're very welcome."

Chloe released the railing. "It doesn't seem like enough, just saying thank you. It would have cost me the better part of a thousand dollars for treatment at the clinic, possibly more with complications. You've saved me a lot of money."

"There aren't many people who'd hock an heirloom to save a mutt. When I meet someone who will, I take my hat off to her. As for thanking me, you just have, and very nicely. Throw in a cup of coffee, and I'll call it even."

Inviting a man she barely knew into the house didn't strike her as being wise, yet off the top of her head, she couldn't think of a good excuse to say no. She did owe him.

"Coffee. Sure. I can do that."

She joined him on the porch to dig for her keys again. With him standing over her, she felt awkward. What did she think she was doing? He had killed someone. Bobby Lee had warned her to stay away from him. Sue had seconded that vote. And here she was, letting him into the house.

After finally locating the key, she inserted it into the hole upside down on the first try, and then was unable to make it turn on the second.

"Here, let me."

He plucked the key from her hand and unlocked the door with enviable ease. At her startled look, he grinned. Dropping the ring back in her purse, he said, "It's all in the wrist."

"My dad says it's all in how he holds his mouth."

He chuckled. "That, too, I suppose."

Once inside, she glanced at the motley collection of furniture she'd picked up for a song after selling all her nice stuff to pay off some of the credit-card debt. Compared with his place, hers looked pretty shabby. "Welcome. It's not much, but it's home. If the floor gives under your weight, don't be alarmed. My landlord assures me it won't fall through."

"It's clean and comfortable. That's all that counts."

As Chloe led the way to the kitchen, she was acutely aware of him looming behind her. The room wasn't large to begin with, and with him taking up space, it seemed minuscule. He sat at the table with his back to the window. His shoulders looked as wide as the window frame. *Impossible.* She'd measured the opening for new curtains last week, and it was forty-eight inches wide. It was only the angle—or a trick of the light. The flickering fluorescent tubes cast a bluish glare, creating a shimmering nimbus around him.

Pausing by the stove, she said, "Regular or decaf?"

"Regular, please. I work most of the night."

Chloe recalled Lucy Gant's saying that he had no job and mooched off his mother. His reference to work piqued her curiosity. "So, what is it that you do in the wee hours of the morning to earn a living, Ben?"

"This and that."

She drew the basket from the coffeemaker. He'd given her the same answer that morning, which was no answer at all. "Is your profession a secret?"

"Not really. I just make it a rule never to talk shop."

As explanations went, that was pretty lame. Okay, fine. He didn't wish to discuss his work. That worried her. Most people didn't clam up when asked about their jobs. What was he trying to hide? More to the point, why was he trying to hide it? Recalling Lucy Gant's allegation that he was dealing in drugs, Chloe decided to let the subject drop. If he was doing something illegal up on his ridge, it was no business of hers—and she wanted to keep it that way.

She quickly rinsed the filter basket, spooned in enough grounds for a half-pot, and filled the carafe to the five-cup mark. Fearful that caffeine at this hour would keep her awake, she nuked a mug of water in the microwave for instant decaf while the coffee machine began its brewing cycle.

She could feel his gaze on her in the silence. She spilled instant coffee on the counter as she scooped a rounded teaspoon from the jar. She needed to say something, but her sleep-deprived brain remained stubbornly blank.

"Excuse me for a moment," she said, and went to the back of the house to awaken her child.

As children will, Jeremy stirred when she shook his shoulder, but he didn't wake up. When Chloe lifted him from the bed, he buried his face against her shoulder and made a mewling sound of protest.

"I'm sorry, sweetie. Someone's here to see you."

"Who?"

"It's a surprise," Chloe whispered, praying that she wasn't making a mistake.

Ben's gaze sharpened when she entered the kitchen. He started to push up from his chair, then sank down again. Chloe turned so Jeremy could make eye contact over her shoulder. "Hey, sweetie, look who's here. Mr. Longtree came to tell you some wonderful news."

Jeremy's head popped up. He blinked sleepily and rubbed his eyes, then managed a slurred, "Hi."

"I just stopped by to tell you your puppy's doing better."

Jeremy grinned. "He's all better?"

"Headed that direction, anyway."

The child beamed, his bleary eyes lighting with happiness. "I *knew* you could make him better. I just *knew* it!"

With a wiggle and push, Jeremy freed himself from Chloe's embrace. The instant his bare feet touched down, he raced around the table and launched himself into his benefactor's arms. Clearly unaccustomed to children, Ben caught Jeremy to his chest to keep him from falling, but then seemed uncertain what to do with him.

"Thank you, Mr. Longtree! Thank you, *thank* you!"

Jeremy cried, hugging the man's neck with his skinny arms.

One hand hovering over the child's narrow back, Ben said nothing for a moment. Then the tension slipped from his big body. "You're very welcome," he replied in an oddly husky voice.

Chloe suspected that Ben would have set the child off his lap, but Jeremy had other ideas. He twisted sideways, snuggled close, and began grilling the poor man.

"How much better is he?"

"He's still very weak. I can treat the virus, but only time will put meat back on his bones. He needs to build his strength back up."

"But he won't die. Right?"

"No, I don't think so. Not unless something unexpected happens."

"Is he still getting a drink in his vein?"

"Yes."

"Is he still swallowing up?"

"Vomiting," Chloe translated.

"Oh, no. He's no longer vomiting."

"Is he still sleeping on your table?"

"No, I made him a nice bed in a box before I came over here. I was afraid he might wake up and fall off the edge."

"Is he moving lots?"

"Not a lot yet, but more than he was."

Mindless of where he poked with his knees, Jeremy rose to hug Ben's neck again. "He really is better, then!"

Ben shifted the boy's weight to protect his vulnerable spots, smiled slightly, and returned the hug more easily this time. Watching from across the room, Chloe suspected it had been a while since this man had experienced any kind of physical closeness, and possibly never the exuberant affection of a child.

To his credit, Ben took to it quickly and was soon running a big hand over Jeremy's shoulders, patting and massaging him back to sleep. It was unusual for Jeremy to so quickly bestow his trust on a stranger, but the child rested his curly head on Ben's shoulder and made no move to pull away. Man and boy had clearly forged a friendship that morning.

They were a picture, the two of them, Ben so midnight dark and Jeremy so fair. Ben's skin gleamed in the flickering overhead light like varnished oak seasoned to umber. His glistening jet hair, so straight and thick, looked almost unreal compared to the child's fiery curls. *Daylight and darkness.* Ben's splayed fingers encompassed the entire span of the boy's back. For just an instant, Chloe found herself wondering how it might feel if he were to touch her that way. The instant she realized the track her thoughts had taken, she busied herself wiping counters that were already clean. *What madness.* She would never submit to the intimate touch of any man's hands again.

When it became apparent that Jeremy was going to fall asleep in Ben's arms, Chloe softly observed, "He likes you."

Ben turned his cheek against the child's hair. The gesture touched Chloe in a way she couldn't define. "The feeling's mutual. He was scared to death when we first met this morning." He flicked her a look. "Much to my shame, I tried to run him off. He stood his ground, insisting I hear him out."

"And once you did, you couldn't turn him away."

"He's quite a boy." His eyes warmed on hers. "Takes after his mother, I think."

She turned to pour his coffee. When she glanced back, Ben was still rubbing his jaw on Jeremy's curls, his expression conveying pleasure and no small amount of wonder.

If he enjoyed children so much, why had he never had any of his own? Chloe was about to ask when she recalled her vow to keep her distance. Yes, the man seemed nice. And, no, he didn't strike her as being crazy. But she didn't have the credentials to make that judgment. He had killed someone with one blow of his fist.

Ben suddenly stood. At his questioning look, Chloe led the way to the bedroom. She hurried around the bed to draw back the covers, then watched as he lowered her child to the mattress, handling him as if he were made of glass.

She was about to pull up the covers when Ben drew them up himself. He executed the task with such gentleness that Chloe had to turn away. A year and a half ago, Jeremy's father had tucked him in just like that. Until this moment, Chloe hadn't realized how much she missed that nightly ritual.

Once back in the kitchen, she added sugar to her decaf. Over the chinking of the spoon, she heard the scrape of Ben's chair as he resumed his seat. She looked away, wondering how one man could elicit such polar responses from her—one moment making her question her sanity, the next reminding her of the good times and making her mourn all that she'd lost.

It wasn't like her to yo-yo, and Chloe could only take it as a warning sign. Ben was indeed dangerous, only maybe not in the way Bobby Lee thought.

"You've made a friend for life." She slid his mug of coffee across the table and sat down. "It's an honor. My son doesn't make friends easily."

"That's two of us." Lifting the mug, he inhaled the steam. "Ah, a woman after my heart." He took a slow sip. "One thing I can't make is good coffee."

Chloe figured he was just being nice. It was pretty hard to go wrong with coffee. "It's one of my few culinary accomplishments."

He shrugged. "I'm a fair hand in the kitchen. Coffee's the only thing I can't seem to master. If it's not too strong, it's way too weak." He took another appreciative sip. "Perfect."

The ensuing silence had Chloe tapping her fingertips on the table. At the sound, Ben glanced at her hand. Then he grinned. Recalling the frostiness of his gaze that morning, she marveled once again that a mere smile could make such a vast difference in someone's face.

Now, if he would only shrink a little, she might feel halfway relaxed with him. He was all darkness and hard angles, masculinity emanating in waves from every pore of his skin. She could smell his aftershave, a brisk, piney scent that reminded her of the woods on a warm day. His hand, curled around the cup, was half again as wide as hers across the back, and his fingers were twice as thick. She remembered the strength of his grip when he'd grabbed her arms at the feed store.

He had been easier to talk to on the phone. Without the visuals, she'd been able to be herself. Such was not the case now. She guessed him to be at least six-five. The name Longtree suited him. And she wished he'd leave now so she could breathe normally again.

"Maybe I should take a rain check on the coffee," he suddenly said. "It's awfully late, and you look tired."

"I'm fine." The moment she spoke, she wondered what had possessed her to protest. "I, um, just didn't sleep much last night."

"My point exactly."

He made as if to rise. Chloe surprised herself by

touching his shirtsleeve. "Please, don't go. I seldom call it a night before one." She checked her watch, thinking that there was no question; she really had lost her mind. "If I crash right now, I'll be up at seven instead of eight. Working the late shift, it's better if I sleep in. Otherwise I'm dragging when I get off."

He sat back, regarding her thoughtfully. "It's not just that you look tired. You seem tense, as well. Not that I blame you." He gestured at the window. "Lights out, all around. The rumors in town don't exactly recommend me."

That was true, and yet . . . she felt as if she did know him, in a way. Yo-yoing again. It had been unwise to allow him inside the house, especially so late at night. But it was done, and so far he'd given her no reason to regret it. "You seem harmless enough."

Holding his mug cupped in his hands, he braced his elbows on the table. "Harmless, huh?" He lifted the cup to his lips. "Then why are you so nervous?"

Fair question. Unfortunately, it wasn't one she felt inclined to answer. "I always feel compelled to talk nonstop when I'm first getting to know someone, and I can't think of much to say. That makes me nervous, I guess."

He smiled again. She liked the way the creases in his cheeks deepened to slashes when his mouth curved up at the corners. "My grandfather maintained that it's better to be silent than to talk a lot and say nothing. The coffee is great. That's what I came in for. I'm not used to talking much. You've met my mom. Since the onset of her illness, conversation hasn't been one of her strong suits."

Chloe could well imagine how lonely his life must be, living alone on the ridge with only a woman with Alzheimer's for company. "It must be difficult for you."

"Not so bad, really. I'm used to being alone."

She had a feeling that he'd been alone far too much. "So . . . when you're not doctoring animals and doing this and that to earn a living, what do you do?"

"Lately my patient load has been such that I barely find time to sleep. All those animals were shot. Someone's been using them for target practice."

"I saw your poster. I can't believe someone's wounding them on purpose."

"Believe it." His dark face went taut. "A .22-caliber rifle is large enough to kill most animals, even a deer if the slug is carefully placed. Whoever's doing it aims at nonvital areas. He's deliberately maiming, not trying to kill."

"Why would anyone do that?"

"Some people are just sick." He ran his fingertip around the edge of his cup. "While we're on the subject, I couldn't help but notice that no cops knocked at my door this afternoon. I take that to mean you didn't report me. I'd like to thank you for that. I'm not sure why you chose to keep quiet, but I appreciate it."

"The letter of the law is pretty inflexible. I can't see how your helping wounded animals is a bad thing." She caught her lower lip between her teeth. Then she smiled. "There was also a certain little boy who never would have forgiven me for ratting."

He gave a startled laugh. "I owe him."

In that moment, Chloe thought she'd never met a more attractive man. It wasn't merely that he was handsome, but also that he didn't seem aware of it. She found that refreshing—and appealing in a way that set her nerves on edge.

"What?" he asked.

Chloe realized she was staring. Heat pooled in her cheeks. "I spaced out for a moment. I guess I'm more exhausted than I realized."

Finished with his coffee, he glanced at his watch, and said, "I'd better be shoving off. My mom was asleep when I left, but she often wakes up about this time and wants some hot cocoa. She likes it made the old-fashioned way, and Alzheimer's and gas burners don't mix. She forgets and lays stuff on the range—like kitchen towels."

"Oh, dear. Has she started any fires?"

"I watch her like a hawk. But we've had a couple of close calls."

"She's a lucky lady," Chloe said, meaning it sincerely. "A lot of sons would put her in a retirement home. It seems to be the way of things nowadays. Kids are too busy with their own lives to have time for parents."

"I'm not very modern-minded." He inclined his head at the mug. "It was great coffee, Chloe. Thanks for having me in."

"It was the least I could do. I only wish I were in a position to pay you."

"Don't be silly." He rose from the chair. "It's not about money."

Chloe laughed. "Where I come from, it's practically always about money."

He conceded the point with a nod. "Seeing that smile on your son's face was all the payment I needed."

Chloe stood to see him to the door. He paused at the threshold, his incredibly blue gaze trailing slowly over her face. "On the other hand, I can think of worse things than having a very pretty lady feeling indebted to me."

For what seemed an endlessly long moment, Chloe thought he might kiss her, and she wondered how it would feel. Her stomach knotted with nerves, and her skin went clammy. She needed to step away, wanted to step away, but she couldn't seem to make her feet move.

Instead of kissing her, he reached up to touch the outside tip of her right eyebrow where a pink hairline scar angled toward the corner of her eye.

Startled, she reached up to grab his hand. The instant she touched him, she regretted the move. His fingers were hard and warm, and they curled to encompass hers; the contact of flesh against flesh was jolting. Bracing his arm against her, he proceeded to trace the scar with the back of his knuckle.

"What happened here?"

"I fell." The memories slid like acid through her mind. "It, um, happened about a year ago."

His jaw muscle started to tic. "Clumsy, are you?"

"Occasionally."

"Your son is a very lucky little boy."

He said nothing more, but it made Chloe feel as if she were standing naked on the courthouse steps. He saw too much. Guessed too much.

She released his hand and stepped around him to open the door. Chill night air rushed in. She welcomed the shock of it—needed it to clear her head.

"Good night, Ben."

He stepped out. The porch creaked under his weight, the sound eerie in the still darkness. "Good night," he said as he moved down the steps.

Chloe leaned her shoulder against the door frame to stare after him. He seemed to be surrounded by a faint aura of blue light. She blinked and narrowed her eyes. Forty hours without sleep was too long. Now she was starting to see things.

As though he sensed her watching him, he turned to walk backwards several steps, his big, rangy body a study of masculine grace. Even in the dimness, his eyes shone like chips of blue crystal. The night wind caught his long hair, whipping the strands across his dark face.

"Sweet dreams," he called.

And then he was swallowed up by the blackness. She stood there, staring at the moon-washed patch of lawn where he had been standing. The overgrown blades of grass shimmered in the silvery light, giving off a glow similar to the one that had seemed to surround him.

Chloe sighed and closed the door. Her sleep-deprived brain had reached overload stage. When she started seeing blue force fields around a perfectly normal flesh-and-blood man, it was time to call it a night and go to bed.

A few minutes later, Ben parked his truck next to his house. For a moment, he just sat there, staring at nothing and listening to the cooling engine ping. He couldn't say why he'd driven down to Whispering Pines to report on Rowdy's condition in person. Even worse, he hadn't a clue why he'd invited himself in for coffee.

There was something about the lady that he found difficult to resist. Maybe it was the expression in Chloe's lovely brown eyes, a mixture of wariness and distrust that made her seem vulnerable in a way that was completely at odds with her composed, self-assured behavior. Not that it mattered. If he saw her again, he'd be playing with fire. Had his experiences with Sherry taught him nothing?

Ben folded his arms over the steering wheel and rested his head on his wrists. He didn't usually have a problem steering clear of women, so why was Chloe different? Ben didn't know. He just didn't know. But he'd be a damned fool if he went near her again.

Chapter Seven

Wearing an oversize Seahawks T-shirt and the pig slippers Jeremy had given her for Christmas, Chloe shuffled into the kitchen at eight o'clock the next morning, her destination the coffeepot. She turned on the water, yawned, and pushed the hair from her eyes as she opened the cupboard to grab the Folgers. Seven hours of shut-eye hadn't been enough.

Her reason for living—and her reason for setting the alarm—burst into the kitchen. "Hi, Mom!" he called.

Even half-asleep, Chloe noted the healthy color in his cheeks and felt thankful. "Hi, sweetie." She blinked and rubbed her eyes. Was she seeing things, or did her son have a shoestring tied around his head? "Jeremy?" She touched one of the dangling laces. "What is this?"

Jeremy beamed at her. "My headband." He went up on his tiptoes to grab the box of toaster tarts from the bread box. "Mr. Longtree wears one."

Ben also wore a medallion, beads, and long hair. Chloe measured out coffee. *This, too, shall pass*. If her son wore a shoelace around his head, what harm could it do? It was a simple case of hero worship. Next week, something new would catch his eye, and the shoestring would be knotted around the washing machine agitator.

Jeremy pulled out drawers to create stairs and climbed up to put his tarts in the toaster. The coffeemaker began its cycle. Chloe sank onto a chair. When she first woke up, she liked to stare at nothing. What she liked and got were usually two different things.

"What're we gonna do today?" Jeremy asked.

Chloe studied his bright face. "What do you have in mind?"

The wall phone rang. Jeremy scampered over and grabbed the receiver. "Hello." His grin broadened. "Hi, Mr. Longtree!" He listened for a moment. "Yup, I 'member. How's he feeling this morning?" He turned toward Chloe. "She's right here. Okay. Tell him I love him lots."

Chloe's stomach got nervous butterflies as she took the phone. "Good morning."

"Good morning. I hope it's not too early."

"I was already up. How's Rowdy?"

"Weak. Diarrhea's gone. No vomiting. Both are good signs."

"That's wonderful." Jeremy was bouncing around in front of her as if he had springs on his feet. "Judging by the exuberance of a certain young man, you've already told him that."

"In part. It does my heart good, hearing him so happy. I'll leave explaining the recuperation period to you. Normally, I'd let Rowdy go home in a few days, but he's not your average pup. Chances are his immune system is next to nonexistent. With your house being a rental, no telling what diseases may be in the soil. The last people could have had a dog with distemper—or God knows what else. To be safe, I'd like to keep him here awhile."

"How long are we talking about?"

"As long as Jeremy can stand it."

Chloe winced. She didn't think Jeremy could stand it for very long. "Rowdy got his first shots. Won't it be safe to bring him here soon?"

"I don't recommend that any pup be exposed to possible infection until it's four months old, and Rowdy is far less robust than most."

Chloe's heart plummeted. "That seems a little overcautious."

"Not with a pup like this. The shots don't work right away. No puppy is fully protected until it's four months old, and even then, there's a slight risk."

"Is there any way I can sterilize our yard?"

"With bleach, I suppose, but it would be hard on the grass—and expensive. Do you have a garage? You could sterilize a concrete floor."

"No garage." Taking in the run-down condition of the house, Chloe sank back in her chair. "Do you have a safe area for the puppy at your place?"

"At the end of the house, a carport. When he grows strong enough to spend time outdoors, I can build him a pen there."

Chloe hated for Jeremy to wait so long, but she preferred that to his losing the puppy. "We'd rather be safe than be sorry. I'll explain it to Jeremy."

A few moments later when Chloe related the situation to her son, he took it better than she expected. "There are bad things hiding in the dirt, Mom."

"What kind of bad things?" she couldn't resist asking.

"Viruses and germs," Jeremy whispered as if they were monsters, waiting to leap out at them. "All winter, they hide under the snow. Then it melts away, and even puppies that never go outside can get sick 'cause people walk through mud and bring germs into the house on their shoes. Rowdy got sick 'cause he sniffed a germ he couldn't see."

This bit of knowledge had Ben Longtree's name written all over it. "Well, we definitely don't want him to sniff any more."

"Nope. He needs to stay with Mr. Longtree till his shots start to work."

Sue was grinning when Chloe got to work a little before three. "You'll never believe it! Jerry got the raise! A hundred and ten a month. Isn't that fantastic?"

With five kids, the Baxters were financially strapped. Chloe was genuinely pleased for her friend. "What're you doing to celebrate? I'll baby-sit."

"Would you, really?"

"Hey, why not? We get the same nights off. At your place, though. My ramshackle rental might implode from the vibration of little feet. It'll be fun. We'll have a barbecue, play lawn soccer, and have a movie fest. Popcorn and ice cream, my treat."

Sue smiled blissfully. "Jerry and I haven't gone anywhere for so long! I could wear my Victoria's Secret bra and panties. They make him wild."

"Well, then?"

"You're on!" Sue agreed. "Let me talk to Jerry about when. Okay?"

"You know my schedule. Any night I'm off is fine with me."

"You're sure?"

"It'll be good for Jeremy. He has a friend across the road, but it's an older boy. He hasn't met anyone close to his own age."

"That won't be the case with my yahoos." There were only two years between each of Sue's five children, and the youngest child was four. "He'll have a blast. It's you I'm worried about. Six kids are a handful."

"I'll manage."

Chloe spent a moment reviewing notes from the first shift. A few minutes later, she had her desk in order and was settling down to work when Sheriff Lang came through the front door. Always respectful around ladies, the middle-aged lawman drew off his Stetson. His graying hair shone as brightly in the fluorescent lights as his silver badge. He wore the same kind of uniform his deputies did, only he didn't fill it out quite as trimly, his belly forming a paunch over his belt, his once-broad chest gone flabby from lack of physical exercise. Despite that, he was still a handsome man with a craggy face turned leathery brown from years of exposure to the harsh Central Oregon elements.

Generally the sheriff was so busy that he paid the dispatchers little heed, but today he looked directly at Chloe. As he approached her desk, she braced for a chewing out, her mind racing as she tried to think what she might have done wrong.

"Chloe, I'd like a word with you," he said. When she started up from her chair, he waved her back down. "It's okay if Sue overhears. It's nothing strictly private. It's just come to my attention that you're getting friendly with Ben Longtree."

That was the last thing Chloe had expected him to say. "Not friendly, exactly. He's treating my son's puppy for parvo."

Lang rubbed his jaw. "Just a word of caution," he said solemnly. "What you do in your off-hours is entirely your own business, but seeing as how you're new to town, I feel it's my duty to give you a heads-up. Longtree has a history, and he's always been a strange one. Be careful around him. I wouldn't want to see you or your boy come to any grief."

Chloe recalled how Ben had rested his cheek against Jeremy's curls last night. "Are there any facts on which you base your distrust, Sheriff?"

The lawman smiled. "After thirty years at this job, I've come to trust my instincts. I can't say why I don't trust the man. Could be that quiet way of his. Or maybe it's just those strange blue eyes, when he looks so Native American otherwise. Something about him just makes me edgy."

"Do you think there's any truth to the stories floating around about him?"

"What I think isn't important. I can't touch him without proof." He winked at her. "That's another thing thirty years has taught me. Proof eventually comes to him who waits. If he's up to no good up there on that ridge, I'll get him sooner or later, and when I do, it'll give me a chance to dig deeper. Until then, be smart."

The phones started blinking crazily just then, saving Chloe the need to reply. The sheriff continued on toward his office. Chloe and Sue exchanged a meaningful look, and then began taking calls. Just like that, they were swamped, with no letup for hours. At some point, Chloe saw the sheriff leave, his passing only a blur. Things were so busy that even Bobby Lee failed to drop in at his usual time. Sue claimed the locals were gearing up for the weekend.

At 8:40, the calls dwindled to nothing. Silence descended over the office like a blanket. After tossing her headset on the desk, Sue rocked back in her chair. "Ah, man! I don't know if I can make it two more hours."

"I hear you," Chloe commiserated.

Sue shot up and grabbed her purse. "Lattes! The stand closes at nine."

"My treat tonight." Chloe rifled through her handbag for her wallet, withdrew a five, and handed it to her coworker. "Would you rather I went?"

"The fresh air may revive me." Sue tucked the money into a side pocket.

"Take your time. I can man the fort for a few minutes by myself."

Chloe took advantage of the lull to do paperwork. She was busy at the keyboard when the door chimed to announce an arrival. Bobby Lee.

"You're late tonight," she said.

He pinched the bridge of his nose. "Been a bitch, then it had puppies."

"I know. The phones have been ringing off the hook. It's quiet now."

"The calm before the storm."

Bobby Lee moved toward her. He shoved things out of his way to sit on her desk. She grabbed her pencil cup just before it toppled.

"Oops, sorry," he said.

She wanted to go back to work, but she couldn't bring herself to be that rude. She didn't like being alone with him. He'd never said or done anything out of the way, but since her divorce, men tended to make her tense.

He began toying with her Japanese lantern. Her heart leaped every time he pushed it to the edge of her desk. "Last night, I drove by your place to make sure you got home safely. I saw Longtree's truck parked out front."

"You drove by my house?"

He nodded and slid the glass paperweight toward the edge of her desk again. Chloe had a very bad feeling—a shivery one that moved up her spine and raised goose bumps on the back of her neck.

"Bobby Lee . . . ," she tried.

He cut her short. "If you're lonely and looking for male companionship, why tie up with a loose cannon like him? I know how to treat a lady."

Chloe couldn't think how to respond. It was one thing for him to feel attracted to her, and quite another for him to become territorial.

"I have no intention of 'tying up' with anyone. I told you that. Right now, all my energies are focused on my little boy, my job, and being a good mother."

He arched an eyebrow. "So why are you hanging out with Longtree?"

"I'm not hanging out with him. I'm just grateful to him for treating Jeremy's puppy, and I offered him a cup of coffee to show my appreciation."

With a sudden flick of his wrist, Bobby Lee sent the Japanese lantern sailing over the edge of her desk. It hit the concrete floor with a deafening pop.

Chloe jumped up from her chair. "Oh, no!"

"I'm sorry. Damn." Bobby Lee crouched down and began picking up the pieces. "I know it meant a lot to you. I'm so sorry. I don't know how I did that."

Chloe could have sworn he'd done it on purpose. Fury lashed her.

Gathering up more glass, he said, "I really am sorry, Chloe."

He could say what he liked, but nothing would convince her it had been an accident. She clenched her teeth to keep from hurling angry accusations. *Ker-clunk—ker-clunk*. The thick pieces of glass hitting the side of the metal waste can resonated in the silence.

Bobby Lee stepped to the back room and returned with a broom and dustpan. As he swept up the slivers, he said, "It's a shame it can't be glued back together." He leaned over to empty the dustpan into the basket. "Some things can't be fixed once they're broken." He straightened. "It's like that with people, too. I'd hate to see something bad happen to you or your little boy."

Before she could respond, he left. She laid a shard of the glass on her desk blotter. It glittered in the light just like Bobby Lee's eyes. He was angry because she'd seen Ben and had retaliated by breaking something precious to her.

People can't be glued back together, he'd told her. On the surface, it could have been nothing more than a warning, meant to steer her away from possible trouble, but Chloe sensed an underlying threat that troubled her immensely.

"I'm back!" Sue called as she pushed in the door. When she came to set Chloe's latte on the desk, she saw the broken glass. "Is that what I think it is?"

Chloe nodded miserably.

"Bummer. How did it get broken?"

Chloe almost blurted out her suspicion that Bobby Lee had broken the lantern on purpose. She liked Sue, and they were becoming friends. But if it meant Sue's job, where would her loyalties lie? Bobby Lee had been a deputy for years and had a sterling record. Chloe was a new hire with no proof the man had gotten out of line.

"It got knocked off my desk," she settled for saying.

"I'm sorry, Chloe. I know it was special."

"Yes," Chloe agreed, "very special."

And Bobby Lee knew it.

Later that night after taking Tracy home, Chloe was still too upset over the incident to sleep. In hopes of exhausting herself, she cleaned like a dervish for two hours, wiping out drawers and cupboards, dusting the top of the fridge, and polishing all her kitchen appliances. If she accomplished nothing else, she would at least have some free time to spend with Jeremy tomorrow.

When the kitchen was spotlessly clean, she attacked the laundry. While sorting the colored clothes, she came across the jeans Jeremy had worn that day. There was dog hair on the denim. She held the pants up to the light. How had Jeremy gotten dog hair on his jeans?

Chloe leaned wearily against the washer. Dumb question. He'd gone to Cinnamon Ridge without permission. She couldn't believe it. She had expressly told him not to go back up there, and he'd promised that he wouldn't.

Sighing, Chloe let the pants slip from her fingers. For just an instant, she felt angry with Tracy. She was paying the girl well to watch her son.

The thought no sooner entered Chloe's mind than reason nudged it right back out again. Tracy was doing her job and doing it fine. She kept the house tidy. She played with Jeremy in the evenings and read to him. She was one of the best baby-sitters that Chloe had ever had. The problem lay not with Tracy but with Jeremy, who had chosen to take advantage of his new-found freedom.

Chloe had moved to this area so her son could have a wholesome, wonderful childhood, running and playing in safety in the pockets of forest that surrounded the old subdivision. Jeremy was on his honor to abide by Chloe's rules, to report back to his sitter, and be where he said he would be. Tracy couldn't be blamed because Jeremy had suddenly developed a devious streak.

Chloe knew she couldn't ignore this. Tomorrow morning, she and Jeremy had to talk.

*   *   *

Chloe was pouring her second cup of coffee the next morning when Jeremy skipped into the kitchen.

"Hi, Mom!"

Chloe smiled. It did her heart good to see him acting like a normal little boy again. "What would you like for breakfast, big guy?"

"Happy-face pancakes!"

"Happy-face pancakes, coming up." Chloe opened a cupboard to make sure she had enough raisins to create eyes and noses. "Berry syrup or maple?"

"Maple!"

"Do you want some bacon today?"

"Just pancakes."

Chloe was surprised. "No bacon?" She checked him for fever. "You sick?"

He shook his head. "Bacon comes from pigs."

She bit back a grin. "Well, yes. Where did you think it came from?"

"I knew it came from pigs. I just never thought about the pigs before."

"Oh. And you've decided you don't want to eat bacon because it comes from pigs?"

In the process of climbing the drawers to get a glass, Jeremy paused, looked over his shoulder, and said, "There's other good stuff to eat."

Chloe suspected there was more to the story, but she opted to let the subject drop. Her son had a shoestring tied around his head again this morning, and he was wearing his moccasin slippers instead of sneakers, reminders of her suspicion that Jeremy had sneaked up to the ridge yesterday.

While she mixed the pancake batter, Chloe tried to think of how to broach that subject with her son. After considering several different tacks, she decided on a straightforward approach. "I noticed the strangest thing last night."

He sloshed milk into a glass. Grabbing a towel to wipe up the spillage, he said, "What kinda strange thing?"

Chloe poured a measure of batter into the hot skillet, quickly formed a happy face with a handful of raisins, and then turned from the stove. "I found dog hair on your jeans." She quickly realized that would allow him far too much wiggle room. "More specifically, on the jeans you wore yesterday."

Jeremy wrinkled his nose and squinted. "I had Rowdy on my bed that first day, 'member? He must've got hair on my bedspread. It hasn't never been washed since then, and I played on it last night before my bath."

Chloe had to give him points for ingenuity. Did all moms feel this awful the first time they caught their children lying? "Jeremy, I want you to tell me the truth. Did you sneak up to Ben Longtree's house yesterday?"

His expression went incredulous. "Why do you think that?"

He was a slippery little eel. Chloe folded her arms, looked him dead in the eye, and replied, "It wasn't only Rowdy's hair that I found on your britches, but Diablo's, as well. Would you like me to get the jeans and show you?"

He hung his head. "No."

"You did go up to the ridge yesterday, didn't you?"

He nodded.

Chloe knew it was stupid to feel betrayed. All kids fibbed to their parents at one time or another. But she and Jeremy had a very special relationship—or so she'd always thought. Hands shaking, she turned to flip his pancake and spent a moment pushing at the edges to make it perfectly round.

"I didn't tell you a real lie, Mommy," Jeremy tried.

Chloe turned his pancake onto a plate. "No, but you did dance around the question. That's the same as lying." Chloe recalled how she had danced around Bobby Lee's questions. "Almost the same, anyway."

"It is?"

She broke off from pouring more batter. "You know it is, Jeremy."

He scrunched his shoulders. "I'm sorry, Mommy. I know it was naughty. But I was afraid you'd be real, real mad if I told you."

"You were right. I'm very upset with you."

She turned off the burner so she could give the conversation her full attention. After sitting at the table, she patted her knee. "Come here, sweetie."

He shuffled over. Chloe lifted him onto her lap. "I love you more than anyone else in the world. Do you know that?"

"Yup."

"Because I love you so much, I make rules to keep you safe."

"I know." He pressed his face against her blouse. "I love you, too."

"You have asthma, Jeremy. The road up to the ridge is steep and dusty. What if you'd had a breathing attack? Tracy had no idea where you were, and neither did I. Did Mr. Longtree even know you were coming?"

"No, I 'prised him."

After seeing Ben interact with Jeremy, it was difficult for Chloe to believe that he might harm the child, but given town opinion and their short acquaintance, she couldn't entirely rule out the possibility. Nevertheless, it seemed wiser not to mention that and to focus on other issues.

"Do you remember the time I had to call the ambulance?"

Jeremy nodded. "I had to go to the hospital."

"That's right. And on the way, the man in the ambulance gave you a shot and oxygen." Chloe didn't want to terrify the child, but she did feel it was vital for him to understand the seriousness of his condition. "What if you'd had a bad breathing attack yesterday? There would have been no one to help you."

Jeremy rubbed his eye with a fist. "I didn't have a breathing 'tack, though."

"You were lucky."

He pouted his bottom lip. "Rowdy's real sick, Mom. I gotta go see him every day—to pet him and tell him not to be scared. I'm his only person."

Chloe hugged him close. "Oh, sweetie, I know you want to see your dog, but you mustn't take off like that without telling me. It's too risky."

What was she going to do? If she refused to take Jeremy to see his dog, he might sneak off and go by himself again. Better that she take him. At least then she'd be there to run interference if Ben Longtree really was as crazy as everyone claimed. "If I promise to take you to see Rowdy as often as Mr. Longtree will allow, do you promise never to go up there alone again?"

"Do you think he'll let us visit every day?"

"Maybe. I'll have to ask him. I'll call him shortly, but only after you and I have settled this to my satisfaction."

"Am I in real big trouble?"

Chloe touched her nose to his hair, which smelled of shampoo and a wonderful essence exclusively his own. "Let's just say I can't let this slide. Lying is a bad habit, and I need to think of a punishment that will make you think twice before you do it again. That being the case, I think your coloring me a picture would be effective."

"What kind of picture?"

She thought for a moment. "Two pictures, actually—one of an ugly old lie, and one of the truth, which has to be really, really pretty. Can you do that?"

Jeremy nodded.

"While you're coloring, I want you to think about how hurtful it is to lie to the people you love—and how happy the truth makes everyone feel."

Ben Longtree answered on the fourth ring, his deep voice slightly edgy.

Chloe identified herself, and then said, "I'm sorry. Have I caught you at a busy moment?" She heard water running in the background. "I can call back later."

"No, no. Around here, one moment's as good as another."

She wrapped the phone cord around her forefinger and watched the tip turn red. "I called to ask if you would mind having company for a little while today. I was hoping to bring Jeremy up to see his puppy."

A clattering sound came over the wire. Chloe pictured him washing dishes. There was something irresistibly attractive about a man in the kitchen.

"No, I don't mind at all."

Despite the reassurance, she detected a note of reluctance in his voice. She thought about saying that they could do it another day, but then she caught a glimpse of Jeremy shoveling down pancakes at record speed, one of his cheeks bulging. The child would be disappointed if he wasn't able to see Rowdy today, and Chloe didn't want him sneaking off again.

"I'm off today," she said. "What time would be convenient for you?"

"I'll be tied up the next couple of hours. Eleven will work."

"You're sure we won't be interrupting?"

"Not at all," he said. "I'll be expecting you."

Muttering under his breath, Ben plunged his hands back into the dishwater, chased around for the dishcloth, and then furiously scrubbed the nonstick pot he'd used for his mother's oatmeal. *Damn it.* He didn't want to see Chloe today—or any other day. Why the hell had he agreed to let her come?

He wasn't a man who courted trouble; it came knocking on his door often enough. The last thing he needed was to get hung up on some woman. He'd been down that path before, and he wasn't making the mistake again.

With a hard jerk, he pulled the sink plug, slapped it down on the counter, and turned on the water to rinse out the suds. *No way.* When a lady affected a man in this way, the smart thing was to avoid her. He should have known after Jeremy's visit yesterday that Chloe would soon follow.

Ben was tempted to send the pup home with them. Even as the thought took root, he discarded it. The pup was weak. If Rowdy caught another virus, it'd be over.

Not even a miracle would save him.

Chapter Eight

Ben smiled as he crouched by his mother's rocker. She didn't glance up from her work, an afghan she was making for his niece Bonnie. He watched her nimble fingers for a moment, glad that she could still crochet. The hobby kept her occupied and out of his hair for hours on end.

The thought filled Ben with guilt. Hap had been a terrible father, but Nan had always tried to make up for it. He owed this lady, not just for her efforts to make his younger years tolerable, but also because she had accepted him just as he was. To Ben, that was a blessing for which he would always be grateful.

"Mom? I'll be out for a bit. Is there anything I can get you before I leave?"

Scowling at the interruption, she straightened her shoulders. "I'll be fine, sweetie. You run along and play. When you get back, we'll make cookies."

Ever fearful that she might start a fire in the kitchen, he said, "Making cookies will be fun. Just don't turn on the oven before I get back. Okay?"

"Oh, no. That's the fun of making cookies, doing it together."

Confident that she would crochet until he returned,

Ben grabbed his pack and the watercooler, then began the hike up to the cave to care for his other patients. The appreciation that settled over him as he walked through his woods never failed to soothe him. The huge, cinnamon-colored trunks of the Ponderosas evoked a sense of serenity within him that he could find nowhere else. He loved the moldy scent of the forest floor. Though the wind whispered in the trees, and birds and squirrels chattered ceaselessly, he could still hear his feet crunch the pine needles that carpeted the earth. He flexed his shoulders, enjoying the warmth of the sunlight that penetrated his cotton shirt.

A rabbit bounded from behind a bush, stopped in his path, and then hopped slowly away, pausing to look back at him. Ben accepted the invitation to follow, and moments later, he found himself standing over a baby bunny with its hind foot caught in a coil of wire snagged on the roots of a tree.

"Hey, little fellow." Ben set aside his gear and squatted over the helplessly trapped youngster. "Just be still. I'll have you loose in two shakes."

The baby rabbit went motionless the instant Ben touched it. Taking care not to pull the wire tighter, he struggled to extricate the little guy's foot. He was relieved to see that no permanent damage had been done.

The wire untangled easily, and within moments, the baby hopped happily away with his mother. Ben gazed after the pair, feeling necessary in a way that he knew would elude him anywhere else. When he'd first returned to Cinnamon Ridge to care for his mom, he had felt trapped. Now he understood that the true prison had been the life he'd left behind.

You've closed the door to your soul, his mother had accused last night, but that wasn't entirely true. He had opened it partway, he just hadn't found the courage to open it all the way yet. And perhaps he never would.

After ducking between the strands of barbed wire that marked his property line, Ben began searching the earth for any sign of human footprints that weren't his own. Since the snowmelt, someone had been invading these woods almost daily to wreak havoc on the animals. What kind of person could cause so much needless suffering and still manage to sleep at night?

The question was still troubling Ben when he approached the cave, situated in the rock face of a cliff, its entrance concealed with brush. Just outside, a doe stood vigil. She was slender and delicately formed, with an easy agility that he envied. He particularly admired the shape of her head and her expressive brown eyes. Many people thought all deer looked alike, but to Ben, they were as individual as humans. This pretty little lady was a sweetheart, and Ben had nicknamed her Sweet Cakes.

As he covered the remaining few feet to the enclosure, he called out softly to warn of his approach. Accustomed to his twice-daily visits, the doe merely wheeled away so he could toss aside the camouflage.

"How's your baby this morning?"

The doe's only response was to nuzzle his discarded pack in search of a treat. Ben opened a side pocket, gave her a slice of apple, and proceeded into the cave with her at his heels. Her fawn, caged just inside the entrance, bleated at the sight of her, hungry for her milk.

Setting aside his gear, Ben threw open the cage door. "With an appetite like that, Kiddo, I'd say you're on the mend."

Unlike the other animals, which had all been shot with a .22-caliber rifle, Kiddo had a compound fracture of the right rear leg, compliments of a careless motorist. Late one night about three weeks ago, Ben had found the poor little tyke lying on Shoshone Road. He'd loaded the fawn into the back of his pickup and driven home at a crawl so the mother could follow. In another six weeks, he would remove the cast and release the fawn back into her care.

Hobbling awkwardly from the cage, Kiddo bleated again and rubbed noses with his mama. When the initial hellos had been said, he moved to her side, nuzzled her underbelly, and began to nurse. Smiling, Ben watched for a moment.

A dank, musty smell assailed his nostrils as he turned away to light the lantern. As the lamp's golden glow illuminated the walls of the cave, he softly cursed Bobby Lee Schuck for making it necessary to hide his patients here. The accommodations were inadequate, with poor ventilation, moist air, and a rocky floor that made leveling the cages a pain in the ass. Ben did his best to keep the pens clean and the water fresh, but with so many critters in a confined space, housekeeping was an uphill battle. There was also the constant worry that one of the animals might have a setback, which was why he came twice a day to check on them.

Before starting to work, Ben visited the cages to give each occupant a little one-on-one. The badger loved to have his belly scratched. Carefully protecting his hurt shoulder, the animal rolled onto his back and gave Ben a beady-eyed, imperious look. While Ben rubbed the demanding fellow's belly, he visually examined the wound. There was less seepage on the bandage this morning, a good sign. The antibiotics were clearing up the infection.

"You're just a big old baby," he accused as the badger arched his back for more scratching. "Like I have time to give you a belly rub?"

After petting the badger a few more seconds, Ben moved from cage to cage, speaking softly to the other animals and giving each some special attention. It wasn't really necessary to their recovery, but it was Ben's policy to make petting as important a part of the routine as medical treatment. He believed his patients recovered more quickly as a result.

He made no sudden movements as he crouched by the rabbit's cage. She was a timid little thing even with Ben, yearning for attention but nervous when she received it. "You don't trust easily, do you, Valentine?" The muscles along her spine twitched as he lightly stroked her fur. "That's okay. Neither do I." He drew a piece of carrot from his pocket, which he'd brought just for her. "It doesn't mean we don't need a little TLC now and again, does it?"

Her pink, heart-shaped nose twitched as she sniffed the offering. He'd sliced it thin because she preferred her carrots that way—little slivers that she could munch easily. While she enjoyed the morsel, he gently examined her left haunch, where she'd been shot two weeks before. The wound, which he no longer kept covered, was healing nicely. She'd be lame, but over time, she'd learn to compensate.

His heart squeezed as he moved across the cave to visit the raccoon and coyote. In the final stages of recovery from a bullet wound to the front shoulder, the smaller animal was doing well, but the canid lay listlessly in his pen.

"Hey, Sly." Ben opened the coyote's cage to examine the wound, located high on his back. The slug, lodged dangerously close to the spine, couldn't be removed without risking permanent paralysis. Ben could only wait and hope that the damaged nerves healed themselves. For now, the coyote had only partial use of one hind leg. "You're not looking too chipper today, my friend."

Waiting and doing nothing for the creature bothered Ben deeply. That's what came of making exceptions, he supposed. Like an ex-smoker who'd sneaked a cigarette, now that he'd bent the rules for Rowdy, he found himself wanting to go the extra mile all the time.

He gently stroked the coyote's shaggy fur, and the tension went out of its body. Ben sighed and ran his palm over the animal's flank. "That's the best I can do for you. I'm sorry."

The coyote's eyes had drifted shut. Ben made a mental note to administer an injection of morphine before he left. That would keep the animal comfortable until he returned tonight.

After feeding all his patients and changing their water, Ben made his rounds, checking wounds and temperatures, applying fresh bandages, and doling out medications. The fawn had finished his breakfast and was leaning happily against his mama by the time Ben finished. He hated to cut the cuddle session short, but his guests would be arriving soon. If he didn't get back, his mother would have Chloe cleaning the oven.

Ben had just started to fix his mother's lunch when he heard a car pull up out front. That was undoubtedly Chloe, arriving on the dot. Why that annoyed him, he didn't know. He hated to be kept waiting. Maybe that was what rankled, he decided as he walked to the entry hall with Diablo trailing behind him. He wanted her to do something to make him dislike her, and she wasn't cooperating.

Most of the time when he got to know a woman, he grew critical. He didn't like the way she simpered, or he discovered that she was a rotten mother, or the way she laughed began to needle him, or her conversation bored him. The list was endless, and it was a rare female who didn't fall short in some way.

So why hadn't Chloe? So far, she was too damned perfect to be real.

Standing back from the tall, narrow window that flanked the front door, Ben angled his head to peer out. Ms. Perfect was rounding the front bumper of her car, one hand held out to her son. Even with the door closed, Ben could hear the cheerful lilt of her voice and felt warmed.

And a little empty, he decided as he watched her and Jeremy together. The love between them was almost tangible—a relaxed, offhand affection that made both of them smile at each other. How might his life have turned out if Sherry had been that kind of woman—tenderhearted and loyal, with a loving nature?

Ben shoved the thought away. He couldn't let himself move in that direction. Didn't dare. Developing a fondness for Chloe Evans would be emotional suicide. He'd *never* open himself up to that kind of hurt again.

The doorbell chimed, and Ben jumped a foot. Muttering curses at himself for acting like such an idiot, he reached to open the door, then stopped himself because he didn't want to seem eager. And if that wasn't stupid, he didn't know what was. What did he care if she thought he was eager? He wasn't. That was the bottom line, and what she thought didn't matter.

Right, a little voice whispered mockingly at the back of his mind. *You care what she thinks. That's what's eating you.*

Ben braced himself as he drew the door open. What he needed was a one-night fling to get his libido under control. He'd been too long without a woman; that was all. Any female would look good to him right now.

And, damn it, she does look good.

Holding her son's hand, she stood in a pool of bright sunlight, wearing faded jeans and a baggy Seahawks T-shirt. Her auburn hair had been slicked back from her face into a French braid, but tendrils had whipped free in the breeze to saucily frame her face. As near as he could tell, she wore no makeup, but the naturally dark gloss of her lashes lent her eyes definition, and the rosy flush on her cheeks was all the color she needed.

"Hi," she said.

Her smile was sweet, and her gaze, though still wary, was more direct today. Dressed as she was, she obviously wasn't out to impress him, so why was his hand sweating on the doorknob? "Hi."

Jeremy tugged free from her grasp and dashed past Ben into the house. "Jeremy!" she cried. When the child kept going, she shrugged. "I'm sorry. He's six. What more can I say?" Diablo turned to follow the child. Flicking a look at Ben, she asked, "Is your dog okay with him barging in like this?"

"They've met a couple of times. I'm sure it's fine." Ben moved back to let her in. "He's generally cantankerous only with adults."

Observing her as she stepped through the doorway, Ben wondered how she managed to look so good without trying. The T-shirt clung softly to her shape, outlining a small bust and a trim waist that flared temptingly to nicely rounded hips. From the hem of the shirt down, the faded jeans took over, showcasing slender legs with just enough plumpness at the thigh to draw a man's eye.

For a slightly built woman, she packed a hell of a wallop.

Neck craned to gaze after her child, she said, "He really shouldn't rush in like that. I thought I taught him better manners."

Ben's gaze was fixed on the V of her collarbone, exposed by the stretched-out neckline of the T-shirt. Her skin there was creamy and looked as soft as a baby's. There was a freckle just above the ribbed cotton, and seeing it, he yearned to see if she had more under the shirt. He shoved his hands in his pockets. The thought of trailing kisses from freckle to freckle made him miss what she'd said.

She glanced up. "He's acting like he owns the place."

"He came up yesterday to see the pup. He knows he's welcome."

"I wanted to speak with you about that. About him coming up here, I mean. He neglected to ask permission."

"He didn't stay long. It really wasn't an imposition, if that's your worry."

"There's that, too, I suppose. But that isn't my main concern." She swallowed and tugged nervously at the hem of the T-shirt. "If he should show up again, would you please call me? I really don't want him coming up here alone."

Ben felt as if he'd been sucker punched. Just that quickly, he was pissed. Where, exactly, did she get off? He hadn't blamed her that first day for being afraid for her child. She hadn't known him then. But she did now, and he'd given her no reason to fear that he might harm her boy.

"I'll do you one better. When you leave, I'll send the pup home with you. That way, Jeremy won't have a reason to come up here again. End of problem."

She flashed him a startled look. "But I thought you said that would be risky for the puppy."

"I was under the impression I was helping someone who appreciated it. May I point out that I'm giving your dog round-the-clock medical care, free of charge? It's pretty damned rude to accept the favor and then insult me."

Looking bewildered, she said, "Insult you?"

"How else should I feel when you imply that I might hurt your kid?"

Her expression turned incredulous. "What?"

"You heard me."

"Whoa. Back up. I'm afraid we're getting our wires crossed. I just—"

"My wires aren't crossed. I understand *exactly* what your concerns are, Ms. Evans. Ben Longtree, the crazy man who murders hapless hunters when they trespass onto his land. One small boy should be a cinch."

She held up a hand. "Wait just a second. That isn't—I wasn't—"

"You weren't what?"

She moistened her lips. "It's true that I have concerns about some of those rumors. I won't deny that. Nor will I pretend I wasn't alarmed when he came up here that first morning. But in all fairness to me, what mother wouldn't be? I still know very little about you. Even so, I never for an instant meant to imply that you might harm him, and that isn't the reason I don't want him coming up here alone."

An ache spread through Ben's chest, which only made him angrier. He didn't want to care what people thought of him—especially her. And he sure as hell wouldn't allow it to hurt. "Right. We're having soup for lunch. Would you and Jeremy care to stay? I've picked out all the finger bones."

All the color washed from her face. "You know, Ben, there's such a thing as being a little too sensitive."

"Really?"

"Yes, really. My son has a severe breathing problem. He shouldn't be riding his bike up that steep hill."

An awful sinking sensation assailed Ben's stomach.

"He has asthma. I won't get into the details, but sometimes the attacks come on suddenly and for no apparent reason. Along with a host of other things, overtaxing himself physically seems to bring them on."

Ben had seen Jeremy have an attack, and now he felt like hell for jumping down her throat. Just looking into her eyes told him that she was telling the truth. While she might have a few concerns about his character—perhaps even more than a few—her main reason for being so protective of the child had little to do with him.

"The road up here is really dusty," she went on, "and it's extremely steep. I don't want him riding up here because I'm afraid he'll collapse. Most times, he recovers on his own, but once I had to call an ambulance." She fixed him with an imploring look. "I honestly believed he might die. It was horrible. I can't take a chance that it might happen again when he's all alone."

No, of course she couldn't. Ben had acted like a jackass a few times in his life, but this took the cake. Resting his hands on his hips, he bent his head. "I jumped to conclusions, I guess."

"Yes, you did."

"I just thought—well, it's obvious what I thought."

"Ben?"

He brought his head up. "What?"

"You don't need to apologize." Her soft mouth curved into a smile. "Can we just back up and start over?"

"Since I'm the one with my foot in my mouth, I won't argue with that."

She laughed, a light, musical sound that moved over him like sunlight. "I haven't completely discounted all the rumors about you," she said candidly, "but I can say I think a number of them are preposterous. I don't believe that you killed those hunters, for starters. And, in my opinion, the theory that you fed the evidence to your animals is the product of twisted minds. People repeating that poppycock need to get a life."

Ben searched her small face, wishing she could discount all the stories with as much certainty. Even as the thought took root, though, he knew it was unrealistic. To feel certain none of those stories were true, she'd need to know him a lot better than she did now. "My sentiments exactly."

"There, you see? We're on the same page." She touched his arm. "I'm sorry for not making myself clear. I can see how you might have taken it wrong. I didn't mean to offend you."

His voice grated like sandpaper as he said, "I guess this should be a lesson to me not to jump to conclusions."

Her fingertips seared his skin through the sleeve of his shirt, and low in his guts, desire knotted like a fist. As though she sensed that, she quickly drew her hand away, looking a little startled. Wide with wariness, her eyes flicked to his. She ran the tip of her tongue across her bottom lip.

"Well." She tugged on the T-shirt and laughed again. The sound had a shrill edge. "Is that invitation to lunch still open? I've never had hunter soup."

She might have carried off the attempt at humor if her voice hadn't twanged with nervousness. Ben watched her fidget, wishing he could smooth over the moment, but he was as uneasy as she was. *Not good*.

"I'm fresh out of hunter soup. Pizza's on the menu today."

"Darn. Just my luck."

She was so pretty that Ben couldn't stop staring at her face. It was heart-shaped, he realized, curving gently to a pointy chin. Sunlight slanting through the doorway ignited the fine overlay of downy hair on her cheeks, making her look as if she'd been sprinkled with gold dust. The scent she wore, a musky floral, drifted to his nostrils and made him want to lean closer to get a better whiff.

The attraction arced between them like a high-voltage force field. Searching his dark face, Chloe knew he felt it, too. If they had been alone, that smoldering heat in his eyes would have had her nerves leaping. Who was she kidding? Her nerves were leaping now.

She took a deep breath and glanced over her shoulder. "Shall we? My son's going to think we got lost."

He gestured for her to go ahead of him. She could feel his eyes on her back as she moved toward the kitchen. She let her arms dangle loosely at her sides. Then she hugged her waist. Then she let her arms hang again. She felt like an elephant walking on ice.

In a strange way, it felt good, she realized. *Exciting.* It had been a long time since a man had had this effect on her. She felt alive, and young, and—well, pretty. She supposed any woman appreciated that feeling.

As she stepped from the entry hall, Chloe came to such an abrupt stop that Ben's chest collided with her shoulder blades.

"Oh," was all she could think to say as she took in the fabulous view of the mountains afforded by the floor-to-ceiling windows at the east side of the house. She'd been so upset and worried about Jeremy during her last visit that she'd failed to really look at it. "How lovely."

Ben moved to stand beside her. "Like it?"

"What's not to like?" The view was panoramic, with a 180-degree expanse of mountains laid out before her. Chloe's attention was caught by a craggy summit still dusted with snow. "Is that Shoshone Peak over to the left?"

"Yes." He touched her elbow. "We'll go out on the deck later so you can really enjoy it."

His touch made her nerves hum. She was acutely aware of him looming beside her. The top of her head didn't clear his shoulder. She needed to get away from him, she thought stupidly. And once she did, she needed to stay away.

To distract herself, Chloe gave the house a sweeping glance, paying attention to detail. Broad expanses of terra cotta stretched to the living room on the right and to the family room on the left, with inlaid teal carpet striking a pleasant contrast. Massive river-rock fireplaces were the focal points of each end wall, the faces reaching to the peak of the cathedral ceiling. A large gourmet kitchen divided the two sitting areas, light maple cabinetry complementing the sunny brightness of the adjoining living areas and the sunroom beyond.

As they entered the kitchen, the owl with the injured leg blinked at Chloe from the bar. The membranes over its eyes narrowed to slits and then opened wide.

Over the top of the bar, she could see Nan Longtree ensconced on a rocker in the adjoining family room, happily preoccupied with what looked like a crochet project, Diablo and Methuselah lying at her feet. When Chloe said hello, the older woman didn't glance up.

Ben pitched his voice low for Chloe's ears alone. "She's off in La-La Land today."

Chloe rubbed her hands on her jeans. "You don't need to explain. I understand."

"I just don't want you to think she's ignoring you on purpose." He frowned as he studied his mother, his eyes a blaze of blue in his dark face. "She wouldn't want that, either."

The affection in his voice touched Chloe. No man who cared so deeply for his mother could be a bad person, surely. If the day ever came that she grew ill, Chloe hoped Jeremy would be as patient—and as loyal.

Stepping away to put some much-needed distance between them, Chloe scanned the kitchen. "You were about to fix lunch. Please, don't let us interrupt. Jeremy and I will say our hellos to Rowdy and get out of your hair."

"No rush."

The faint scent of fresh bread dough drifted to Chloe's nose. She was surprised. When Ben had said pizza was on the menu, she'd envisioned the ready-to-bake kind.

"I don't know how you manage," she said, and she honestly didn't. "With your mom and all the animals to take care of, I mean. When do you find time to work?"

"I don't get much sleep." He flashed her a lazy grin that did strange things to her pulse rate. "Lately, I seem to spend most of my time cooking or taking care of critters."

He stepped over to the work island and pushed the skillet onto a back burner, an unnecessary movement that told her he was as tense as she was. She stepped around him to crouch with Jeremy beside Rowdy's box. The puppy lifted his head and listlessly wagged his tail.

"I can't believe how much better he looks," she observed. The tail thumping picked up speed as she ran her hand over the dog's yellow fur. "I can tell just by looking at his eyes that he feels better." She glanced over her shoulder. "Thank you, Ben. You've performed a miracle."

"That's nothing compared to the miracle I can perform with pizza. Why don't you and Jeremy stay to eat? Why go home and fix something? I'll just put you to work here, and we'll all chow down together."

Chloe was about to refuse when Jeremy piped in. "Please, Mom? Can we stay? Please?"

Ben sweetened the invitation with another one of those grins that she was quickly coming to believe should have a Richter-scale rating.

"Let me make amends for my behavior at the door," he said huskily. "I really do make a mean vegetarian pizza."

Chloe just wanted out of there, the faster the better. "I, um—"

"Please," he persisted. "I'd really love the company. It gets lonely up here on my ridge. Besides, it'll give Jeremy more time with his puppy."

"Please, Mommy? I wanna be with Rowdy. You don't have to work today."

Pushing to her feet, Chloe heard herself say, "Only if you actually put me to work."

Ben inclined his head at the sink. "You're on. Wash up. I'll let you rinse the vegetables. That's the job I hate most."

Within seconds, Chloe stood at the sink, wondering how she had gotten talked into this. Maybe Bobby Lee's accusation hadn't been so far off the mark as she liked to think. Did she have a thing for Ben?

Her hands began to ache as she rinsed the leaves of baby spinach. Behind her, Ben was sautéing garlic and onions in the large skillet. The smells made her salivate.

And so did the man.

This was madness. She'd never been one of those women who was drawn to danger. So why was she so attracted to him? He'd killed someone, for God's sake. How did she know that some little thing wouldn't set him off?

He came up beside her to rinse his hands. His hard arm rubbed against hers as he turned his wrists under the faucet. She stared at his wide, callused palms and work-hardened knuckles. With one swing of his fist, he could knock her flat. She should never have come here. She should have been firm with Jeremy and threatened him with severe repercussions if he disobeyed her again.

"This water is like ice," he said. "Artesian. Even in the dead of summer, it's cold. If it's making your hands hurt, adjust the temp."

Chloe could no longer feel her hands. "I'm fine."

He grasped her fingers in his. The warmth of his grip felt wonderful. She looked up into his blue eyes and couldn't look away. Her blood slogged in her veins, each push of her laboring heart making a loud swish in her temples.

"Your fingers are freezing." He released her to adjust the faucets. "That'll help."

"I've never eaten vegetarian pizza," she said inanely. "Is it good?"

"Good?" He looked at her lips. "You'll think you've died and gone to heaven."

Chloe searched his heated gaze and wondered if he was talking about pizza—or something else.

Chapter Nine

Nudging Chloe out of the way to put the pizza into the oven, Ben wondered what in the blue blazes had possessed him to invite her for lunch. Had he or had he not decided to nip his attraction to her in the bud? It wasn't like him to waffle like this. Once he made a decision, he usually stuck to it.

Frustrated with himself, he opened a drawer to get the pizza cutter. The problem, he decided as he rifled through the cooking utensils, was going too long without sex. Five years, for Pete's sake. That was enough to make any man a little crazy. Chloe was a beautiful woman. The crux of it was, he wanted her.

So what did he intend to do about it? He shot her a sidelong glance—noted the way her hips moved as she reached to put spinach leaves in the colander—and went back to rifling. Except he couldn't remember what in the hell he was looking for.

Damn. Okay. Deep breath. Sex. He wanted sex. No big deal. He was making it complicated when it didn't need to be. She was an adult—and a divorcée, to boot. The chemistry between them was combustive. Why not make some moves on her and see where it got him?

"Where in the blue blazes is it?"

Chloe jumped and whirled, her slender hands dripping water. "What are you looking for?"

"Damned if I know. Something important."

Her mouth twitched. A dimple flashed in her cheek. "And I thought I had a corner on forgetfulness."

"The pizza cutter," he remembered. "A little round thing to cut the dough." Just as he spoke, Ben found it. "Voilà!"

Nan chose that moment to leave her chair and rest her arms on the bar. Only seconds ago, she'd worn a vacuous expression. Now her blue eyes looked as bright and alert as a chipmunk's.

"How are you today, Nan?" Chloe asked.

"Very good. And you?"

"No complaints." Chloe took a deep breath of the delicious smells wafting from the oven. "Except for the fact that your son is making me hungry. Pizza is one of my favorites."

"Ben's pizza will be a real treat for you then."

Today Nan wore jeans and a blue blouse that enhanced the hue of her eyes. A faint blush of pink at her cheeks gave her pretty face a healthy-looking glow.

"Are you a fan?" Chloe asked.

Nan shook her head. "Not anymore. We have central air."

Ben caught Chloe's eye. She ducked her head to hide her smile.

After a delightful lunch, Chloe helped Ben tackle the kitchen cleanup while Nan returned to her crocheting and Jeremy resumed his vigil beside Rowdy's box. The lull in conversation as they worked seemed tense, but recalling Ben's grandfather's adage that it was better to be silent than to talk a lot and say nothing, Chloe resisted the urge to fill the air with chatter.

When the dishwasher was loaded and she'd wiped off the counters, she turned from the sink, intending to hustle Jeremy to the door as fast as was humanly possible. But her gaze moved past Ben to the bookshelf over the desk, and she forgot what she meant to say.

"You've got Brett Caldwell books?"

Still wiping off the stovetop, he jerked up his dark head, looked at the hardbacks, and growled something that sounded vaguely like, "Yeah."

Jeremy, too, whipped around to stare at the collection. "Wow!" he said. "You've got lots!"

"I'm a fan of his," Ben said gruffly. "Nothing but a big kid at heart, I guess."

"Me, too." Chloe wandered closer to study the titles. She was even more surprised to see that he had the entire collection. She smothered a grin. Little wonder he was embarrassed when he had no children in the house to provide him with an excuse. "I got turned on to Caldwell's work about a year ago when a friend recommended that I buy *Bandit* for Jeremy."

"Ah." He wiped out a burner plate. "So what did you think of it?"

"At first, I was dubious because the story is for older kids, and I was afraid it might be a little too realistic, but he loved it. After that, I began buying every Caldwell book I saw. Did you know he won a Newbery award?"

"Really?" He bent to scrub another burner. "Now that you mention it, that does ring a bell."

"It came as no surprise to me. His work is incredible." Chloe drew *Bandit* from the shelf. Turning the book in her hands, she examined its edges. No page corners had been turned down. She believed the way a person treated a book revealed a lot about his character. "This is my all-time favorite. I'm surprised it hasn't gone to the big screen. It has all the elements of a classic."

"You liked it that much, did you?"

"Loved it. How about you?"

He shrugged. "I like all his work. I can't really say I have a favorite."

Chloe set it back on the shelf. "Well, Jeremy?"

Her son gave her a gloomy look. "So soon?"

Chloe walked over to crouch beside him. "I know it's hard, sweetie." It was very tempting to say they could come back tomorrow, but she didn't think that would be wise. "It's time to say good-bye."

"Can we come back tomorrow, Mr. Longtree?" Jeremy asked.

Chloe wanted to clamp a hand over her son's mouth, but the question was already out.

"That would be great," Ben replied. "In fact, I've been meaning to talk with your mother about that."

Chloe threw him a surprised look. "You have?"

He tossed the dishcloth into the sink and hunkered down next to them. It didn't escape Chloe's notice that his broad shoulders pulled his shirt taut across his chest or that the muscles in his arms bulged under the sleeves each time he moved. Having experienced firsthand the disadvantage of lesser strength, Chloe found it difficult to breathe when she was so close to a powerfully built man. She knew it was silly. Her father was robust, and there had never been a gentler soul. She had the same sentiments about her older brother Rob. Why, then, with other men, who might be every bit as nice if she gave them a chance to prove it, did she get this awful breathless feeling?

Ben checked the IV and then fondled the pup's curly ears. "You've mentioned a couple of times that you'd like to pay me for Rowdy's treatment. Were you serious about that?"

"Of course. I'm a little tight right now, but in a couple of weeks, I—"

"I'm not talking about money." He lifted his gaze to hers. "I was thinking more along the lines of you helping me out around here."

Chloe got that awful feeling at the base of her stomach that always came when she stepped forward, expecting solid ground, and met with open air instead. "Oh. I see."

He gestured at the animals. "Twice a day, every one of these cages needs to be cleaned, the bedding has to be changed, and the animals must be fed and watered. I'm working under a deadline. It'd really take some of the pressure off me if you could swing by twice a day to take care of the animals." His mouth curved into a slow smile. "Only as long as Rowdy's here, of course."

Chloe couldn't think what to say. No was the smart response, only how could she possibly turn him down? He was saving her almost a thousand dollars, possibly more, and it was true that he probably needed help.

"The arrangement would work nicely for Jeremy, too," he added. "He'll be able to see Rowdy twice a day." He reached out and ruffled the child's hair. "Maybe I'll even put him to work."

"I can work! I'm a good worker, huh, Mom?"

"Working nights, my time is pretty limited," Chloe tried. "I don't see how I could possibly—"

"It really won't take very long, a half hour at most once you learn the routine." He flashed one of those bone-melting grins. "I was thinking maybe eight in the morning and then again right before you go to work, say one o'clock? You could get ready for work before you come here in the afternoon, and then you could drop Jeremy off at your house on your way to town."

Chloe pushed to her feet, hugged her waist. She

couldn't shake the feeling that he had neatly maneuvered her into a corner.

"Please, Mommy? I'll help lots. Please?"

"I, um—sure," she heard herself say. "I guess I can
do that."

Ben stood as well. "Great." His shimmering gaze
trailed slowly over her face. "Perfect, as a matter of
fact." He shifted his attention to Jeremy. "I need to
build Rowdy a pen soon so he'll be able to get some
sunshine and fresh air."

"He'll have to be in a pen, even up here?" Jeremy asked.

Ben nodded. "Coyotes can carry the parvovirus. It's
extremely important that Rowdy not be allowed on
any soil that may be contaminated."

"If I'm gonna be here lots, I can help build it,"
Jeremy said excitedly.

"That's exactly my thought," Ben agreed. "It'll be
nice to have an extra pair of hands." To Chloe, as if
he sensed her reservations, he quickly added, "It'll be
good for Jeremy. He'll be able to take care of the
puppy himself. That'll teach him responsibility."

Chloe couldn't argue the point. It probably would
be good for Jeremy. She just wasn't sure it would be
good for her.

"Well," she said, trying to hide her agitation, "it's
settled then. I guess we'll see you at eight o'clock in
the morning." She glanced at her watch and thrust out
a hand to her son. "I think we've imposed on Mr.
Longtree's hospitality long enough, sweetie. If we're
going to come here twice tomorrow, I should take
advantage of my day off to get some errands done."

Grumbling, Jeremy obeyed. After clasping his hand,
Chloe called good-bye to Nan and thanked Ben for
having them to lunch.

"I'm glad you could stay," he assured her as he

walked with them to the entry. "I always cook more than we can eat and end up with leftovers."

The warmth of the summer day rolled inside when he opened the door. Chloe took a deep breath of the pine-scented air. "It smells wonderful up here."

Ben stepped outside with them. The door frame behind him gave measure of his height and the breadth of his shoulders, once again causing Chloe to marvel at his size. He was so trim and leanly muscled that he didn't look bulky, but there was no denying that he was a good deal larger than most men.

He remained on the porch as she led Jeremy to the car. She'd just reached for the handle of the passenger door when the loud report of a gun rent the silence, making her jump. Ben scaled the steps in one leap, strode out to the driveway, and stared off through the woods, his jaw clenched in anger.

Chloe turned to look up the hill. "That sounded close."

"Yes, it did," he agreed. Glancing at Jeremy, he said, "You should go now, Chloe."

With that to serve as a farewell, he struck off, his strides brisk and long. Chloe stared after him. Then she called, "Is it wise to go up there? You have no weapon."

Never breaking pace, he turned to walk backwards. "I'd never use a gun if I had one. I just want to ID the guy. The law can handle the rest."

Chloe was still standing there, gazing after him, when he disappeared over the rise west of the house. What would happen if he actually caught the shooter in the act?

After doing the ironing, going grocery shopping, and washing her car, Chloe was more than ready to spend a pleasurable June evening with her son. On the back porch, she set up her small gas barbecue, attached a propane canister, and grilled garden patties for dinner. They enjoyed the simple but tasty meal at the rickety picnic table under a pine tree in the back-yard. Just over the fence, the neighbor's lilac bush was in full bloom, attracting hummingbirds.

"They're havin' their supper, too, huh, Mom?"

Chloe reached over to wipe a drip from Jeremy's chin. "Yes. We should get a feeder and hang it by the kitchen window. I love watching them."

Cheek bulging, Jeremy studied the tiny birds. "Do they ever land?"

"Sure. And when they do, you can actually see what they look like. They're darling little things—so tiny they almost don't look real."

Watching the birds, Jeremy devoured the rest of his garden burger. After clearing away the mess, Chloe challenged him to a game of Frisbee, which kept them happily occupied until almost dark.

"Time to go in," she called when Jeremy missed a catch and almost got hit in the face. "In this light, it's too hard to see. We're both getting clumsy."

Jeremy sank onto the grass. Concerned, Chloe moved across the patchy lawn to him. "You okay, sweetie?"

Jeremy nodded, but she could see his chest heaving and heard the rattle of his windpipe. She sat down beside him. "Jer?" She touched a hand to his clammy forehead. "Hey, big guy."

He fumbled in his pocket for his inhaler. Chloe helped him extract the canister and cupped the back of his head as she released two blasts of medication. The child's lungs grabbed frantically at the mist. Her heart squeezed with fear. He'd been doing so well lately, bouncing around and acting like a healthy, normal little boy. She'd dared to hope that he might have no more incidents.

The doctor in Washington believed the attacks were a reaction to emotional stress, but nothing she could think of had happened to trigger this one.

It was so hard to remain calm—to watch and do nothing while her child struggled to breathe. But the doctor claimed that a panicked reaction from her would only make things worse. With every wheezing breath Jeremy dragged in, her stomach knotted and her muscles tensed.

It seemed to Chloe that the attack lasted forever. When Jeremy was able to breathe more easily again, she sat on the grass and put an arm around him. "Better now?"

He nodded, but Chloe could tell by his expression that he was upset about something. "What's wrong, Jeremy? Can you tell me?"

He shrugged his skinny shoulders. Then he turned his face against her T-shirt and sobbed. Chloe's heart caught. She gathered him close.

"He hit me," the child whispered raggedly. "On the head with the Frisbee. Lots and lots of times. He got mad 'cause I didn't catch it. He said I was stupid and clumsy."

For an instant, Chloe could barely breathe herself. She realized she was hugging him too hard, and she made a conscious effort to loosen her arms. "Oh, honey." She searched her memory, trying to recall the incident. "You never told me Daddy hit you with the Frisbee."

He shook his head. "I didn't wanna make you cry."

Chloe pressed her cheek to the top of his head and started to rock him. "He can't get mad at you ever again," was all she could think to say. "I'm so sorry he did things like that, Jeremy. So sorry."

She fell quiet for a time, trying to convey her love for him with every touch of her hands. Guilt made a fist in her chest. Though she'd remained in the marriage for only a few months after Roger came home from the hospital, she had stayed too long. Much too long.

"I'm so sorry," she whispered again.

The words remained in Chloe's mind long after they went inside. *Sorry* couldn't erase the horrible memories from her son's mind. *Sorry* couldn't undo the damage that Roger had done or heal the wounds he had inflicted. It was hard to deal with, even for Chloe, and she was a grown woman.

After putting Jeremy down for the night, she lay awake in her bed, staring sightlessly at the ceiling. Sleep eluded her. As far as she knew, Jeremy had never blamed her for any of the things Roger had done. But, oh, God, she blamed herself. Every time he struggled to breathe—every time his lips turned blue—it was her fault. *Mine. All mine.* How would she ever be able to forgive herself for that?

Chapter Ten

The following morning, Chloe wondered what on earth she had been thinking when she'd agreed to show up on Ben's doorstep every morning at eight. She worked until eleven, and it was always after one o'clock before she to got to sleep. Last night it had been two because she'd lain awake agonizing over her child. With only five hours of sleep, she would be exhausted by the end of her shift that night.

"Are you sick, Mom?" Jeremy asked as she parked in Ben's driveway.

"Not sick, just tired." She unfastened her seat belt and leaned across to kiss his forehead, which was bisected by the shoestring again. "I'll perk up."

Jeremy left the car and skipped ahead of her to the steps. "Don't you wish we lived on a hill?" he asked.

Chloe paused on the walkway to take in the glorious view. "It'd be nice."

Jeremy scampered up the steps. "Maybe we'll marry Ben and move in with him!"

Chloe was so flabbergasted by the suggestion, she was speechless. Before she could manage so much as a sputter, Jeremy was racing across the porch. To her dismay, she saw Ben standing in the doorway. Judging by the look on his dark face, he'd overheard what Jeremy said.

Chloe wanted to shrivel up and disappear. That not being an option, she considered trying to explain. Only what could she say? That she wasn't angling for a marriage proposal?

Happily oblivious of the bomb he had just dropped, Jeremy said, "Hi, Ben!"

"Hi, tyke." Ben patted the child's head. "How are you this morning?"

"Real good."

Ben glanced at Chloe. "Hi, there."

He looked good enough to be illegal, wearing a simple white T-shirt that did marvelous things for his well-muscled chest and a pair of freshly laundered, faded blue jeans that skimmed his powerfully roped legs like a second skin. "Hi." She watched Jeremy race into the house. "About the marrying business . . ."

His mouth twitched, and a twinkle warmed his eyes. "If you're about to tell me you're as surprised as I am, don't bother. He's six. At that age, children are pretty linear in their thinking."

Chloe relaxed, but only slightly. There was something about the way he looked at her this morning— a determined gleam in his eyes—that was unsettling. He stepped back to allow her entry.

As she crossed the porch to him, she asked, "So— what happened after we left yesterday? Did you find out who was doing the shooting?"

"No, unfortunately, and I couldn't find the wounded animal, either." He pushed the door closed and walked with her. "We're surrounded by woodlands up here. Trying to find anything is like searching for the proverbial needle in a haystack."

He cupped her elbow in a big, hard hand as they

entered the kitchen. His touch on her bare skin sent a jolt of sensation up her arm.

"It's going to take patience and determination," he said, his mouth quirking at one corner as though he were laughing at a private joke. "But I'll triumph in the end."

"I hope so."

His lips curved. The blue of his eyes caught the sunlight, shimmering and shifting like quicksilver. "Do you?" he asked softly.

It seemed a strange thing for him to say. Of course she wished him luck in stopping the shooting incidents. She studied his dark face, all her feminine instincts jangling. He seemed different this morning. The way he looked at her was more intent and somehow— calculating. His fingertips moved lightly over her skin in a tantalizing caress, reminding her that he was still holding her arm.

"Look, Mommy, he's kissing me!" Jeremy cried, his face scrunched with blissful distaste as the puppy lapped his chin. "He feels lots better today. The needle's even out of his leg!"

"Don't let him lick your mouth, Jeremy. He's got germs." Relieved to have a reason to put distance between herself and Ben, Chloe set her purse on the counter and went down on one knee to pet the puppy. "Just look at you!" She laughed when the puppy hooked his paws over the edge of the box and tried to wriggle his way to freedom. "You are so darling."

The puppy's feathery tail whipped back and forth, drumming a tattoo on the cardboard. He bathed Chloe's fingers with a raspy little tongue. She picked him up to look at his eyes. They were large, liquid pools of innocence and curiosity, the glazed, feverish blankness entirely gone. He twisted in her hands, braced a hind foot on her arm, and took her completely by surprise with a sudden sweep of his tongue over her mouth.

Chloe sputtered. Jeremy giggled so hard he almost choked.

"He loves you, Mommy!"

She handed her son the puppy, wiped her mouth with the back of her wrist, and said, "Yes, well, I love him, too, but that's a bit much."

Rowdy slipped free of the child's grasp and wobbled across the tile. He seemed amazingly energetic for a puppy that had so recently hovered at death's door. Jeremy scrambled after him, but not in time. The puppy squatted and made a puddle.

Jeremy grabbed some paper towels to blot up the mess. "I'm gonna be real busy taking care of him this morning, Mom. I think you're gonna have to clean cages by yourself."

"I can see that."

Chloe stood up. She'd decided on the way over that the only way to handle the situation was to be all business. She was entirely too attracted to Ben to play it any other way. If she worked out a routine, she could get the cages cleaned and the animals fed in no time and wouldn't have to be here long.

Watching them from across the kitchen, Ben stood with his hips braced against the counter's edge. He looked better than any man should so early in the morning, his black hair still damp from the shower, his burnished jaw sporting a shine from the recent pass of a razor blade. The short sleeves of his T-shirt were stretched taut over arms that rippled every time he moved.

"Well," Chloe said, rubbing her hands together, "I'm ready to get this show on the road. Can you tell me where to start?"

"Coffee first," he said. "You look like you need a cup." Without waiting for her assent, he grabbed a mug from the cupboard. After filling it, he topped off another on the counter. "I fixed Mom a fruit plate this morning. When she gets up, all I'll have to do is toss some bread in the toaster."

When he turned, Chloe expected him to hand her one of the cups, but he walked right past her. "The deck is fabulous this time of day," he said over his shoulder.

Chloe glanced at Jeremy, who was happily enthralled with his puppy. No help there. She trailed after Ben. The French doors were already open. Well ahead of her, he was already sprawled on a patio chair when she joined him outside. With a nod of his dark head, he indicated a chair beside him. After she sat down, he handed her a mug.

Warmed by the sunlight that bathed the east deck, Chloe took a careful sip of the coffee. The rich flavor flowed smoothly over her tongue, and the aroma was divine. "I thought you couldn't make coffee."

"Lucky hit. Sometimes I get it right."

He gazed out at the view as he took a swallow from his cup. His big body was relaxed, his expression distant and dreamy.

"Have you read the *Thunder over the Ochoco* series?" he asked.

Chloe had heard of the Ochoco National Forest, but so far, she'd had no time to take Jeremy exploring. Nevertheless, she was glad for something impersonal to talk about. Some of the tension eased from her body, yet she was still aware of Ben in every pore of her skin. "No, I haven't. Are they good books?"

"Informative. Entertaining as well, if you're interested in local history. In large part, it's about my people." He swept his hand in a wide arc and inclined his head at the mountains. "Shoshone hunting grounds, as far as you can see."

Given the fact that his mother was white, Chloe found it strange that he identified so strongly with his Native American ancestors. "Your mother—she isn't Shoshone. You're what, a quarter?"

"It's common knowledge in town that I'm a quarter-breed. When people say my name, they usually tack that on in the same breath. That being the case, I'm fairly sure you know the answer to that already." He arched a black eyebrow at her. "So what's your point?"

"Not a point so much as bewilderment. If you're three quarters something else, why do you feel the Shoshone blood runs strongest?"

He turned the full impact of his gaze on her. "Look at me," he said simply. "What do you see?"

Chloe saw a man who was beautiful, rugged, and masculine. She also had to concede that, except for his eyes, he looked to be pure Shoshone. Even his chiseled facial structure was classically Indian. "I see a—" She bent her head, flicked at a spot of lint on her jeans. "You look very Indian. Native American, I mean."

"You don't have to be politically correct with me. Indian works. I prefer it."

"You do?"

"My grandfather put it much more eloquently. He rapped my chest so hard with his finger, he introduced my diaphragm to my backbone, and said, 'Benjamin, you are Shoshone. Your forefathers fought and died for this land, and they were proud to be called Indians. If it was good enough for them, by God, it is good enough for you!' " He gave her a sidelong look that twinkled with warmth. "I never argued with Grand-father—or disobeyed him."

"I wish I could have met your grandfather. He sounds delightful."

A distant expression came over his face. "He was a deep, soulful man. He saw the world in a way you and I can barely comprehend, and everything in it had spiritual significance to him. You think I look Indian—you should have seen him. His hair was streaked with silver and hung well past his waist. He wore a long braid at each temple, as Shoshone braves of old once did. When he moved, his beads made a soft clacking sound. He never heard the term 'politically correct' and would have called it poppycock if he had."

He paused for an instant and closed his eyes. "I still hear the sound of his beads when I remember him. And I loved his smell." His voice went gravelly and thick. "Leather, tobacco, wood smoke, and an under-lying earthy scent because he spent so much time out-doors. He hated walls. I think being inside made him claustrophobic. Toward the end, I can remember Mama helping him out to sit under the woodshed lean-to after he grew too weak to make it by himself. It was the dead of winter and bitterly cold, but he preferred to be out there. Before I went to school, I'd build him a fire, and she'd put wood on it throughout the day. In the afternoon when I got home, I did my chores as fast as I could so I could sit at his knee and listen to him talk." He fell silent again, staring at the horizon. "He told me fascinating stories of his boy-hood—and of his father's before him. Once, when I asked him why he sat out there, gazing off at nothing, he said that he was waiting. I didn't understand then. I do now. He was very old and ill. His life had stopped, but his heart had not. I was just a little guy, about a year older than Jeremy, when his wait was finally over."

Chloe heard the intense sadness in his voice and knew he still grieved.

He shifted and resettled, then took a sip of coffee. "He would have liked you." He gave her an assessing look. "You have true eyes."

"Do I? True, huh? I've heard of honest ones."

"Grandfather believed honest eyes could be faked. 'Look to the heart,' he used to say. 'If you see no heart, run.' "

Chloe laughed again. Ben did a beautiful job of mimicry, and she could almost see his Indian grandfather lecturing him. "You must miss him terribly."

"He left a great hole," he said huskily.

It was an odd way to put it, but Chloe understood exactly what he meant. When people you loved died, they did leave a great hole, and no one else could ever fill it up again. She wished it had happened that way with Roger—that he had simply died so they could mourn him and miss him. Modern medicine had managed to save his body, but it had failed to repair his mind, or recover the man he'd once been.

"Chloe."

She jerked herself back to the moment. "Sorry."

"You went to a sad place."

She tried to school her expression, knew she failed. "Yes, a sad place."

"I'm glad you're back." He inclined his head at the deck railing. "Listen."

Chloe did and smiled. In the trees growing on the steep slope below, the birds raised their voices in song. "How lovely."

" 'My worm's bigger than your worm,' " he sang softly.

She burst out laughing again. "That isn't what they're saying."

"What, then?"

She thought for a moment. "They're saying it's a beautiful day. An incredibly beautiful day."

They enjoyed the remainder of their coffee in silence, listening to the sounds of nature around them. It seemed to Chloe that everything was clearer, sharper, and infinitely lovelier than it had been before.

After showing Chloe how to clean the cages and feed the animals, Ben fixed his mother's toast, set her up to eat breakfast in the family room from an oak TV tray, and then applied himself to cleaning the kitchen. He tried to ignore Chloe as she skittered around him, taking care of critters, but he found that difficult when every time he looked her way, she had her sweetly rounded fanny poked in the air.

He'd just finished polishing the stovetop when Jeremy turned from the puppy's box to say, "My mom's sure been outside a long time."

"You're right. She has been gone for a bit."

Ben dried his hands and stepped over to the door that opened from the family room onto the back deck. Sure enough, his assistant in training appeared to be having an in-depth conversation with Pokey, the convalescent skunk, who was housed in a cage just outside the master bedroom's French doors.

He leaned his shoulder against the door frame to watch her. With a double layer of glass separating them, he strained to hear what she was saying.

"I really am a nice lady. If you'll just lower your tail, I'll prove it by cleaning your cage and giving you food and fresh water."

Tail poked proudly out behind him, Pokey hobbled in a tight circle inside the wire enclosure.

"Okay." Chloe settled her hands at her hips. "Let me put it another way. Either lower your tail or starve. Your choice." She wrinkled her nose. "Has anyone ever mentioned that you smell to high heaven? No offense intended, of course. I'm sure lady skunks find your cologne very sexy."

Ben was grinning when he opened the door. At the sound, Chloe jumped so violently that he was surprised she didn't part company with her sneakers. Hand at her throat, she shot him an accusing glare. "Don't *do* that."

He stepped onto the deck. "What seems to be the major malfunction out here?"

She touched a finger to her lips. "Not so *loud*. I'm in his line of fire."

Ben chuckled and approached the cage, shuffling his moccasins and making more noise than he usually would to prove a point. "He isn't going to spray you, Chloe."

"He's agitated," she insisted. "See how he's circling? And his tail is up."

"He normally carries his tail trailing out behind him like that. When skunks spray, they whip their tails high over their backs and throw their butts in the air."

"No need to get graphic."

Ben could see she was seriously worried. He bent to open the animal's cage. "He's just anxious to be fed," he assured her, "and you're torturing him."

"Yes, well, I worry about silly things, like how I'll buy groceries if I can't go to work."

Reaching inside the pen, he stroked the skunk's striped back. "Pokey, meet Chloe. She's a little paranoid, but she'll get over it." As he said that, Ben realized that he honestly believed she might. The skunk arched its spine for petting, much like a cat. "There, you see? He just wants breakfast."

Tensed to bolt, she inched closer. Judging by the wary looks she kept shooting his way, Ben wasn't sure which of them made her more nervous, him or the skunk. *Time,* he assured himself. They'd had a nice few minutes on the deck this morning, and though it had taken some doing on his part, she'd finally relaxed. With twice-daily exposure to him, she'd soon stop being so skittish. He burned to know why there were shadows in her eyes in the first place. Her husband, probably. Only somehow the pieces to the puzzle didn't quite fit. She didn't strike him as the type to stay in an abusive marriage. . . .

He turned his attention to replacing the newspaper lining the bottom of the cage. When he glanced back up at her, he forgot what he was about for a moment. She'd left her hair down today, and it cascaded to her slender shoulders in a wild array of curls. With the morning sun behind her, the tendrils caught the light and blazed like sun-struck copper, creating a brilliant nimbus around her head. He understood now why Shoshone warriors of old had been so fascinated by redheads. She was beautiful. The kind of beautiful that made a man yearn to touch—and lay claim. His grandfather definitely would have approved.

"What?" she said.

Caught staring, Ben tried to think of an excuse, but his mind had gone as blank as a sheet of copy paper. "I, um—nothing. I'm sorry."

She plucked at her pink knit top, which should have clashed with her hair but didn't. It also clung to her breasts, revealing delightful details. Wise move, plucking it away from her chest that way. He didn't know if it was the breeze or an instinctive female reaction to a man's heated regard, but something had hardened her nipples.

"Are you okay?" she asked.

Hell, no, he wasn't okay. He wanted her. And five years of denial was making it damned hard to convince his body that he could wait.

"I'm sorry. I just went spacey for a second."

She moved closer to the cage. She was wearing that soft, musky scent again today. "I can't believe you call him Pokey."

"He isn't navigating very fast with that foot."

"Still." She crouched beside him to study the skunk. "He's too elegant for a name like that."

Her top gaped away from her chest as she leaned forward to gingerly pet the animal, giving Ben a glimpse of perfectly shaped, creamy breasts. He could now say with absolute certainty that there were freckles below her collarbone. A man could entertain himself for hours, connecting the dots. "What name do you suggest?"

She studied the skunk for a moment. "Sir Galahad."

"*Sir Galahad?* Aw, come on. You can surely do better than that."

"It's better than Pokey." She thrust a finger through the wire and wiggled the tip, which brought the skunk hobbling toward her. "There, you see? He's grateful. Pokey? That's demoralizing."

Ben took another gander at her breasts, which were edged with the scalloped lace of her white, front-clasp bra. It had been a while since he'd fumbled with hooks and eyes, but he remembered the gratification that came when man triumphed over frustration.

"Yeah, well, when you work with as many animals as I do, you run out of clever names. Not that Galahad is particularly original."

"How about Winston?"

He was starting to wish she'd stop bending forward that way. "Winston works."

"Winston it is, then." Scratching the skunk's sloped nose, she said, "He's darling." She leaned farther forward, God help him. "You are, yes, you are," she crooned. "Now I feel silly for being afraid of you." She glanced up. "If you start calling him Winnie, I'll help him get even."

Ben chuckled in spite of himself. "Winnie's a girl's name. I wouldn't insult him like that."

"What happened to his foot?" she asked.

"The bastard with the .22 shot him."

"In the *foot?*"

Ben nodded. "He's got good aim, I'll say that for him." He was okay now, he thought. She had straightened to look at him. That helped. Tops like that should be outlawed—along with front-clasp bras. "Whoever he is, he's either had formal training with weapons, or he's spent a lot of hours practicing."

Ben tossed out the skunk's water, added fresh from the jug Chloe had carried out, and set the dish back in the cage.

"Why are you convinced it's a man?" she asked.

He considered the question for a moment. "Women are vindictive."

"Watch it, buster."

He chuckled and shook his head. She made his heart feel light. "Well, it's true. I mean it as a compliment. Women need a reason. Even if it's only an imagined reason, they usually don't do stuff like this unless they have one." He gestured at the skunk. "What do you suppose he ever did to make some woman shoot him in the foot?"

She watched Winston eat for a moment and then rose to a standing position. "Shooting an animal in the foot is—" She broke off and shook her head. "Only a very sick person would do such a thing."

"Exactly."

He bent to retrieve the cat food. Chloe collected the jug.

"Now I understand why you've posted such a large reward. Whoever's doing this has to be stopped. It's terrible."

"I just hope somebody calls me." Ben studied the woods. "And the sooner I get a call, the better. He could be out there right now." He centered himself on the thought. His blood pressure, which he felt certain had been clear off the chart a moment before, dived to an acceptable level. "Sometimes, I hear the shots. Other times not. When I do, I always go looking for the animal."

"Oh, Ben." Her voice rang with sadness. "When you can't find them, it must make you feel so helpless."

Her comment jerked his gaze to her face. Her brows were knitted in a frown, and her eyes were filled with shadows. "Yes, it does. I know if I hear a shot that there's probably a wounded animal out there, needing my help." He nodded toward the trees. "One night last week, I searched with a flashlight until almost midnight. They can't call out to me like a person. I have to be fairly close to sense that they're there. I keep zigzagging, afraid that I've missed them. It's hard to give up. If the injury allows, I know they'll come to me the next day, but I hate like hell to let them suffer all those hours."

When he looked back at her, he saw that she was studying him with bewilderment. "What?" he asked.

She smiled and shook her head. "Nothing. You just—" She gave her head a harder shake. "Nothing."

Ben went back over what he'd just said—and realized that he'd relaxed his guard and revealed too much. "Here in my woods, I know most of the animals." Pointing to the deer feeders and salt lick, he added, "As you can see, they come in for treats. They've grown used to me."

"Ah." She nodded. "That explains why they approach the house, then. And they probably talk among themselves, don't you think?"

His attention sharpened. "Talk?"

She turned toward the woods again. "Like in the Caldwell books, they communicate. When you help one animal, it tells all the others. Pretty soon, they know to come here if they're hurt. I wonder what their word for *vet* is?"

Dangerous ground. "Beats me."

"If they come to you, they must understand you're a vet," she said. "They know you have magic in your hands and will make them feel better." She tapped the toe of her sneaker on the wood. "The blue jays have loud, raucous voices. Maybe they go around telling all the animals in the forest about you."

Ben stared hard at her profile. Was she serious—or pulling his leg? She suddenly turned toward him. Her cheeks went pink with embarrassment. "Now you're laughing at me."

"No."

"Sure you are." She shoved her slender hands into her jean pockets. "Animals talking. I'm sure it's a chick thing that only another woman would understand." She shrugged. "I honestly think they talk."

Ben didn't just think; he knew. She bent her head to stare at her toes. Then she rocked back on her heels, angled him a teasing look, and said, "I'm glad I'm not a man."

"What?"

"You're all so pragmatic and *boring*. Didn't you ever watch *Bambi*?"

*   *   *

A few minutes later, Ben was standing at the stove again, fixing his mother a cup of hot chocolate. Sometimes, he felt as if invisible chains bound him to the kitchen. As he stirred the flavored milk over a medium flame, he watched Chloe put fresh bedding in Rowdy's box. In the family room, Jeremy sat on the love seat with his puppy.

Didn't you ever watch Bambi? Recalling Chloe's question, Ben bit back a smile. He was doing a lot of that lately. Strange. How could a man go for five years living a humorless existence, and then suddenly feel like laughing so often? *Chloe. Such a simple answer, wrapped in such a complicated package.*

She cared, he thought. She truly did care about the animals, not in a purely scientific way, but about how they felt and suffered. He'd seen it in her eyes. That, too, felt strange. His ex-wife Sherry would have shrugged, yawned, and bent to peer through her microscope again.

Ben heard Chloe say something and glanced up to see her crouched by the raccoon's cage, one finger thrust through the wire to scratch the animal's head. Apparently she'd shelved her concerns that the raccoon might bite.

"Hey, Rēvo," she said softly. "Feeling better now that you've eaten?"

Ben tapped the spoon on the edge of the pot. "Rēvo?"

"Yeah, he looks like he's wearing shades. Rēvo works. He's got a classy look about him."

It was true, he decided. Rēvo worked, and so did she. The kitchen, filled with lemon-yellow sunlight, seemed brighter with her in it. After building this house, he'd tried to make it homey. One wall of the living room held a collection of Shoshone artifacts, neatly arranged, around paintings of the area done by local artists. Over the last three years, he'd picked up other pieces of art. His mother's penchant for crocheting had provided cozy touches, as well: afghans, decorative pillows, doilies, and lap throws.

At a glance, the place looked like a home, but the plaster and wood had always been ominously silent. When he moved from room to room, no memories whispered, and the air felt empty. It sounded crazy, even to him, but that was how he felt, that the house had no life.

Chloe was changing that. She lent the rooms traces of her essence, making them feel friendly. When she laughed, the sound seemed to linger.

"Does Einstein need a towel over his cage?" she asked, jerking Ben from his musings.

He stared blankly at her. "Who?"

"Einstein." She hooked a dainty thumb at the owl.

Ben found himself about to smile again. "Who named him Einstein?"

"Mc. *Owl* seems unfriendly. He looks smart, don't you think? All hc lacks is a mortarboard with a tassel." She studied the bird. "Isn't he nocturnal?"

Ben nodded. "I don't cover his cage, though."

"Why?"

"Because he's accustomed to sleeping outdoors. In the wild, he just perches on a limb where it's shady."

She leaned across the counter to move the owl's cage forward to get him completely out of the sunlight. "There, that's better, isn't it, Einstein?"

The owl made a tutting sound and lifted his wings as though to thank her. Chloe gave the top of his cage a pat. "Good night, wise guy. Sleep tight."

As she started from the kitchen, she stopped at the end of the counter where Ben had left a stack of manuscript pages by the cookie canister. He circled the work island to grab the papers and shove them in a drawer.

"Personal stuff," he muttered.

Her brows lifted. She threw a curious glance at the drawer. Then she shrugged and left the room. Ben gazed after her, wanting to kick himself for leaving the printout lying in plain sight. If he was going to have her in his home, he had to start being more careful.

Chapter Eleven

When Chloe and Jeremy returned to Ben's that afternoon, he greeted them at the door with a barely discernible hello. Jeremy whispered back, "How come you're being so quiet? Is your mom sleeping?"

Ben motioned the child back out, joined them on the porch, and eased the door shut. "My mom's taking a nap, but that's not why I'm whispering. Buddy, a raccoon friend of mine, is just waking up from surgery." Ben gave Chloe a long look laden with meaning. "He got hurt yesterday, and it's taken him all this time to find his way to my house. I like to keep things quiet the first day after an animal has an operation." Placing his hands on his knees, he leaned down to get eye to eye with the child. "Buddy's a wild animal, and his head is fuzzy from the sleeping medicine. He isn't used to people."

"Oh," the child said solemnly. "We might scare him, huh?"

Chloe rested a hand on Jeremy's shoulder. "Would it be better if we skipped this afternoon, Ben?"

"No, I just wanted to explain the need to keep our voices down." He reached behind him to open the door. "Imagine, if you will, waking up in a lion's lair—with the lion pacing all around you and roaring."

Jeremy's eyes grew huge. "We aren't lions, and we don't roar."

"To Buddy, we're as scary as lions, and our voices sound like roars."

Jeremy tiptoed behind Ben into the house. As they entered the kitchen, the child crouched down some five feet from Buddy's cage. In a stage whisper, he asked, "How did he get hurt?"

Chloe threw Ben an uncertain look. To her dismay—or was it relief?—he knelt beside Jeremy to field the question. Curling an arm around the boy's shoulders, he murmured, "Buddy was shot, Jeremy."

"With a gun?" At Ben's nod, Jeremy glanced back at the animal. "But how come?" he whispered. "Raccoons aren't to eat, and he's not big enough to hurt anybody."

"There's a sickness in some people. They do bad things we can't understand. There's no justifying it, no explaining it. They're just very mixed up."

Jeremy leaned closer to Ben. "Do you think the person who shot him got his head hit by a 'peller blade?"

Ben glanced at Chloe, his expression bewildered.

"My daddy got his head hurt," Jeremy whispered. "He fell out of our boat, and the 'peller blade got him. Before it happened, he was real nice, and he loved me and my mom lots. But afterwards, he got mad all the time and did bad things."

Ben's black brows drew together in a frown. He stilled his big hand on Jeremy's narrow back. "I'm sorry, Jeremy. That must make you feel sad."

"My mom says he's lost and can't find his way back to us no more." Jeremy's face looked pinched, and the ache in his eyes made Chloe's heart twist. "The last time he got real mad at me, all I did was spill my milk. Not on purpose or nothing. But he yelled and grabbed my neck."

The child's eyes went bright with tears. He stared for a long moment at the raccoon. Then his mouth started to quiver. "He squeezed so hard, I couldn't breathe. My mom tried to make him stop." He gulped and expanded his lungs as though remembering how it had felt. "He got mad and hit her in the face. She's lots littler than him, and he made her fall and cut her eyebrow."

Chloe felt as if a fist had slammed into her stomach. *I couldn't breathe. He squeezed so hard, I couldn't breathe.* The doctor had told her Jeremy's breathing attacks stemmed from some kind of emotional trauma, but until now, she'd never made the connection between the child's symptoms and what he had lived through that night. *Oh, dear God.* Roger had tried to strangle him, and Jeremy had been having breathing problems ever since.

Chloe wheeled away, her only thought to find a place where she could be alone for a moment. She circled the cages at the end of the bar, passed through the family room into the sunroom, and stepped out onto the deck through the French doors. At the railing, she curled her hands over the wood, cocked her knee against a lower slat, and bent her head as she struggled against tears.

She felt so stupid. So awfully, horribly stupid, and completely inadequate as a mother. It all fit. *I couldn't breathe.* As the truth sank in, she had trouble breathing herself. It hurt. What had happened that night had traumatized Jeremy so badly that he was reliving the incident over and over again. His wonderful daddy, the man who'd once tossed him in the air and tickled him, had flown into a mindless rage and tried to kill him over a glass of spilled milk.

The sunlight caressed Chloe's shoulders with gentle warmth, and the breeze dried her tears. She hauled in a deep breath and slowly released it. *Oh, God, what have I done? I should have left the very first time Roger grew violent. I never should have let Jeremy go through all that.* At the time, she'd felt duty bound to remain with her husband and take care of him. It had seemed so wrong to file for divorce and abandon him when he'd needed her so much. *In sickness and in health.*

Now her son was paying the price for her misplaced loyalty.

"You okay?"

Chloe jumped at the sound of Ben's voice. Keeping her head bent, she saw his big, dark hand come to rest on the railing next to hers.

"I'm fine," she managed to squeeze out. It was a lie, of course. "Is Jeremy all right?"

"He's a little upset. Nothing to worry over. I left him in the family room with Rowdy. They're having a cuddle session on the love seat."

"Oh." She wished he'd go away and leave her alone. "That's good."

"Can you talk about it, Chloe?" he asked.

She shook her head. "It's, um—no, I don't think so."

How could she talk about what had been not only the end of her marriage, but a defilement of everything she'd believed in and come to trust as well?

He shifted beside her. She had an almost overwhelming urge to turn into his arms—to lean against him and cry her heart out on his sturdy shoulder.

When she found the courage to show her face, he was staring off at the mountains. "I guess it's not really necessary for you to talk about it," he murmured. "Going by the things Jeremy just said, I know you've been through a hell of a time."

He spoke of the hell as though it were over. She wanted to correct him. It wasn't over. Sometimes she wondered if it ever would be.

He turned his gaze to her. She wanted to look away, but couldn't.

"Can I say just one thing?" he asked.

"Of course," she said thinly.

His hard mouth tipped into a smile. He touched a fingertip to her cheek, brushing at a spot of wetness and then pushing back a tendril of her hair. Chloe instinctively wanted to shrink away, but something, she wasn't sure what, held her fast.

"You did the right thing," he said huskily. "By getting Jeremy out of it, I mean."

A burning sensation came up the back of her throat, and she was afraid her eyes might fill with tears again.

"Normally, I have little if any respect for people who end a marriage over the illness of a spouse, but your situation was extraordinary. You did the right thing, Chloe. Children aren't just a gift; they're a God-given responsibility, and in cases of abuse, a mother should never—and I do mean *never*—let anything else come first, not even her husband."

Tears did fill her eyes then. "Yes, well, that was a lesson I took a while learning. After Roger came home from the hospital, I stayed for almost five months, hoping he'd get better, that the—" She gulped to steady her voice. "You can't stop hoping, you know? I told myself there might be postsurgery swelling, or that maybe the incisions deep inside hadn't healed completely. He was such a good man before the accident, a wonderful man. We had a solid marriage." She pressed her fingertips to her temples. "I was conditioned, I guess—to think in terms of always. It was so hard for me to end it, and because it was, I waited too long."

"Five short months," he corrected. He caught her chin on the edge of his hand and tipped her face up again so he could look into her eyes. "Five months, Chloe. If he was a good man before the accident, you owed him that much. What kind of woman waltzes out on an injured husband without giving him time to heal? And there's not a damned thing wrong with being slow to give up on what was once a great marriage. Did you stay after the milk incident?"

"No, he—" She panted for oxygen. "He was choking him, and I couldn't get him off. I knew then." She averted her face, breaking the physical contact between them because it unsettled her so. "I filed for divorce the next morning. That didn't entirely stop Roger from disrupting our lives—thus my decision to move here—but at least it was never Jeremy in his line of fire again."

He nodded. "So, there, you see? When push came to shove, you jumped ship. Stop beating up on yourself."

"It's hard not to. When I see what it's done to my son, it's almost impossible not to."

"You did your best. Jeremy's out of it now. That's the bottom line. You didn't stay with his father and make him live like that for eighteen years."

The bitterness in his voice brought Chloe's head around. He met her regard evenly, his face set in grim lines. "My mother had her reasons for staying," he whispered. "I don't blame her, and I never will. But I can tell you this. I'd be carting around a lot less baggage if she had divorced him when I was Jeremy's age."

Having said that, he turned and went back inside the house, leaving her alone to digest what he'd said and to gather her composure. She fleetingly wondered how he had managed to zero in on the things that tormented her most. Even more bewildering, he'd succeeded in making her feel better.

Jeremy was still on the love seat with Rowdy when Chloe reentered the family room. The child gave her a shamefaced look. "I'm sorry, Mommy."

"For what, sweetie?"

"For telling 'bout Daddy. It's s'posed to be our secret, and I forgot."

Searching her son's troubled gaze, Chloe had cause to wonder if her decision to make their past a taboo subject with strangers wasn't yet another count against her.

That was a worry for later, though. Ben entered the room just then. After taking in Jeremy's downcast expression, he glanced questioningly at Chloe. "My mom's still asleep. After lunch, she generally naps for two or three hours. I was wondering, would you and Jeremy like to play hooky with me and take a walk?" He gestured toward the kitchen. "You got so much done this morning, I can do the chores this afternoon, no problem."

Chloe checked her watch. "Oh, I—"

"About a mile from here, there's a pretty little creek, and I spotted a beaver dam there the other afternoon. I thought Jeremy might enjoy seeing it."

"Can we, Mom?" Jeremy asked in a stage whisper. "Please?"

Chloe sighed. Her son knew just the right note of pleading to inject into his voice. She also knew that Ben had suggested this outing to cheer the child up, and she had to admit it was probably a good plan.

"It's really not that far," Ben assured her. "We can easily make it there and back, leaving you plenty of time to get to work."

"Well . . ." After the conversation with him on the

deck, she would have preferred to go home where she could lick her wounds in private, but she decided that would be selfish. A walk might be just what Jeremy needed to push the unpleasant memories from his mind. "Okay. Why not? I've never seen a beaver dam."

For the next hour, Ben gave them a tour of his world. As they trailed behind him through the forest, he stopped occasionally to point out sights Chloe and her son might have overlooked.

"Look there, Jeremy," he said, gesturing at the top of a dead tree. "See that nest? It belongs to a bald eagle."

Just as he spoke, the mother bird swooped down to perch on the untidy collection of grass and small branches. Chloe would have sworn the eagle looked directly at them. Beautiful with a reddish-brown body and snow-white head, the raptor lifted her wings and did a half-turn, as though to show off for them.

"Oh," Chloe said softly, her skin tingling with awe. "She's fabulous, Ben. The bald eagle is our national bird, Jeremy."

Jeremy stood there, head back, expression solemn. He kept his voice hushed. "Does she have babies up there?"

"Probably," Ben replied. "And because she does, we really shouldn't linger. No point in making her nervous."

He struck off through the trees again, moving with a fluid grace that Chloe found amazing in so large a man. He was, she thought nonsensically, as sturdy as the huge Ponderosa pines that defined the terrain.

Soon Chloe heard the rushing sound of a stream. Ben held out a hand, signaling them to halt. Then, with an exaggerated lightness of step, he led them around a copse of manzanita. When the stream came into view, he crouched behind the brush, motioning for Chloe and Jeremy to do the same.

"There," he said softly.

Just as he spoke, a beaver slapped the surface of the water. Jeremy jumped. Then he giggled. "Look, Mom!" he whispered.

Chloe was already looking. The beavers had impeded the water flow, creating a pool just above the dam. As she watched, three heads appeared. "It's a family," she exclaimed softly. "Oh, Jeremy, that's a mama with her babies."

His expression thoughtful and searching, Ben glanced at Chloe over the top of the child's head. "Glad now that you came?"

"Oh, *yes*."

Chloe could have stayed forever. The animals cavorted in the water, as agile as seals. The babies, still inexperienced at slapping their tails, seemed to be practicing the technique. Occasionally the mother demonstrated how to do it properly, sending up an impressive spray of water.

"That's their danger signal," Ben explained to Jeremy. "The mama beaver teaches them how when they're very young. It's important to their survival."

"Wow." Jeremy looked at Chloe. "Isn't this cool, Mom?"

Ben glanced at his watch. "I guess it's about time to head back if you're going to make it to work on time."

"Oh, darn," Jeremy said, his voice ringing with regret. "I don't wanna go."

"We'll come again," Ben promised. "Fun's over for today, though. Your mom will get in trouble if she's late to work."

"When can we come back?" Jeremy pressed.

Chloe expected Ben to put Jeremy off with a vague

reply. Instead he said, "Tomorrow, if you like. I can always squeeze in a half hour to watch the wildlife."

As they followed Ben back through the woods, Chloe studied him with a new understanding of who and what he was: not a mere wilderness expert, but as much a part of this rugged country as the animals that lived here.

When they came upon a rocky area, he grasped Chloe's arm, took Jeremy's hand, and guided them to a hollow under a boulder. "Shh," he said as they approached. "No talking at all, Jeremy. Okay?"

The child nodded. And he kept to the rule, even after Ben gently lifted the end of a large rock to reveal a nest of baby chipmunks. They looked like newborn mice, their tiny pink bodies squirming in the soft, billowy collection of nesting material.

After allowing Jeremy to look his fill, Ben carefully returned the rock to its original position. As he straightened, Chloe yearned to ask how he had discovered the newborns. But, like Jeremy, she observed the rule of silence. At her questioning look, he smiled and grasped her arm again, this time more lightly, his fingertips trailing like whispers over the sensitive underside of her arm. The sensation made her nerves thrum, and something low in her belly thrilled in response. For just an instant, she tried to imagine how it might feel to have him touch her that way everywhere.

When she realized what she was thinking, a strong urge to escape crashed over her. She didn't want to feel this way—couldn't allow herself to feel this way. It was dangerous. She'd loved once—and trusted once. The very thought of making herself vulnerable like that again filled her with panic, an awful, clawing panic. Roger had been her prince, and then he'd become her jailor. Even though she knew it hadn't been his fault, there was a part of her that couldn't trust so easily again—a part of her that recoiled from any kind of physical closeness.

As though he sensed her need to escape, Ben stilled his hand, his palm and fingers radiating warmth into her flesh that spread in pulsing tingles to her shoulder and then into her torso. At the first shock, Chloe threw him a startled look, but before she could analyze the sensations rolling through her, she lost her ability to focus. The fear flowed from her like water from a sieve, and a delicious languor replaced it, making all her muscles relax. She felt like a wax candle going soft in a spill of sunlight, and she found herself leaning toward him.

He didn't immediately release her as he led them away from the rocks. When he finally did turn loose, she felt oddly bereft. He fell into a walk with Jeremy at his heels. Chloe trailed several paces behind them.

"Those baby chipmunks were born much too late," he said over his shoulder. "Usually they come before the snow melts. When they're a bit older, I'll bring nuts and corn for them to horde for winter. If left to their own devices at so young an age, they'll never make it till next spring."

"Are late births common?" Chloe rubbed her arms, still feeling oddly euphoric. She'd never tried any recreational drugs, but she imagined this was how they'd make her feel—light as air and absurdly happy. She couldn't remember now why the touch of Ben's hand on her arm had upset her. It was the oddest thing. "I thought Mother Nature orchestrated things more precisely."

"Percentage-wise, it's not common," he replied, "but it does happen every year. Somehow the natural cycle gets bumped off course, the young are born too late, and they die when winter comes."

Not for the first time, he stopped and lifted his face

to the breeze. Chloe couldn't shake the feeling that he was picking up scents on the wind that she couldn't detect. Sometimes he got a distant look in his eyes that made her wonder if he was even aware of them beside him. He had described his grandfather as a deep and soulful man. Watching Ben now, Chloe wondered if he realized that he had also been describing himself.

"It'll rain tonight. That will be good. The forest can use the moisture."

Chloe studied the clear sky. "What makes you think it'll rain? I don't see any clouds blowing in."

"Can't you smell it in the air?"

Chloe couldn't, but she had no doubt that he could.

As they continued the return trek to the ridge, she noticed Jeremy mimicking Ben's every move. Where the man stepped, the child stepped. When Ben stopped to sniff the air, Jeremy tipped his head back, too. Chloe could understand her son's enthrallment. Ben Longtree was everything most little boys yearned to become—big and strong and fearless.

"Which way is north?" he asked Jeremy about half-way down the incline. When the child couldn't say, he showed him how the moss grew on the north side of the trees. "Which way is water?" he asked another time. When Jeremy frowned, Ben said, "Always head downhill if you're lost and thirsty. Eventually you'll find water if you don't come to a road first. Either way, you'll eventually get a drink." A few minutes later, he began pointing to dry deadfall that would easily ignite. "Sometime soon, I'll show you how to make a fire without matches," he promised. "You can also use that deadfall to build a temporary shelter. If you ever get stranded in the woods, build a windbreak and roof with limbs, then gather pine needles to make a bed. In a pinch, they're nearly as good as a blanket. Just pile them in a heap and burrow in for the night, like our brother the bear."

"The bear's not my brother!" Jeremy exclaimed with a giggle.

"Sure he is." With a sweep of his arm, Ben indicated the forest. "You're related to everything, even the trees and grass. The Shoshones always understood that. Scientists are proving now that they were absolutely right. Everything's made from the same tiny particles."

Jeremy's eyes went wide. "Everything?"

"God just put the particles together differently to create bears and trees and other things in our world. We aren't alike on the outside, and yet, essentially, we're the same. I am in you, and you are in me, and we are in the animals and the trees. Someday, I hope all of mankind will come full circle back to the basic truths that Jesus tried to teach and the Shoshones knew without ever having met Him—that we're all one with each other, millions of tiny pieces in a huge jigsaw puzzle. If we destroy just one of the pieces, we risk destroying it all."

"Is that how come you don't eat animals, 'cause you think they're your brothers and sisters?"

Ben chuckled. "Vegetarianism is a personal choice. As long as there are supermarkets and I can fill my cupboards with other good foods that keep me healthy and fit, I prefer not to eat animals, that's all."

"What if all the stores closed?"

Ben laughed again. "Well, in that case, I would hunt as my forefathers did. And, following their example, I would say thanks to the animal's spirit for giving its life to sustain me. First, though, I think I'd try my hand at gardening."

Ben suddenly dropped to a crouch. Gathering Jeremy close to his side, he pointed to some brush just ahead of them. "Look," he said softly.

A tiny fawn, almost invisible against a backdrop of multicolored leaves, stood stock-still, staring at them. Chloe hadn't noticed the fawn until Ben pointed it out, but she couldn't shake the feeling he'd known it was there all along.

The child gazed raptly at the fawn. He'd seen pictures of baby deer, and so had Chloe, but nothing compared to actually coming upon one in the forest. The small animal was exquisitely formed. Its huge brown eyes reminded Chloe of Jeremy's. Oddly, the little guy didn't seem frightened. Chloe decided that fear of humans might be a learned behavior.

Ben made a shrill bleating sound. Chloe stared at his throat, watching the tendons work in a strange undulation to produce the noise. She was incredulous when the fawn took a faltering step forward. The baby deer seemed far more worried about Chloe than he was about Ben and Jeremy. She held her breath and stood absolutely still. One hesitant step after another, the fawn kept coming.

When the baby finally reached them, Ben reached out a big hand and caressed its fragile body.

"You can pet him if you like, Jeremy."

"Won't he be scared?" Jeremy whispered.

"Has he reason to be?"

Jeremy shook his head.

"Well, then, I don't think he will be."

Jeremy thrust out a hand to touch the fawn's forehead. "Hi, baby deer."

The fawn smelled Jeremy's hand. And then, to both Chloe's and her son's surprise, the youngster caught one of the child's fingers in his mouth and began to suckle. Jeremy giggled. "He thinks I'm his mom."

"No. He understands who his mama is. She has left him for a bit, probably to forage for food. He's supposed to stay hidden while she's gone, but he knows me and isn't afraid, so he's breaking the rules."

"Will his mom be mad?"

"No. She knows me, too. She comes to the house a lot to eat cracked corn. He understands that it's okay to break the rules with me."

The fawn grabbed another of Jeremy's small fingers.

"He's getting your taste and scent." Ben nudged the child forward. "If you give him your breath, he'll always remember you."

"How can I give him my breath?"

"Just breathe into his nostrils."

"But my mom says animals got germs."

"They do, and so do we. His won't make you sick. Share your breath with him. When he's an antlered buck, he'll remember, and he won't be afraid if he sees you in the woods."

Jeremy scrunched up his face, bent forward, and pressed his pursed lips to the fawn's nose.

"Breath out. Open your mouth." Ben kept a hand on the child's shoulder. "Let him taste you."

"His tongue's scratchy," Jeremy exclaimed with a giggle when the fawn licked him on the mouth. "I'm gonna 'member his taste for always," he said a moment later, scrubbing hard at his lips with the back of his hand.

"And he'll remember yours." Ben cupped the child's chin in his hand and made eye contact. "You've made a sacred promise to him, Jeremy. Do you understand what sacred means?"

"Like in church?"

Ben nodded. "Exactly, only this is a church without walls, and God, no matter what name you call Him by, is the Father of all that you see. You've made a

promise to the fawn that you'll always be his friend.
He trusts you now. If you break that trust, it will be
a very bad thing."

"I won't break it."

Jeremy no sooner finished speaking than the fawn
butted him. It was only in play, but the child was
knocked clear off his feet. Rump planted in the dirt,
arms braced behind him, he looked indignantly at the
baby deer and said, "That wasn't nice."

Ben laughed and helped the child stand up. While
brushing off the seat of Jeremy's pants, he said,
"Young deer play with each other that way. He
doesn't understand that you're a boy and don't know
how to tussle with him."

"If we see each other in the woods when he's big,
will he do that again?"

Ben gave the child's pants a final swat. "Nah. He'll
grow up and become full of himself." He sent Chloe
a warm look. "Some of us forget how to play when
we grow older, and more's the pity." He stroked the
fawn again. "When he gets horns, be careful of them.
Sometimes they swing their heads at a fly or something and hit you accidentally. You don't want a prong
in your belly."

"I'll be real careful. Is he really gonna be my friend
from now on?"

"For always," Ben assured him solemnly.

It was an impossible promise. Rationally Chloe
knew that. Yet watching Ben's dark face as he said
the words, she could almost believe they were true.

They walked in silence for a while after leaving the
fawn. Then, out of the blue, Jeremy asked, "Did God
make those baby chipmunks, Ben?"

"He did."

"Are all of them my brothers and sisters, too?"

"They are," Ben said in that same oddly quiet way.

"And if you remember that when you become a man, Jeremy, you will be extraordinary."

"What's *'strordinary* mean?"

Ben thought for a moment. "It means you may have to walk through life alone, that few will come behind you and only a very special, rare person will choose to walk beside you."

"Won't that be lonesome?"

Ben flicked Chloe a searching look. "Sometimes, yes. But if you know you're walking the right way, you grow to accept the loneliness."

Chapter Twelve

That evening, Bobby Lee stopped in to do his paperwork only minutes after Sue left to go buy the nightly lattes. When Chloe glanced up and saw the deputy entering by the front door, she moved her pencil holder to the far end of her desk. It wasn't nearly as precious to her as the lantern had been, but it was a gift from her sister Phoebe, and she always smiled when she read the message. I'VE WORKED HARD FOR THIS NERVOUS BREAKDOWN. BACK OFF AND LET ME ENJOY IT.

Bobby Lee's uniform shirt was wet with rain. He tugged at his collar. "If you don't like Oregon weather, be patient and it'll change." He wiped his boots on the mat. "June, and it's pouring. Can you believe it?"

Chloe leaned around to peer out a window. Sure enough, rain sluiced over the glass. She remembered Ben's prediction and said, "Who would have thought it? The sky was clear as a bell this afternoon."

Chloe resumed her work, hoping Bobby Lee would take the hint and go straight to his office. No such luck. After clearing a space, he propped a hip on her desk. Chloe ignored his presence.

"Hi," he said when she didn't look up.

Chloe sighed and abandoned her work, wondering as she did if his timing was a coincidence or if he'd been waiting for Sue to leave so he could catch her alone. She leaned toward the latter theory, which made her uneasy.

"What's up?" she asked

"Only this." He thrust a rain-spattered white bag with gold lettering into her hands. "It was the least I could do."

Chloe recognized the name of a classy little curio shop over on Sunrise Loop that catered to tourists. "What on earth is this?"

Bobby Lee swept off his sand-colored Stetson and raked his fingers through his black hair. "Open it and see for yourself."

Bemused, Chloe sat back in her chair with the package on her lap. "I know it may sound hopelessly old-fashioned, Bobby Lee, but I don't accept gifts from men outside my family."

"It's not a gift. More a peace offering." He hooked his hat over his knee. "I felt so bad about breaking your lantern that I went shopping to find you a replacement. It's a lighter shade of blue but the same size. I know it can't replace the one your dad gave you, but I bought it anyway." He waited a beat. When she still didn't open the sack, he said, "Hey, come on. It's not a gift. When you break something that belongs to someone else, it's customary to replace it."

He had a point, and normally, Chloe wouldn't have felt hesitant. She just didn't want to get herself into a sticky situation with a male coworker, and she'd sensed from the beginning that it would be easy to do with this man.

Setting aside her reservations, she lifted the fancy white box from the bag. When she tugged up the lid, she saw a tissue-wrapped Japanese lantern nestled inside. It was almost identical to the one Bobby Lee had broken, and she knew he must have searched several stores before he found it.

As she lifted the sphere carefully from the box, she felt like a worm. She'd been so certain that he had broken her other lantern on purpose. This was inarguable proof that she had been wrong. Genuine Japanese lanterns were a rarity these days, and the scarred surface of the sun-tinted glass told her this was the real McCoy. "Oh, Bobby Lee, I don't know what to say. You really shouldn't have. This must have cost you an arm and a leg."

"Nah, only an arm. And it'll be worth every penny if it convinces you to take my name off your shit list."

She gave a startled laugh. "You aren't on my shit list. I was upset about the lantern, I admit. It was very special to me. But I knew it was an accident." *Liar.* "I'm sorry if I led you to think otherwise."

"I'm the one who's sorry. I shouldn't have been fiddling with it." He watched her hold the lantern up to the light. "It's not a reproduction. They said it wasn't, anyway, and charged accordingly. Even so, I know it's not the same."

Chloe set the new lantern on her blotter. "Nothing can replace the one my dad gave me, but it means a lot to me that you went to the trouble and expense to buy me another one. It was very sweet of you."

"Sweet enough to warrant your going out to dinner with me?" He held up a hand. "Before you say no, hear me out. I don't mean a date, just a nice meal between friends. I got off on the wrong foot with you. I'd like a chance to set things right. We are coworkers, and we'll be seeing a lot of each other. It seems to me it'll be better, all around, if neither of us bears the other any animosity."

He reminded her oddly of Jeremy in that moment,

his eyes open and honest, his expression imploring. For a fleeting instant, she remembered what Ben's grandfather had said. *If you see no heart, run.* Could she see Bobby Lee's heart in his eyes?

Chloe wasn't sure. He looked sincere, yet there was something—something she couldn't name—that made her uneasy. Of course, to be fair, most men made her uneasy these days. Maybe she needed counseling.

She wadded up the sack and tossed it in the trash. "No one can have too many friends, Bobby Lee. It's just—well, you gave me the distinct impression you were—"

"Looking for more?" He shrugged. "When you first came to work here, I was. I won't lie about it. You're a pretty lady."

"My mirror contradicts you, but thank you for the compliment."

He rubbed his jaw. "I realize now that you aren't interested in me that way, so you can stop looking wary. We can still be friends, can't we?"

She rocked back in her chair again. "Of course. I'd like nothing more."

"Well, then? Let me start over with a clean slate."

Chloe had never been one to hold a grudge. "It's really not necessary to take me to dinner, Bobby Lee. We can start over fresh by mutual agreement."

"I want to buy you dinner, all right? The High Desert Inn is a family restaurant. What better way is there to clear the air and really get acquainted than over a nice meal?" When she hesitated, he rushed to add, "Come on. Be a sport and say yes. It'll give me a chance to prove I'm not such a bad guy."

"I'd love to say yes, but I hate being gone from home on my nights off."

"We'll make it an early evening. I'll have you back in time to tuck Jeremy in, I promise."

She ran a hand over the lantern. "You're making it very difficult to say no."

"Then don't. Dinner out with a coworker. What harm can it do?"

"None, I suppose." She relented with a nod. "All right. Sure. Why not?"

He flashed a relieved grin. "Great. How's Friday night at six sound?"

"Six will be fine. I can feed Jeremy and do the dishes before I leave."

He pushed up from her desk. "Friday at six, then. I'll look forward to it." He settled his Stetson back on his head. "You won't regret it, Chloe. I promise."

She sincerely hoped not.

Over the next five days, Ben was always at the house when Chloe and Jeremy arrived to clean cages and feed the animals, and the routine established that first day became a pattern. Each morning, he insisted that Chloe join him on the deck for a cup of coffee before she started work. Their conversations had an overall tone of lightness that made her relax and laugh but also gave her something to think about later.

Ben had a way of slipping profound observations into an exchange, taking her off guard and sucking her in before she realized the communication had turned serious. "Do you know why most plants are green?"

"Photosynthesis."

"Ah, but why so many shades of green? My grand-father believed it was God's favorite color. That was easy for me to buy. Then I went to college and discovered it was actually all about the fibrous composition of different plants and the spectrums of light different plant structures absorb and reflect. In books, there's a fact to explain every mystical thing my grandfather ever taught me."

He sounded so sad. Chloe stared into her coffee, trying to imagine him at nineteen and twenty, with his nose in biology books. He was so rugged and elemental that the image wouldn't gel. "Just because the books proved him wrong doesn't mean he was any less beautiful as a person."

"For a long time, I became convinced he was just an ignorant old man who had concocted a story to explain every damned thing. I felt betrayed—and angry, which compelled me to learn all that I could so I'd never be stupid and ignorant like he was. That makes me feel ashamed now." He gave his coffee a slow swirl. "I lost touch with the truths he taught me, began to scorn them. I had to come home and walk through my woods again before I came full circle. Green *is* God's favorite color. We've only to look at the plant life to know that. He masterminded photosynthesis and created different plants to absorb different wavelengths and light spectra. My grandfather was right all along. God painted the world green.

"Everything is linked, the sun to the plants, the plants to the earth, and the earth to all its inhabitants. Nature is a complex dance with countless partners. Without opening a book, my grandfather understood the magical choreography of it all and stripped it down to simple truths. In our arrogance, we give fancy explanations for everything when a simple one would do just as well." He winked at her. "The plants are different shades of green because God painted them that way with a divine brush."

"Of course. Why make it complicated? Simplicity is much more beautiful."

"Exactly," he murmured. "Why make it complicated, Chloe?"

The questioning note in his husky voice made Chloe's nerves jangle. She understood the unspoken invitation—to simply let go and allow her feelings to take over. They were strongly attracted to each other, yet she was balking, letting concerns that had nothing to do with him spoil something that could be beautiful. *Problem.* Until Ben opened up to her, how could she let down her guard with him? She still didn't even know what he did for a living.

Another morning, right after they took their usual positions on the deck, Ben pointed to the patches of earth visible in the distance between the expanses of trees. "Do you know why the soil here is red?"

Chloe smiled. "Because red is God's second favorite color?"

He shook his head. "The Shoshone died fighting for this land, and they stained the earth red with their blood. Ashes to ashes, and dust to dust, they became part of it again." He turned an ear to the woods. "If you listen closely, you can hear their voices riding on the wind." He flashed a quick grin. "Sometimes the breeze catches the dust just right and funnels it toward the sky. When that happened, my grandfather always stopped what he was doing, lifted his arms in prayer, and wished his ancestors a safe journey. He believed lingering souls were being lifted by angels into the Great Beyond."

"How lovely." Chloe stared into the distance. "I'll never look at the red earth here again without thinking of him—and all those who went before him."

"Neither will I," he said softly.

Each afternoon, Ben helped Chloe change animals' bedding so she and Jeremy could accompany him into the woods. During those walks, Chloe watched as her son was slowly transformed from a troubled little boy who was withdrawn around strangers, especially men, into an outgoing child with a sturdy, tan body and a healthy glow. Sometimes the things Jeremy revealed to Ben embarrassed Chloe, but she held her tongue. Ben was like a balm to her child's battered heart. She saw it in Jeremy's expressions and heard it in his words. Ben was making Jeremy believe in magic and miracles again, possibly because the man himself believed in them so deeply.

By the third day, Chloe realized she would not be surprised by anything that happened when they were with Ben Longtree. His world was intricately layered, rich with mysteries another person might never see. On the surface, his woods looked like any other, just a bunch of trees and brush. And then Ben would reveal something incredibly beautiful.

Jeremy loved the walks and absorbed information like a sponge. On one such trek, he saw a monarch butterfly hovering over a bush and asked Ben where butterflies came from. After a good deal of searching, Ben parted the foliage of a manzanita bush to reveal the dangling remains of a chrysalis.

"That's where butterflies come from," he explained, touching the fragile shell with his fingertip as he explained the metamorphosis from caterpillar to pupa and then to butterfly. "When I was about your age, my grandfather found one of these, and we watched it every day until the butterfly finally came out."

"You got to see it?"

"Actually, no, but there was a butterfly flitting around when we found it empty, and my grandfather believed that it had come out of its chrysalis just before we got there. He was dying at the time, and I was very young. I think he was trying to prepare me for that final good-bye. He'd been trying to teach me the difference between our bodies and our souls. You know what a soul is, don't you?"

"The part of us that goes to heaven?"

"That's right. It's the beautiful part of us that no one

can see. It's how we think, and how we feel. More important, though, it's how we make other people think and feel when we're with them. When we die, they bury our bodies, but our souls aren't inside us anymore. They've flown away, just like a beautiful butterfly from its chrysalis."

"Oh."

"I'm sure I don't need to explain that to you. You saw it happen with your father, right?"

Jeremy frowned. "My daddy isn't dead."

Ben toed the dirt and pine needles. After a long, quiet moment, he crouched and bent his dark head, running his fingertips over the forest floor. "Technically, you're right. His heart is still beating. But when the propeller blade hit his head, it did serious injury to the part of his brain where his thoughts and feelings lived. His soul place." He fingered the chrysalis again. "This is all that's left of your daddy now, just his shell, because there's no place for his soul anymore. It flew away, like a beautiful butterfly."

"Is that how come he can't find his way back to us anymore, 'cause his soul went to heaven?"

Ben glanced up at Chloe, before settling his solemn gaze on the child again. "He isn't your daddy anymore, is he? When you're with him, he doesn't make you feel the way he used to. That has to mean all the important parts of him—the parts that made him your dad—have flown away like the butterfly to a beautiful place."

Jeremy's eyes went sparkly with tears. "So he's kind of like dead?"

"Yes, in every way that counts, Jeremy. Only his body is left. Your mom says he was a really good daddy before he got hurt. That he loved you a lot."

Jeremy nodded.

"Well, then," Ben said softly. "That means he had a good soul—a beautiful one, just like the butterfly. Most people believe that good souls always go to heaven. Judging by that, I'd say that must be where he went."

Jeremy gulped. "Then I don't have a dad anymore."

"I didn't say that." Ben glided his hand through the air. "When we die, a part of us lingers with the people who knew us and loved us. That part of us is called our essence. If you hold on tight to your dad's essence, he'll always be with you."

"How can I hold on to something I can't see?"

"You do it in your heart." Ben pressed a fist to the center of his chest. "Make a special place there, just for your dad, and put all your good memories of him in there so you'll have them with you always. When you feel lonesome for him, you can reach inside for a nice memory, and he'll be with you again."

Chloe hugged her waist. Tears had filled her eyes, and they burned like acid. For so long, she'd been focused so completely on the ugliness that she'd mostly forgotten the beautiful things about Roger— his essence. Ben was absolutely right. She needed to forget the bad stuff and hold tight to all the beautiful memories, not just for herself but also for her son.

She took a deep breath and turned her face to the pine-scented breeze. It felt as if a huge weight had been lifted off her heart. *He's dead*. For all intents and purposes, Roger was dead. All this time, she'd been unable to grieve or say good-bye because he still walked and talked and breathed. But the man he'd become wasn't her husband. Her husband had died that awful afternoon on the Puget Sound as surely as if his heart had stopped beating.

On the way home a few minutes later, Jeremy

turned on his seat to stare wide-eyed at Chloe. "Mommy, why didn't you ever tell me that Daddy died?"

Chloe rolled the car to a stop under the log archway that marked the end of Ben's driveway. "Because, sweetie, he didn't die the same way most people do, and I didn't have Ben's grandfather to help me understand in a way I could explain to you. It's complicated with your daddy. Like Ben said, the part of his brain that made him your daddy is dead. But his shell is still alive."

Jeremy turned to look sadly out the windshield. "The shell isn't my dad, though."

"No. The shell is nothing like your daddy. He loved you so much, Jeremy. He never would have hit you with the Frisbee or grabbed you by the throat for spilling your milk."

"So my real dad is in heaven."

Again, Chloe fell back on what Ben had said. She was too confused and upset to think clearly herself. "Yes, I'd say so. All the good parts of him have left. And he was *so* good, I have to believe those parts of him went to heaven."

The child let his head fall back against the seat. "I'm glad he's not lost, Mommy. In heaven, he won't feel lonesome for us, will he?"

"No," Chloe assured him. "In heaven, everyone is completely happy. That's why it's called heaven, because it's perfect there."

"Do you 'member the train he got me? It wasn't my birthday or nothing. He bought it for me, just because."

Chloe was startled by the sudden change of subject. "It's been forever since I thought of that. He came home, carrying a great big box, and the two of you spent hours putting it all together."

"After we got it running, you and me and him had a picnic on the floor." Jeremy stared past her at nothing, his small face glowing. "Daddy put raisins on top of the cars. We played a game, trying to grab raisins as the train went past."

Chloe's heart hurt at the memory. Roger's deep guffaws. The easy affection he'd shown his son. That was the man she'd married, the man she'd promised to love in sickness and in health. How had she reached this dismal point where a stranger had to remind her of that and put everything into its proper perspective?

The remainder of the way home, Jeremy talked about his train. Once, when Chloe glanced over at him, she saw him pressing his small fist to the center of his chest. Ben had given her son a precious gift, simply by showing him the chrysalis of a butterfly.

"I still got my train," Jeremy informed her when she parked in front of the house. "It's in my closet in that same big box. I haven't looked at it for a long, long time 'cause it made me feel bad inside."

Chloe killed the car engine. As silence settled, she turned to study her son. Jeremy probably couldn't remember many of the wonderful things his father had done. For so long now, Chloe had been unable to speak of Roger. Now she was starting to realize that she'd been doing her son a terrible injustice.

"Your dad was the best," she said, her voice taut with emotion. "Do you remember when your gerbils got loose?"

Jeremy shook his head.

"We couldn't catch them, so he set out food so they wouldn't starve. For months, they ran loose in the house. And then—" Chloe laughed at the memory, and it felt absolutely wonderful "—then they had babies! I'll never forget how your father looked, crawling around the house on his hands and knees, peeking under the furniture. Every once in a while, he'd yell, 'God, Chloe, they're everywhere!' We didn't know what to do. The neighbor said to put out rat poison, but they'd been your pets, and your dad refused to kill them."

"What did he do?"

"One afternoon, he came home from work with this thing called a live trap. He eventually captured all the gerbils without hurting any of them. We had so many that he gave most of them away to other kids on our block."

"Ben says traps are cruel. I'm glad my dad didn't get one that would hurt my gerbils." Jeremy smiled. "My dad was nice. Wasn't he, Mom?"

"Yes, Jeremy, he was." Chloe reached a decision. "You know what? It's my night off. Why don't we dig that box out of your closet and put your train together? Would that be fun?"

"Can we grab raisins when we get it running?"

"I may be low on raisins, but we'll come up with something." She drew her keys from the ignition. "And I'll tell you bunches and bunches of stories about your dad."

Chapter Thirteen

The following morning after returning from her eight o'clock rounds at Cinnamon Ridge, Chloe was sitting at the table, enjoying a leisurely cup of coffee, when the phone rang. Jeremy raced in from the adjoining living room to answer the call. Then, stretching the cord as far as it would reach, he brought the phone to Chloe. "Sue," he whispered.

Grasping the receiver, Chloe said, "Hey, girl, what's up?"

"Steven, stop that! Sorry. He brought his squirt gun in the house. *Steven!*"

Chloe held the phone away from her ear.

"Kids!" Sue complained. "I just washed that window, and I only do it about once a year. Now it'll have spots all over it until next June. Toby! Do *not* throw that water. If you guys want to have a water fight, take it outside!"

"It sounds like you have your hands full."

"I always have my hands full, and I swear, they time the worst of it for when I'm on the phone. I don't know how Jerry manages. He says they're good as gold on his shift. Are you *sure* you want to keep them while we go out to celebrate his raise?"

Chloe had forgotten about making the offer. "I'm positive. Name the time."

"We were thinking tomorrow night."

Chloe winced. "Oh, Sue, I can't. I'm so sorry. I've got a dinner date. I can do it next Friday, though."

"That works. We've waited this long without dying. Another week will seem like a nanosecond. A dinner date, huh? With a guy?"

"Yes, but not like that. It's just Bobby Lee. A friendly thing."

"Oh, yeah? Hmm."

"What's that mean?"

"Nothing," Sue assured her. "It just doesn't sound like Bobby Lee."

"He understands that I'm not interested in anything romantic. He and I got off on the wrong foot. He wants to have dinner and chitchat to clear the air. Afterwards, we'll call it an evening." Chloe related how the deputy had replaced her Japanese lantern. "I couldn't say no after he did something so thoughtful."

"That really was nice of him," Sue agreed. "And, hey, what can happen at the Desert Inn? The restaurant section's pretty tame. On Friday nights, they have a band in the lounge, but even that's low-key, no rowdies or anything."

Chloe glanced at her watch. Swing shift was the pits. She had to go shopping before she left for work, and there were a dozen other things she needed to do as well. She never had any real downtime, going in at three.

She took another sip of coffee and settled back to listen while Sue screamed at her kids. When the brunette came back on, she said, "I've got to go. Tiana just melted Barbie's hair with my curling iron."

"Uh-oh."

Chloe could hear the child crying in the background.

Sue made clucking noises. "She's fine, Tiana. Mommy will fix her." To Chloe, Sue added, "Barbie goes butch. My curling iron will never be the same."

Chloe was still grinning when she hung up the phone.

When Chloe arrived at work that afternoon, she found a single red rose lying on her desk blotter. She raised her eyebrows at Sue. The plump brunette lifted her hands and shrugged. "Not I. I've been dying to read the note, but I slapped my hand and stayed away."

Bemused, Chloe slipped the card from the folds of flocked cellophane. She stared at the local florist shop logo on the front of the envelope.

"God, would you just *open* it?"

Chloe laughed. "But it's so much fun torturing you."

"Read it aloud or die."

Grinning, Chloe opened the card. Inside, a masculine, uneven scrawl read, *"I'm looking forward to dinner tomorrow night. Love, Bobby Lee."*

Chloe's smile blinked out.

"What?" Sue cried. "Who's it from?

"Bobby Lee. It says he's looking forward to dinner tomorrow night."

"Smooth move."

Chloe tossed the card in the trash. "I guess that's what worries me. If he were having dinner with, say, Frank Bower, he wouldn't leave a rose lying on his desk. He'd just say in passing, 'Hey, man, we still on for tomorrow night?' " She looked at Sue over the top of the rose as she sniffed its delicate petals. "He signed the card, 'Love, Bobby Lee.' "

Sue pursed her lips. "Uh-oh."

"Yeah." Chloe sighed and laid the flower down.

"You think he's blowing smoke about not being interested in anything romantic?"

Sue steepled her fingers. "He wouldn't be the first guy to try sneaking in a side door."

Chloe leaned her hips against her desk. "Maybe I should cancel."

Sue thought about it. "Lots of people sign cards using the word *love.* They don't mean anything by it." She shrugged. "And, like it or not, you aren't exactly Frank. Guys treat women differently than they do other men. I'd go on the date. If he gives you any bad vibes, you know he's not being up-front about his intentions, and you can be otherwise engaged when he asks again."

Chloe nodded. "You're right. I'm overreacting, aren't I?"

Sue held up her hands. "I'm just saying that canceling the date might be too extreme. He's a nice guy. A lousy lover, but that's a story for another day."

"Speaking from experience?"

"Heavens, no. Just an opinion I've formed, observing him in action over the years. You know that saying, 'Love 'em and leave 'em?' Bobby Lee invented it. Once he gains the inner sanctum, he loses interest and moves on to the next challenge."

Chloe stowed her purse in the cubbyhole. "Well, I'm not going to sleep with him so that he'll lose interest."

Sue chuckled. "Would I suggest that?" She gave Chloe a sidelong look. "Although it might be stimulating. He's pretty cute."

"Not my type."

"Who is?"

"No one."

"And why is that?" Sue asked. "You're a pretty lady. I'd kill for that figure. After so many kids, I look like the Goodyear blimp. Life can't stop just because you're divorced."

"I just don't feel like dating yet, is all."

"My point exactly. You're, like, way too uptight. A sweaty romp with Bobby Lee might be a nice diversion."

Chloe laughed and shook her head. "Aerobics are more my speed. Maybe I'll take up jogging."

Sue groaned. "You are so boring."

Chloe put the blue dress back on the hanger. *Too clingy.* She plucked a taupe suit from the rod. *Nope, too dressy.* She sighed, planted her hands on her hips, and glared at her wardrobe. She didn't want to look too casual, but she wasn't sure she wanted to wear a dress, either. A woman's choice in clothing made a statement. The message she wanted to send was, "Friends, only."

Half her closet had been emptied onto the bed before she finally settled on gray linen slacks and a matching summer blazer over an ecru silk blouse. For accessories, she chose a simple gold chain and tiny diamond earrings. *Done.* She looked nice enough to go out to dinner with a coworker, and that was exactly the note she wanted to strike.

A half hour later, Bobby Lee knocked at the door. In civilian clothes, he looked so different she almost didn't recognize him. He wore chinos and a blue pinstripe that complemented his dark complexion and brought out the color of his eyes. In his hands, he held a drum of Lincoln Logs.

"For Jeremy," he said, thrusting them at her.

Chloe accepted the gift. "Oh, Bobby Lee, you really shouldn't have. Jeremy, come see what Mr. Schuck brought for you!"

Jeremy, always timid around strange men, approached hesitantly, but the wariness in his eyes was replaced by a glow of excitement when he saw the drum. "Wow!" He grabbed the container, dashed back to the living room, and dumped the contents on the rug. "Thanks, Deputy Schuck! I've been wanting some of these for forever."

"Hi-yee, Bobby Lee!" Tracy called from the kitchen.

"Hi, there, Trace." Bobby Lee shoved his hands in his pockets. Arching a black eyebrow at Chloe, he said, "You ready?"

Chloe was as ready as she'd ever be. She kissed Jeremy good-bye, reminded Tracy that she would be dining at the Desert Inn, and joined Bobby Lee on the porch. Keeping his hands in his pockets, he preceded her down the rickety steps.

"Thanks again for the logs," Chloe said. "He loves them."

"Hey, there's a method to my madness." He fell into step with her en route to the Bronco. "I figured you'd enjoy yourself more if you knew he was having fun, too."

He opened the passenger door. As Chloe climbed into the vehicle, she was grateful she'd chosen to wear slacks. From ground to running board was a high step, which she couldn't have executed with any grace or modesty in a dress. The inside of the Bronco was tidy and smelled of new vinyl and leather. While Bobby Lee circled to the driver's side, she fastened her seat belt.

Here goes nothing, she thought as he started the engine.

An hour and a half later, Chloe was laughing at herself for having been so nervous. Bobby Lee was an engaging companion, talking almost nonstop over the meal about his experiences as a deputy. When Chloe wasn't chuckling over an absurdity, she was asking questions, sincerely interested in his answers.

"So teen drug use is on the decline in Paulina County?"

He topped off their glasses with merlot. "Yes. Stricter enforcement, along with the support of school administrators, has had an impact. Two years ago, I busted thirty percent more teenagers for possession."

Chloe took a sip of wine. One glass was usually her limit, but he had been keeping her goblet full, and she'd lost track. She felt relaxed and pleasantly tipsy.

Their waiter approached the table. "Dessert?"

Chloe held up a hand. "That steak was huge. None for me, thank you."

"I'll pass, too," Bobby Lee replied.

The young man discreetly laid a black leather folder at the edge of the table. "When you're ready, sir."

Chloe got her purse. Bobby Lee narrowed an eye. "Don't insult me."

"Friends, remember? You shouldn't have to pick up the entire tab."

He spread a large hand over the book. "This is on me. Please."

Chloe could see he was determined. She put her purse back on the floor. "Thank you, Bobby Lee."

He lifted a hip to get his wallet. The credit card he drew from inside gleamed gold in the candlelight. While they waited for the waiter to process the ticket, they sipped their wine in companionable silence.

Moments later when they rose to leave, Bobby Lee gently grasped her arm. "How about an hour in the lounge? It's only eight, and the Rounders are playing. Great country-western band."

Chloe drew back her sleeve to check her watch.

"What? You think I can't tell time?" He steered her toward the swinging doors. "It's against my religion to end an evening before nine."

It was still early, Chloe decided. And she enjoyed country-western music. "Okay, but at nine sharp, home we go. Right? You did promise I'd be back in time to tuck Jeremy in."

"And I never break a promise."

It took Chloe's eyes a few seconds to adjust to the dimmer lighting inside the lounge. By the time she could see clearly, they were seated at a small table, tucked away in a back corner. Bobby Lee signaled the waitress, ordering a glass of merlot for Chloe, and a Jack and Seven for himself. It worried Chloe that he was still drinking when he knew he had to drive.

"I really shouldn't," Chloe protested. "I don't usually drink so much."

"You're fine," he assured her.

The band started a new song. The music throbbed from speakers around the lounge. Leaning close so Bobby Lee could hear, Chloe said, "They're good!"

He nodded, tapping his hands on the table in time to the beat. Several couples converged on the dance floor. Before Chloe could guess his intention, Bobby Lee pulled her up from her chair.

"Oh, I—"

Ignoring her protests, he drew her to the dance floor. Turning, he slipped an arm around her waist and pulled her tightly against him so his thigh pressed against her pelvis. The next thing she knew, he was doing a swing version of the two-step. To save her feet, Chloe followed his lead, wondering if he realized where his leg was rubbing.

She started to sweat, not from exertion but from nerves. The lock of his hard arm around her brought back memories she preferred to forget. When the number ended, the band started another, and Bobby Lee continued dancing. Chloe felt trapped, and she heartily wished now that she'd said no to an hour in the lounge.

When the second song finally ended, he led her back to their table. Chloe nursed her wine. He tossed back the Jack and Seven, then signaled the waitress for another round.

"Not for me, thanks." Chloe set her nearly full goblet back down on the table. "I'm a lightweight. I probably won't finish this."

At the end of an hour when they returned to the Bronco, Bobby Lee had a gleam in his eye that made Chloe uneasy. When she asked if he should drive, he waved aside her question and laughed, saying he was fine. As he drove from the parking lot, she said, "This has been fun, and I really appreciate your ending the evening early."

Expecting him to hang a left onto Shoshone, Chloe flashed him a startled look when he kept driving north. "Uh—Bobby Lee—you passed my turnoff."

He flipped on the stereo. "Relax, honey. Just one little detour."

Chloe's alarm mounted when she realized he was driving toward the river. "It's getting late, Bobby Lee. I really do need to get home."

Ignoring her objection, he just kept driving. Chloe's muscles knotted with tension when the lights of Jack Pine were eclipsed by woodland darkness. To increase her apprehension, there were no other cars on State Rec Road, which made her feel frighteningly disconnected from other people.

A few minutes later, Bobby Lee parked near the river, cut the engine, and unbuckled his seat belt.

Without the dash lights to brighten the Bronco's interior, Chloe could barely make out his features. He leaned across the console to unfasten her safety restraint as well. Then, without a word, he snaked out a hand, clamped it over the back of her neck, and dragged her toward him.

"Bobby Lee, what are you—?"

The breath whooshed from her lungs when his other arm clamped around her. Despite her panicked attempt to extricate herself from his hold, he pulled her across the plastic compartment between the seats and onto his lap. His mouth covered hers, his teeth shoving her lips back as his tongue thrust deep. For several moments, Chloe was plunged back into the past, and fear almost paralyzed her.

He was strong. Terrifyingly so. And to Chloe's frightened mind, he seemed to have six hands. She struggled helplessly against him, her brain so frozen with shock that she could recall none of the self-defense moves her brother Rob had taught her.

She heard buttons pop, felt the front of her silk blouse fall open, and then his hands were on her, his fingers digging brutally through the lacy cups of her bra. Chloe whimpered into his mouth, shoved ineffectually at his shoulders. *Oh, God.* He meant to rape her. With her hip wedged under the steering wheel, she couldn't get enough distance between their bodies to knee him in the groin.

Chloe's mind reeled with memories of Roger and how helpless she'd felt the few times he turned his strength against her. If anything, Bobby Lee was even stronger. A burning sensation scored her breast. She realized he was clawing at the cups of her bra, and that he'd scratched her in the process.

Red blurred the edges of her vision. With a violent

twist of her head, she managed to wrench her mouth from his. "Let me go, Bobby Lee!"

He made a fist on her hair, bringing tears to her eyes. His face hovering a scant inch from hers, he grated out, "You got something against cops? If you want to keep your goddamned job, you better treat me nice. With one word, I can get your sweet little ass fired."

Chloe rammed the heel of her right hand hard against his nose. He grunted and grabbed for his face. She seized the moment to scramble away from him. *Thank you, Rob.* Once on the other side of the Bronco, she grabbed her purse, threw open the door, and spilled gracelessly out of the vehicle.

Shaking with outrage, she spun to cry, "I don't care that much about the job, you jerk! You can shove it where it'll never again see daylight!"

Recovered from the nose jab, he tossed open his door, as well. "Oh, yeah?" he cried as he piled out. "Think long and hard about that, darlin'. You'll be hard-put to feed that kid, standing in the unemployment lines."

Afraid he might jump her again, Chloe ran toward the woods. "I'd rather go on welfare than be touched by the likes of you!"

"Good, 'cause that's where you'll end up, on welfare!" he yelled after her. "I don't spend a hundred bucks on a woman without getting something in return."

Chloe wasn't about to delay her escape long enough to remind him that she'd offered to pick up her own tab. When she reached the trees, she ducked behind a stout trunk, pressed her spine to the bark, and tried to breathe shallowly so he couldn't follow the sounds. *Something in return?* She'd heard of men who thought that way, but she'd never had the misfortune of actually dating one.

"You're a long way from town, little lady," he hollered.

Little lady. What a pompous, chauvinistic ass he was. She should have heeded her instincts and canceled the date.

"I'll leave you out here, damn it. Put out or walk, your choice."

Put out? He was disgusting. Chloe shivered, silently sending up heartfelt prayers that he'd get back in the Bronco and drive away.

"There are bears and cougars out here!" Anger throbbed in his voice now. "I'm the lesser of two evils. You were quick enough to start fucking Longtree. Why not me?"

Chloe gulped down a retort. That was undoubtedly his intent, to make her so furious she gave away her location.

His voice turned wheedling. "Come on, Chloe. All I did was get fresh. I'm a little drunk, okay? Come back, and I'll behave myself, swear to God."

Right. She was staying put. If she hadn't landed a good one on his schnozzle, she'd be in big trouble right now.

"Fine, then. You wanna walk? Okay by me!" She heard him stomp back to the vehicle. A door slammed. Then, "The cell phone reception sucks out here, by the way. Enjoy your hike home. Just desserts, if you ask me."

A second door slammed closed. An instant later, the Ford's engine roared to life, and its tires peeled out on the loose gravel. Chloe stayed put for several minutes to make sure he didn't come back. When she deemed it safe, she drew her phone from her purse with shaking hands. When she turned it on, the illuminated window said, NO SERVICE. Unlike the Seattle area, Central Oregon was rife with dead zones where cellular signals couldn't reach.

"Blast it!" she cried.

An owl hooted somewhere nearby, then swooped from its perch, filling the air with a rushing sound just above her head. Chloe ducked, swung to one side, and dropped the cell phone. "Damn it, damn it, *damn* it!"

The faint glow of the phone saved her from having to crawl around on her hands and knees to find it. She grabbed it, stuffed it into her purse, and made her way back to the parking area. In the dark, she tripped every few steps, which drove home to her that she was way out in the woods somewhere. If she fell and got hurt, no one but that jerk would know where to look for her.

Once on the road, Chloe draped her purse strap over her shoulder and tried to fix her blouse. Hopeless. In the moonlight, she could see a long, deep scratch on her right breast, just above the edge of her bra. The knowledge that Bobby Lee's fingernail had inflicted the wound made her feel contaminated.

Remembering how he had pawed her, Chloe started to shake, and her belly rolled with nausea. She'd meant it about the job. Nothing, absolutely nothing, would induce her to work in the same building with him again. He might catch her alone. No way. She didn't need any job that badly.

Hugging her blazer close against the night air, she trudged along the shoulder of the road, her fury mounting with every step. Her two-inch heels were comfortable walking shoes in town, but they'd not been designed for country roads. She kept stepping on rocks and almost turning her ankle.

She was seriously tempted to file charges. He'd threatened to get her fired from her job, hoping to coerce her into having sex with him, and he'd tried to use physical force as well. If she lodged a formal complaint, he would be in deep trouble. *Ha! Maybe he'll be the one standing in the unemployment line.*

The notion no sooner took root in Chloe's mind than she discarded it as a bad plan. If she filed charges, it would be her word against his. He was a law enforcement officer, and she was nobody. Who was a judge going to believe? She didn't need that kind of stress in her life right now when no good was likely to come of it.

She wasn't sure what she'd do for money until she found another job. If worse came to worst, she could always call her dad. She hated to ask him to dip into his retirement fund, but she knew he'd do it if she really needed help. If it came down to that, she'd pay him back with interest.

One thing was for certain: tomorrow morning she would tell Sheriff Lang what had occurred and quit the job without notice. If anyone else asked why, she'd just say she had irreconcilable differences with one of her superiors.

The thought of being without an income was frightening. As the first wave of panic washed over her, she straightened her spine, squared her shoulders, and lifted her chin. She could have been raped. She would not, absolutely would *not* whine and whimper because the stupid job hadn't worked out.

The owl hooted again, reminding her how completely alone she was. Better to stay focused on her present problems than to obsess about empty cupboards and unpaid bills.

Lengthening her stride, she plucked the cell phone from her purse again to see if it was working yet. No such luck. Okay, fine. She was young, and in fairly good shape. If she couldn't call for a ride, she'd just have to hoof it.

Chapter Fourteen

Ben turned left onto Shoshone Road, taking the turn so sharply that the grocery sacks slid across the seat toward him. The deejay at Country Best, 105.3, came over the radio, saying, "And now, listeners, we've got George Strait to serenade you as the clock strikes midnight."

The song began, and Ben had just started to sing along when a woman walking along the edge of the road loomed in his headlights. She wore gray, of all the stupid things. What was she trying to do, get herself killed?

Just as Ben thought that, the woman veered off the road, jumped across the bar ditch, and plunged into the thick brush and small trees growing at the other side. Watching in his rearview mirror, Ben caught only a glimpse of her from the front, but that was all it took to make him slam on the brakes. *Chloe?* What was she doing out here at this time of night? And why was she diving for cover?

Battling the grocery sacks, he leaned over to throw open the passenger door. *Locked. Damn it.* Easing off the brake pedal, he shifted into first gear, steered the pickup onto the gravel that bordered the asphalt, and then backed up so the headlights were trained on her hiding place. There wasn't enough room to get the vehicle completely out of the traffic lane, so he turned on the flashers, shifted to neutral, and set the emergency brake.

"Chloe?" he called as he exited the Ford. *No answer*. He strode over to the ditch. Aided by the headlight glare, he glimpsed movement in the brush. He narrowed his eyes. "Chloe?" he said again, wondering why she wouldn't answer him.

Growing truly alarmed, Ben jumped across the ditch. The instant his feet touched down, she flew up from the bushes. Blessed with sharp night vision and lightning-quick reflexes, Ben saw her swinging a branch at him and threw up an arm to shield his head. The force of the blow snapped the tinder-dry weapon in half, rendering it useless.

She sobbed and scrambled backwards, almost tripping and falling when her feet caught in the tangle of roots. In the glare of the headlights, her face was stark white, her eyes huge pools of fear.

"Get away!" she cried, poking at him with the broken stick. "I mean it. One step closer, and I'll stab you!"

In that instant, Ben realized the lights were blinding her and she couldn't tell who he was. And her blouse, stained with blood at the bodice, had been ripped almost off her.

"Chloe, it's me, Ben," he tried. She didn't seem to register the words. "Ben Longtree?"

Her already huge eyes went even wider as she strained to see his features. "Ben?" she repeated shakily.

He turned so the light would touch his face. She stared up at him. Then, trembling with delayed reaction, she slowly lowered the stick. "Oh, God, I hit you. I'm so sorry. I thought it was him."

Him?

"At this time of night," she went on, "there isn't much traffic. I thought it was him. Are you all right? Did I hurt you?"

If it hadn't been for the condition she was in, Ben might have smiled. Babe Ruth couldn't have swung that rotten branch with enough force to inflict injury.

"I'm fine," he assured her, thinking that the same couldn't be said for her. She was shaking violently, and her small face was so pale it alarmed him. He was afraid to move for fear he might startle her. The sprawl of his shadow, cast by the headlights, reminded him just how large he must appear to her. "The question is, are you okay?"

The fact that she didn't try to straighten her clothing and cover her chest told Ben she was treading perilously close to shock. He wanted to lend her the support of his arm, but he was afraid to touch her.

"Oh, I'm okay," she said hollowly. Then she looked stupidly at the stick in her hand as if wondering how it had come to be there. Her hair was a wild tangle of curls around her heart-shaped face, the strands peppered with twigs and bits of leaves. "Just a little shaken up."

Ben decided the best course of action was to focus on the practical, giving her a moment to collect herself. "When I first saw you, you were carrying a purse. Do you know where you dropped it?"

She turned to stare blankly around. "Somewhere," she replied, which was no help at all.

Ben executed a search, taking care that he made no sudden moves. He found her handbag lying at the base of a bush. "Here it is." The top wasn't zipped, so he parted the folds and tipped the purse toward the light to peer inside. He didn't think anything important had fallen out. Her wallet and cell phone were there.

Keeping his distance, he offered her the bag. She dropped the broken branch to take the purse, holding it in front of her by the straps. Ben had the uneasy feeling she might clobber him again if he got too close.

He gestured at the ditch. "Ladies usually go first, but let's change the rules this time so I can help you across."

She nodded. He leaped over, then turned to offer her a hand. He wasn't sure if she'd take it, but she surprised him and laid her slender fingers across his. Closing his grip, he steadied her as she made the jump, catching her from falling when she reached the other side.

Before guiding her onto the road, Ben glanced in both directions to make sure no cars were coming. Then he turned back to Chloe. She just stood there, staring at him. He released his hold on her and retreated a step, giving her the distance he sensed that she needed.

"What are you doing out here, Chloe?" he asked, pitching his voice to be heard over the truck engine.

She took a moment to digest the question. Ben saw the confusion in her expression give way to relief and then a flash of anger. "My forking cell phone wouldn't work. Can you believe it? I couldn't call anyone to come get me."

Forking? If he hadn't been so concerned about her, he might have smiled. "The phone reception's usually good in Jack Pine."

"I'm not coming from Jack Pine. I got stranded at the river. I took that dirt road that cuts across from the State Rec Road."

"You *walked*?" It was a five-mile trek. He wanted to ask how she'd found her way in the dark, being so new to the area, but for now, he had more pressing concerns, namely to get one very upset lady into his pickup before they caused an accident. "That's a far piece."

Ben took a cautious step toward her again, assessing her physical condition. He hadn't been seeing things; there was blood on her blouse. Now that they were closer to the headlights, he could determine the source, a deep scratch, perhaps two inches long, just above the lacy cup of her bra.

"Are you badly hurt?"

"I'm fine." Her chin came up. "Mad, but fine."

It looked to him as if she were holding herself together by sheer force of will. He wanted to gather her into his arms. The proud lift of her chin forestalled him. "Get in," he settled for saying. "I'll give you a ride."

"What're you doing out here?" she asked.

"Grocery shopping while my mom's asleep. I don't have to worry about her that way."

Giving her a wide berth, he went to the passenger side of the pickup. After opening the door, he set two of the grocery sacks on the backseat of the quad cab to make room for her up front, then moved well away so she could approach the vehicle without feeling threatened.

She took a lurching step toward him. His gaze shot to her feet. In the headlights, he saw that the heel on one of her pumps had broken off. When she reached the truck, she just stood there, staring as if she couldn't think how to climb in. Ben's heart caught. He grasped her elbow to give her a boost and said, "There's a hand grip to your right."

Still, she just stood there. Ben thought, *Well, shit, this is worse than I thought.*

"When you pulled up, I thought it was him again." She pushed ineffectually at her hair with a trembling hand. "After driving off the first time, he parked at a pull-off along State Rec Road and waited to ambush me when I got there. It scared me half to death when he came roaring up behind me. I hid and waited until he finally gave up and left, but after that, I kept expecting him to come back."

Judging by the state of her clothing, she'd had reason to be terrified. Ben bit down hard on his back teeth. His hands knotted into fists. By nature, he wasn't a violent man, but there were times when an injustice could be righted only with a good ass-kicking.

She dragged in a quivery breath. "He would have been sorry, I can tell you that. My hip's not wedged under a steering wheel now." She angled him a burning look. "My brother taught me self-defense."

Ben couldn't think what to say, except that it looked to him as if the self-defense lessons had failed her when she needed them most.

"Get in, okay? We're sitting in the middle of the highway."

She finally climbed in the truck. Ben reached across her to push at the grocery sacks and make sure her belt was fastened. At the graze of his hands at her waist, she flinched and sent him a wary look.

After joining her in the cab, he cranked up the heater, not because it was all that nippy, but because she was still shaking so hard. She made a grateful sound and held her trembling hands to the vent. "Ah, thank you, Ben. I don't know why I feel so frozen."

As the truck rolled forward, he asked, "Are you sure you're all right? Do I need to take you to the hospital?"

"I don't think a hospital is necessary."

If she was in shock, she might not realize how badly she was hurt. He couldn't see any more blood, but that didn't mean she had no other injuries. "Chloe, did he—you know—hurt you?"

She tugged her blouse together. "I've survived worse. He didn't rape me, if that's what you're asking. I shoved his nose gristle into his brain and got away from him."

Ben hadn't realized he was holding his breath until it came whooshing out of him. "Thank God you're all right." He waited a beat. "Who did this, Chloe?"

If she heard the question, she chose to ignore it. "I'm plotting his demise. Something slow and extremely painful. You got any treacherous ideas?"

He knew then that she was going to be okay. He increased speed and shifted to third. Yeah, she would be okay. He just wasn't sure he would be. Emotions were pelting him like scatter spray from a shotgun. "Before I plot a man's murder, I like to know his name. Will you share that with me?"

She cast him a shadowy look. "I'd just as soon not. I'm afraid you'll do something stupid."

"I never do anything stupid."

"I'm all right. That's the important thing, Ben."

He wasn't so sure about that.

Chloe found herself wedged between the truck door and three grocery bags. She shifted, relieved to be reasonably comfortable, protected from the chill night air and finally off her feet.

"I'm sorry about the lack of space," Ben said.

"I didn't know we had an all-night supermarket in Jack Pine."

"Don't. They lock up at one."

Chloe let her head fall back and closed her eyes. She felt oddly disconnected from reality, due, in part, to exhaustion, she felt sure. Now that her adrenaline levels were dropping, she realized she hurt all over. Her feet ached, the gouge on her chest stung, and her breasts throbbed where Bobby Lee had dug in his fingers. She shuddered at the memory. Where did he get off, thinking he could treat a woman like that?

"Need to talk about it?" Ben asked softly.

Chloe lifted her lashes and let her head loll sideways to look at him. "Right now, I'm just enjoying getting warm." She almost added that it felt good to feel safe, too, but the thought, coming to her through a web of muddled perceptions, seemed vaguely alarming. She still knew so little about Ben. "Thanks for giving me a lift."

In the green glow from the dash, his sharply chiseled countenance gleamed like seasoned oak rubbed to a high sheen. "You're very welcome," he replied, his voice pitched low.

A short time later, he pulled into her driveway, killed the engine, and turned off the headlights. In the sudden silence, his voice moved around her like warm smoke as he asked yet again, "You sure you're going to be okay?"

Chloe laughed shakily, the sound brittle and forced. "I came very close. I can't really say I'm okay. Tomorrow, I'll feel better. Right now, I'm headed for the wine cupboard. Another glass of merlot should set me right."

She started to open the door, but he caught her arm. She jumped with a start even as she registered how gentle his grip was compared to the bruising pressure of Bobby Lee's. "You need to fix your clothes and hair before you go in," he reminded her. "You don't want Jeremy or the sitter to see you like this."

Chloe hadn't thought of that, which drove home to her that she'd given little consideration to the practicalities, period. Tracy would be very late getting home, and her folks were probably concerned. She'd have to call Frank and Mary Kay, then give the girl a ride. "I doubt Jeremy's still up, but you're right. I wouldn't want Tracy to see me like this."

She pushed at her hair, fumbled with her blouse.

"It's no use. Maybe I can tug my jacket closed and slip past her to the bedroom before she sees me."

Ben huffed at that idea and leaned over to pop open the glove compartment. After digging through the jumble, he found a large safety pin. Without seeking permission, he drew the front of her blouse together, the fingers of one hand slipping to the underside so the pin wouldn't stab her. Chloe's lungs hitched, making her breath stutter up her windpipe. Coming so close on the heels of Bobby Lee's attack, the touch of another man was unsettling.

"Easy," he murmured. "I'm not getting fresh, just trying to repair the damage." In the dim light, his white teeth flashed in a grin. "Just relax."

For Chloe, under even the best of circumstances, that was easier said than done. His hard knuckles lightly grazed her throbbing breast. He went suddenly still, his shimmering gaze holding hers. The heat of his hand radiated over her skin until it felt almost hot, and a tingling sensation moved through her, taking away the pain. It was the loveliest feeling, like sunlight sparkling inside her. At the edge of her mind, Chloe was surprised. The physical contact should have made her heart leap. Oddly, though, she felt neither threatened nor nervous now. Instead she just felt wonderfully relaxed and yearned to lean toward him. He smiled slightly as he moved away.

"Now for the hair." He lifted a hip and drew a comb from the back pocket of his jeans. "Look at me."

"I can fix it."

He crooked a finger under her chin. "I know, but you're still a little shaky."

He attacked her tangled curls, taking care not to pull when the teeth of the comb snagged. His gentleness worked on her battered emotions like a balm.

"I love your hair," he whispered. His mouth twitched at one corner, and even in the faint moonlight, she saw a twinkle enter his eyes. "All the curls, I guess, and that fiery copper color when the sun strikes it. Mine's dull black and straight as a board."

Chloe thought his hair was beautiful—a glistening jet black that shone like polished obsidian.

"I like your skin, too." He stopped combing to grin at her. "If only we'd met a hundred and fifty years ago, I'd snatch you up, toss you over my horse, and ride off with you into the sunset."

Chloe could picture him—gloriously dark and strong, wearing nothing but buckskin pants and moccasins, his muscular chest streaked with war paint. "I would have been a very uncooperative captive."

He abandoned all pretense of fixing her hair and cupped her chin in his hand. "Pretty to look at, though. And worth the trouble, I think."

Chloe had never engaged in such a silly conversation. "You really are a little crazy, Ben Longtree."

"Maybe so. Probably so. I'll definitely wish I hadn't done this tomorrow."

Chloe knew then that he was going to kiss her. She wasn't sure how she felt about that. With the grocery sacks running interference, it took him a moment to close in.

"Ben?" she whispered.

His only response was a low, "Hmm?"

Chloe couldn't remember what she'd meant to say.

Then, his voice throbbing in the darkness, he said, "Don't be nervous. I'd never hurt you."

"I know. I just—"

"You just what?"

His dark face drew closer. His breath wafted over her cheek, smelling faintly of coffee and mint, a pleasant combination. "I don't—it's been a year and a half. I'm not sure I remember how."

He chuckled. "It's like riding a bike."

"The last time I rode a bike, I crashed and peeled the hide off my knees and elbows."

"Ah, but this time, you have me here to steady your balance."

Slowly, ever so slowly, he bent his dark head and feathered his lips lightly over her cheek. The teasing caress made her breathing hitch again, and she forgot all about the mechanics. Suddenly all she could see, all she could feel was this man, and her thoughts scattered like chaff in the wind.

He made her feel—oh, Chloe couldn't think how to describe it. Wonderful. Ben made her feel wonderful. When their lips finally touched, she melted into the kiss, and her hands found their way to his shoulders, where muscles played in an enticing ripple of strength. Yet he was so gentle. Taking his time, he nibbled lightly at her mouth, tasting her as if she were a rare delicacy.

Chloe's bones felt as if they were dissolving, and it was all she could do not to cling when he started to pull away. He gazed down at her afterwards, his expression gentle. "When you go to sleep tonight," he whispered, "take the memory of that with you into your dreams. Try to forget what happened earlier."

She realized then that he knew she was far more upset over the incident than she was letting on. She was touched that he cared but not really surprised. She was quickly coming to understand that Ben's feelings ran deep and that he was sensitive in ways a lot of men weren't.

At the thought, Chloe put on her mental brakes. She couldn't let herself start to care for him. When it came right down to it, she still knew very little about him, and he didn't seem inclined to correct that situation by sharing information about himself.

She reached for the door handle. "Thank you for the ride, Ben. I was a little farther from home than I realized when you stopped to pick me up."

"You take care," he said softly. "And don't worry about coming up to the ridge in the morning. Sleep in and rest up. What I don't get done in the morning, you can finish in the afternoon."

She nodded and opened the door. "I may take you up on that. Sleep sounds really good right now."

After she climbed from the truck and slammed the door, he backed from her driveway. Chloe stood there to watch him drive out of sight, but he stayed on the road, waiting until she safely reached her door. She smiled as she hurried up the steps. Maybe she didn't know all that she would have liked about Ben Longtree, but she felt sure of one thing: He never would have treated her the way Bobby Lee had tonight.

Ben drove fast and crazily the remainder of the way home, not caring when the truck hit chuckholes and almost bounced off the road. He was in over his head and going under fast. At the outset, all he'd wanted was sex, damn it—mutually enjoyable and uncomplicated sex. He'd yet to come close, and now things were getting very complicated.

He kept reminding himself there was no future in it and that caring for Chloe would only bring him pain, but his heart wasn't listening. *Why the hell did I kiss her?* Now that he'd had a taste of her, he craved more. He needed to get his head on straight. If he didn't, and damned fast, he was going to be so far gone, there'd be no turning back.

Nan was awake and rattling around in the kitchen when Ben entered the house. Juggling grocery sacks, he stepped over to the security console to turn off the alarm, which he always set when he left her alone at night.

"Hi," he said as he entered the kitchen. Diablo came over to greet him. Ben set the bags on the counter and bent to stroke the wolf's head as he took in his mother's activities. "Mom, you know how I worry when you use the stove. Let me put this stuff away, and I'll make the cocoa."

Nan shuffled over to the table and sat down. Her eyes never left Ben as he quickly emptied the grocery bags. When he turned to finish making her hot drink, she said, "You're troubled about something."

Ben threw her a surprised look. It never failed to unsettle him when her mind suddenly clicked into gear. "Not really."

"Remember me? I'm your mother. I know when you're upset."

Ben supposed there was a lot of truth to that. He tapped the spoon on the edge of the pot and laid it on the butcher block. "That's a pretty robe."

Nan smiled and smoothed a hand over the embroidered yoke. "Don't try to distract me."

The blue of the garment complemented her eyes. She was still a lovely woman, Ben thought. Sometimes when he looked at her—really looked—he wondered how his father could have taken her for granted all those years. Unfortunately Hap had—and he'd broken her heart a fair thousand times in the process. At some point, he'd almost killed her love for him. What a waste. Ben would have given his right arm to have a woman love him like that.

"What are you so upset about?" she asked.

The milk began to steam. Ben gave it another stir,

removed it from the flame, and poured it into the mug his mother had set on the work island. "Here you go, madam. Anything else I can get you?"

"This is lovely. Thank you. Now answer my question."

Ben turned his attention to preparing Diablo and Methuselah their nightly snack. "I'm not upset, just exhausted. For two cents, I'd hit the sack early and forget about working tonight."

"Do it, then. How long's it been since you got a full night's sleep?"

"I've lost track."

She turned the mug in her slender hands. "I worry about you."

"Yeah, well, my deadline looms. I don't have much wiggle room right now. Surgery on the bear took a big chunk of my time today."

"How's he doing? Will he live, do you think?"

"I dug out the slug, and I've got him on strong antibiotics. He'll recover fine. It was just a hectic day."

She nodded. "You're misjudging Chloe." When Ben gave her a baffled look, she smiled. "She wouldn't turn you in. She's proved that, hasn't she?"

"I'm not still worried about her turning me in, Mom."

"What, then?"

Ben closed the meat drawer. "How many wild pets can I conceivably have? I keep making excuses, and so far, she's accepted them. But an excuse wouldn't fly with a full-grown black bear."

"So you went to incredible lengths, building that travois and hauling the poor thing up to the cave? Why not just tell her the truth?"

A tight feeling banded Ben's chest. He avoided meeting his mother's eyes. "The truth? I tried that once. It destroyed my marriage and damned near landed me in jail for the rest of my life. It was a hard lesson, but I learned it well. It's best, all the way around, to keep some things to myself."

"Chloe isn't Sherry, Ben. She's got a heart of gold."

"Can we talk about something else?"

"Your gift is beautiful, Ben, not something to feel ashamed of. I can understand your not wanting just anyone to know, but Chloe has become a good friend. She won't tell anyone."

Ben held up a hand. "Mama, I love you, but you're stepping over the line. End of discussion, all right?"

After taking Tracy home, Chloe returned to the house, poured a glass of wine, and headed to the bathroom to disinfect the abrasion on her chest. After unearthing the peroxide, she unpinned her torn blouse, peeled back the silk, and froze in midmotion. Where was the gouge? She blinked, thinking maybe she was so exhausted that her eyesight had gone blurry. But upon closer inspection, there was still nothing there but a smear of dried blood. She drew back the other side of her blouse, thinking it might have been on her other breast. Nothing.

Bewildered, she touched a fingertip to the streak on her skin. Then she tugged the lace cups of her bra away to check inside. Both her breasts looked perfectly fine, and even more amazing, they no longer ached from the brutal dig of Bobby Lee's fingers. How strange.

Okay—so where had the blood come from? She raised her chin to check her throat. Nothing. Stripping down to her slacks, she twisted at the waist to examine all sides of her torso. There wasn't a mark on her, not even a bruise.

She remembered how Ben's hand had pressed against her—the tingling warmth that had moved slowly through her. The burning and aching in her breasts had stopped then. *What am I thinking?*

She needed to get a grip. There was a perfectly rational explanation. The scratch—or what she'd mistaken for a scratch—had been nothing but a smear of blood, which had undoubtedly come from Bobby Lee's nose when she punched him. She'd given the jerk a nosebleed.

She grinned at her reflection. *Way to go, Chloe.* Her brother Rob would be so proud of her. As far as that went, she was pretty proud of herself. *Take that, you schmuck.*

Schuck—schmuck. Chloe giggled at the similarity. It was so good she almost regretted that she couldn't go in to work the next night and call Bobby Lee that to his face. *Good evening, Deputy Schmuck. Is it my imagination, or is your nose a bit swollen?*

Chloe released a big sigh of regret. Ah well. She'd gotten in a good lick. She turned off the bathroom light and smiled all the way to the bedroom. A nosebleed. Imagine that. He'd think twice before he messed with her again.

Chapter Fifteen

Ben seldom drank, but he made an exception that night. After pouring himself a precise measure of whiskey from a bottle left over from Hap Longtree's stores, he adjourned to the living room to sit by the fire. He thought of Hap as he took the first sip of liquor.

The smell of the stuff almost turned his stomach. Disgusted by the memories that swamped him with each whiff, Ben tossed the remaining contents of the tumbler onto the fire. A whoosh of flame momentarily brightened the room, the fiery flashes of red reminding him of Chloe's hair.

Ben conjured a picture of her face, mentally tracing the delicate curve of her cheek and the stubborn tilt of her small chin. He particularly loved her eyes, all big and wary much of the time. And therein was half his problem, he decided. It was difficult to run scared when she obviously feared the feelings erupting between them even more than he did.

He remembered how sweet and tremulous her mouth had felt when he kissed her. Her lower lip had been slightly swollen, undoubtedly from the grind of the other man's teeth. The thought had Ben knotting his fists and wishing for five minutes alone with the bastard. Chloe had been right to withhold the man's name. He was in a murderous mood, all his pacifist convictions overshadowed by fierce feelings of protectiveness.

He sighed and let his head fall back to stare sightlessly at the ceiling. When his mother entered the room moments later, he pretended to be asleep. He was in no mood to talk with her any more tonight.

Nan came over to lightly touch his hair. He nearly smiled when she checked his forehead for fever. No matter how confusing his life became, some things never changed, and her love was one of them. It humbled him to admit it, but he often felt like a lost child when she grew disoriented and didn't know him. It filled him with a terrible sense of loss and dread, because deep down he knew that someday soon she would slip away and never come back.

If his life had been a normal one, the thought of losing his mother to the disease might not have made him feel quite so bereft. Ah, but there was the hitch. He wasn't normal, and he'd long since accepted that he never would be. Other men fell in love and built lives apart from their parents, but Ben no longer had that hope. Forty years from now, he would be a palsied, frail old man, isolated on a mountain ridge with only the animals for company. There would be no woman with snow in her hair to sit beside him on the porch at night and reminisce about days gone by, no kids to flock home for the holidays, and no grandchildren to comfort him in his old age.

In short, when he lost his mother, he would lose his last link to family. His sister Karen had her own life now—one that she'd worked hard to build. Ben rarely saw her or her children. He had a hunch it was avoidance by design, and he didn't blame Karen for that. Her memories of her childhood were as unpleasant as his. Granted, Hap's venom had been directed mostly at Ben, but Karen hadn't entirely escaped, and neither had their mother.

Thinking of that, Ben reached up to clasp his mom's hand. Drawing it from his forehead, he kissed the backs of her fingers. Feeling the fragility of her bones made his chest go tight. She was a study of contrasts. As a small child, he'd wished a thousand times for her to simply walk out, but Nan hadn't been cut from that cloth. She'd remained loyal to the man she loved, even when his vision had been so blurred with drink, he couldn't see her.

Some people might brand her a coward for not taking a stand to shield her children, but Ben never would. She had put herself in harm's way too many times, taking the brunt of Hap's rage while he hid in the closet with his arms crossed over his head to block out the terrible sounds. Later, when he grew older, he'd stood his ground and taken the beatings himself rather than see his mother be hurt. But, even so, he had never forgotten the times when he hadn't.

Courage was a word with countless definitions. Chloe had a glorious strength and determination that were visible to all who knew her. A woman like Nan Longtree seemed pale and timid by comparison. But for all that, Ben admired his mother. Nan was a brave woman in her way, and she'd done her best. When Ben started to feel bitter because her best hadn't been good enough, he had only to remember the countless injuries she had endured for his sake. How could he feel resentment toward someone who had proved over and over that she loved him more than she loved herself?

"Love you, Mom."

She curled the tips of her fingers over his. "I know," she whispered.

That says it all, Ben thought.

He pretended to drift back to sleep, and as he hoped, his mother took that as her cue to shuffle away. Lifting his lashes, he gazed after her as she vanished into the deepening shadows. *Yes, vastly different from Chloe,* he thought.

And since when had Chloe Evans become his gold standard for women? Ben studied the moonbeams that shone through the window, recalling the shine of her hair. No matter where his mind wandered, it seemed to circle back to her. That worried him. And frightened him. Maybe he should take his mother's advice and be up-front with her about everything. That would send her running—and end this madness, once and for all.

Thinking about it gave Ben a headache. Rubbing his eyes and leaning back in the recliner, he willed himself into that shadowy, half-aware state just this side of sleep, his body relaxed, his mind drifting. Perhaps because he'd just been thinking of his childhood, images of his father slipped into his mind. Hap, staggering into the house late at night with a half-full jug of cheap whiskey dangling from his fist. Hap, slapping a cold pot of spaghetti off the stove and bellowing at Nan because she had no hot meal waiting for him at midnight. Hap, standing on the back porch of a morning, badly hungover and whiskey mean, shooting at the animals that had wandered into the yard overnight.

As those memories took center stage in Ben's mind, he shifted and slowly surfaced back to full awareness. But even awake, he felt chilled. His father's aim had been poor after a night of hard drinking, and his unfortunate targets had often escaped into the nearby forest to endure slow, agonizing deaths. It had fallen to Ben to find them later and try to help them. Unfortunately, his gift for healing had always had its limitations. It had been his inability to help so many of the animals that had first made him dream of becoming a vet.

"Damn," he whispered raggedly, willing the memories away.

Kicking down the footrest, he sat forward on the recliner, elbows braced on his knees, head in his hands. Over the last several weeks, with so many wounded animals seeking him out, Ben had thought more than once that he was living through some kind of weird reenactment of his childhood. He knew it was madness. But sometimes he couldn't shake the feeling that his father was reaching out from the grave.

On one level, Ben knew it was impossible. Hap was dead, for God's sake. He couldn't be responsible. And yet the similarities couldn't be ignored. Each time Ben found a wounded animal, he was swept back in time, and everything he did, everything he thought, seemed eerily the same, as if the last twenty years had never happened, and he was a kid again, trying to undo the damage done by his father.

It definitely wasn't Hap shooting the animals; Ben knew that. But couldn't it be someone else who knew of those incidents and was deliberately reenacting them to get back at Ben for something? All the animals had been shot near his house. Someone, it seemed, wanted Ben to find them.

Ben got up to pace. The more he thought about it, the more certain he became that he'd just solved part of the puzzle. It made an awful kind of sense. Everyone knew how he felt about animals. What better way to hurt him than to go after the things he loved most? Now, to answer the next most obvious question, whom did he know who might hate him that much?

Bobby Lee Schuck.

Braking to a stop, he stared thoughtfully into the fire. An almost forgotten memory came rushing back to him of Bobby Lee stumbling upon him in the woods while he was working over a wounded coyote. He'd been about fourteen at the time, Bobby Lee a year older. Bobby Lee had snorted in disgust and laughed at Ben for being such a bleeding heart. There had been a bounty on coyotes at the time.

"Any normal person would whack off his ears and collect the ten bucks," Bobby Lee had jeered. "But not pussy Ben. I got a dollar that says it was your daddy who shot it, too!"

Ben had leaped to his feet, angry enough to forget everything his grandfather had taught him. "Go away, Bobby Lee!" he'd cried. "You're trespassing on Longtree land."

"Yeah, so you say, but true Shoshones didn't believe in owning land."

"How would you know?"

"Because I can read, you dumb ass. I know lots of stuff about them. A Shoshone warrior could have several wives. Did you know that? And he was automatically married to any woman he took. The wedding ceremony that came after was just for looks, and a warrior's firstborn son was always number one, no matter who his damned mother was." Bobby Lee pointed a finger at Ben and laughed again. "The way your father screws around, no telling how many kids he's got in Jack Pine. And by Shoshone law, every one of them has as much right to his name as you do!"

"Get out of here!" Ben cried.

"Who's gonna make me? Not a pussy like you, that's for sure." The coyote had gone into its death throes just then, prompting Bobby Lee to mimic the muscle jerking. "Oh, do I see tears? Duh poor widdle coyote's gonna die. Where's your Shoshone magic now, dickhead? Did you forget to bring your grandpa's medicine pouch?"

Ben was shaking when he surfaced from that memory. He closed his eyes, willing the rage to abate, but it was a very long while before it did.

The next morning, Ben jerked awake to the sound of his mother's voice. He blinked and rubbed his eyes, wondering why there was sunlight hitting him in the face. He rarely slept in the daytime. In fact, for the last few weeks, he'd barely slept at all

"You were so exhausted you passed out in the chair," Nan scolded. "Now, I ask you. Wouldn't you have rested better in bed like a normal person? But, oh, no, there's that deadline of yours. As if you got any work done, sitting up all night."

Ben groaned and flexed his shoulders as he sat up. "Mom?" He squinted to bring her into focus. When he saw that she was wearing jeans and sturdy boots, he said, "What time is it?"

"Seven-thirty." She gestured at the windows behind him, which caught the morning sun. "It's so gorgeous out. I thought I'd take a little walk."

Ben rubbed his face again. After seven? He needed to go check on the bear and tend to the other animals up at the cave. He was glad now that he'd told Chloe to sleep in and skip coming up this morning. He was running so late he'd never get out of here before eight, and he didn't want to explain where he was going.

"A walk?" He struggled to clear his head as he met his mother's worried regard. "Will you be sure to stay on the property?"

"Of course. Down to the log deck and back. That's about as far as these tired old legs can carry me anymore." Nan ran a hand over his hair. "At least you got some rest, even if it was in a chair. That's better than nothing, I guess."

Ben stifled a yawn. "Take Diablo with you, all right?" Whenever Nan ventured from the yard, Ben sent the canine with her. If, by chance, Nan grew confused and got lost, the wolf could lead her home or, failing that, at least show Ben where she'd gone. "I don't like you walking alone."

"Diablo's a good walking companion. I'll be happy to take him." She started to turn away, then paused. "I'll rest for a bit by the log deck before I walk back. If I'm gone a bit longer than you think I should be, don't fret."

It was only a quarter mile to the log deck. Even if she took a break, she'd be back before he was ready to leave for the cave. "I'm going to grab a shower." He pushed to his feet and kissed her cheek. "We'll have a little breakfast when you get back. Something easy this morning. How does oatmeal sound?"

"Lovely." Nan snapped her fingers. "Let's go, Diablo. This crazy old woman isn't allowed to go walking without an escort."

Ben smiled and shook his head. His mother was in fine form this morning. She rarely had lucid spells that lasted this long. Last night, she'd been feeling pretty good, and now this morning, she still was. It was nice, and made him feel as if he had his mother back.

Fifteen minutes later, Ben heard voices when he stepped from the shower. He cocked his head, listened for a moment, and then swore under his breath as he toweled off. Chloe. He'd told her to forget coming this morning, but that was definitely her voice.

He made fast work of throwing on some clothes

and didn't bother to shave. One benefit to being part Indian was a sparse beard and little body hair.

"Oh!" Chloe reeled to a stop when he emerged from the master bedroom directly into her path. She held a bundle of soiled bedding in her hands. Her hair, caught at the crown of her head in a wildly curly ponytail, looked delightfully mussed and made a man want to mess it up even more. "You startled me. I saw your mom on the road. I figured you were out walking with her."

He shoved at his wet hair. "I sent Diablo with her."

Her cheeks turned a pretty pink. "Well," She smiled and shrugged. "Hi."

Jeremy wheeled into the hall behind her and braked to a fast halt when he saw Ben. He launched himself at Ben's legs. "You're here!"

Ben laughed, grabbed the child under the arms, and tossed him in the air. "I live here. Why the big surprise?"

Jeremy caught his face between his hands. The feel of the child's little fingers pressing against his cheeks made Ben's heart catch. He caught the boy to his chest on the downswing to steal a quick hug. Never in Ben's recollection had any embrace felt so right.

"I missed you," he whispered.

Jeremy clung to his neck. "Me, too."

Ben tucked in his chin to frown in mock bewilderment. "You missed yourself?"

"No!" Jeremy giggled. "I missed you!"

Ben shifted the child onto his hip. Chloe was still standing in place, the soiled bedding held slightly away from her body, her hands knotted over the cloth with such force that her knuckles gleamed white. With one glance at her hands, Ben knew this was as difficult for her as it was for him—and that he wasn't the only one alarmed by the feelings between them.

Oddly, seeing the hesitation in her big brown eyes made him feel braver. He swung Jeremy to the floor. "That pup of yours could use a walk. There's a leash hanging on the coat tree in the entryway. Just keep him by the deck so he doesn't sniff any germs."

Jeremy was off like a shot.

Chloe gestured with the bedding. "I was on my way to the laundry room."

Ben stepped aside so she could pass, then turned to follow her. *Not smart.* But he could no more pretend last night hadn't happened than he could deny his Shoshone blood. He had to talk to her. It wasn't a decision. It wasn't a choice. He just had to.

When they reached the utility room, he positioned himself in the doorway so she couldn't escape and watched as she stuffed the bedding into the washer. She knew he was there. Her fidgety, nervous movements were a dead giveaway.

"How are you this morning?" he asked.

"Oh. I'm fine. I slept like a baby."

Ben ran his gaze over her. She was wearing tight blue jeans that lent a whole new definition to the term *packed*. Her green knit top had a scoop neckline that revealed the creamy upper swells of her breasts, which he was happy to see bore no marks this morning. She was too sweet to be defiled. Damn, he liked the way she was made.

"Is something wrong?"

He searched her wide brown eyes. The innocent look became her, but he wasn't fooled. She knew very well what was wrong. Or, more precisely, what was right, namely practically everything. Usually when two people clicked like this, they jumped in with both feet.

"No, nothing," he forced out. "I've just been worried about you. I'm glad to see you're okay this morning. I could have sworn you had a bad scratch on your chest."

She flattened a slender hand over the spot. "I thought so, too, but it was only a smear of blood."

Now there was an interesting explanation. "Whose?"

"Bobby Lee's. I—" She broke off, her cheeks flaming.

"Bobby Lee," he repeated. "I see."

She blinked. "I didn't mean to say his name."

"I realize that. Although why you'd try to protect the bastard escapes me."

She glanced past him into the hall and touched a finger to her lips. "Please, Ben. Don't forget Jeremy."

"He's outside with the pup." Ben struggled to make sense of it all. He'd already determined that Bobby Lee was the shooter, but it hadn't occurred to him that he'd also been the man who jumped Chloe. What did that mean? More important, was there a connection? Had Bobby Lee guessed that Ben was coming to care for Chloe? Was this just another twisted way to make Ben suffer? It made no sense, yet Ben had an awful feeling he was right. Chloe had become a target. "The man's worse than a bastard."

"He'd had too much to drink. Things got out of hand. It was—"

"Bullshit. I can drink whiskey until my eyes turn amber, and nothing would induce me to force myself on a woman."

"That's good to know. But maybe it's different for him. Not everyone can handle alcohol, and maybe he just—"

"I call bullshit again." Ben's blood was pumping through his head with such force he could hear the swish against his eardrums. "Drunkenness is no excuse. It's *never* an excuse. Any man who hurts a woman, claiming booze is to blame, needs his ass kicked from here into next week."

She hugged her waist, staring at him from eyes gone soft with compassion. "I'm sorry. I think this subject may strike a little too close to home for you to discuss it rationally."

Bobby Lee had gone after Chloe. That was all Ben could take in. *Sweet Christ.* When he thought of all the animals that had endured horrible pain at the deputy's hands, he broke out in a cold sweat. "You're not going back there."

"Back where?"

"To work. I won't have it."

The widening of her eyes was no act this time. "I beg your pardon?"

Ben saw the stubborn lift of her chin and knew he'd screwed up. A woman like Chloe couldn't be ordered around. She'd get her back up every time. "Please," he tacked on. "I'm afraid he'll hurt you, Chloe. Please, don't go back."

She held up a hand. "Save it. I've already quit. Not officially, but I did call and give notice this morning so they could get someone to cover my shift tonight. I'll submit a written resignation when I go in this afternoon to clean out my desk."

Ben's skin felt prickly. "Let me drive you."

She arched a finely drawn eyebrow. "I'm a grown woman, Ben. I don't need anyone to hold my hand while I quit a job."

"I won't hold your hand. I'd just like to be in the parking lot."

"Why?"

"Because I don't want him to catch you alone."

"He won't. At least one dispatcher is on duty at all times. Besides." She flapped her hand. "It's not as if he's dangerous or anything."

Oh, yes, very dangerous. Only Ben had no proof to convince her of that. "He damned near ripped your blouse off last night."

"But he did stop."

"You said he waited along State Rec Road for you. If you hadn't run into the woods to evade him, do you think he would have stopped a second time?"

Shadows darkened her eyes. "It's a different set of circumstances in town, with people all around. I'm not worried that he'll bother me."

"So why did you have his blood on your chest?"

She blinked and scratched under one eye. "Oh, well, that."

"Yes, that. Why was he bleeding?"

"Because I bopped him a good one on the nose."

Ben relaxed marginally. Maybe, he decided, those self-defense lessons had saved her bacon, after all. Nevertheless he was worried about her going near Bobby Lee again. She was a slightly built woman. Any man could knock her ass over teakettle with one punch, and Ben had a very bad feeling that Bobby Lee wouldn't hesitate.

"I have errands I need to run in town. Just a couple. I could swing you by there, and then—"

"No." She said it softly, but the word rang with decisiveness. "I appreciate the offer, but I don't lean on anyone. I'll handle my own affairs."

Ben studied her face. He'd realized last night that he was falling in love with her. Feeling afraid for her had given him that final push over the edge. If anything happened to her, he didn't know what he'd do. "Why don't you lean on anyone?"

"Because just about the time you grow to count on the support, it isn't there anymore."

She moved toward him. Ben could see that their conversation was over. He was trying to decide if he

should let her pass or stand his ground until they settled this to his satisfaction when he heard the front
door crash open.

"Ben!" his mother shrieked. "Ben?"

Chloe followed Ben back up the hall, her running
feet slapping the tile twice for every stride he took.
An instant later, they entered the kitchen to see Nan
standing by the work island. Her short hair was in
wild disarray, her blue eyes gigantic in her pale face.
She stumbled over to her son, made frantic fists on
his shirt, and rested her forehead against his chest.
Ben curled his arms around her trembling torso.

"Mom? What's wrong?"

"A dead body!" she cried. "I just saw a man burying a body on the hill above the log deck!"

Ben cupped a hand over the back of her head.
"Ah, now."

"No, no! I didn't imagine it, I swear. I really, really
saw it happening! A body, Ben. Right here, on our
land!"

Ben met Chloe's gaze and waggled his eyebrows.
By the gesture, Chloe knew he was trying to tell her
not to take this seriously. Chloe understood. The older
woman wasn't always in touch with reality. Nevertheless, she was very convincing now.

Speaking in soothing tones, Ben pressed his mother
onto a chair, fetched her a glass of water, and then
stepped to a cupboard. Chloe watched as he withdrew
a hypodermic needle, sterilized a cool vial of medication, and expertly filled the syringe. "Here, Mama,"
he said gently. "This will make you feel better." He
drew up her sleeve to dab at her upper arm with a
cotton ball. "A fast prick. Hold still, okay?"

"No!" Nan cried, attempting to pull away. "That'll
put me to sleep! I don't—"

Ben firmly grasped her arm to hold her and expertly administered the injection. Afterwards he capped the needle, put it on the table, and crouched to curl an arm around her. "If it makes you sleepy, that's okay. I'm here to handle everything."

Nan shook her head. She looked imploringly at Chloe. "You *have* to listen!" she cried. "I saw a man burying a dead body!"

When Nan had calmed down enough to talk, Ben asked her questions. Nan shakily repeated the story, giving specifics. The man burying the body had been tall and dark. "He was wearing a baseball cap, an Oregon Ducks sweatshirt, and sunglasses," she said, her words growing slightly slurred. "The same kind of glasses your father used to wear." She grabbed a quivering breath. "Diablo—oh, *God*. He tried to go up there. I grabbed his collar, but it was all I could do to hold him back. I hid with him behind the logs. I was so afraid he might bark. I know he doesn't usually, but he was so upset I was afraid he might. What if that man saw us?

"Finally, he went back up the hill to bury some other stuff—a pack of some sort, I think—you know, the kind hikers use. While he was up there working, I tightened my hold on Diablo's collar and ran." Nan threw a frightened look at Chloe. "I just pray he didn't see me. I'm a witness. What if he decides to shut me up?"

Ben kissed his mom's forehead. Imagined or not, the incident had frightened her badly. He tried to massage the tension from her shoulders. "He can't hurt you now. I'll keep you safe."

"I'm not lying, Ben. I swear I'm not. You need to call the police. The log deck isn't that far away, a quarter mile at most. If he saw me, he's liable to come up here."

Too much late-night television, Ben thought. This story had all the plot elements of an old Hitchcock thriller. Jeremy hugged his puppy protectively to his chest and glanced fearfully at the windows. Ben gestured subtly at the child, cluing Chloe that she needed to do some damage control. She crouched beside her son, whispered something in his ear, and a moment later, Jeremy carried his puppy from the kitchen.

Chloe gazed after the boy until he was safely out of earshot on the front deck. Then she came to put an arm around Nan's frail shoulders. "It'll be okay," she said soothingly. "Let Ben go check it out."

Nan shook her head. "No, no, *no*. He could get hurt. That awful man. He's killed once. What's to stop him from doing it again?" Nan pressed a hand over her heart. "We should just let the police handle it."

Ben patted his mom's arm. "I'm not stupid, Mama. I'll be very careful." He winked at Chloe over the top of her head. "Rest assured, if I see a fresh grave up there, or anything that looks the least bit suspicious, I'll call the cops."

When Ben left the house a few minutes later, Chloe sat at the table and held Nan's hands. The injection had done its job, and Nan's fingers felt limp. She stared blankly at nothing. Her pupils had grown dilated, and the light had gone out in her expressive blue eyes. Chloe sighed and trailed her thumbs over the protruding veins just below Nan's wrists. Ben wouldn't be gone long, she knew. He would take an obligatory drive up to the log deck, scan the hillside, and then come back to tell his mother that he'd seen nothing.

There was, after all, nothing up there to see. It had all been a product of Nan's confused mind.

"Chloe?" Nan managed to focus on Chloe's face. Speaking slowly, as if her tongue had gone thick, she said, "Will you do something for me?"

"Of course," Chloe replied. "Just name it."

"Call the sheriff's department for me. Please? Ben doesn't believe my story, but I swear to you, I'm not lying. We have to report this."

After thinking over Nan's request, Chloe nodded and stood. "Sure. I can do that for you." Everyone at the department knew of Nan's illness and wouldn't take the call seriously. "I'll even speak directly to the sheriff. How's that?"

Nan closed her eyes and smiled shakily. "Thank you, Chloe. I'll rest easier, knowing it's been reported."

Stepping over to the desk, Chloe dialed the number, waited for an answer, and then asked to be put through to Sheriff Lang. He listened quietly to what Chloe said. Then he replied, "Having a bad day, is she?"

Chloe kept her back to Nan. "Yes, and she's terribly upset."

"You tell her I'll have it checked out. That should calm the poor thing down. A murderer burying a body, huh?" Lang chuckled. "Sounds like the plot of a movie I watched a few nights ago. Maybe she watched the same one. Or maybe she's seen that boy of hers, up to no good."

Chloe's hand clenched on the phone. She yearned to set Sheriff Lang straight on that score, but because Nan was listening, she chose to let it pass. "How soon can you come out to have a look, Sheriff?"

"Sometime before Christmas if I find a moment when I've got nothing better to do," the lawman said with a chuckle. "Tell her I'll be out in thirty minutes, and that I'll call if I find anything. That should ease her mind."

Chloe related the message to Nan when she hung up the phone.

"Oh, good," Nan said drowsily. She pushed up from her chair, blinked, and then yawned hugely. "I need to lie down. Will you wake me when he calls?"

As Chloe expected, Ben returned quickly. He entered the kitchen to find her and Jeremy sitting at the table. "I finished with the animals," Chloe explained, "but I thought I'd better stay until you showed up." She quickly related her conversation with the sheriff. "Your mom felt better, thinking it was reported."

Ben's mouth tightened. "The last thing I need is for Sheriff Lang to come up here, snooping around."

"He won't bother. Trust me on that. He knows your mother is ill."

The tension went out of his shoulders. "Is she asleep?"

Chloe nodded. "That shot must have been a doozie. Did you see anything up by the log deck?"

He shook his head. "Not that I got out and really looked. She does this sometimes. When I tried to take her to Pineville to see a specialist three months ago, she saw aliens with laser guns all along the highway. She got so hysterical, I had to bring her home and sedate her."

"Maybe next time you should sedate her before you leave."

"There's a thought." He shrugged and passed a hand over his eyes. "It's probably just as well I don't take her to anyone else. She's comfortable with her doctor here in Jack Pine. I don't have much faith in him, but all and all, she's done amazingly well under his care. It's going on five years now since Karen first called to tell me Mom was acting funny. In the three years since Dad died and I came back to care for her, I really can't say she's grown worse. Most Alzheimer's patients do, and rather quickly, I think. Her doctor must be doing something right."

It made Chloe sad to think of Nan growing more demented and irrational. In her lucid moments, she was such a lovely person, warm and caring. "Some people are luckier than others. The old man who lives next to my folks was diagnosed about ten years ago, and he's still doing pretty well. He drives my dad crazy sometimes. One morning, Daddy found him in their garage calling his cat. Tinkerbell has been dead for fifteen years."

Ben smiled and sank onto a chair. "Maybe my mom is one of the lucky ones, and she'll be driving me crazy for a long time to come."

Chloe nodded. "I felt so bad for her, Ben. Real or not, she genuinely believes she saw a body."

"I know." Ben sighed and rubbed the back of his neck. "Maybe it's good that she heard you call the sheriff. It will probably bewilder her when he doesn't call back, but at least she'll know it was reported and be able to put it to rest after a few days."

"She'll sleep most of the day now," Chloe pointed out. "Maybe when she wakes up, she'll have forgotten all about it."

"Maybe so."

The shovel made a loud clattering sound when Bobby Lee threw it in the back of his pickup, the dirt-encrusted blade thumping over the ridged bed before it struck the back of the cab and stopped. The thunderous sound made the deputy's nerves leap, and he cursed vilely, slapping the dust from his clothes and spitting debris from his mouth. *Close call*. Ben had almost caught him in the act. All that had saved Bobby Lee from being seen was a headlong dive into a wash, overgrown with scrub brush.

The batty old woman had seen him and gone running home to tell the tale, he guessed. Bobby Lee wasn't overly concerned. Nan Longtree was certifiably nuts. Who was going to listen to her wild ranting? Not even her son, judging by the quick turnaround Ben had made by the log deck. If he'd just climbed from his truck and walked the hillside, he might have stumbled upon the freshly turned earth behind that cluster of manzanita.

His pulse still hammering, Bobby Lee strode to the front of his old pickup, which he always took from his garage for these forays. The county vehicle he usually drove was white and would be too easily spotted. The dusty brown Chevy blended in with the terrain, greatly reducing the chance that Bobby Lee might be seen, or even worse, identified.

He threw open the driver's door to grab his .22. A little target practice would soothe him. The results, several more wounded critters, would also keep Ben distracted. Under no circumstances did Bobby Lee want the bastard up here, sniffing around. The evidence that he'd just buried on the hillside would be found eventually, but only when Bobby Lee decided the time was right.

He smiled to himself, eagerly anticipating the moment when he could watch Ben being hauled away to the hoosegow in handcuffs. He would go to prison for murder this time, and Bobby Lee would finally have his revenge. On that fine day, he hoped the smoke in hell cleared away long enough for Hap Longtree to look down and see what was happening. So much for the grand family name the bastard had gone to such lengths to protect—and so much for the prissy younger son he'd chosen to acknowledge.

Every dog had its day, and Bobby Lee would finally have his.

Chapter Sixteen

While at the sheriff's department to empty her desk that afternoon, Chloe stepped into Lang's rear office to have a quick word with him. The sheriff kicked back in his chair and frowned. "If you're here to report another body, my sense of humor has worn thin. I just got the word that you're quitting."

Chloe laid her letter of resignation on the desk. "Yes." As briefly as possible, she related to him the events of the prior evening. "I'm not here to file a formal complaint. Bobby Lee was drunk, and if this is his first offense, perhaps it'll never happen again. I did want you to be aware of my reason for quitting, though, just in case another female employee should encounter difficulties with him in the future."

"You're accusing one of my best deputies of attempted rape?"

"And sexual harassment, if that's the appropriate term when a woman's superior threatens her with her job when she refuses to have sex with him after a friendly dinner date."

Lang's cheek muscle started to throb. "That's a very serious accusation."

"Yes. His behavior was despicable."

"It's difficult for me to swallow. I've known the man for twenty years."

Chloe lifted her hands. "Believe me, don't believe me. I've done my duty. You've been made aware. If one of my successors comes to you with a grievance, perhaps you'll be able to swallow it then."

Chloe wasn't about to leave Jeremy sitting in the car while she debated the issue. She turned, left the inner office, and collected her box of desk items. She left the Japanese lantern sitting there. Let Bobby Lee decipher that in any way he pleased, but she wanted nothing even remotely connected to him.

After leaving the department, Chloe drove to the nearby Dairy Queen to get Jeremy a cone. As she was pulling away from the drive up, she glimpsed a HELP WANTED sign in the window of the Christmas Village. She stepped on the brake. Why not? The pay probably sucked, but it couldn't hurt to check it out.

Chloe wondered if her eyes were as wide as Jeremy's when they entered the store. It was a huge place, and every inch was a Christmas wonderland. Chloe had avoided coming in here until now because she'd been afraid she might spend money. Now she knew her instincts had been sound.

"Can I help you find something?"

Holding Jeremy's hand for fear he might break something, Chloe turned to find the proprietress standing behind her. She was an elderly woman with rosy cheeks, merry blue eyes, and hair the delicate lavender of lilac blossoms. She wore a blue jersey dress and clunky black shoes.

Jeremy tugged on Chloe's hand. "Is she Mrs. Santa Claus?"

The elderly woman smiled. "No, sweetie." She leaned down to look him directly in the eye. "I do happen to be one of Santa's full-time helpers, though."

"You are?" Jeremy asked in an awestruck voice. *"Wow!"*

"I'm Mrs. Perkins." She thrust out an arthritic hand. "And you are?"

"Jeremy." The child wiggled free from Chloe's grip to shake hands. "Have you met Santa? The real one, I mean? Not the fake one at the mall."

Mrs. Perkins laughed. "Oh, my, yes. I see Santa nearly every day." She patted the child's head. "It never hurts to have an inside track to Santa, does it?"

"No, ma'am."

Mrs. Perkins clearly liked Jeremy's manners. She smiled warmly at Chloe. "Were you looking for something special, dear?"

"Well, yes, Mrs. Perkins, I—"

"Hattie."

Chloe shook hands with her. "Chloe Evans. I just noticed the sign in your window—about needing help? I wanted to inquire about the job."

"Oh! My goodness! You're my first applicant." Hattie pressed a hand to her throat. "Do you like what you see?"

Chloe thought it was a strange question to ask a prospective employee. "Well, yes." She looked around the shop again. "It's magical." She felt silly the moment she spoke. "I mean—well, you know—like wishes that came true."

Hattie nodded and smiled. "That was exactly my aim."

Chloe hated to be rude, so she bit her tongue to keep from asking what the hourly wage might be. She doubted it would come close to what she'd been making—and the chance that Mrs. Perkins offered benefits was almost zilch.

"Let me show you around," Hattie said.

And so began one of the most delightful tours in Chloe's memory. The store was laid out in sections, and in each, a Christmas tree, beautifully decorated for the holidays, held court. All the ornaments were for sale. Small hand-painted dog ornaments hung from one tree, cats from another.

"Oh," was all Chloe could say when they came upon a dollhouse section where several assembled kit houses, decorated gaily for Christmas, were displayed on electric turntables. Chloe bent to admire the detail. Each little house was lighted from within, and the surfaces of the turntables had been landscaped like yards. "Look, Jer, there's even a milk can on the porch."

"Welcome to the world of miniatures." Hattie gestured at the shelves. "Everything you see can be purchased here. The houses must be assembled, of course." She pointed to a workbench. "Many people want the entire display just as it is, so I do the work and charge a handsome price."

"How fun!" Chloe loved to do crafts.

"That's exactly what I hoped to hear." Mrs. Perkins led them deeper into the store. After giving them a full tour, she led the way back to the front. "I'm not as young as I used to be. I'll have to sell my shop soon. In the interim, I'm looking for a responsible person to manage the business for me."

Chloe couldn't help but feel excited. Okay, so her aspirations weren't very high. Working in a Christmas wonderland had a lot of appeal. *Stop,* she cautioned herself. The pay couldn't be very good, even for a manager. And she'd only stopped in to check it out, after all. The instant she heard, "Minimum wage," she'd be out the door. "I hate to ask, Mrs. Perkins, but what's the pay?"

"The manager will receive a percentage of the daily gross, plus an hourly wage."

Chloe glanced over her shoulder at two couples that had entered the shop. She heard the women making appreciative sounds as they explored with their husbands. In only a couple of minutes, the shoppers had made their selections and approached the register. Chloe couldn't believe her ears when she heard Hattie tell each husband that his tab was well over a hundred dollars. Even more amazing, the foursome left looking pleased.

The moment the door swung closed, Hattie smiled and said, "Here's the deal. Five percent commission, plus minimum wage."

There they were, the death words: *minimum wage.* Only Chloe wasn't heading for the door. Five percent? Her brain went into warp speed as she tabulated the take on the last sale. *Slow down,* she cautioned herself. This place couldn't possibly get a steady flow of customers.

"I do a booming business here, all year long," Hattie added. "Practically everyone loves Christmas. This is a resort community. When people are on vacation, they enjoy buying Christmas pretties as mementos of their stay. I also do a steady business with locals."

Chloe recalled the many times she'd wanted to come in here to look around. The Christmas Village definitely had curb appeal.

"I'm looking for someone very special," Hattie went on. She smiled conspiratorially at Jeremy. "Someone who loves the magic of it all and believes in Santa Claus. Jeremy, would you, by any chance, like the job? Or better yet, maybe you'd like to come in during the day and help your mom."

Chloe squeezed her son's shoulder. To work where Jeremy would be welcome sounded too good to be true. "If the money's adequate, I'd enjoy working here," she assured Mrs. Perkins. "I love Christmas. I always have. It would be fun to be surrounded by that feeling all year long." She glanced around. "Even dusting the merchandise would be a pleasure."

"Dusting is a never-ending task." Mrs. Perkins looked directly into Chloe's eyes. "There's a catch," she said softly.

Chloe had been afraid of that.

"I'm looking for someone who may be interested in buying the shop in a year. I'm getting old." She rubbed the back of a gnarled hand. "It's time for me to scale back. My husband and I want to travel."

Chloe's heart sank. "I see. Well, that counts me—"

Hattie cut her off. "This place has given me a wonderful income for many years, but it's time to relax a little and enjoy my husband."

Chloe had recently had a similar discussion with her parents. "You really shouldn't wait too long, or you may not be in good enough health."

"Exactly." The older woman nodded decisively. "I'd like to find a buyer who'll work hard at learning the business, someone who'll love this shop as much as I do."

"I can see myself loving it," Chloe said with a laugh. "I just can't afford it."

As if she hadn't spoken, Hattie said, "If you're the person I'm looking for, the finances can be worked out. I'm willing to give you a one-month trial period. If it goes well, we'll discuss the possibilities. I can guarantee that you'll earn enough in commissions to support yourself and your son while you save enough to make a respectable down payment on the business at the end of a year."

Chloe's stomach clenched.

Hattie raised her eyebrows. "I'll carry the contract. For the right buyer, I will adjust the terms so the payment won't be too steep."

Chloe didn't know what to say.

Hattie smiled slightly. "I like you, Chloe Evans. I've always made decisions by the seat of my pants, and when I opened this shop, it was no exception. It seems only right that I end the way I began, going on instinct. If you're interested in my shop, how soon can you start?"

When Chloe got home, she had mixed emotions, part of her wanting to dance with excitement, another part almost afraid to believe. If Hattie Perkins was on the level, she had a job! And not just any job, but one that would enable her to buy a business. She was so thrilled that she almost hugged the breath out of her son several times. After feeding Jeremy and putting him down for the night, she was still floating on a cloud when the phone rang. It was a little after nine, and she couldn't think who might be calling. She'd spoken with her folks three evenings before, and her brother and sister called only once a month.

"Hello?"

"Hi, there. Call me a worrywart. I had to call and check on you."

Ben? Chloe was surprised. Then, almost as soon as she registered the thought, she wondered why she should be. If it was true that bad luck came in threes, why couldn't the same hold true for good? The first time she'd seen Ben Longtree, she'd felt strongly attracted to him. How many other times had a man made her feel that way? Exactly once. Maybe she had been destined to move to this magical little town, and maybe she was supposed to have quit her job and stopped by the Christmas Village to inquire about the position there. And maybe, just maybe, the best part of all had been meeting Ben Longtree.

"Are you there?" he asked.

Chloe laughed. "Oh, yes. Sorry."

"Are you okay? No problems with Bobby Lee, I hope."

"No, none. I didn't even see him when I stopped by to clean out my desk."

"That's good. And how are things otherwise? You sound—I don't know—different. Is there a problem?"

"No, no. I had a slightly heated discussion with the sheriff. Dumb me. I had it in my head that I needed to report Bobby Lee's transgression."

"I take it he didn't appreciate being enlightened?"

"He's known Deputy Schuck for twenty years. Need I say more?"

"He's the stupid one, Chloe."

"Yes. The good-old-boy system is busily at work. I knew last night that I'd get nowhere, filing charges. I'm too new in town. He's been here all his life. I did my duty by reporting it. What the sheriff does with the information is up to him. I'm ready to close that chapter now and move ahead."

"Good for you. It's better forgotten."

Chloe was dying to share her news, but she was almost afraid to say anything for fear she might jinx the deal. "I'm feeling fantastic tonight. Well, maybe I should qualify that. If everything pans out, I'll feel fantastic."

"Now you've piqued my curiosity. If what pans out?"

"I think I've got another job—a fabulous one that may turn out to be the opportunity of a lifetime."

"Details."

"You'll laugh. It's one of those situations that sounds too good to be true, and men are always such wet blankets about such things."

"Bite your tongue. And I promise not to laugh."

Hesitantly, Chloe recounted her conversation with Hattie Perkins. When she finished, Ben said, "That's wonderful news. Hattie is a neat lady."

"You know her? I mean, well, obviously, in this small town, you probably know her. But do you know her well?"

"I used to work for her when I was in high school. Evenings. I dusted merchandise. It's a fabulous shop, isn't it? And she's not pulling your leg about the business she does. That place is always hopping."

"Really?"

"Absolutely. If she's willing to sell to you on contract and tailor the terms, how can you pass it up?"

"I just can't believe she offered it to me. I mean—*why*?"

He chuckled. "Only you would ask. All anyone has to do is look in your eyes to see your heart shining through, and it's a warm heart, to boot. I think Hattie has made the perfect choice."

Chloe felt as if she'd just gotten a telephone hug. What was happening here? When she counted the days, she knew she hadn't known Ben all that long, but it seemed as if she'd known him forever. When she remembered how wary she'd been of him in the beginning, she could only laugh at herself. She never should have listened to Lucy Gant.

Ben ended the conversation by saying, "I'm happy for you, Chloe. This calls for a celebration. I have some champagne that I've been saving for just such an occasion. Would you mind some company?"

Chloe's hand flew to her hair. "I, um—sure, why not?" She could slap on some makeup before he got there. "If Hattie Perkins is for real, this does call for champagne. I'm so excited I'm about to bust."

"Maintain the mood, and I'll see you in ten minutes."

When the phone clicked and went dead, Chloe stood there for a moment, smiling at the receiver.

Chapter Seventeen

Ben arrived fifteen minutes later with champagne on ice. When Chloe answered his knock, she could only stare for a moment, wondering if the darkness beyond the threshold was playing tricks with her eyes.

"Your hair," she said stupidly.

He stepped inside. "I got my ears lowered." He smiled slowly at her. "Does it look that bad? I let Mom cut it."

"Your *mom?*"

"I figured she needed the distraction. It kept her from worrying about why the sheriff hadn't called. I finally convinced her that the man she saw was probably doing something harmless—like burying a shirt with lipstick on the collar that he didn't want his wife to find."

Chloe gave a startled laugh. "With an imagination like that, you should be a writer."

He grinned and shrugged. "Maybe so. The haircut got her to thinking about something else. She wandered off only twice. It was a little worrisome at one point when only half my head was done, but she finally came back on-line."

"She did a great job. I'm just used to it long. It looks good."

Very good, she thought. The headband had vanished, and his black hair, shorn to a much shorter length, lay in disarray over his high forehead, the mussed strands gleaming like polished jet. He seemed taller somehow, and he looked handsome and sexy enough to be illegal. It was just—well—he looked so different from the Ben she'd come to know.

He juggled the burden in his arms. "Champagne on ice causes frostbite."

He'd stuffed the bottles into plastic bags filled with ice cubes, which he held close to his chest. He went to the kitchen and set the bags in the sink. Chloe rose onto her tiptoes to retrieve two wine goblets from a shelf.

"Sorry," she said as she set them on the counter. "When I was hitting garage sales, there were no crystal flutes available."

"After the divorce, you didn't get half the household belongings?"

Chloe had felt fortunate to escape with her skin intact. "I'm a peace-at-any-cost person. What Roger didn't get, I sold to pay his medical and credit card bills."

"He's still able to live by himself?"

"Yes. In my opinion that's a mistake, but I've got no say-so anymore."

She couldn't stop staring at his hair. He looked so different—like someone she barely knew. The woven sash that he'd always worn had been replaced with a wide leather belt, and he was also wearing western boots.

"What happened to your sash and moccasins?"

"I retired them to the closet and unearthed my old

standbys. I caught a glimpse of myself today and decided I was carrying the Shoshone look too far."

Chloe suspected there was more to the story. Jeremy would be disappointed. He'd been working so hard to get the Ben Longtree look perfected.

The thought no sooner settled in Chloe's brain than another came hard and fast on its heels. "Oh, Ben," she said softly.

He shot her a wary glance. "What?"

"You did this because of Jeremy."

He ran a hand over his hair. "Let's not go there, okay? I got a haircut. No big deal."

"I thought you refused to wear leather for moral reasons."

He rested a lean hip against the counter. "He's been copying me."

"Yes."

"Other kids will make fun of him. I know what that's like, and I don't want it happening to him." He shrugged. "I disapprove of killing animals for food or clothing, but sometimes you can carry things too far. Millions of people in this country consume beef. The hides will be used to make leather goods whether I wear leather or not. You have to pick your battles."

"I can't believe you'd do this for my son."

He finally met her gaze. "He's a good kid. I'm fond of him. It's hard enough, moving to a new school, without stacking the deck against yourself. Maybe he'll get rid of that silly shoestring now and start wearing sneakers again."

"True, and that will be good, I suppose. It's just that I don't like to see you compromise your ideals this way."

"You can't have him looking like that. The other kids will crucify him."

Chloe sighed and conceded the point with a nod. Smiling up at him, she said, "The haircut looks fabulous. I liked it long, but it's attractive this way, too."

"The hair doesn't make the man. Neither do the clothes." He raked his fingers through the thick strands. "It's a lot less troublesome, cut short. It was always falling in my eyes, even with the headband."

He began peeling away the foil from one champagne bottle to reveal a wire doohickey over the cork. Using his thumb, he gave it a hard push. With an explosive *pop*, the cork cannoned from the bottle and hit the window above the sink. The glass shattered as though a cannonball had struck it.

"Shit!"

Chloe leaped back. Glass went everywhere. When her initial shock subsided, she clamped a hand over her mouth to stifle her laughter. Ben just stood there, the bottle still aimed at her window, his dark face a study of incredulity. "I can't *believe* I did that."

Laughing so hard she could scarcely breathe, Chloe clamped an arm over her waist. He slanted her a mock glare. "You think it's funny? I busted your window."

She nodded again and managed to squeeze out, "I noticed." She wiped tears of mirth from her eyes. "I'm sorry," she squeaked. "It's just—the look on your face. *Priceless.* I'm sorry."

He set the bottle on the drain and shook champagne from his hands.

"At least you didn't hit yourself in the nose." Her voice went shrill. "Did you see that movie?"

Smiling, he shook his head as he filled the glasses and handed her one. "Congratulations on the job." He touched his goblet to hers. "Bottoms up. Drain the glass, or it'll bring bad luck."

"I've never heard that one." Chloe wrinkled her

nose as she gulped down the champagne. Ben immediately gave her a refill. "Whoa! I'm a lightweight."

"To the future. I hope it all works out, and you're a wealthy business owner five years from now."

Chloe couldn't pass on a toast like that. As she lowered her empty glass, she felt the warmth of the alcohol moving through her, and she smiled. Setting the glass aside, she said, "I was too excited to eat much dinner. On an empty stomach, that stuff packs a punch."

His glass joined hers on the counter. He moved toward her. Before Chloe realized what he meant to do, he cupped a hand over the back of her head and hauled her up against him. This time, he wasted no time on preliminaries. He just took her mouth in a deep, searing kiss.

Chloe went from laughter to yearning so quickly that her brain barely registered the change before her body ignited. The force of her need alarmed her. She'd believed herself incapable of ever wanting a man again. *Wrong.* The heat of him—the hardness of him. She suddenly wanted him more than she'd ever wanted anything.

Just a kiss, she promised herself. *There's no harm in that.* When it was over—after she'd gotten just a taste of him—she'd pull away and end it.

She dug her fingers into his shoulders, pressing her body to his. He slipped his free arm around her, his hand splayed over her side. He was fire and ice, making her burn with need and shiver with delight. That tingling warmth she'd come to associate with his touch moved through her in waves. She felt as if she'd been plugged into a high-voltage socket and every cell of her body were being charged.

Suddenly she couldn't think, didn't want to think. When he moved his hands under her top—when she felt his palms on her bare skin—she stepped up onto his boots to gain height, hugged his neck with both arms, and hungrily feasted on his mouth, reveling in the thrills that pulsed so wildly through her system. His hand found her breast. *Yes.* She wanted this, needed him. The layer of nylon and lace that protected her nipple from his clever, searching fingertips was such a frustration that she wanted to scream. *There. Oh, yes, just there,* she thought dizzily when he captured the sensitive protuberance and teased it with light rolls of his fingers that sent electrical buzzes through her body.

Chloe moaned and shivered. He caught her at the waist and set her on the counter. She felt his hands making fast work of her blouse buttons, felt the strength rippling in his shoulders, gloried in the tingling heat that poured from him and into her. *Ben.* He parted her blouse and unfastened the front clasp of her bra. Her breasts spilled forth into his big, warm hands. When his thumbs touched the tips of her nipples, hums of delight shot through her. The ribbons of sensation tangled in her belly, forming a white-hot mass of longing.

She made fists in his hair, struggling to wrap her lower legs around his thighs, the feminine place at the apex of her own screaming for contact with his hardness. Visions of making love with him swirled through her brain, their bodies entwined, the sheets damp with their sweat, the magic forming a cocoon around them. Nothing existed in that moment but him and the way he made her feel.

"Sweet Christ," he whispered, wrenching his mouth away and resting his forehead against hers. She felt him trembling, and by that she knew he wanted her as much as she wanted him. "I can't," he shuddered out. "Foul play. I can't do this."

Chloe blinked stupidly. She dragged in a jagged

breath as he fumbled to get her breasts back into the flimsy cups of the bra. Every graze of his fingertips ignited her, adding fuel to the fire he'd already started. Why was he stopping? This wasn't how it usually went. It was the woman who was supposed to have second thoughts.

"You're not ready for this, Chloe. You're not ready, and I'm a jerk."

She was ready. She'd never been more ready for anything. Only how could she articulate that when—what was it about his hands that made her whole body feel as if it were melting and humming, all at once?

He managed to refasten her bra. "I'm sorry," he murmured, trailing kisses along her cheek. "When I'm touching you, I can't control myself. I'm sorry. It isn't fair. I'm sorry."

She had no idea what he was talking about, and she made a sound of protest when he drew back to button her blouse. A dozen questions spiked in her mind, but his closed expression told her he wouldn't provide answers.

Shaking, she pushed his hands away to finish the buttoning herself. Embarrassment washed her face with scaring heat. She couldn't bring herself to look at him. "Well, now." Her voice quivered. "That was—fun."

He didn't want her. The realization hovered in her brain like a black cloud. She'd been all over him, practically begging him for sex, and he'd been the one to stop.

When her mind cleared, Chloe jumped down from the counter and began gathering the glass shards in the sink.

"Chloe."

He touched her shoulder. She flinched away. "What a mess!" she managed to say with a laugh.

"It's not what you're thinking."

And how did he know what she was thinking? Right then, she was seriously questioning her sanity. What, exactly, had come over her? She'd long since vowed never to let another man put his hands on her. Now that her blood had stopped racing and her body was starting to feel halfway normal again, she was appalled by her behavior. They easily could have ended up in bed. What then? If she'd regained her senses right in the middle of it and asked him to stop, he would have been angry, and perhaps rightfully so.

"It's fine, Ben," she said quickly. "Let's just blame the champagne, shall we?"

"I've hurt your feelings. I never meant—" He broke off and muttered, "Shit. I want you, Chloe. That wasn't why I stopped."

She picked up a large piece of glass and put it in the trash.

"You shotgunned two glasses of champagne," he said. "I don't get women slightly drunk and then seduce them."

By now, Chloe wasn't sure what upset her more, the fact that he'd pulled away, or that she'd been so eager. It wasn't like her. Of all the things she missed about being married, sex wasn't one of them. It was humiliating to have lost control like that, humiliating to remember how she had shivered and moaned, wanting more. It had been a very close call, too close for comfort.

She had the glass cleared away in short order. Taking his cues from her, Ben let the subject drop. "Do you have a flashlight? A lot of it probably went outside."

"I have a flashlight, but it can wait until morning. I'll have plenty of time before work to take care of it."

"You don't happen to have any cardboard, do you?"

Chloe went to her bedroom, emptied a partially unpacked box in her closet, and took it to him. He cut the cardboard to fit the window opening while she fished through her junk drawer for some tacks and a hammer.

When the window had been covered to his satisfaction, he poured each of them more champagne. Chloe almost turned it down. Maybe she was tipsier than she realized, and that accounted for her inexplicable reaction to his kiss.

She reluctantly took the goblet, assuring herself that she had the situation under control now. As long as he didn't touch her again, she'd be fine.

"I'll replace the glass tomorrow while you're at work," he assured her. "You'll need to tell your sitter that I'll be stopping by."

"Don't be silly." She took a sip of champagne. "It was an accident. I'll take care of it."

"You know how to replace window glass?"

"It can't be very difficult."

"Answer enough. I'll fix it. These old-fashioned things require caulking. There's a trick to applying it. I've done it a few times." His mouth twitched. "I'm almost as slick at replacing windows as I am at breaking them."

Chloe turned the goblet in her hands, staring at the bubbles that rose to the surface. They were both pretending nothing had happened now, and tension filled the air between them.

"Chloe?"

He said her name softly, but it brought her head up as if a rifle had just gone off. "What?"

He held her gaze. "Do I need to apologize for stepping out of line?"

Chloe seriously considered playing that card. But the truth was, she'd drawn no line.

"I can't see why you should."

"Good," he said. "I really hate apologizing when I'm not sorry."

It was her cue to smile, only she didn't feel like it. "Are we going to drink this champagne or just look at it?"

He lifted his glass. "I know I already did this, but it bears saying twice. Congratulations on the new job and possible business venture. It's great news."

Chloe chinked her glass against his. The bubbles tickled her nose when she took a sip. This time, she wasn't foolish enough to drain the glass. She was a woman who learned from her mistakes.

The phone rang. Afraid Jeremy might awaken, she dashed to answer it. "Hello." No reply. She thought she heard someone breathing. "Hello?"

"Hmm," she said as she broke the connection. "A wrong number, I guess." She started back to the table only to be stopped short by the phone ringing a second time. "My sister Phoebe, I'll bet. Her cell phone, messing up. It does that sometimes." She grabbed the receiver. "Hello?"

"I thought I told you to stay away from him," a raspy voice said.

Chloe froze. *Bobby Lee?* It didn't sound like him, but, aside from the sheriff, who surely didn't make prank calls, Bobby Lee was the only man who'd warned her to steer clear of Ben.

"It's stupid, going up to his place all the time," the voice went on. "Even stupider to let him come there. I saw you, letting him paw you. You know what happens to stupid women, Chloe? They get themselves—"

She broke the connection. It *had* been Bobby Lee. She felt certain of it. She glanced at the front windows. The dining area curtains were slightly parted. He was out there in the darkness, looking into her house.

"You okay?"

Chloe rubbed her arms. She didn't want to get Ben involved in this. She'd seen the anger in his eyes last night and this morning. If he got it into his head that she needed protection from a county deputy, he could get himself in big trouble.

"I'm fine." She stepped over to adjust the curtains. Her hands were shaking. *He's out there,* she thought. "It was just a wrong number."

"Are you sure? You're white as a sheet."

"I am?" She touched her cheek. "I probably forgot to put on blusher."

She jumped nearly a foot when the phone rang again. Ben started up from his chair. "No, don't," she said. "Please, don't."

He sank back down, his gaze sharp on hers. "Who is it?"

She shook her head.

"It's Bobby Lee, isn't it?"

Chloe didn't want to involve him, but she didn't want to lie to him, either. Her hesitation seemed to be all the answer he needed.

"That bastard."

"Ben, please." She held up a hand. "I just won't answer. He'll stop. It's not any big deal."

He stared at the ringing telephone. When it finally fell silent, he passed a hand over his eyes and said, "Chloe, sit down. You and I need to talk."

"About what?"

"About Bobby Lee."

She tugged on the curtains again before she sat down. Ben said, "He's watching the house, isn't he?"

She threw him a startled look. "No, I—"

"Damn it, Chloe, don't lie to me. You immediately closed the curtains after the second call. He said something. You know he's out there."

She nodded. "Yes. He knows you're here."

"What else?"

"I hung up. He didn't get a chance to say much else. Only that I was stupid."

Ben sighed and closed his eyes. When he lifted his lashes, he grated out, "He's hated my guts for years. I have no idea why, only that he despises me."

"What has that got to do with me?"

"He probably thinks we've got a thing going. Aside from the fact that you're very attractive, that's reason enough for him to make moves on you."

Moves? He'd tried to rape her. Chloe wrapped her arms around her waist. "I'm not following."

"Neither am I. I've never understood it. I only know that he gets off on causing me grief. From the fifth grade on, it was as if we had an unspoken competition to outdo each other, only I wasn't in on the game. If I got a B plus on a test, Bobby Lee busted his ass to get an A on the next one. In high school, it got even worse. I had one girlfriend. Only one. Her name was Peggy Lee Bradshaw. She wasn't popular or very pretty, but I liked her, and we started dating. The instant Bobby Lee got wind of it, he was after her like bears for honey. He was a star football player, very popular. The girls waited in line for him to ask them out. Peggy Lee was flattered by the attention. She'd been ignored by boys most of her life, and suddenly the school hunk liked her."

"What happened?"

"She dropped me and started going with him. I tried to tell her he was bad news, but she was floating a foot above the ground. He got her pregnant. Tossed her aside like so much trash. Four months later, her folks sent her away to live with her aunt. I never saw her again. Her parents were born-again Christians, very strict. They still live here in Jack Pine. If Peggy

Lee has ever come home for a visit, I've never heard about it."

"So essentially, he ruined her life." A week ago, Chloe wouldn't have believed this story, but after her experience with Bobby Lee last night, she couldn't discount it. "All because she went out with you."

"That's right. I know it sounds absurd, Chloe, but I'm afraid for you. There's something—hell, I don't know—something not quite right with him. You know what I'm saying? You got away from him last night. But what if you hadn't? And who's to say he'll stop there? His calling here like this alarms me."

Chloe fleetingly recalled the press of Bobby Lee's fingers on her arms, and she decided Ben could be right.

"I'll be careful, Ben. Thank you for warning me."

He raked a hand through his hair. "Damn it. The window. I don't suppose you'd consider staying the night at my place until I get that fixed. He could cut through the cardboard, and you'd never hear a thing."

The thought made Chloe's body go tense. After the kiss they'd recently shared, she didn't think staying all night at his place was a good idea. "I'll take precautions." She was an expert on precautions, thanks to Roger. "Jeremy's already in bed. We'll be fine here for the night."

Ben's jaw muscle started to tic. "I think he's responsible for all the wounded animals."

Chloe fixed him with an appalled stare. "What?"

"You heard me. I think Bobby Lee is shooting the animals."

"He'd have to be mad to do such a thing. If he got caught, it would end his career."

"If he's over the edge, he may not worry about things like that. He's always been arrogant." He tapped the table with rigid fingertips. "Chloe, would you promise me something? Don't take any chances. If he comes into the shop and does anything that alarms you, don't hesitate to call the police."

"I won't," she assured him. "Count on it."

He glanced at his watch and pushed slowly to his feet. "Are you sure you won't consider staying at my place?" He hooked a thumb over his shoulder. "That broken window worries me."

Making sure to keep her distance, Chloe walked with him to the door. "We'll be fine."

He put a hand over hers when she reached to turn the doorknob. She knew he meant to kiss her, and she pressed a hand to his chest to hold him off. "Ben," she whispered. "What you said earlier, about me not being ready? You were absolutely right. I'm not in the market for a relationship. I think—"

"Don't think," he ordered softly as he took her mouth.

His lips moved against hers like satin. Then he tasted her, delving deep. The heat that ignited between them was searing. Chloe's legs went weak. She sank against him. He ran his hands lightly over her back, making her skin hum with pleasure. It frightened her to want him so badly, but not so much that she could bring herself to pull away.

He finally curled his hands over her shoulders to set her away from him, sipping sweetly from her lips as he ended the kiss. "Good night, Chloe," he whispered.

Before she could blink to bring things back into focus, he was closing the door behind him. "Precautions!" he called through the door.

Chloe rested her head against the wood. Precautions. Perhaps, she thought dizzily, she was protecting herself against the wrong man.

* * *

Ben deleted the word *walked* and replaced it with *ambled,* then found himself staring stupidly at the computer screen, his mind on Chloe and Jeremy instead of his work. He sighed and rocked back in his chair, rubbing the grit from his eyes. He kept forgetting the storyline and the names of his characters, his head filling with images of a knife slicing through cardboard.

He turned to stare at the phone. It was three in the morning. He shouldn't call and wake her. But, damn it, he was worried. What if Bobby Lee broke into the house? Chloe prided herself on those self-defense moves she knew, but he didn't put much stock in them. A woman her size was no match for a man like Bobby Lee Schuck, who wouldn't pull his punches or give a rat's ass if her child got in the way.

Unable to stand it a moment longer, Ben picked up the phone. He knew her number by heart. He'd looked it up a dozen times since he'd left her house. He dialed, cringing at the first ring. He could almost see her jerking awake, confused and disoriented.

"Hello?" she said, cutting into his thoughts, her voice clear and alert.

"It's me."

"Ben?" There was a smile in her voice. "I thought well, never mind that. Why are you calling at this hour? Is everything okay?"

"It is now. I've been worried about you. Sorry for ringing so late. I hope I didn't wake Jeremy."

"No. He's sound asleep." A rustling sound came over the line. He pictured her sitting up in bed. "I wish I could say the same. I have the wide-awakes."

"Any more calls?"

"No. Not until now."

"Sorry. I know it's crazy, calling you at three in the morning."

"You shouldn't worry, Ben. We're perfectly fine. I brought the phone into Jeremy's room. The door is locked, and for extra measure, I put his toy box in front of it. I'm also armed."

"With what?"

"His ball bat."

Ben smiled and relaxed. He should have known she would be okay. Bobby Lee would get a hell of a surprise if he opened that bedroom door.

"We're fine. I've got my cell phone in here, too. You know all those shows where the intruder cuts the wires? Got it covered."

He chuckled. "I guess I'll get back to work, then."

"You're working?"

"Mmm."

"Mmm," she echoed. "I won't even ask. This and that, right?"

He was grinning when she broke the connection.

The following morning flew by. After caring for the animals at Ben's, Chloe raced home to clean up the glass outside, do a few chores around the house, and get ready for work. She chose a light blue summer suit to wear her first day at the Christmas Village. In honor of the occasion, she even used a curling iron on her hair, hoping to tame the flyaway tendrils. The result was just fatter curls, going every which way.

By the time she parked her car behind the Christmas Village, her skin had gone clammy with tension. A quick check in her visor mirror told her she looked okay. Not good, but okay. She climbed from the vehicle, locked the doors, and took several calming breaths, telling herself that she was placing far too much importance on this job. Yesterday at this time, she hadn't even met Hattie Perkins.

With that thought to bolster her, Chloe entered the

shop. Hattie waved to her from the dollhouse section. "There's an apron under the counter. Lose the jacket. You'll roast."

Well, Chloe thought, *so far, poor marks.* She'd worn the wrong clothes. She put her purse on a shelf in the check stand area, draped her jacket over a stool, and grabbed the apron, slipping it on as she went to join her new boss.

Hattie held up a paintbrush tipped with cotton-candy pink. "Isn't it going to be cute?"

Chloe stood back to appraise the dollhouse in progress. It was Victorian, her favorite style. Hattie had done the siding in pale mocha, and now she was doing the gingerbread in a rainbow of sherbet shades.

"It's darling." Chloe looked in a window. "How will you do the inside?"

"Quaint and old-fashioned. I got a new miniature catalog with some of the cutest furniture kits. I spent all last evening working up an order." She put the brush in a cup of murky water and wiped her hands. "Playtime is over. I'd better start training you."

An hour later, Chloe was struggling to master the electronic cash register and credit-card processing. "I'm sorry," she told Hattie when the customers departed. "I've never done any of this. After I left my husband, I was a cocktail waitress. I took orders and the bartender handled the register."

"No worries. You'll learn." Hattie laid a price sheet beside the register. "During the lulls, do your best to memorize this. It makes a transaction go more smoothly. If you make a mistake, holler. I'll come bail you out."

The elderly proprietress was true to her word. She bailed Chloe out several times over the next seven hours. By the time the shift was over, Chloe's head was swimming with department numbers, merchandise codes, price sheets, and procedures. She despaired of ever learning it all. The only thing she could honestly say she'd done well was the dusting. She did know how to clean.

After doffing her apron and collecting her purse and jacket, Chloe turned to Hattie. "Do you want me back tomorrow?"

The older woman laughed and handed her a price sheet. "It's just a copy. If you lose it, don't panic. Perhaps you can look it over tonight."

As she drove home, Chloe divided her attention between the price sheet and the road.

Jeremy met Chloe at the door. "Ben came while you was gone!" he cried.

"He did?" Chloe bent to grab a hug, no easy task since her target was making like a jumping bean. "Wow. You liked that, did you?"

"He fixed the window," Tracy explained. Eager to be gone, the teenager was already slipping on her jacket. "He is, like, too cute," she said, wiggling her penciled eyebrows. "Way to go, Chloe."

"No, no." Chloe laughed. The sound was whistle thin and rang false. "It's not like that."

"Bummer." Tracy grabbed one of Jeremy's curls and tugged. "Bye, brat." To Chloe, she said, "Trent's picking me up. We're going bowling."

Chloe waved from the doorway as Tracy skipped across the yard. Then Jeremy distracted her by tugging on her hand.

"You gotta come see our window!"

Chloe allowed herself to be herded to the kitchen. Sure enough, the glass had been replaced. She leaned close to look at the caulking. Ben had been so precise that the line might have been done by machine. She wondered if he was as meticulous when he made love.

The question no sooner slipped into her mind than she chased it right back out.

While Chloe fixed dinner, Jeremy entertained her with a blow-by-blow account of Ben's visit. It was Ben this, and Ben that.

"He did a good job of putting in the window, huh, Mom?"

"He sure did."

"Ben's good at everything."

He was especially talented at kissing, Chloe thought. She just wished—oh, she didn't know what she wished. For a different mind-set, maybe? Why couldn't she be one of those women who could take their pleasure where they found it? Life would be a lot more fun that way. But, oh, no, she had to take everything so seriously. As a consequence, Ben had her feelings in such a tangle, she could barely think.

By the time the dishes were done, Chloe was numb with exhaustion. She was throwing on jeans to go to Ben's when the phone rang. Jeremy answered in the kitchen.

"Mommy, it's Ben!"

Chloe grabbed up the phone, which she'd returned to her bedroom that morning. "Hello?" Jeremy had the television blaring. "Just a sec." She clamped a hand over the mouthpiece. "Hang up, Jeremy! I can't hear!" When she heard the other phone click, she said, "Hi, again."

"Now I can't hear. You should have been a drill sergeant."

She laughed. "I *am* a drill sergeant. Sorry if I hurt your eardrum."

He chuckled. "You didn't. I'm impressed, though. Give you a megaphone, and I bet they'd hear you clear in Pineville."

"Have you had your fun?" Chloe tucked the phone

under her chin to snap her jeans. "Don't mess with me tonight, buster. I've had a hard day."

"I figured. That's why I called. I took care of the critters tonight. You can crash and relax."

Chloe sank onto the bed. "You angel. If you were here, I'd kiss you."

"I can be there in three minutes. Hold tight to that thought."

She snorted. "On second thought." Silence. She straightened her legs and stared at her bare feet. Ugly toes, skinny with knobby knuckles and big balls on the ends. Definitely the feet of a woman who plodded through life. No flitting for her. "I think maybe we need to talk about that."

"About what?"

Chloe took a deep breath, slowly exhaled. "Sex."

"Make it two minutes."

Silence descended while Chloe sorted her thoughts. "Ben?"

"I'm still here. What about sex?"

She laughed again. She didn't know why. The way she felt wasn't funny. "I don't do one-night stands."

"That's good. After last night, I don't think one night will be enough."

"You know what I mean."

Another silence. "Do we have to discuss this right now?"

"Yes. I, um—hmm, how shall I put this?" Chloe squeezed her eyes closed. Flexed her shoulders. "I'm not very modern-minded about relationships. I wish I were. But that isn't how I'm made."

"Chloe, has anyone ever mentioned that you complicate everything?"

"Maybe so. But I am who I am. I don't do uncomplicated. I'm also—"

"Also what?"

The words were aching at the back of her throat, but somehow, she just couldn't dredge up old ghosts and tell him about the last few months of her marriage. Some things were better left unsaid.

"What do you want from me?" he asked softly. "Just tell me how complicated you want it, and I'll let you know if I can step up to the plate."

"That's the problem, don't you see? I need you to figure that out for yourself."

His expelled breath wafted loudly across the wire. "Can you at least give me a hint?"

"This and that," she said softly.

He swore under his breath. "Chloe."

Her body tensed. "I need something more than an introductory handshake, something more than stories about your grandfather. You have secrets, Ben. If you can't trust me enough to reveal at least one of those, how can we deepen our friendship or even think of having a relationship?"

"My profession isn't who I am."

"At least it's a starting point. It bothers me that you won't reveal the simplest things about yourself. It's like refusing to tell me your name. How can we move forward? You accuse me of complicating things. Maybe it's the other way around."

Silence. He was still there. She could hear him breathing. But he said nothing. It was, Chloe realized, all the answer he was willing to give her. After a long moment, she let the receiver drop back into its cradle.

Chapter Eighteen

Over the next few days, Chloe was so busy that she fell exhausted into bed each night. She loved her new job, but there was so much to learn, all sandwiched in between her visits to Cinnamon Ridge, her responsibilities as a mother, her household chores, and her mounting alarm about Bobby Lee. Her schedule was so packed that she was forced to cancel babysitting for the Baxters.

Several times when she arrived at work, Chloe saw the deputy's Bronco next door in the Dairy Queen parking lot. Bobby Lee sat inside, and despite the fact that he wore sunglasses, she knew he was watching her. It gave Chloe the creeps. Even worse, he ventured into the shop a few times. He always bought some little trinket, using that as an excuse for his visit.

After his third appearance, Chloe telephoned Sheriff Lang to complain. The lawman made light of her concerns, saying Bobby Lee had as much right to buy Christmas decorations as the next person. Besides, it was his job to check on the local businesses and see how things were going. By the end of the conversation, Chloe was furious.

While Chloe wrestled with her demons, Ben was dealing with a few of his own. Whenever Chloe came to the ridge, the tension between them was almost palpable, and no matter how he circled it, he knew it was his own damned fault. It wasn't unreasonable of her to want to know what he did for a living, and the truth was, his original reason for withholding the information no longer held water. Chloe wouldn't go rushing back to Jack Pine to tell everyone she saw that he was a famous writer. Her silence about Methuselah and the other animals was proof of that.

So why didn't he just tell her?

Each time Ben asked himself that question, he circled back to the same answer. He was afraid that once he got started talking, he wouldn't be able to stop, and he might tell her everything—about his father, about his gift, and even about Sherry. He wanted to believe it wouldn't matter to her. But what if it did? He was in love with her. Hopelessly. Completely. If she couldn't accept the truth and walked away, he didn't know what he'd do.

All of Ben's life, keeping secrets had been a matter of survival. He hadn't even been completely open with his mother for fear she might unintentionally betray him to his father with an unguarded expression or gesture. He'd spent his childhood keeping his own counsel, and the habit had followed him into adulthood. The only time he had shared the private parts of himself with anyone, it had ended in disaster.

He felt as if he were standing at the edge of an abyss and Chloe was urging him to jump. Whenever he tried to tell her about his job, the words got trapped at the back of his throat.

"You can't keep it from her forever," his mother chided him on Saturday night. "You love her, Ben. I see it in your eyes every time you look at her. You can't move forward without complete honesty between you. That's no way to begin a relationship."

"I know that, Mom. I'll tell her. The right moment just hasn't presented itself."

"And when do you think it will? Have you even told her about your writing yet?"

"No."

"Why, for heaven's sake? It's nothing like the other. A lot of people are writers."

"But a lot of people aren't freaks. Is that what you're saying?"

Nan paled. "You are not a freak."

"What am I then? Just an oddity?"

"You're a wonderful man with a beautiful gift."

Ben struggled to draw a full breath. He always felt as if he were suffocating when he thought about talking to Chloe. "This *gift* ruined my father's life, and now it's ruining mine. I love her, Mom. I lost Sherry over it. From the moment I told her, she looked at me differently, and it was never the same between us again."

"Sherry had no heart. You didn't fit tidily into her intellectual understanding of the universe."

"We had a lot in common, both of us being vets. Until I ruined it, she loved me."

"No." Nan touched her feet to the floor to put her rocker in motion. "That wasn't love, Ben, or even a pale imitation. You were young and you perceived it to be love."

"If I had kept my mouth shut, we might still be together."

"Then she didn't love the real you, did she?" Nan picked up her crocheting and started to hum.

Frustrated because she'd chosen this precise moment to drift away from him, Ben stomped from the family room. As he circled the kitchen desk, his mother called after him.

"Do you miss her?"

Ben stopped. "Who, Chloe?"

Nan smiled benignly. "Just as I thought. Sherry is no longer first in your thoughts. Real love isn't extinguished quite that easily."

Ben turned down the hall, heading for his office. What did his mother know about real love? he wondered angrily. She'd been Hap Longtree's punching bag for over thirty years. That didn't exactly recommend her as an expert on healthy relationships.

Fuming, Ben sat at his desk, only to have Rowdy rear up to plant oversize paws on his knee. Glancing down, Ben came face-to-face with another problem. It wouldn't be long before the puppy could safely go home. When that day arrived, Ben would lose his only link to Chloe and her son.

The following Sunday evening when Chloe came to clean cages and feed the animals, Ben noticed that Diablo had joined Methuselah in following her around the house. *Damn.* Maybe it was the perfume she wore.

Only he knew it wasn't. The essence that had beguiled him and his critters couldn't be bottled. It was Chloe's complete and absolute sweetness that drew all of them to her. Even the animals in their cages gazed after her as she moved around the kitchen, each of them hoping for another little scratch or a soothing pat. Ben could have used a pat himself, and he definitely needed his itch scratched. Instead he got that stubborn lift of her chin and an arctic blast from her eyes.

"Is my mom mad at you?" Jeremy asked just before it was time for them to leave.

Busy in the kitchen, Ben shut off the water and glanced down. Jeremy peered up at him with a troubled frown. "I don't know," Ben replied. "Do you think she is?"

Jeremy pursed his lips. "Yup, I think so."

Ben grabbed a towel to dry his hands. "What makes you say that?"

The child shrugged. "I don't know. She's just gets that mad look when I talk about you." He pleated his brows in a frown. "Have you said you're sorry?"

"For what?"

Jeremy scrunched his shoulders. "I dunno. Don't you?"

Now he was getting relationship counseling from a six-year-old. Ben stepped into the family room to give his mom her pills. Nan smiled up at him. "That girl is so sweet. Have you noticed how Methuselah and Diablo have taken to her?"

Ben was starting to feel like a lone soldier in enemy territory. He thrust the glass of water under his mother's nose. "Take your pills, Mom."

She popped them in her mouth, took two sips of water, and passed the glass back to him. "Along with you now. I have to get this row done before supper." She resumed crocheting. And humming. He really, really wished something besides "Hang down your head, Tom Dooley" would stick in her brain.

Once back in the kitchen, Ben decided he was cranky. Okay, bitchy. He should be glad all his critters liked Chloe. What bothered him was his knowledge that wild animals had good instincts when it came to people. They seldom trusted someone who might do them harm. Methuselah and Diablo were giving Chloe the highest of recommendations.

What if? he wondered. Chloe was nothing like Sherry. Wasn't there a chance, if only a slim one, that Chloe might be able to accept him, not only for who he was, but also for what he was?

Fat chance. Ben had never even understood himself. How could he expect Chloe to? He couldn't give her what she needed. That was the bottom line. Being honest with Sherry had damned near destroyed him. When he considered taking that gamble again, he broke out in a cold sweat.

In a few more weeks, Rowdy could go home. No more Jeremy, no more Chloe. Life on the ridge would return to normal.

The thought made Ben feel desolate. When Chloe and Jeremy left, the rooms would be silent again. He didn't know how he would bear it.

The following afternoon, right after Hattie left for the bank, Bobby Lee came to the shop again. The instant the bell above the door rang, Chloe felt him—much as a person might feel a blast of cold air. She straightened from a box of merchandise she'd been unloading onto a shelf, saw him standing by a display table near the door, and contemplated ducking down to hide.

Her pride wouldn't allow it. If he wanted a confrontation, she would oblige him. Knotting her hands into hard fists, she wove her way toward him. When she reached the check stand, she said, "Good evening, Deputy Schuck. How can I help you?"

"You can listen," he said with the same phony sincerity that had fooled her once, but never would again. "I know I screwed up. I was drunk, Chloe. Please give me another chance."

The sound of his voice made her skin crawl. "I understand that alcohol can have an adverse effect on human behavior, but using that as an excuse is a cop-out."

He spread his booted feet, planted his hands on his hips, and hung his head. He was the picture of dejection, but she wasn't buying it. "Come on. Have a heart. I messed up. I admit it. I'm sorrier than you can know."

Chloe set herself to the task of emptying the trash. As she twisted a tie around the top of the plastic bag, she said, "I have no heart, Bobby Lee, not for you. If you aren't here to buy something, please leave."

He plucked up a sale item without even looking at it. After setting it on the counter, he drew his wallet from his hip pocket. "How much?" he asked.

"It's two ninety-nine."

He laid three ones on the counter. Chloe quickly rang up the item, bagged his purchase, shoved it toward him, and said, "Have a nice evening," just as she would to any stranger.

"I'll be back."

He turned and left. She stared after him, feeling hot and cold both at once. She had a very bad feeling that he'd make good on that promise, and she wasn't sure what to do. He'd clearly developed some sort of fixation about her. She didn't know if it was because of her supposed relationship with Ben, or if he'd just chosen her at random, but the man definitely had a problem. He was watching the shop. He made an appearance only when Hattie was absent.

A few minutes later, Chloe's boss returned from the bank, only to leave again to go home and check on her husband. The older woman had been gone only a few minutes when Bobby Lee made a trio of visits, the span of time between them so short that they were almost back-to-back.

Inside, Chloe trembled each time she saw him. She ignored the man's presence—didn't glance up, didn't speak. Perhaps he would stop doing this if he could get no reaction from her.

The last time he came, he spoke in that whiny, have-mercy voice she was coming to despise. "I'll go bankrupt doing this."

Chloe sacked his merchandise. "Please, do. My commission is five percent of gross."

"Chloe, please." He flashed her an imploring look. "What really happened that night? I stopped, didn't I?"

"Did you want to buy something more?"

He nudged up the brim of his hat. "You're a hard woman."

She was a smart woman. Chloe turned her back on him and began sorting the daily receipts. Inside, she was shaking. On the outside, she was deadly calm.

"Okay, fine. We'll play it your way. I have a bankroll. If you want five percent of that before you'll forgive me, I'll give it to you."

She wouldn't forgive him for all the tea in China. When the overhead bell chinked to announce his departure, the trembling inside her attacked her hands. She dropped a bunch of receipts, which fluttered to the floor. She was still crouched down picking them up when Hattie returned to the shop.

"Are you all right?" Hattie asked when she saw Chloe's face.

Chloe had never wanted to confide in anyone quite so much, but Hattie had problems enough of her own. She'd just learned that her husband, Bill, had diabetes, and his blood sugar was yo-yoing radically in reaction to the insulin injections. "I'm fine, Hattie. How's Bill?"

Hattie launched into a long explanation of diet and insulin types that Chloe only half attended. Bobby Lee had made four appearances in the shop that day. She could no longer kid herself. The deputy was stalking her. Even more alarming, he was being very careful, making sure she was alone when he came. After the phone calls he'd placed to her residence the night Ben was there, she also knew he was watching her house. In situations like this, most women could call the law, but Chloe had already done that and received no help.

She didn't know what to do. She toyed with the possibility of calling the state police and filing a complaint. The problem was, did she have any legal grounds to actually file charges? Sheriff Lang would pooh-pooh her story, saying it was Bobby Lee's job to patrol all the local businesses on a daily basis. Jack Pine was so small, it was not yet incorporated, so the community had no city police force and fell under county jurisdiction.

From the start, Chloe had been determined not to involve Ben in this mess. Her reasons still held. If she told Ben what was happening, he might confront Bobby Lee. No civilian could take a law officer to task and come out a winner, not in this town, especially not Ben.

Chloe considered calling her folks for advice, but decided otherwise. There was nothing they could really do, and she didn't want to worry them.

In desperation, Chloe waited for Hattie to leave and called Sheriff Lang again, hoping against hope that the lawman might listen to her this time.

"Well, now, Chloe," he said sagely. "Stalking is a pretty serious charge."

"Trust me. I'm on the receiving end. I understand how serious it is."

"I think you need to calm down and look at this objectively," he replied. "As I explained once before, Bobby Lee patrols all the businesses in Jack Pine. It's part of his job. I can't very well reprimand the man for doing his duty, now can I?"

"These aren't duty calls, Sheriff." Her voice quaking with anger, Chloe reminded him of her dinner date with the deputy. "If I hadn't gotten away from him, he would have raped me that night! I quit my job at the sheriff's department to avoid any further contact. Now he's spying on my house and driving me nuts at my new place of employment. He never comes in when Hattie's here, only when I'm alone. Today, he was here four times."

"I have to admit that four visits to one store is a little excessive."

Chloe clenched her teeth.

"Chloe, has it occurred to you that Bobby Lee may sincerely regret his behavior and want to make amends? He's a good man. Been with the department for twenty years without a single mark on his record. That has to count for something."

In Chloe's opinion, all that proved was that Bobby Lee had managed to hide his true colors for almost a quarter of a century. "As spotless as his record may have been, Sheriff, that's no longer the case now. A good man doesn't try to force himself on a woman, and he doesn't threaten her with her job when she refuses him. I'll also remind you that he ambushed me later alongside the road and nearly ran me down with that Bronco. If I hadn't jumped the ditch and run into the woods, he would have hit me."

Lang sighed heavily, making Chloe feel like a recalcitrant child trying his patience. "Is he buying something each time he comes into the shop?"

"Yes."

"Well, then? Maybe he's just been in the Christmas spirit lately."

Chloe could see she was wasting her breath. She sarcastically thanked Sheriff Lang for his time and broke the connection. A dull ache had settled behind her eyes. As she fished through her purse for some ibuprofen, her hands trembled so violently that she could barely control them. Acid rolled up the back of her throat.

Taking a deep breath and slowly expelling it, she tried to calm down. Only she couldn't. Bobby Lee was dangerous. She could see it in his eyes. All her instincts warned her to do something, but for the life of her, she couldn't think what. The obvious course of action, calling the law, had gotten her nowhere.

The situation was nightmarishly similar to what she'd gone through for months after leaving Roger. For days now, her nerves had been raw. If something shifted when she opened a closet at home, she leaped with fright. She no longer enjoyed playing in the yard with Jeremy for fear she'd turn and find Bobby Lee standing behind her. She was tense when she took Jeremy on an outing, watching for a white Bronco everywhere she went and dreading the moment when she'd have to go home to an empty house.

Recalling those trials with Roger came to Chloe's rescue now. Bobby Lee frightened her, and she hated his visits to the shop, but she'd been through worse. Maybe he was just slow on the uptake and honestly believed he might wheedle his way back into her good graces. Soon, he'd start to realize that no amount of cajoling would convince her to forgive him. Maybe, at that point, he'd grow weary of the game and leave her alone.

Before Ben knew it, Chloe had been working at the Christmas Village for nearly two weeks, Rowdy was three months old, and time was running out. Soon the puppy would be old enough to go home. Chloe's debt to Ben would be paid in full, and she'd no longer have a reason to visit the ridge.

He told himself he'd just as soon not see her if her

only reason for coming was a sense of obligation. But deep down, he knew it was a lie. *Chloe.* He loved the throaty, musical sound of her voice. He loved the way she sang to herself as she worked. She filled his home with warmth and laughter.

One evening, it finally came time for Winston to be returned to his natural environment. Chloe walked with Ben deep into the woods, cheerfully said farewell, and then started to cry as the skunk disappeared into the woods. Clearly embarrassed, she averted her face so Ben wouldn't see her tears.

"It's one of the drawbacks," he told her as they walked slowly back toward the house. "You fall in love with each one of them, and it always hurts when your time with them is over."

She rubbed angrily at her cheeks. "I'm sorry. This is stupid. He's just a silly old skunk."

A skunk she'd come to love like a pet, Ben thought. It was much easier for him. He knew he'd see Winston again. His patients always returned for visits. "Maybe he'll drop by now and again."

She gulped and wiped at her cheeks again. "Yes, well, it's unlikely that I'll be around to see him, isn't it?"

Ben caught her by the elbow and turned her into his arms. "Hey," he whispered. "It's not so bad as all that, is it?" He suddenly had a bad feeling that saying good-bye to Winston was merely a catalyst and not the true source of her agitation. He rubbed gently at her wet cheeks, noticing the dark circles under her eyes where he removed her makeup. He drew back slightly to better assess her face. Without the touches of camouflage, she was frighteningly pale, and she looked drawn and exhausted. "Chloe, what is it? What's troubling you?"

Her eyes went bright with tears again, and she just

shook her head. "It's nothing. I, um—just some difficulties at work."

"What kind of difficulties?"

She shrugged and pulled away to hug her waist and stare off through the trees. "Nothing that I can't handle."

Ben resisted the urge to reach out and touch her again. "Sometimes a problem is easier solved when it's shared with a friend. Talk to me."

Her gaze flicked up to his. "The way you talk to me?" Her voice rang with bitterness. "Friendship goes two ways, Ben."

This was his chance, he thought. He swallowed. The words she wanted to hear gathered in his throat. He tried to push them out. He honestly did. Only, somehow, all he made was a soft grunting sound. She stood watching him—and waiting. His blood began to pound in his temples.

At last, he managed to speak, only the words that came weren't what he meant to say. "I talk to you, Chloe."

Her big brown eyes, already shimmering with tears, filled with pain. Knowing he was the cause made Ben feel ashamed.

"Fine," she said shakily. "Take all the time you need. Forever, if you like. It no longer matters to me one way or another. Keep your precious secrets."

She turned and started to walk away. Ben snaked out a hand and grabbed her by the arm, whirling her to face him. "You can't turn your back on this."

"On what? I fail to see what I'm walking away from."

"This, damn it!"

Ben knew it was stupid—a move he was bound to regret—but he jerked her into his arms and kissed her with everything he had. He half expected her to fight.

Instead, she only stiffened and started to push away. Then she moaned and melted against him.

Warning bells went off in his head. *His touch.* It was unfair to use that as a weapon against her. Only this time, fear of losing her outweighed his sense of honor. He backed her against a tree, feverishly kissing her as he ran his hands over her body. She hooked a slender leg at the back of his knee and offered no protest when he pushed up her top, unfastened her bra, and began fondling her breasts. She wrested her mouth from his and let her head fall back, her body jerking as he tweaked her nipples.

She dug her nails into his shoulders, clinging to him as if she were about to fall. "I love you, Ben. I love you. Kiss me, please?"

He'd already kissed her. As inflamed as he was, it took him a moment to understand where she wanted his mouth. He didn't need to be asked twice. Cupping her small breasts, he pushed them up and drew on her pink nipples. They went instantly hard. He could feel every slam of her heart in the vulnerable tips.

She shuddered and then sobbed. Ben continued to tease her breasts as he reached for the snap of her jeans. The instant his knuckles grazed her belly, her eyes opened, wide and disoriented. Then, with a suddenness that took him completely by surprise, she shoved hard on his shoulders.

"I can't *do* this!" she cried. "I just *can't.*"

Ben thought they'd been making damned good progress. Grabbing for breath, he turned to watch her scramble away from him. "Chloe," he said hoarsely.

She gave him her back as she struggled to right her clothing. "That's it. I'm out of here. I was afraid this might happen if we were alone again."

"What do you mean, out of here?"

"I mean I'm leaving." She turned to fix him with

an accusing look. "All you want is an easy lay who doesn't ask questions. Sorry, but that's not the way I'm programmed."

Before he could collect his wits, she stomped away. "Chloe, wait a minute. Can you just wait a minute?"

She never broke stride, her slender hips rotating seductively with every angry step. Ben stared after her for a moment. Then, feeling deflated, he leaned against the tree, closed his eyes, and willed his need of her away.

When he felt he could follow her without embarrassing himself, he fell into step behind her. As he walked, he mentally circled the problem. He'd obviously come to a crossroads, and he had to make a choice. If he didn't start talking, and fast, she would make tracks, and he might never see her again.

Only it wasn't that simple for him. He honest to God didn't know how to be open, even about little things, and the thought of sharing the big things scared him half to death. What would she say if he told her the whole truth? Not just part of it, but all of it. Even more important, how would she react? Would she stay with him, regardless? Or would she run like hell?

When he entered the house a few seconds later, he found her collecting her son and the puppy. His stomach dropped to the region of his knees. She really was leaving.

She handed Jeremy the squirming pup. "Go on out to the car, sweetie. Mommy will be along in a second."

Jeremy sent Ben an "I told you so" look before he scampered from the house. When the front door thumped closed, Chloe smoothed her hands over her slacks.

"What about the viruses?" Ben knew he was grabbing at straws. That wasn't what she wanted to hear, and it wasn't what he needed to say. "If you take the pup home, he'll be at risk."

"I'll pour bleach on a small section of lawn. For the next few weeks, Jeremy can take Rowdy potty there and keep him off the rest of the grass."

"Do you know how much bleach that'll take?"

Even as he asked the question, Ben wondered if he'd lost his mind. As if bleach were what he wanted to talk about? She loved him. She'd said as much. *Sweet Christ.* That was what he should be focused on, not bleach.

She shrugged. "Several gallons, I'm sure. Whatever it takes." In a quivery voice, she went on. "The local vet would have charged me a thousand dollars to treat Rowdy. I believe I've worked off a fair fourth of that. As soon as I'm financially able, I'll mail you a check for the remainder to settle the debt."

"Don't be silly, Chloe. I don't want your money."

She refused to look him directly in the eye. "I can accept help from good friends, but not from strangers. Call it silly pride if you like, but I pay my own way."

"I'm not exactly a stranger."

She didn't argue the point. She didn't need to. When she turned toward the door, her actions spoke more loudly than a dozen words.

Ben trailed after her to the entryway. "Chloe, don't end it like this. Please."

"End what? From where I'm standing, nothing ever began."

That hurt. His only consolation was that he could see in her expression that it pained her as much to say it as it did him to hear it. "We need to talk," he said. "I'll tell you whatever you want to know, I swear."

"Because I've pried it out of you?" When she met

his gaze, he saw no lingering anger in her eyes, only a
hurt that ran so deep her voice shook with it. "Sharing
between two people who really trust each other should
come freely, not upon request. I waited." She made a
hopeless gesture with her hand. "For two weeks I've
waited, Ben. Until now, you haven't offered to tell me
anything, not even what you do for a living."

What he did for a living was only a start. He had
much more to tell her than that. Only Chloe didn't
understand that. To her, it was cut and dried, a refusal
on his part to come clean about things other people
divulged without a thought.

"There's a lot more to it than that," he said. "A lot
of things you don't understand, Chloe. Things that—"
He broke off and swallowed hard. "I, um—I've always
been a private person. You know? It's not as easy for
me as it is for other people. It's not a matter of choosing not to tell you things. It's just that I can't think
how to start—and I'm afraid of your reaction."

He hoped that might soften her, but instead she
opened the door. As she stepped out, she said, "Then
you really shouldn't tell me, Ben. Trust is key. Without that, we don't have much."

He started to follow her out, but she held up a
hand. "I'm serious, Ben. Whatever it is you can't think
how to tell me, keep it to yourself. Hearing it from
you now won't mean anything. I'd always feel that I
forced it out of you."

The door closed in his face. He considered following
her out and forcing her to listen, then discarded the
idea. She was very upset with him right now. That
didn't bode well for a meaningful heart-to-heart, and
too much rode on the outcome for him to have rotten timing.

Nan, who'd evidently been awakened from her nap
by the sound of their voices, appeared like a wraith

beside him. She hugged his arm and rested her cheek against his sleeve, looking with him through the window at Chloe's departing car.

When the last bit of dust had finally settled, she said, "She's a sweet girl, Ben."

"She's not coming back," he whispered.

"Of course she will. You've only to go after her."

Ben glanced down. "You overheard our conversation."

She nodded. "Yes, and if you're a typical man, I imagine you're bewildered. When you're finally ready to spill your guts, she refuses to listen."

Ben was more than a little confused on that count. "She said it wouldn't mean anything now."

Nan smiled and kissed his shirtsleeve. "She just doesn't comprehend the magnitude of what you have to say. From her standpoint, you've been impossibly secretive about silly things. When you talk to her, it'll mean a great deal to her."

Ben bent to rest his cheek atop her head. "I'm afraid, Mom. I want to tell her, but the words won't come."

"Give it a little time then."

"She won't wait."

Nan sighed. "Then tell her just enough to satisfy her for now while you work your way up to confessing the rest."

Chapter Nineteen

Suffering from an incurable case of depression, Chloe was relieved to finally get Jeremy and Rowdy tucked in for the night and have a blessed quiet settle over the house. Determined not to think about Ben, she snuggled on the sofa with a glass of iced tea on the end table and an issue of her favorite magazine opened over her bent knees. She leafed back to the recipes.

She saw a broccoli and cauliflower au gratin recipe that sounded good, and then a vegetarian burrito recipe that made her think of Ben. She glanced at the clock, wondering what he was doing right now. Working, she decided resentfully. He always did "this and that" until the wee hours of the morning.

Her heart twisted painfully as a picture of him formed in her mind. She'd tried her best not to fall in love with him, knowing that the last thing she needed was to complicate her life with relationship problems. Now look at her. An aching lump was lodged at the back of her throat, and she felt all-over miserable. It was highly tempting to wallow in her misery and go on a good old-fashioned crying jag.

The harsh peal of the phone startled Chloe so badly she jumped. Tossing aside the magazine, she swung off the sofa. In four easy strides, she reached the wall phone. "Hello?"

"Hi."

It was Ben. She squeezed her eyes closed, loving the sound of his deep voice. How was it that she could feel so completely certain she needed more from him than he was willing to give, yet still find it so difficult to cling to her resolve? "Hi," she managed to push out.

"I, um—" She heard him release a weary sigh. After a long moment, he said, "I'm not very good at this. Bear with me, all right?"

"Not very good at what?"

"Apologizing and asking for another chance."

She rested her shoulder against the wall. The lump in her throat grew larger. "Oh, Ben."

"When you walked out the door tonight, I felt as though I'd just lost everything that's important to me."

Stinging moisture washed over Chloe's eyes. "Are we important to you, Ben?"

He expelled another breath, the sound of it huffing over the line. "More important than I can convey with words." Silence again. Then, "I miss you, the animals miss you. Even the walls miss you. I tried to work. I can't. My mind won't stay focused. When I tried to eat dinner, I damned near choked, trying to swallow. I thought about getting drunk, but that didn't strike me as being a grand idea, so I decided to call you instead."

Chloe couldn't think what to say. She closed her eyes and rested her cheek against the textured paint.

"Can I come over later?" he asked. "There are things I have to tell you. I've thought about it all evening, and you're right. Without trust, we have nothing."

Chloe smiled tremulously. "I don't want you to feel pressured into it."

"Don't even go there. There are things you don't know, Chloe. Serious things. When I've talked to you, maybe you'll understand why it's been so hard for me, why I can't think how to start."

He sounded as if he were coming over to have a wisdom tooth extracted without novocaine. She stared at a spot of dirt on the wall. "What can possibly be that bad?"

"You'll understand when we talk." She heard him sigh. "For now, just know one thing. I do trust you, Chloe." His voice rang with sincerity. "I trust you more than I've ever trusted anyone."

Tears did come to her eyes then. "When will you be here?"

"I've got to make sure my mom's tucked in for the night. I worry about leaving until she's sound asleep. Can we keep the time open? It may be less than an hour, or as long as two, depending."

"Sure," she said softly. "I'll be waiting."

She expected him to end the conversation then. Instead, he said, "Chloe?"

"Yes?"

She could almost feel the warmth of his grin radiating through the phone line. "I feel better already."

She felt as if a thousand pounds of sadness had just been lifted from her chest. "Me, too, Ben. Me, too."

After hanging up the phone, Chloe hugged herself and twirled until she was dizzy. It had been hours since Ben had kissed her, but her lips still tingled as if it had happened only minutes ago. Recalling the radiant warmth of his hands moving over her skin, she yearned to be in his arms again. She honestly didn't care what he might tell her when he finally arrived. What mattered—what really, *really* mattered—was that he cared enough to finally confide in her. She wasn't worried in the least that he'd tell her something appalling. Ben was—well, Ben was just Ben, one of the kindest, gentlest men she'd ever known. She didn't believe—couldn't believe—that anything he revealed could change how she had come to feel about him.

Chloe had just stopped twirling when she heard the back door rattle. Her skin prickled. She stepped cautiously into the kitchen to peer into the laundry room. The worn linoleum felt cold and rough under her bare feet. The light was out in the other room. She wasn't able to see the back door clearly, but she thought she saw the knob turn.

Her heart jumped into her throat. Had she remembered to lock it? Because of Bobby Lee, she'd been pretty paranoid lately about securing the house at night, but, oh, God, what if she'd forgotten?

The door rattled again, and this time, Chloe was certain she saw the knob turn. Her pulse pounded so loudly in her temples that she could scarcely hear. Someone was trying to come in. *Footsteps.* She turned, following the sounds around the side of the house. Then they suddenly stopped, and a scratching sound came at the window over the sink. A sharp rap against the glass followed.

Chloe whirled and grabbed the phone. With wildly shaking hands, she started to dial the sheriff's department. Then she changed her mind and dialed 911 instead. The last thing she needed was for Bobby Lee to show up on her doorstep.

When the dispatcher answered, Chloe said in a loud voice, "I need to report a break-in in progress!" She hoped the intruder would hear her and run. "Someone is trying to enter my house."

"What's your name, ma'am?" the man asked.

Chloe started to reply, but just then, she heard another loud crack against the glass. "Oh, *God*. He's trying to break the window. Chloe Evans. My name's Chloe Evans."

The dispatcher asked for her address. Chloe was so frightened she blanked out for a moment. She thought she heard running footsteps, but her heart was pounding so hard, she couldn't be sure.

"Please, Ms. Evans, just stay calm. I'll remain on the phone with you until an officer arrives. Where are you located?"

"Ponderosa Lane." She listened again but heard nothing. Whoever had been at the window had apparently left. She wanted to believe the would-be burglar had heard her calling the police and run. Only what if he hadn't? "I'm in the Whispering Pines subdivision out by Shoshone Reservoir." She hurriedly recited the address. "How long will it take to get a car clear out here?"

"I'm dispatching the call right now."

Chloe thought she heard voices out in the front yard. She turned, straining to hear. "There's two of them," she told the dispatcher. "I think I hear them talking."

"Help will be on the way shortly. Where are you in the house, Ms. Evans?"

"On the kitchen phone. I'm only a few feet from the window."

"Do you have another phone?"

"Yes, in my bedroom."

"Can you lock that door?"

"Yes."

"Leave this phone off the hook and go to the bedroom. Lock the door, and then get on the other line. I'll wait until you pick up."

Just then another loud bang rattled the front window in the dining nook. Chloe dropped the phone, raced to her bedroom, and unplugged the telephone from the wall. She dashed back out into the hall, barged into Jeremy's room, and slammed the door with a loud *thwack*.

"Oh, God, oh, God." After turning the lock, she grabbed the toy box, dragged it over the worn carpet, and shoved it hard against the portal. Only then did she retrieve the phone from where she'd dropped it on the floor.

"Damn it, damn it," she whispered shakily as she stabbed the cord connection at the phone jack. "Go in, damn you, go in."

Finally she reestablished the connection. "Hello? Are you there?"

"I'm here. Are you in the bedroom with the door locked?"

"Y-yes." Chloe was shuddering so violently that she could barely hold the phone. "I'm frightened."

"Of course. Help will be there soon. A car is on the way as we speak."

"I live a long way from town."

"We have an officer in the neighborhood. Stay calm, Ms. Evans. Even if the burglar gains entry, he'll have to break down the bedroom door to reach you."

Chloe huddled on the floor beside Jeremy's bed. Rowdy stirred and crawled across the mattress to poke his cold nose in her ear. She almost jumped out of her skin.

"The officer just radioed back. He's in front of your house, and he's checking your yard with a spotlight. Do you see the light?"

Chloe saw something flash through Jeremy's drawn curtains. "Yes. Yes, I see it."

"He'll check outside first and try all your doors to make sure the house is secure. When he has established that no one has gained entry, he'll knock at your front door. It will be safe then for you to leave the bedroom. If he doesn't knock, it means he's found a door or window that's been forced open. In that event, remain in the bedroom until he gives you an all clear."

"I'm in a nightshirt. I'm in my son's room. I have nothing in here to put on."

The dispatcher spoke to someone else. When he came back, he said, "Do you have a bedspread or something to wrap up in?"

"Oh. Yes. I, um, yes."

"Do that. He'll be knocking in a moment. That'll be your all clear. He'll want to ask you some questions, but I'm sure he'll give you a moment to get dressed first."

Chloe nodded. She was about to say something more when she heard someone knock at the front of the house. Then the doorbell pealed. "He's at the door. I hear him. Thank you so much."

"You're more than welcome. That's what I'm here for."

Chloe hung up, wrapped Jeremy's Winnie-the-Pooh bedspread around her waist, and shoved the toy box out of the way to enter the hall. She eased the door closed behind her. Why she bothered, she didn't know. If her son could sleep through the racket she'd just made, she doubted the sound of voices in the living room would wake him.

She hurried through the house, threw on the porch light, and then fought with the dead bolt and chain guard to get the front door open. As it swung wide, she just stood there, frozen in disbelief.

Bobby Lee Schuck stood on her porch.

Bobby Lee's smile was like oil sliding over glass. "Good evening, Ms. Evans. I understand you've had some trouble here?"

Chloe locked her knees. The door was open, the deputy stood two feet from her, and she wasn't wearing any underwear. "Bobby Lee, you're—what are you doing here?" Her brain clicked, lagged, and lost the connection. She struggled to hold on to a thought. Finally, she blurted, "I called the state police, not the sheriff's department."

"I monitor the police channel. I was in the area, so I took the call."

Chloe couldn't feel anything from the waist down. She'd been neatly maneuvered. It had been Bobby Lee who had rattled her doorknob, Bobby Lee who had rapped something against her window. She knew it as surely as she breathed.

Without invitation, he stepped inside. "I need to ask you a few questions, Ms. Evans. Would you like me to wait while you go to the bedroom and dress?"

Chloe was afraid he might follow her to Jeremy's room. How long would it take for a tall, well-muscled man to kick in a door and move a toy chest? She could try to phone for help, but chances were that Bobby Lee would anticipate that and prevent her from dialing out. No matter what, she had to keep her son safe, and that meant keeping this man as far away from him as possible.

She clutched the bedspread so it wouldn't accidentally slip. "No, no. I've got the blanket. This will take only a couple of minutes, right?"

He pulled out a pad, plucked a pen from his pocket. "At what time did the attempted burglary occur, ma'am?"

He was speaking to her as if they were complete strangers. This was a wicked game, and he was playing a role, silently laughing as he said his lines. Her blood ran icy. He'd staged a break-in, knowing she would panic and call the police. He'd wanted her to let him inside the house, whether to simply frighten her, or for other, more nefarious reasons, she didn't know.

Chloe couldn't think what to do except play out the scene, doing her best not to enrage him in the process. All her feminine instincts told her that this man was dangerous, extremely dangerous. "It was ten after eleven," she replied. "I'd just looked at the clock shortly before I heard someone try the back door."

She wished Ben were already on his way over. An hour, maybe two. *Oh, God.* She needed him right now.

Bobby Lee jotted down the time she'd given him. "I checked for footprints outside. You say you heard noises at the back door and one of the windows. Which window was it?"

She pointed. "That one, above the sink. Then, a bit later, at the front window in the dining area."

"Hmm. I didn't see any footprints out back. That isn't always significant, though. We've had no rain for a while. The earth may be packed down pretty hard."

"I know what I heard. Someone tried to break in."

Trying not to be obvious, Chloe inched toward the dividing wall between the living room and kitchen, where the wall phone was located. Even though she knew he would be on her before she could dial, she felt safer.

"To your knowledge, is there anyone who might want to frighten you?"

She stared incredulously into his blue eyes. He was mad, she thought. It was the only explanation. A normal adult male didn't do things like this.

"No," she forced out.

"Are you aware of anyone who might want to harm you?"

"No," she said faintly, wanting him to end this pointless charade.

"Did you happen to look out either window and see anyone?"

"No. I was afraid to. I've always heard that's unwise."

He nodded. "If the burglar is a man, it tells him you're probably home alone." He clipped his notebook over his belt. "I know you've been badly frightened, but chances are it was only teenagers. Over summer vacation, they get bored and look for trouble. As we move toward August, they get more creative. We always have a rash of incidents the last month or so of summer."

Teenagers? Chloe didn't believe it for a minute.

"Unfortunately, it's difficult to collar youngsters. They usually live in the neighborhood, and they strike and run, jumping fences and crossing yards to get back home. Most of the time, they're long gone before an officer arrives on the scene." He smiled again, his eyes gleaming at her. "Just in case it wasn't teenagers, however, you'll want to be extra cautious. Make sure all your doors and windows are secured before you retire tonight and that you have a phone near at hand. As an added precaution, I'll call the department and have someone patrol the neighborhood every hour or so."

"That will greatly reassure me," Chloe said, barely able to keep the outrage from her voice. "Good night, Deputy Schuck."

"Good night." He turned and moved to the door. After opening it, he glanced back over his shoulder. "If you have any more trouble, please, don't hesitate to call. To that end, you really should hang up that phone. If you should forget and go to bed with it still off the hook, your extensions won't work."

After he stepped outside and closed the door, Chloe just stood there for a moment, trembling so violently she couldn't trust her legs. She braced a hand on the wall to steady herself. She was so glad he had left. *So* glad. Her gaze caught on the dangling phone. She grabbed the cord with a shaking hand and dropped the receiver back in its cradle. Then, locking her knees so her legs wouldn't buckle, she started toward the door.

She'd taken only a step when it swung open again. Bobby Lee smiled as he came back inside. He pushed the portal closed behind him and drove the dead bolt home. Chloe's whole body went rigid.

"Thank you. Conversation over, all nice and tidy." He inclined his head at the telephone. "I asked the dispatcher to stay on the line and listen to our exchange."

Knotting her hand over the ends of the bedspread, she asked, "What do you want, Bobby Lee?"

"Just to revisit an issue. You look scared half to death. There's really no need to be. I'm here. No one else can bother you now. Only me."

Chloe grabbed for the phone.

"Please, don't," he said. "You can't possibly dial the number and make a connection before I stop you. All you'll do is piss me off."

Chloe froze with her hand clenched over the receiver. "Get out! I mean it, Bobby Lee. Get out of my house right now."

"Shh. You don't want to wake your little boy. He might come out to see what's wrong. Better to leave your child out of this, don't you think?"

Quaking with fright, Chloe drew her hand from the telephone. "Just leave, Bobby Lee. You can't possibly believe you can get away with this. I'll report you and file charges. Your career in law enforcement will be destroyed."

"Nah." He took another step toward her, his body

relaxed, his smile cajoling. "I took precautions. You can file charges all you want, and no one's going to believe you." He gestured at the telephone. "When I asked the dispatcher to stay on the line, I explained how we dated once—and how bent out of shape you were when I didn't want to see you again. Women can be so vindictive when they get their noses out of joint. A law officer is an easy target for false accusations. We can't be too careful."

Chloe could only stare at him.

"The dispatcher heard me tell you good night and leave the house. All by the book, no hint of a problem. If you start making wild accusations now, no one's going to buy it." He winked at her. "If you're thinking of fighting me, please reconsider. You don't want your little boy to get hurt, do you, Chloe?"

Jeremy. Oh, dear God. Chloe was too frightened now to speak. She shook her head.

"There's my girl." He took another step closer. "My sensible Chloe."

He stopped just far enough away that she couldn't kick him or knee him in the groin. "So," he said, rubbing his hands together. "Let's start this little party off right, shall we? Drop the bedspread and take off the shirt. I've been dying to get a look at that body. You've got gorgeous tits. Has anyone told you that?"

Chloe's head went dizzy. For a horrible moment, she thought she might faint. "I won't do this," she said weakly.

"Sure you will. Ever the good little mother. You're going to do this, sweet cheeks. If you don't, I'll bash your son's brains in. Then I'll have you the way I'd really like to. We all have our sexual fantasies, don't we? My secret fantasy has always been to take a woman—no holds barred, no limits, doing anything I want. Afterwards, I'll strangle you. I'll be extremely careful to leave no DNA evidence to incriminate me, of course.

"Tomorrow when I hear the news, I'll go white and shake. 'I was there just a few minutes before it happened,' I'll say. 'Dear God, the intruder must have been lurking outside.'" He shrugged. "Easy. So very easy, Chloe. I have a spotless record. I've been a deputy for almost twenty years. Who's going to suspect me? You've been seeing Ben Longtree, who's already killed once. He'll be the prime suspect. If it comes down to that, I'll plant evidence to make sure they nail him. Nice and tidy, no trouble for me."

He really is insane, she thought stupidly. She could try to scratch him, she thought—if he gave her a chance. He was trained to overpower people effortlessly. She'd seen him squeeze a drunk's neck once, paralyzing the man by merely pressing on a nerve.

"Your choice," he went on softly. "Cooperation and plenty of foreplay, followed by civilized sex. We can have a nice evening between two consenting adults, with you going out of your way to please me. Or we can go the other route—no cooperation and plenty of foreplay, followed by extremely uncivilized sex. Either way, I'm going to have you. Call it a score to settle— or unfinished business. I've wanted you ever since we first met. I always get what I want."

"Do you?" She dampened her lips, her stomach rolling with fear. "Always?"

"Always, one way or another. And I will get away with it, Chloe. I'm a cop. I know all the little tricks, and I've covered myself."

For all of two heartbeats, Chloe sent up silent prayers that Ben would show up. But then cold reality settled in. He wouldn't come until his mother was asleep, and there was no telling how long that might take. She was on her own.

"I much prefer the civilized version," she managed to say. Then she forced a smile. "It's sort of—exciting, actually. I've never known a man who refused to take no for an answer."

It wasn't what he expected her to say. She saw the surprise in his expression—and an awful, sick delight.

"It's going on midnight. Are you off duty now? I just happen to have some champagne. If we're going to do this, we may as well go the whole nine yards and have fun." Dropping the bedspread was the hardest thing Chloe had ever done in her life, but she unclenched her hand and let it slip to the floor. With a swing of her hips, she went to the kitchen, showing off her legs to best advantage en route. As she opened the refrigerator, she made sure to bend over just far enough to tantalize him. "You amaze me, Bobby Lee. I figured with you being a cop—well, you know—that the missionary position with a few unimaginative variations would be your entire repertoire."

From the corner of her eye, she saw that he'd followed her into the room—and that he was ogling the backs of her thighs.

"Most men today are so—" She frowned, then shrugged and smiled. "I don't know. *Tame,* I suppose is the word. I'd heard so many stories about Ben Longtree being dangerous that I hoped he might be different. He turned out to be the biggest dud of all."

She pulled out the unopened bottle of champagne that Ben had left at her house. "Can you get the glasses? Top shelf, to your right."

He hesitated. Then, after glancing around, undoubtedly to check the nearby surfaces for anything she might use as a weapon, he opened the cupboard door, grabbed two goblets, and set them on the counter.

When he faced her again, he said, "Lose the shirt."

Chloe assumed what she hoped was a sultry smile.

"But it'll be so much better with some anticipation."
She inched up the hem of the T-shirt, stopping just
short of anything really interesting. "After all your
work and planning to make this happen, you should
enjoy it."

He smoothed a hand over his fly, and she knew she
had him. "Do that again, only higher," he said softly.

"No rush." She managed another smile. "I've surprised you, haven't I? You had me pegged as the
straight and narrow type. Shame, shame, Bobby Lee.
You never know what a woman's capable of until you
really get to know her." *Or have her cornered.* "Take
me, for instance." She dug at the foil with a fingernail
and walked toward him, keeping her eyes fixed on his.
"You've told me your fantasy. Can I tell you mine?"

His eyes darkened. "Sure," he said gruffly.

"I've always—" She pushed out a laugh. "I can't.
It's too embarrassing."

"Don't be embarrassed. Fantasies are perfectly
normal."

His wasn't. Chloe scratched frantically at the stupid
foil. The edge clung to the glass as if it had been glued
down. "I, um—well. Oh, no, I really can't. It's just
too, *too* wild."

"Tell me."

She changed the angle of her attack on the foil and
finally managed to tear it a bit. *A fantasy.* Please, God,
she needed a ready-made fantasy—something imagi-
native and erotic enough to excite him. She glimpsed
the table behind him. "I've always fantasized about—"
What? Her brain went blank. "Well, you know, about
being taken. And not just anywhere. I imagine it happening on a table. No rules, no stops, just being devoured by a man. A sexy smorgasbord, of sorts, and
I'm the main course."

His Adam's apple bobbed. "That sounds promising."

She worked to catch the tuft of foil between her fingers and finally ripped it away. She dropped the wrapping on the floor. *Close.* She needed to be very close. "Well, there's the catch, you see. You want me to please you tonight, and in my fantasy, I have to be utterly helpless." She laughed and bent her head, pretending to be mortified while she examined the wire doohickey to figure out how it worked. Roger had always opened the champagne. "I could never just—do all the stuff I imagine of my own free will, so I fantasize that he ties me down and gags me. That way I'm completely at his mercy. He just—you know—does whatever he wants, and I can enjoy it with no sense of guilt."

"That can be arranged."

Yeah, I just bet it can. Chloe pressed her thumb against the wire release, then glanced up with what she prayed was a completely incredulous expression on her face. "You'd do that?" *Why wouldn't the wire come free?* "With bonds and everything?"

"Sure." His voice had gone gravelly and thick. "It's my fantasy, too, in a way. I never thought about doing it on a table, but what the hell? It works."

"Oh, Bobby Lee," she said in a breathy voice. "Just thinking about it turns me on. I can't believe you'll really do it for me. What'll you tie me up with? I don't have any rope."

"Belts will work. You've got several. I've seen you wear them at work."

She pushed frantically on the wire. *Please, God.* "Belts?"

"I can loop them around your wrists and ankles, then knot the ends around the legs of the table. You'll be snubbed down so tight all you'll be able to move is your head."

Chloe's stomach lurched, but she managed to keep smiling. She aimed the neck of the bottle at his face and pushed on the wire with all her might. Nothing happened. Sweat trickled down her spine. Ben had made this look so easy. "When I'm tied up, what's the first thing you'll do?" She stepped a little closer. "Tell me," she whispered. "I want details."

"I'll do anything I want," he said throatily. "That's your fantasy, isn't it?"

"Oh, *yes.*"

"And I'll do it as long as I want. You'll be spread-eagle and naked. I'll gag you with a kitchen towel so you can't scream, and I'll do absolutely anything I want. Everything you ever imagined, and a lot more."

He began telling her things he'd always wanted to do, getting more graphic as he went along. Terror built within Chloe, so chilling and thought-obliterating that her whole body started to quiver. She strained so hard to move the damned wire that she shuddered.

"Here, let me do that."

"No, no, almost got it. Don't stop. Tell me more. I'm getting so"—she shoved with everything she had—"aroused. I'll have to be aroused to go through with it. Until now, it's only been a fantasy, never real. I'm afraid I'll chicken out." She flicked him a nervous look she didn't have to fake. "What if you—you know, do things I don't like? I won't be able to make you stop."

He reached out to touch her hair. She felt the wire shift under her thumb.

"You're going to love it," he whispered. "I'll show you a repertoire to blow your socks off, babe. It'll be so good. The best you've ever had."

She aimed the bottle at his face and fired. The cork

shot from the opening like a bullet and hit him in dead center in the forehead. For a horrible instant, he just gaped at her. Then he grunted as he grabbed for his face.

Chloe skittered out of his way, grasped the neck of the bottle in both hands, swung it high, and brought it crashing down on his head. Champagne spewed all over her. He dropped to his knees. She danced to one side and hit him again, groaning with the force she put into her swing. The bottle connected with the crown of his head, making a loud crack. She expected it to knock him out, but he didn't go down.

Before she could hit him a third time, he threw up a hand to ward off the blow. "Enough! Enough. Christ Jesus, I can't see!"

"Get out!" she cried. "*Now!* Or I swear to God, I'll break this over your head and slit your throat. *Out!*"

He crab-walked toward the door. When it wouldn't open, he moaned, dropped to his knees, and cradled his head in his hands. "It's locked."

"Unlock it!"

"I can't see. You hit me between the eyes."

Chloe wasn't about to fall for that trick. "You're so damned good at groping, grope to find the lock. And you'd better be fast about it. I'd just as soon kill you as look at you!"

"I wouldn't have hurt you," he whined. "I'm armed, for God's sake. If I really meant you harm, I'd just shoot you."

No, Chloe thought. The bullet could be traced back to his gun. "Get out," she said, shaking so hard her voice quivered. "Get *out!*"

She tossed down the bottle and grabbed a kitchen chair. He held up a hand again, which told her he could see just fine. "I'm going." He pulled himself to his feet, gave his head a hard shake. "Jesus, lady. I thought you might go for a knife, but a champagne cork?" He fumbled with the dead bolt. "This isn't finished." He swung the door wide. "I'll be back, and next time, your ass is mine. You got it?" He gave her a burning look and staggered outside. Chloe waited until she heard him stumble down the rickety steps. Then she tossed aside the chair and raced across the room. Her heart pounding with fear, she grabbed the door, slammed it shut, and threw her weight against it. Still frantic, she groped for the dead bolt and chain. When she'd finally secured the locks against him, she glanced wildly around. The windows were all closed and locked. She'd been so paranoid since that night when Bobby Lee had phoned while Ben was visiting that she'd been afraid to open them at night, even to let in a breeze. She sobbed and slid down the wood like a pat of butter off a hot biscuit.

She wanted to huddle there on the floor and shake. Her legs and arms were jerking spasmodically, like a puppet's on strings, and she couldn't control the movements. *Think.* He was out there, just on the other side of the door. She'd done him no permanent injury. He'd recover in a moment, and when he did, he would be ugly mad.

She sprang to her feet and staggered to the phone. After dialing 911, she cut the connection. Not the cops again. Bobby Lee might intercept the dispatch. *Oh, dear God. He's out there.* Only glass and thin, hollowed panels of wood protected her. And Jeremy. If he got back inside, what might he do to Jeremy? *Ben. He was only a few minutes away. Ben.*

Chloe knew his number. Nearly mindless with panic, she dialed, clung to the phone, listened to it ring. No answer. "Ben!" she sobbed his name. "Ben."

His voice came on the line. "Hi. You've reached

the Longtree residence. I'm sorry I'm unable to come to the phone right now, but your call's important."

Chloe sank to her knees, holding on to the phone and his voice, because, in her terror, they were all she had.

Chapter Twenty

As Ben left for Chloe's place, he heard the phone ringing. He almost went back to answer it, but then he changed his mind. He rarely received calls this late, and he feared it might be Chloe phoning him to either cancel or postpone their talk. *No way.* He had to get this over with tonight. If he waited and gave himself time to think about it, he might lose his courage.

Juggling the plastic bag that held ice and a bottle of champagne, Ben fumbled in his pocket for his keys. As he withdrew the ring, he lost his grip on it. The metal hit the cement and bounced away into the darkness. *Damn!* He tossed the champagne onto the truck seat and executed a search, bent forward at the waist to see through the shadows. He finally found the keys lying behind the front left tire.

A few minutes later, when he finally pulled in to Chloe's driveway, he sat for a moment, trying to calm down. He didn't want to blow this. When his heartbeat had slowed to a fairly normal rhythm, he grabbed the champagne, stepped from the truck into the chill night air, and slammed the door. Here went nothing.

As he strode across Chloe's lawn to the lighted front

porch, he rehearsed his lines. *I promise not to break a window this time. How's a hole in the ceiling strike you?* He'd be funny, casual. Then he'd slowly lead up to what he had to say. He'd tell her about his writing first. Given her love of Caldwell's books, that would be a pretty big shock, in and of itself. When she'd digested that, he'd somehow find the courage to tell her the rest. No more secrets. He was going to make a clean breast of it. No matter how it turned out, at least he'd know that he'd done everything he could to save the relationship. If it was all too much for her and she chose to end things between them, he'd just have to live with it.

He stepped up onto the porch, took a deep breath, and doubled his fist to knock. The lights were on. She was still up. That was good. Not that he would have let darkness stop him. He had to see her. He kept gulping for breath like a man slowly suffocating on low-oxygen air—grabbing, hauling it in, and still feeling on the edge of frantic need.

He rapped his knuckles against the flimsy door, thinking as he did that he could give her solid oak. Up on his ridge, ensconced in his home like a queen, with wolves and cougars as her loyal subjects, she could have anything his money could buy. All she had to do was accept the unbelievable—the unnatural— the unthinkable.

He heard no footsteps approaching the door from the other side. He knocked again. Waited. Where the hell was she? Peering at his watch, he determined that he was arriving well within the time he'd predicted, only forty minutes since they'd spoken on the phone. She should be expecting him. He was about to knock a little harder when he heard her voice, faint and tremulous.

"Who is it?"

He flattened his hand against the door. "It's me, Ben."

"Ben?"

He heard rustling sounds. Metal clacked. Scrabbling noises ensued. He pressed closer, willing the door to open.

"Say something." Her voice sounded taut and quivery. "Anything so I know for sure it's you."

What the hell? "Of course, it's me. Chloe, are you all right?"

"What's the skunk's name?" she asked shrilly.

"Winston. What the—?"

"And the owl?"

"Einstein. What's with the twenty questions?"

The door nudged open. He had his gaze fixed where he expected her face to be. No Chloe. Movement made him look down. She was kneeling—no, slumped—on the floor, her white face visible in the narrow opening. Her eyes were huge splashes of brown rimmed with red.

"Sweet Christ, what's wrong?" Ben dropped the champagne. It hit the porch with a loud whack. He pushed the door open, bodily moving her in the process, then fell to one knee on the threshold. Seizing her by the shoulders, he leaned down to better see her face. "Chloe? What in God's name—?"

She let out a cry—half whimper, half moan—and threw her arms around his neck. Her whole body jerked with sobs. Awful, horrible sobs. He gathered her against him, vaguely registering that there was nothing under the damp, oversize T-shirt but woman, sweet, warm, trembling woman. A citrus scent drifted to his nostrils.

"Sweetheart." He'd thought the endearment a hundred times, but never uttered it. Somehow it felt absolutely right to say it now as he tightened his arms around her. "What's wrong? Are you sick? Is it Jeremy? Talk to me."

She made a gulping "huh-huh-huh" sound, her nails scoring the back of his neck. "B-Ben? H-he c-came. The p-police. I c-ca-called the police, and h-he came."

He stopped trying to make sense of it and hauled her more tightly against him. "It's okay, sweetheart. It's okay." He threw a worried glance into the house. A kitchen chair lay on its side in the living room. *Jeremy.* Snaking a hand under her butt, he braced his shoulder against the door frame to get leverage and shoved himself erect with her sagging in his arms. He got one foot over the threshold, braced, and bent at the knees to lift her off her feet. He kicked the door shut behind him. "Chloe, where's your son?"

She said something, but the garbled utterance made no sense. Ben knocked a magazine off the sofa and laid her on the cushions. He had to peel her off of him.

"Let me go check on Jeremy. Okay? I'll be right back."

He strode through the house, his heart cracking against his ribs like the fist of a giant. When he opened the child's bedroom door, his legs went weak. Jeremy lay curled up in bed, Rowdy sleeping beside him. Both boy and dog were perfectly fine. Ben was surprised that all the racket in the living room hadn't awakened Rowdy. He decided puppies, like little boys, played so hard that they could sleep through almost anything.

Ben slumped against the door frame. He'd been afraid—so afraid that something had happened to the child. It wasn't like Chloe to fall apart like this.

As he retraced his steps across the living room, he saw that she was shaking as though with chills, her bare legs drawn to her chest, her arms locked around her knees. He grabbed up a bedspread lying on the floor and shook it over her as he knelt on one knee beside the sofa. *Shock?* Fear for her filled him. He had no idea what had happened, only that it had been something really bad.

"Chloe?"

She opened her eyes. In the light from the lamp on the end table, he could see tear tracks glistening on her cheeks. He smoothed her curly hair back from her face, every line of which had been engraved on his heart. After giving her a quick once-over, he could detect no physical injuries, but when he looked into her eyes, they told a different story.

"What happened? Tell me what happened." Ben cupped his hand to her cheek, trailing his thumb over the wet streaks. He loved her. Just the thought of someone frightening her or harming her made him shake with rage. "Who did this to you? Who did this?"

"Bobby Lee," she whispered. "He tried to break in. A trick. When I called the police, he took the c-call. Oh, God, Ben. It was so awful."

He made her repeat the story, interrupting to ask questions. When he'd finally dragged all of it out of her, he said, "You shot him with a cork?"

"It worked on the window."

Ben might have laughed, but her eyes—oh, God, her eyes. She'd just come through a nightmare. If not for the champagne cork, the bastard might have raped her.

"That miserable son of a bitch. I'll kill him."

"No! Just—" She gulped, shivered, and clutched his arm. "Don't leave us. Please, don't leave us. I'm afraid of him. He said he'll be back."

"We'll see about that." Ben smoothed her wildly tangled hair and kissed her forehead. "I won't leave you, Chloe. Count on that. I won't leave you. But I am going to call the police."

"No! No!" She grabbed his shirt. "He'll hear the dispatch."

She rushed on to tell him about all the visits Bobby Lee had made to the Christmas Village, and how he'd parked outside to stare at her as she walked to and from her car. "He's been stalking me. He thinks he's above the law—that he can do anything, and no one can touch him."

"Why the hell didn't you tell me?"

"Because." Her face crumpled. "You put up such a wall between us. I didn't feel right, dumping all my problems on you when you refused to share anything with me."

Dump on him? Ben wanted to give her a good shake, but the urge no sooner struck than a heartfelt regret took its place. This was his fault, entirely his. She was right; he had erected a wall between them. When she'd needed him as a friend, he hadn't been there for her.

"Ah, sweetheart." Ben gathered her into his arms and just held her for a while. "I'm so sorry. No more secrets. Okay? I swear, I'll tell you everything."

She clung to his neck with quivering arms. *Definitely in shock,* he decided. Until she calmed down enough to start thinking straight again, he needed to take control. The first order of business was to call the authorities, just in case the bastard decided to come back. Ben didn't kid himself. Man to man, with even odds, he'd have no problem holding his own with Bobby Lee, but the deputy wouldn't hesitate to fight dirty, using any weapon at his disposal to win.

When he stood, Chloe fixed him with a wildly frightened look. "What are you going to do?"

"I'm going to report this."

"But—"

"Just trust me. All right? I don't want him coming back here any more than you do. When I confront the son of a bitch, I don't want you or Jeremy anywhere around."

Ben went to the kitchen, located the phone book, and called Frank Bower at home. The deputy answered on the second ring, sounding wide-awake, as only a man accustomed to middle-of-the-night phone calls could.

"Frank, this is Ben Longtree. I'm sorry for waking you up, but I've got some trouble on my hands. I need your help." As briefly as possible, Ben recounted Chloe's story. "She's terrified to call the police again, and I can't blame her. He's armed. If he comes back, I may not be able to hold him off."

"I'll be right there," Frank said.

The next two hours passed in an awful blur for Chloe. Ben brought her some panties and jeans, then helped her pull them on before Frank Bower arrived. Then he dampened a cloth and dabbed at her face and neck, his touch so gentle and soothing that Chloe wanted to huddle against him.

"Better?" he asked softly.

"Mm, much." It was true. She did feel better, and not because of the coolness of the cloth. She looked into his eyes, and she knew she was safe, that he'd die before he let anything happen to her or her son. "Thank you, Ben. I'm so glad you decided to come over tonight. So glad. I didn't know what to do."

He ran a fingertip down the bridge of her nose. "Yeah, well, you're still not real steady on your feet. Just let me handle it. Okay?"

Her eyes filled with fresh tears, and her mouth twisted. "I'm sorry I'm such a mess. I don't know why

I'm shaking like this. He didn't touch me. It was just—
I don't know—the threat of it, I guess, and the horrible things he said. He told me he'd bash Jeremy's brains in, Ben. I was so scared. I've never in all my life been that scared, not even when Roger flew into one of his rages."

Ben could well imagine the things Bobby Lee had said. Tightening his arms around her, he closed his eyes, thanking God that she'd kept her head and thought of a way to fight back. As weapons went, a champagne cork wasn't exactly fail proof, but it had worked, and he was proud of her.

He left her to make some coffee. Then he gently guided her to the kitchen table, put a mug into her trembling hands, and sat next to her, rubbing her tense shoulders. When Frank arrived, Ben remained at her side, holding her hand and prompting her when she grew confused while answering the deputy's questions.

When Frank had heard the entire story, beginning with Bobby Lee's breaking her Japanese lantern and ending with his attempted attack on her earlier that night, he sat back in his chair, glanced at Ben, and frowned with concern.

"Chloe," he said softly, "when you and Bobby Lee went out to dinner, are you positive the evening went exactly as you've told me?"

Pale and still shaking, she took a moment to reply. "Yes, Frank. Why do you ask?"

Frank scratched his temple. "Bobby Lee tells a different story."

Ben broke in to say, "Bobby Lee has a story? What version has he been telling?"

Looking uncomfortable, Frank resettled his Stetson on his head. "Well, he says—" He glanced apologetically at Chloe. "Not saying it's so or anything, but he claims he wanted to head home at eight, and it was you who insisted on a few dances in the lounge. Afterwards, he says you asked him to drive down to the river. Once there, you came on to him. He turned you down. You grew furious and ran off into the woods. He tried to coax you back to the vehicle, but you refused, saying you'd rather walk."

"That isn't how it happened," Chloe whispered shakily. Her nails dug into Ben's palm, giving him reason to fear that she'd had all she could take for one evening. "That isn't how it went at all." Her voice rose to a shrill, reed-whistle pitch on the last word. "He's lying."

"That's the version he's told. The next day when he came to work, you'd already cleaned out your desk. You spoke briefly with the sheriff and made some accusations, but you didn't press any charges. If he really tried to force himself on you, why didn't you follow through, Chloe?"

"When I hit him on the nose, he let me go. He'd been drinking." Chloe lifted her hands in helpless perplexity. "What should I have done? I didn't know if he'd ever done such a thing before. I thought maybe it was just the alcohol. You know? I didn't want to ruin his reputation and possibly his whole life over one stupid mistake." She sent Ben a miserable look that made him wish he could make all of this go away. "There was also his badge to consider. I'm new to town. Who would have believed me? Not even Sheriff Lang took my story seriously."

Ben wished now that he had more forcefully insisted on accompanying her to the department that day. Whether the sheriff held him in high regard or not, at least Ben could have corroborated Chloe's story to some extent, which might have made Lang listen up.

"If you didn't think Lang would believe you," Frank

asked, "then why did you bother to tell him about it at all?"

"I couldn't be positive it was an isolated incident," Chloe replied faintly. "I was afraid Bobby Lee might do the same thing again with one of my successors, and I felt it was my responsibility to at least tell the sheriff what had happened, whether he chose to believe me or not. That way, if it occurred again, he'd be more inclined to believe the next woman."

The deputy nodded and then sighed wearily. "I can understand why you hesitated to press charges, and to be absolutely honest, after being in this line of work for so many years, I wish more people would think twice. Unfortunately, that isn't the case. It's also a documented fact that an appalling percentage of women play the rape card just to get even over a real or imagined slight." Frank passed a hand over his eyes. "In most instances, those women bring up past incidents that they failed to report. Unfortunately for you, that's a red flag to an investigating officer."

Chloe's hand felt icy. Ben rubbed his thumb over the backs of her slender fingers, lending her what little warmth he could. "Is it a red flag to you, Frank?" he demanded, not attempting to keep the anger from his voice.

Frank squirmed on his chair. "Let's not personalize this, Ben."

"I'm sorry, but it's starting to feel pretty damned personal. It sounds to me as if you're implying that Chloe may be playing some vicious little game, trying to get even with Bobby Lee. That's not only preposterous, but it's damned insulting."

"I'm not implying any such thing."

Ben tightened his hold on Chloe's hand. "Then you'd better clarify your meaning, Deputy. Going on what you just said, I'm ready to call an attorney and peel the paint off the walls down at that damned sheriff's department. There are laws in this country to protect women, especially in the workplace. How would Sheriff Lang like to have a huge sexual harassment and attempted rape lawsuit filed against him? Correct me if I'm wrong, but he is an elected official, isn't he? Win or lose, if we make enough noise, we could seriously hurt him at the polls."

Frank puffed air into his cheeks. "I don't run the show, Ben. I don't blame you for being angry, but let's keep it in its proper perspective."

"You're basically saying that without any proof to back up her story about tonight, it's unlikely that Chloe can do anything. Isn't that right?"

"I'm saying that her failure to press charges the first time could backfire on her now. That's all. It casts a suspicious light on her whole story." Frank flashed Chloe another hangdog look. "It's not a matter of what I think. I know Chloe personally. I don't believe for a second that she would concoct a crazy story just to get a man in trouble. I'm just laying out the facts and telling you how others may see things."

Ben forced himself to sit back in his chair. He couldn't recall the last time he'd been so pissed. "I picked Chloe up on the highway that night, Frank. I saw the state she was in. Her blouse was ripped half off her. She was smeared with blood. And, in my opinion, she was in shock."

"Where did the blood come from?"

"She whacked the bastard on the nose to get away from him," Ben explained. "It must have given him a nosebleed."

"Do you still have the articles of clothing?" Frank asked Chloe.

"No, I threw them away. I couldn't fix the blouse

or get the stains out of the undergarment, and I couldn't bring myself to wear either of them again."

Frank pursed his lips and jotted more notes. "I believe you, Chloe. Please don't misunderstand. But the sheriff has to abide by the law, look at the situation and allegations, and decide, to the best of his ability, if Bobby Lee actually did anything wrong. As it stands, the deputy didn't finish what he came here to do, so we don't really have much on him. There are no marks on you to corroborate your story about this evening, nothing to prove he reentered the house after he left the first time."

"Are you saying that nothing can be done because I managed to stop him from raping me?" Chloe sent Ben an incredulous look.

"I understand your frustration," Frank commiserated, "but we have to have proof before we can make an arrest. And even if we can come up with some proof, we're still talking about an almost rape, not an actual one."

He made it sound so trivial. An almost rape. By the sudden tightness of Chloe's grip, Ben knew the words had struck home with her, and that they hurt.

"He threatened to kill my son," she whispered. "He said he'd bash his brains in if I didn't cooperate. And you're telling me that he may be back on patrol tomorrow as if nothing happened?"

"I'll do everything I can to see that doesn't occur. If what you've just told me is true, he shouldn't be wearing a badge."

"If?" Ben sat forward in his chair again.

"I don't make the rules, Ben. I just follow them. That being the case, I can't make any promises." Frank looked tired. "When Deputy Schuck told Chloe that he'd covered his ass, he wasn't blowing smoke. The state dispatcher heard the exchange." He swung his hand. "He didn't force a door or window to enter the house. The only footprints outside are undoubtedly his, and he had a reason to be out there, which makes it appear that she fabricated the attempted burglary. There's also the dinner-date incident to corroborate his story. He's laid the stepping stones very carefully."

"If he weren't a deputy, what follow-up would be done on a call like this?" Ben asked evenly.

Frank shifted on the chair and flexed his shoulders. "If you're implying that Bobby Lee may get preferential treatment, I won't argue. He's been a deputy in this county for going on twenty years, and he has a spotless record. I'll also remind you that if he weren't a deputy, he never could have pulled this off."

"Point taken." Ben gave Chloe's hand a reassuring squeeze. "It just seems to me a piss-poor way to do things, Frank. What if he follows through on his threat and comes back? Chloe will be hung out to dry."

Frank nodded. "Unless I can come up with more than I've got right now, you're probably right. I'll do my best. That's all I can say."

Ben stood to see Frank to the door. "However it turns out, I appreciate your coming over. I know I dragged you out of bed."

"Not a problem," Frank assured him. "Trust me. Good cops don't like bad cops. If I had my druthers, Schuck would be suspended until further investigation." He tipped his hat to Chloe. "Let's hope that champagne cork blacked both his eyes and he's got goose eggs on his head. If so, maybe, just maybe, I can nail him."

After Frank left, Chloe just sat and stared at the surface of the table. Ben rubbed a hand up and down her spine. She felt violated. It made no sense, because Bobby Lee had barely touched her, but he'd raped her with words. The images that he'd painted in her mind would remain there for a very long while.

"Sweetheart, you sit tight, okay? I'm going to gather up your things in pillowcases."

Chloe blinked. "What?"

"I'm not leaving you and Jeremy here. You're coming to the ridge."

"I can't do that. I have a job and—"

"I'll drive you back and forth to work." He caught her chin in his hand. "I'm not leaving you alone. Understood? You're coming with me."

Once at the ridge, Chloe felt as if all the starch went out of her spine. It was all she could do to walk to the door. Diablo greeted them in the entryway. He was so happy to see Chloe that he actually wagged his tail. While Ben disappeared to put Jeremy to bed, she sank to her knees to hug the wolf.

"Oh, Diablo, I wish you'd been there," she whispered against his ruff. "You would have protected us. I know it."

Diablo snuffled her hair and whined. Recalling the first time she'd ever seen him, she buried her face in his fur and sobbed. She felt so battered. So filthy. She remembered the sick delight in Bobby Lee's eyes and started to shake again. In an attempt to collect herself, she struggled to focus on other things. *Diablo*. And *Ben*. And *Methuselah*. She had been reluctant to come here, but now she was very glad that Ben had insisted. This place had become more of a home to her than where she actually lived.

There was no denying it. Her family was here. All the animals she'd cared for every day and come to love—and the man, with his raven hair and soulful eyes. She belonged here, not in that awful little house down on Ponderosa Lane.

"Chloe?"

She jerked her head up and wiped her wet cheeks. She'd tried so hard to stand on her own two feet. Now, here she was, on her knees in Ben's entryway, sobbing her heart out with her arms around his dog.

"I'm sorry. I don't know what's wrong with me."

"Damn it, don't say you're sorry." He crouched beside her. After studying her face for a moment, he smiled slightly and brushed at her cheek. "Diablo is a generous soul. He'll share his coat with anyone."

Chloe scrubbed a trembling hand over her mouth and sniffed. "He can share it with me any time he wants." Tears sprang to her eyes again, which made her impatient with herself. "Someone opened the floodgates. I'm not usually a sniveler."

"Sweetheart, you're not being a sniveler now. You've had a hell of a night."

"It's just—" She shuddered. "I keep flashing back. You know? I couldn't get the wire thing off the champagne bottle. I pushed and pushed. It was all I had as a weapon, and for what seemed like an eternity, I stood there, shoving on it, listening to him go on about the things he wanted to do. It was—" A knot formed in her throat, and she couldn't say more, so she settled for shaking her head.

Ben sighed and curled a big hand over the back of her neck. "Come here," he urged.

At the back of her mind, Chloe knew it was irrational to so deeply yearn for his touch, but at that moment, what dimly made sense and what was clamoring at the forefront of her mind were in direct opposition, and the clamoring won out. She leaned forward, letting him gather her close. His arms curled around her, strong yet gentle. As always, the instant he touched her, a tingle of warmth moved through her.

"You know what you need?"

"No, what?" she whispered against his shirt.

"A huddle cuddle."

"A what?"

"It's my mom's phrase. When I was a kid and bad things happened, she'd hold me on her lap in the rocker, and we'd just talk. A huddle cuddle."

Before Chloe could anticipate what he meant to do, he scooped her up into his arms as if she weighed no more than a child. "As for what's wrong with you, Chloe, he might have killed you and Jeremy, as well. I think you've held yourself together amazingly well, considering."

She loved his strength—the wonderful dizziness that came over her as he walked with her in his arms to the living room. When he sat on the sofa with her cradled on his lap, she liked that, too. Hugging his neck, she pressed her nose to his throat and took deep breaths like a junkie sniffing glue.

At the back of her mind, she wondered if she was losing it. She'd come very close to being raped, one of the most horrible experiences a woman could endure, and she'd escaped by the skin of her teeth. She should be recoiling from Ben's touch right now and needing her space. Only this was what she wanted, to be with him—heart to heart, flesh to flesh, with his hardness and heat forming a shield of safety all around her. Maybe it was weak of her, but for now, the stores of strength that had seen her through so many difficult times seemed to have drained out of her.

His touch was completely asexual, the kneading motion of his hand on her arm, shoulder, and side searching out all the knotted muscles and melting away the tension. Soon Chloe felt like a puddle of warm gelatin smeared over his broad chest. She closed her eyes.

"You have magic in your hands," she whispered. "Little wonder the animals love you so."

She felt his lips graze her hair. "Yeah," he said huskily. "Magic in my hands. But that's a subject for another day. For tonight, I think we need to concentrate on you and how you're feeling."

Right then, Chloe felt as if she had no bones. She nuzzled her nose against his collar. She'd cared deeply for Roger, and in many ways, she would always love the memory of him. But her feelings for him had never run this deep. Or been so completely consuming.

"I love you, Ben."

He was silent for a moment. Then in a low whisper, he said, "You love your idea of me. You may feel differently when you learn who I really am. There are things I haven't told you, remember. Maybe it'd be better if you keep those feelings on ice for a while until we can talk."

"It won't matter." As Chloe said those words, she knew they were absolutely true. She'd learned some invaluable life lessons tonight. "You can know a great deal about someone, Ben, and discover you really know nothing. And you can think you know nothing, only to realize you actually know everything." She pressed even closer against him. "I know everything about you that I need to know. *Everything*. You're the most wonderful man I've ever known. That's all that counts. When I realized it was you on the other side of the door tonight, I knew it would be okay, that nothing could happen to us because you were there."

His arms tightened around her. "Ah, Chloe."

"It's true. I'm sorry I got so nasty about all the little stuff. I don't know why it seemed so important to me.

Details, only details. If you never tell me what you do for a living, I don't care. It doesn't seem important to me anymore."

He ducked his chin to smile at her. His dark face shone like burnished oak in the dim lamplight. "Thank you. That's one of the nicest things anyone ever said to me, and I know that at this moment, you mean it from the bottom of your heart. But let's not lose sight of the fact that you may feel differently tomorrow."

When she started to speak, he touched a blunt fingertip to her mouth.

"We have to talk. Not tonight, but soon. Even if you don't need to hear it, there are things I need to say." His deep blue eyes went cloudy with tenderness. "It helps knowing that there's a good chance you'll love me anyway, no matter what I tell you. I'll hold that thought close."

"If you're worried about it, just tell me now."

He kissed her eyes closed. "I think you've had enough dumped on you in one night. It'll keep until you get your feet back under you."

Chloe sighed. "He's sick, Ben. He told me tonight that he likes to inflict pain during sex."

He ran a hand slowly up her arm. "There's a lot of sickness in our world, Chloe. We see it every day on the news. It just strikes a lot closer to home when it's someone you actually know."

"I can't get the things he said out of my head. I was afraid—so afraid—that he'd do all those things to me, and that afterwards, he'd kill my Jeremy. It was like a horrible dream, only I couldn't wake up."

When Ben said nothing, Chloe continued to talk. She wasn't sure where the words came from. They simply spilled from her, disjointed, sometimes making no sense, but like with her tears earlier, she couldn't seem to hold them back. As she talked, she became vaguely aware that she was occasionally dropping Roger's name into the mix and recounting offenses that he had committed against her during the last few months of their marriage.

When she finally fell silent, Chloe couldn't recall exactly what had prompted her to begin—or why she'd stopped. She only knew the pressure inside her had been released—as if Ben had pricked an abscess within her and all the poison had drained out.

Boneless, drifting, she lay in his arms, disconnected from reality, feeling at peace. Sleep stole over her in insidious waves of blackness. Her last conscious thought was that she and Jeremy were absolutely safe. Bobby Lee couldn't get them now, not with Ben and Diablo standing guard.

Chapter Twenty-one

Ben carried Chloe to a bedroom that was adjoined to the master suite by a large bathroom. Ever the optimist, he'd originally designed the room to be a nursery, just in case he was ever lucky enough to marry and have a child. Tonight it would serve as a room for Chloe, separated enough from his to give her privacy, but close enough to hear her if she needed him during the night.

After laying her on the daybed, Ben drew a coverlet over her and sat on the mattress to study her sweet face. In the moon-kissed shadows, she was incredibly lovely, her skin glowing like alabaster, her dark lashes forming crescents on her cheeks, her hair spread like a fan over the pillow.

With the back of a knuckle, he traced the delicate hollow of her cheek, loving her as he'd never loved anyone. Tonight, when she'd pressed so trustingly against him, he'd yearned to make love to her, the devil take tomorrow. But as much as he'd wished for that, he hadn't been able to bear the thought of seeing regret in her eyes in the morning.

She was right; he'd erected a wall of evasion between them. As soon as she had recovered from the trauma of this evening, he meant to tear it down, secret by secret, until there was nothing left between them but absolute honesty. Afterwards, if she still wanted him, there would be time enough for love-making.

He could wait. All things worth having were worth waiting for, and Chloe was infinitely more precious to him than anything else ever had been.

Sighing, Ben stood and left the room. He kept the connecting doors open, glad of the fact that he'd always been a light sleeper. If she so much as stirred, he'd know it. Moving out into the hallway, he cut around to the foyer and set the alarm, just in case a certain deputy decided to pay them a predawn visit.

After stripping down to his boxers, which he left on in case of emergency, he slipped into bed. For a long while, he stared blankly at the ceiling, unable to drift off. Anger roiled within him. He'd managed to hold it at bay in front of Chloe, but now that he was alone, the emotion built pressure in his chest like a volcano.

He imagined himself standing toe-to-toe with Bobby Lee Schuck and delivering blows to the bastard's face. He abhorred violence but felt driven to it now. He wanted to pound Bobby Lee into the dust. Oh, God, how he wanted to.

Some time later, Ben jerked awake. For a moment, he didn't know what had disturbed his sleep. Then he heard a whimper and a moan, coming from Chloe's room.

He leaped from the bed, dashed through the adjoining bathroom, and was beside her in seconds. She was thrashing, the coverlet and sheets tangled around her slender body, her face twisted as she struggled in her dreams with some imagined horror.

"Chloe?" Ben bent over her. "Sweetheart, wake up. You're dreaming."

"No, please, no!" she murmured, her words slurred with sleep. "No!"

Ben touched her shoulder. The contact brought her jackknifing up, her eyes huge in her sweat-filmed face, her fists pummeling the air. He ducked to avoid a swing, caught her wrists, and said, "Chloe, wake up!"

Somehow she twisted free of the cover and nailed him dead center in the chest with one foot. Ben emitted a pained "*Umph!*" He lost his grip on one of her arms. She flew at him like a wild thing, kicking, clawing the air, and trying to bite.

"Chloe! Wake up! You're dreaming!"

She froze and stared stupidly up at him. "Ben?" Then, as recognition dawned, she covered her face. "Oh, Ben, I'm sorry."

He sank down beside her. "It's okay, Chloe. I'm not hurt." He didn't ask what her dream had been about. He knew. "Hey, it was just a nightmare. You and Jeremy are safe now. I have the security system on. If anyone tries to enter the house, the alarm will go off."

A sob jerked her shoulders. "The cork! It wouldn't fire. He grabbed me, and in my dream, I knew he was going to kill me. I kept thinking I had to protect Jeremy, only I couldn't get away from him."

Ben gathered her into his arms, despising Bobby Lee with a virulence that turned his mouth acidic. "It's all right. The cork did fire, sweetheart. You nailed him a good one, and followed up with several swings of the bottle. I would love to have seen the look on his face. The bastard probably didn't know what hit him."

Between sobs, she giggled and almost choked. The next instant, she was scrambling from under the covers to sit on his lap. His boxers provided precious little barrier between a certain recalcitrant part of his body and her soft, delightful bottom. Ben clenched his teeth and returned her hug. Her tears trickled from the hollow of his shoulder to his chest. He ran a hand into her hair, struggling to control his physical reaction so he could provide the comfort she so desperately needed.

The smell of her drifted to his nostrils—an enticing blend of scented soap, shampoo, perfume, and an underlying essence exclusively her own. Ben wanted to start at the top her curly head and devour every sweet inch of her. Then he wanted to bury himself in her moist warmth and carry both of them into oblivion.

Evidently she felt his hardness. She lifted her head and gave him a searching look. Ben swallowed, hard. "It's, um—I'm sorry. You don't have to worry. I can't control the reaction, but I can control what I do about it."

She ran her slender hands over his chest. He nearly groaned. Her palms felt like fire-warmed satin on his skin. Her face shimmered in the moonlight coming in through the window behind him, the tear tracks on her cheeks shot through with silver, her eyes liquid pools of darkness, outlined by spiked lashes. She somehow managed to look angelic and sultry, both at once.

"When you touch me," she whispered, "and even when I touch you, the most glorious feeling moves through me. It's like sunlight and electricity, and I can barely think. All I know is I can't get enough of it."

And therein lay the problem. When she gave herself to him, he wanted her to make the decision to do so with no stimulus from him to sway her. Ben didn't want to push her away, but at the same time, he accepted his limitations. If she wiggled her butt one more time, he was going to lose it.

"How about some hot cocoa?" he suggested.

She studied him as if he'd lost his mind. "No,

thanks." Her shoulders jerked with a residual sob. She wiped her cheeks. "Hot cocoa isn't really what I want."

"What would you like then?" Ben was willing to fix a seven-course meal if it would get her off his lap before he did something he'd regret. "I've got some whiskey. You want a hot toddy?"

"You," she whispered. "I want you, Ben."

"What?"

Dumb response. But what else could he say? There were unresolved issues between them. She might not realize their importance, but he did. When they were intimate, it wouldn't be mere sex between two consenting adults, as he'd hoped for in the beginning. When she gave herself to him, she'd be expecting forever to be part of the package. Before she made a commitment like that, she needed to know everything about him, even the parts that he wished he didn't have to tell her.

"Chloe, I can't," he said, his voice thick with regret. "I want you. More than I've ever wanted anyone. But there are things we need to discuss, things that—"

She cupped her hand over his lips to stop him from saying more. Her gaze, aching with emotion, clung to his as she whispered, "I don't *care* about any of that now. I just need you to make love to me, Ben. *Please?* Erase the memories of Bobby Lee from my mind and replace them with new ones."

She shifted off his lap, only to turn and straddle his bare thigh, which was infinitely more torturous for him than her prior position had been. She wore only lacy panties and the T-shirt, and the feel of her bare inner thighs bracketing his leg was about to push him over the edge.

"Do you love me?" she asked.

"Yes. I love you with all my heart."

"What else really matters?" she asked breathlessly.

Ben had no answer for that. She rose up, her nipples dragging his chest through the flimsy T-shirt as she sought his mouth with hers. *Spontaneous combustion.* It had always been this way with her. One kiss, and he was a goner.

Ben slipped an arm around her, his body igniting with a desire so intense it almost blinded him. His blood hammered in his temples. His heart was knocking so hard he feared it might crack his ribs. She felt so good in his arms. How could something that seemed so absolutely right be wrong?

Still kissing him deeply, she twisted and fell back against the pillows, drawing him down with her. Grabbing for breath, she arched against him. "Touch me, Ben. Just touch me. Make me feel the magic again."

Ben knew he should pull away, but at that precise moment, he had difficulty recalling why. Jeremy was securely tucked away in the guest room at the far end of the hall where he wouldn't hear, and his mother had taken her sleeping pill, so he felt fairly confident that she wouldn't awaken. He and Chloe were alone. She wanted him, and he wanted her. He'd tried to do the right thing. Now all his willpower had been burned away by physical need.

"No second thoughts?"

"No second thoughts. None. I need you."

It was all Ben needed to hear. Feverishly, he peeled her panties off of her, loving the silkiness of her skin as his palms moved down her slender legs. "Ah, Chloe," he said on a sigh. "You are so sweet."

She reached for the hem of the T-shirt with trembling hands. Bracing his weight on his arms, Ben watched her tug up the cotton and twist her hips to pull it off over her head. His heated gaze skimmed over her small, perfectly shaped breasts, the indentation of her slender waist, and the delightfully full curve of her hips. "You're beautiful, Chloe. Absolutely beautiful."

"You're the beautiful one. Hold me, Ben. I need to feel your arms around me."

Ben had never wanted to do anything more. But he couldn't simply react to his own need, forgetting all else. "Chloe, I haven't been with anyone for over five years. I have nothing here to protect you."

A beatific smile lighted up her face. "Oh," she whispered, running her hands into his hair. "Oh, Ben, that's so sweet."

Sweet? To Ben, it was a red light. "Chloe," he began. "I can't just—"

"Yes, you can. It's not my dangerous time," she assured him. "I don't think pregnancy is an issue, not tonight. And safe sex isn't a worry. You haven't been with anyone for five years, and I've never been with anyone but Roger."

Ben wanted her so much that he didn't need any more encouragement. *Not her dangerous time. That worked.* He lowered himself beside her and gathered her close. The instant his arms closed, he felt her shiver with delight. Flesh to flesh, they turned to face each other. She trailed kisses up the center of his chest, setting his skin afire. "You're like a drug," she whispered against his neck. "Or wine. Yes, wine with electrical surges going through it."

He smiled against her hair. *Chloe.* She had no idea how much electricity he could actually generate. What he was putting out right now was involuntary. With a little concentrated effort, he could easily heighten the effect.

Thinking along those lines drew Ben's gaze to the room around them. He could only hope she didn't notice the blue glow that radiated from him. It was more obvious in the dark like this, especially with the moonlight to emphasize it.

"Love me, Ben," she whispered.

He didn't want to rush this. The first time between them needed to be savored. Slowly, ever so slowly, he set himself to the task of igniting each and every one of her nerve endings. He began by trailing slow, feather-light kisses up her arm, lingering at the sensitive bend of her elbow and then moving higher to nibble at the satiny flesh that led to her underarm. She shivered and lay perfectly still, her breaths coming in shallow, jagged spurts that told him he was pleasing her. He loved the way her lashes fluttered closed and the soft moans she made. He loved even more the way she surrendered herself to him. Her absolute trust in him nearly brought tears to his eyes.

He kissed his way back down to her wrist and then trailed his lips lightly up her side until she shivered again and arched in the sweetest of ways, offering him her breasts. Gently, carefully, he took her left nipple into his mouth. The dusky tip went as hard as a rivet against his teasing tongue.

She gasped at the shock. Her spine arched, and her body sprang taut. "Oh, Ben! It's like lightning going through me."

He wasn't sure if that was good or bad. Raising his head, he asked, "Do you want me to stop?"

She made fists in his hair and drew him back down to her. At that point, he stopped trying to control the power inside him. With Chloe, it just happened, an unleashed energy that arced between them like bolts leaping from one cloud to another. It had never happened this way with Sherry. Ben knew now that it was because he'd never loved Sherry like this—with all his heart and with such intensity that every cell of his body awakened when he touched her.

"I love you, Chloe," he whispered. "I swear to God, I'll never hurt you. Never. I'd sooner cut off my right arm."

"I know," she said simply. "I know. Just show me how much you love me, Ben. Just—show me."

The words worked like a key to a complicated lock inside him. No longer afraid to let go, no longer concerned about how it might screw things up, he closed his mouth over her nipple, gently seized the tip in his teeth and laved it with his tongue, giving her everything he had. Her hips bucked, her spine arched, and with a strangled sob, she cried, "Oh, God!"

All Ben registered was that her cry was one of pleasure, and for the first time in over twenty years, he gloried in his gift.

He abandoned her breasts to trail kisses down her belly. He knew by the convulsive spasms of her body that she'd already come, and he wanted to taste the sweetness that he had wrought. He smiled to himself at the shudders that ran through her with every brush of his lips over her taut belly, anticipating the moment when he would reach his ultimate target, the most sensitive place on her body.

At the press of his hand there, she parted her legs for him, allowing him access. He cautiously nuzzled the nest of curls at the apex of her thighs, eager yet cautious, for he'd never taken a woman this way and had no idea how she might react.

The instant he found that feminine nubbin with his tongue, she gave a muffled, strangled cry and lifted her hips, offering herself to him. He could no more resist what she offered than he could stop breathing. He moved down on her, drawing her firmly into his mouth. With another strangled cry, she climaxed almost instantly, and then, with a violent shudder, he felt the tension in her body mounting yet again. With a few more passes with the tip of his tongue, he made her cry out again, and she arched even higher, climaxing even as she silently pleaded for more.

All his life, his mother had been telling him that he had a special gift, something extraordinary that he should embrace and rejoice in. Until now, Ben had never believed that, never felt special. He'd made love with women, but always with the power tightly leashed. With Chloe, he couldn't hook a collar around it. It was simply there, pulsing from his skin, radiating from his pores, as uncontrollable as the beating of his heart.

And it was beautiful.

As Chloe convulsed a fourth time, tears came to Ben's eyes. In bed, at least, with the woman of his heart, the power within him *was* an extraordinary thing.

When he finally drew away to let her catch her breath, she stared up at him with unfocused eyes, relaxed and glowing. "Oh, *Ben*," she whispered. "That was—" She broke off and blinked sleepily. "That was incredible."

He couldn't help but grin. She was about to drift off to sleep in a puddle of contentment. He had news for her. The satisfaction thus far had been one-sided, and now it was his turn. He nudged her thighs apart, settled himself into position, and slowly thrust himself into her. The moist heat and tightness almost undid him, but if her reaction was any indication, the feeling was even more intense for her. Her eyes flew wide, and she stared up at him in startled amazement.

"You okay?"

"Oh, *Ben*! Oh, God, I feel like I'm soaring."

Ben hadn't even begun to show her how high they could fly. He shoved forward, exulting in the thought that he was completely in control, if not of his power, then of the act itself.

He had a surprise in store. Chloe generated an electricity all her own. When the soft, wet walls of her convulsed around him, the sweet jolt immediately sent him rocketing toward orgasm, and all thought, all maneuvers, went up in a flame of need he couldn't orchestrate or hold back. He came with a violence that shocked him. Hard thrusts brought an excruciating tightening of his body, and then—a violent release that hurtled him into oblivion.

Afterwards Ben collapsed on top of her. Ever so distantly, the thought occurred to him that he outweighed her by at least a hundred pounds and was probably squashing her. But, God help him, he couldn't put bones into his arms to lift himself off her. When he tried, she hugged his neck and whispered, "Don't. Stay with me. Please, I don't want you to leave me."

He relaxed, shifting one hip to rest most of his weight on the mattress. *My Chloe.* He gathered her to his chest, rained kisses over her face, buried his nose in her curls. Dear God, how he loved her. When he tried to think of words to describe the depth of his feelings for her, he came up blank.

"I love you," she whispered. "I love you, love you, *love* you."

He managed a throaty response. "And I love you, Chloe. You're my everything."

Then black folds of exhaustion overtook him.

Chloe drifted up from a deep sleep sometime later to find herself right where she wanted to be—closely enfolded in Ben's arms. Even relaxed, his hands limp in sleep, the weight of his palms and the loose press of his fingers made her skin hum with pleasure. It was the only way to describe how his touch made her feel—a fabulous, magical glow that permeated to her bones. He was thunder. He was lightning. He was the blue, electrical glow she'd seen hovering around him in the moonlight that first night, someone magical and otherworldly, yet hers, entirely hers, and so solid, she reveled in every breath he drew and every rise of his chest against her own.

In the shadows, it was so easy to imagine that the world had fallen away, that they were the only two people on earth. Just her Shoshone warrior and her— lost in feelings of discovery and need. They had joined together in a marriage of flesh, strength and softness melting into each other and becoming one in a way that she hadn't thought possible.

She'd felt no shyness with him. When he'd lifted her breasts to suckle and tease the tips, she'd arched shamelessly up to him, wanting and needing him in a way that couldn't be denied. Never had she climaxed merely from the draw of a man's mouth on her nipple, but she had tonight, with a combustive surge that had ignited her and made her crave more.

Now, even in the lethargic aftermath of deep slumber, she wanted him again. Sleepily—lustily—she kissed his neck and nibbled on his ear. He groaned and moved a big hand up the curve of her back, yet even as he mumbled a protest, she felt his body awakening. Chloe pressed closer, undulating her hips against him. He responded with a throaty growl. The next instant, she was flat on her back, his dark face hovering only inches above hers.

"You asking for trouble, lady?"

Chloe looped her arms around his strong neck. "You got any to dish out?"

He chuckled sleepily and bent to kiss her. With the

first brush of their lips, Chloe was ready. At the back of her mind, a voice of reason whispered that it was only the newness of it all that made his kisses seem so potent. In time, when their lovemaking became old hat, she would no longer thrill to his every touch.

But that was for later, and this was now. As she melted into the kiss—and into him—she dimly registered that the world itself was celebrating their union.

In the night sky there hung a gorgeous blue moon.

Chloe awoke the next morning alone in bed. She ran her hand over the sheet where Ben had lain beside her during the night, and a feeling of magic engulfed her again. She smiled, yawned, and sat up. Sunlight poured through the window, as yellow as the filling in a lemon meringue pie, and Chloe felt as light and airy as the topping.

She slipped from bed, grabbed her T-shirt and jeans. In seconds, she was dressed and stepping from the bedroom, her hair a wild tangle that fell over her eyes. The house was silent. She almost felt like tiptoeing. Once in the kitchen, she saw that the coffee in the pot was cold. She set herself to making fresh, thinking how right this felt. Ben, the house, and the titter of Einstein, who watched her curiously from his perch, all combined to give her a feeling of having come home. The feeling moved through her as surely as her blood through her veins. She belonged here.

With a start, she noticed the time on the kitchen clock. It was ten of twelve. Chloe couldn't believe she'd slept so late. She was due at work by noon. Her hands flew to her hair. She'd never make it on time. It was a twenty-minute drive.

She raced back to the bedroom, found her pillow-case of clothes, and searched for something suitable to wear. Ben had packed, helter-skelter, taking things only from her drawers. All her nice things hung in the closet. Chloe settled on a blue knit top and jeans. Hattie would understand once she heard about last night.

Chloe stepped into the bathroom to quickly brush her teeth, comb her hair, and wash her face. On the counter, she found a note. *Go back to bed*, the masculine scrawl read. *I told Hattie what happened, and she called in Ethel Martin to sub for three days.*

Chloe laid down the comb and touched her fingertips to the Post-it note. It was yellow, like the sunshine outside and inside her heart. Smiling, she went to the kitchen for coffee. After filling two mugs, she went in search of Ben. She found him in his office working at the computer.

Holding the mugs out to each side of her body, she crept up behind him, planning to surprise him with a kiss. Just as she reached her target, she glanced over his shoulder at the computer screen. He was typing furiously. The page was capped with a heading that flashed clear in her vision. BEAVER MARSH—BRETT CALDWELL—SYNOPSIS. Chloe straightened so quickly, she slopped coffee onto her hand and scalded herself, which made her yelp and brought Ben lunging from the chair.

"Chloe."

"Ben." *Brett*. Chloe stared up at him. Then her gaze shifted to the collection of Caldwell books on his bookshelf. "I see."

He whipped around, moved the mouse, and minimized the program window. But he was too late.

"Oh, Ben," she whispered.

"It's not how it looks," he said, shoving a rigid hand through his hair. "Well, actually, it is how it looks, but I can explain."

Chloe set down the mugs of coffee before she spilled them entirely. "I know you tried to tell me last night. I'm not upset. Really." As she uttered those words, she knew they were the absolute truth. She wasn't upset, just—well, shocked, she supposed. "You're *the* Brett Caldwell?" She studied him through new eyes. "Of course. It makes perfect sense. I always knew when I read his books that he loved animals. It comes through in everything he—everything you— write." She laughed shakily. "Why don't you have brick walls around your estate and drive a Rolls?"

"I'm not famous. Brett Caldwell is a fabrication. He doesn't really exist."

Chloe stared hard at the computer. "And writing is the 'this and that' you wouldn't elaborate on? For weeks, I thought maybe you made a living doing something illegal. Why didn't you just say you were a writer? I've never known a writer. It's incredible."

"That first night when you asked what I did for a living, I couldn't possibly tell you." His eyes ached with regret. "I wish now that I had because I do trust you, Chloe. But at the time, I didn't know very much about you, and you didn't know me. My career hung in the balance." He rubbed a big hand over his face and blinked. "It's not just about the writing. There was an incident in my life before I sold the first book, something that could seriously damage my career as a children's writer if the news media ever found out. I write under the pen name to protect my anonymity, and I rent a post office box in Pineville to receive all correspondence from my publisher. There are a lot of people in this town who would delight in ruining me. One phone call, that's all it'd take, and my sales could plummet."

Understanding dawned. How many mothers would

buy his books if they knew a killer had written them? "Oh, Ben. Surely, after a time, you realized I wouldn't tell anyone."

"Yeah. Early on, I realized you wouldn't. But it goes deeper than that, Chloe. You seemed so in awe of Caldwell when you talked about him." He shifted his weight and looked away. "I needed you to fall in love with *me*. I didn't want the Caldwell thing to enter into it—not the fame, not the money. I wanted you to love *me*." A suspicious brightness entered his eyes. "No one ever has. You know? Only my mom, and a man's mother doesn't count."

Chloe had never met anyone more extraordinary than Ben Longtree. But since her divorce, she'd experienced her own share of insecurity, and she understood that feelings weren't always rational. "Well," she managed to say with a note of levity, "at least now you know that I loved you with all my heart before I found out you were famous."

"Yeah." He smiled slightly. "And that feels really good." He cleared his throat and rubbed beside his nose. "I, um—I suppose now you'd like to know more about the incident I mentioned."

"It's common knowledge in Jack Pine. I know that you accidentally killed a man."

His gaze sharpened on hers. "Without hearing the details, you automatically believe it was an accident?"

"I *know* it was an accident." The incredulity that crossed his dark face made Chloe's heart hurt for him. "I was a little wary at the beginning, I admit. But once I got to know you a little better, I knew you didn't have it in you to deliberately harm anyone or anything. It follows that it had to be an accident."

"It *was* an accident," he acknowledged. "But that doesn't negate the fact that he's dead, or that it was my fault. People in town think I got off scot-free without any punishment. They're wrong. I have to live with what I did for the rest of my life."

Chloe understood exactly what he meant. "We all make mistakes, Ben. An unfortunate few of us make fatal ones." She hugged her waist. Her next words weren't easy to say. "Roger's accident was my fault. I was manning the controls. The tide was going out, and as we headed out for the deeper water of the sound, I slowed down just a bit. I didn't know that speed made the boat skim over the surface of the water. When I backed off the throttle, the prop caught on a sandbar. We tried shifting from forward to reverse several times, hoping the rocking motion would free the blades, but it didn't work, and Roger had to use a pole to push us clear. When we finally floated into deeper water where the prop was free, I gave it too much throttle. Roger was still standing on the seat at the back of the boat. He lost his balance and was thrown overboard."

"Oh, sweetheart," Ben said, his voice barely more than a whisper. "How awful for you."

Chloe had long since learned to live with what had happened. "We all have our crosses to bear, I guess. A split second, and you can regret it for the rest of your life. A person's whole life can change with a shift of the wind or a turn of a leaf."

He nodded.

"I understand that it can't be easy for you to talk about," she added, "so we needn't discuss the details."

"I want you as a permanent part of my life, with a ring and promises and a license framed on the wall. How can you wave it off and say we don't need to discuss it? I killed a man. Surely you at least want to know how it happened."

Chloe thought about it for a moment. And while she was thinking, she remembered what he'd just said about needing to feel loved for who he was. "No," she said softly. "If the time comes that you're burning to unload it, I'll listen, but I don't *need* to know. It's a nonissue as far as I'm concerned. You're a beautiful person, Ben. You try to save baby chipmunks from certain death because they were born too late to survive the winter. You can walk up to a fawn in the woods, and the fawn trusts you implicitly. How can I do less?"

He hooked a hand behind her neck and hauled her against him. For several seconds, he just clung to her, his big body vibrating with the intensity of his emotion. That wonderful feeling of electrical warmth moved through her. "I love you, Ben. Just you, Ben Longtree, for better or worse, no matter what. I'm sorry I pestered you to tell me about your work. It seems so silly of me now."

"I'm so sorry I kept it from you."

She smiled against his shirt. "Wanna make it up to me?"

"How?"

"Let me read the synopsis."

He laughed and set her away from him. Catching her face between his hands, he searched her eyes, the blue of his delving deep. "You really aren't mad?"

"Nope." She wrinkled her nose. "Well, it depends. If you don't let me read the synopsis, I could work my way up to it."

"I think that can be arranged. I'm not very far along with it yet, though. I, um—well, the boy is patterned after Jeremy. With everything so up in the air between us, I've been having trouble staying focused. Suddenly, this morning, I woke up burning to get it down."

"Patterned after Jeremy? I *am* burning to read it now." Chloe retrieved her coffee. "Get to work and finish it. I'll fix breakfast. Or should I say lunch?"

"I can stop for now. No hurry."

"Oh, yes, there is. I can't wait to read it. Brett Caldwell. I can't believe it. Just imagine that." She started from the room, then braked to a stop. "Where is Jeremy, by the way?"

He gave her a slow grin. "He's on the deck, learning how to crochet."

While Chloe made preparations for the midday meal, the reality of her discovery started to sink in. Ben was famous, she thought giddily. He was Brett Caldwell, children's writer extraordinaire. He'd won a Newbery Medal. As she got ready to scramble eggs for sandwiches, she drew a spatula from the drawer and held it up, half expecting it to be gilded with gold.

Ben joined her in the kitchen a few minutes later. "My concentration's blown." He leaned against the counter to study her. "I can't believe you're not mad."

"Nothing for me to be mad about. I can see the necessity of your using a pen name, and I also understand why you can't be open with people about your career." She began slicing onions and broccoli to go in the eggs.

"Thank you for that. You're an extraordinary lady."

"Trust me, I'm not the extraordinary one. You are." She got a bowl from the cupboard to whisk the eggs. "How did you first get started? I am curious about that. You're a vet. How does a vet, with all those years dedicated to the profession, end up telling stories?"

"When my father died, I came home to care for my mother. Her condition was such that I couldn't leave her alone while I worked. I thought about starting a practice here, but zoning ordinances prohibit it. So for a while, I cut firewood for a living. I could take my mother into the woods with me."

"And you kept the wolf from the door that way."

"Occasionally, he scratched to get in. Money was tight. You can't cut wood here in the winter. The snow's too deep. And the woods are open only part of the summer. One August afternoon, when the forests were closed to cutters due to extreme fire danger, I got bored and wrote a story about my childhood dog, Bandit."

"And Brett Caldwell was born."

"So to speak. Later, I submitted the story to a publisher. I never really expected to sell the thing or to become so successful. It just happened."

"Bandit." Chloe sighed. "It's such a beautiful story. But, then, each and every book you've written is beautiful, teaching kids to be kinder, wiser, and more thoughtful about the creatures around them." For the first time, Chloe really understood what made Caldwell's stories so incredibly special. Ben had an almost spiritual bond with animals, and that came across in his writing. "Was *Bandit* autobiographical?"

"In some ways. I did have a faithful dog named Bandit, the dog did die, and he's buried under the oak tree out back. There, truth and fiction separate. I wrote the story as I wished it had happened, with Bandit living to a ripe old age and being painlessly put down at the end. Unfortunately, my dog wasn't that lucky. He wasn't sick when he died, and his passing wasn't painless. One afternoon, when my father was upset with me, he got drunk and shot him."

Chloe almost dropped an egg. "Oh, Ben." She stared at him in startled amazement. His eyes had turned frosty with remembered pain, and a haunted look had settled over his dark face. She knew in that moment, *knew* beyond a shadow of a doubt, that he'd never shared this with anyone else. The love she felt for him wasn't one-sided. This man needed her as much as she needed him. "How horrible."

He sighed—a weary expulsion of breath that re-laxed his shoulders. "I've never told anyone about that until now. I'm sorry. I didn't mean to dump on you."

Chloe turned off the gas flame and went over to hug his waist. For several minutes they just stood there, loosely wrapped in each other's arms. "I'm just sorry your father did such a thing. How awful for you."

As she spoke, it sank home to Chloe that once, years ago, this man had been a boy, standing over his beloved dog's grave, and that there had been no happy ending for him. She yearned to give him one now—a happy ending that would make up for all the sadness in his life.

"I never got another dog until Diablo. He didn't come along until twenty years later. Somehow, it just never felt right until then."

She had already determined that Ben was a man who felt things deeply. It made perfect sense that he would grieve over a dog for twenty years, especially when she thought of how the real Bandit had died. Ben must have hated his father for what he did. He might still to this day.

Silence settled between them. Chloe held on to him, never wanting to let go.

"Now it's my turn to ask a question," he said against her hair. "Why didn't you tell me that Bobby Lee was pestering you? Was it only because I wouldn't tell you about my job?"

Chloe closed her eyes. "I wanted to tell you. Yesterday afternoon when we had the fight, I wanted to so badly that I ached."

He tensed and drew back to study her face. "And?"

"I was afraid of what you might do. I didn't want you to take Bobby Lee on and get in trouble."

He relaxed slightly. "I'm not dumb, Chloe."

No, she thought, but he was protective. "All's well that ends well," she quipped.

"True," he agreed. "Let's just hope it's over."

He burrowed through her curls to kiss her ear, doing fabulous things to her nerve endings. "Scared?" he asked.

"Yes. I'd be lying to say I'm not."

"Me, too," he whispered. "I'm not sure how to deal with him. He has the power of the law on his side."

With that thought to trouble them, they simply stood there, holding on to each other and feeling anxious together.

Chapter Twenty-two

A few minutes later, Jeremy dashed in from outside with a misshapen hank of yarn dangling from his hand. "Look, Mom! See what I made?"

"What" was unidentifiable. Chloe made appropriate sounds of appreciation. "Is it for me?"

Jeremy frowned. "What do you want it for?"

There was a question. Thinking quickly, Chloe replied, "Well, because you made it, and I've always wanted one."

"One what?"

Again Chloe considered carefully before answering. "One of those things."

Jeremy held up the bedraggled mass of variegated worsted. "Really? You mean it's something? I thought it was only for practice."

Uh-oh. Chloe sent Ben an appealing look. He came to the rescue. "You made that, just practicing? Wow. That's a fine-looking—key chain."

Jeremy beamed. "It is?"

After flashing an apologetic look at Chloe, the child handed the bedraggled mess to Ben. "If you like it that much, you can have it. I'll go make my mom another one. Pink is her favorite color, but she doesn't wear it very much 'cause she thinks it clashes with her hair. But she could have a pink key chain."

After Jeremy dashed from the house, Ben gave Chloe a long look. "I think I just inherited your favorite thing."

She giggled. "At least we'll have matching key holders."

After lunch, Jeremy returned to the deck to practice his crochet stitches with Nan while Chloe and Ben joined forces to clean up the kitchen. They'd just finished when the phone rang. Chloe watched as Ben picked up the receiver. Her stomach bunched with anxiety when she heard him say, "Hi, Frank. We've been hoping you might call."

A long silence followed. Judging by the expressions on Ben's face, the news wasn't good. A few seconds later, he politely thanked Frank for trying. As he hung up the phone, Chloe said, "So, with no fuss or further ado, Bobby Lee's going to get away with it?"

Ben sighed. "He's covered his ass, nine ways to hell. Frank had a private meeting with the sheriff this morning. Before going in, he went over everything and spoke with the dispatcher. On the surface, it looks as if you and Bobby Lee have a history, and last night was an attempt on your part to cause him grief."

"That's so absurd." Chloe was so angry she was shaking. "The man is dangerous, Ben. He's going to hurt somebody. I'd just as soon it not be me or my son."

"Me, too." He gestured helplessly. "Frank says Lang has a lot of other stuff on his mind right now. A local man has gone missing, a young guy about twenty-five named Jimmy Suitor. A month and a half ago, he took off to go camping. I guess he's an outdoor enthusiast who loves to hike, and every summer, he spends a couple of weeks exploring the surrounding wilderness areas. This year he never came home. Frank says that Suitor's never been one to hold down a job for long, so at first his mom wasn't concerned. She just figured he'd decided to stay in the mountains longer than planned. When he was two weeks overdue, she reported him missing."

"I'm sorry to hear that," Chloe said.

"Right after she filed the report, Frank says they searched hot and heavy—did a sweep of the area where he was supposed to be hiking. No sign of him. That was shortly after you quit your job at the department."

"Ah. That explains why I haven't heard about it until now."

"Plus the fact that they didn't hype it up because of Suitor's penchant for vanishing. Everybody just figured he was off doing his own thing again. Then yesterday, a hiker came across a ball cap covered with blood."

"Oh, no. Was it Jimmy Suitor's?"

"His mother says it is. They've sent it off for tests. It looks like foul play, and all hell is breaking loose today. Every lunatic for a hundred miles is calling in to say they've seen him—or something suspicious. Frank says a case like this brings all the fruitcakes out of the woodwork. Lang is going nuts, and so is everyone else."

"And he really can't afford to put Bobby Lee on suspension right now because he needs all the manpower he can get? Gotcha."

"I know it sounds callous. But to them, your run-in with Bobby Lee last night ranks about a two on an importance scale of one to ten."

"I see."

"Frank has nothing solid to pin on him, Chloe."

"I understand," she said faintly. "Bobby Lee outsmarted me at every turn, and I got off lucky. If he tries again, I may not be so lucky. In that event, then the sheriff will be all over it."

Silence. Chloe immediately felt awful. "I'm sorry, Ben. I know this isn't your fault."

She sat on a bar stool and pressed her face to her hands. Bobby Lee was going to get away with it, just as he had predicted. He'd threatened her life and sworn to kill her son. He would have brutally raped her if she hadn't had a bottle of champagne in the house. And the incident was being swept under the rug.

Ben came to stand behind her and rub her shoulders. "I'm the one who's sorry. Sometimes our justice system totally sucks."

"I just don't know what I'm going to do," she confessed. "As long as he's loose, I won't draw an easy breath."

"I can tell you what you're *not* going to do," he said softly. "You're not going home. You and Jeremy are safe here. I'll feel a lot better if you stay with me on the ridge."

"I can't just move in here, Ben."

"Why not?" He leaned around to search her face. "Are you having second thoughts about us?"

"No. Of course not. It's just—"

"Just what? I've got plenty of room."

"I have a job, and all my work clothes are down there."

"You have three days off. We'll go collect your clothes before you have to go back. As for going to work, for the next couple of weeks, I'll drive you and pick you up, just to play it safe. Bobby Lee may enter the shop when you're on shift, but I seriously doubt that he'll dare to cause any trouble in a public place. He'd much prefer to catch you off alone. I aim to see that doesn't happen."

Chloe was about to respond when the phone rang again. She tensed, believing it might be Frank calling back. Ben stepped over to the desk to pick up. Piecing together his side of the conversation, Chloe decided it wasn't Bower on the other end of the line. Ben said something about a horse. Then he mentioned 4-H.

"Actually, that's never been one of my aspirations, but I appreciate the thought, and I'll definitely consider it." He listened for a moment. "Yeah, sure. Day after tomorrow will work. Around one? I'll see you then."

After he hung up, Chloe asked, "Who was that?"

He sent her a knowing look. "Lucy Gant. Her horse has a bum knee, and it's become inflamed. She asked if I'd drop by and have a look." He studied her solemnly. "It seems a certain lady at the Christmas Village has been singing my praises. Lucy stopped in one afternoon last week and got her ear bent. She's now convinced that the town has given me a bum shake, and she just invited me to be the 4-H vet this year."

"Oh, Ben. That's wonderful."

He fiddled with some papers on the desk. Watching him, Chloe noticed his decided lack of enthusiasm and wondered why. It seemed to her that he should be pleased. The people of Jack Pine had been unfair to him, and it was high time public sentiment underwent a change.

When he glanced back up, he said, "I really appreciate the good word, Chloe. And I'll honestly consider the 4-H thing. It's just—" He broke off and smiled. "I guess I don't have a lot of faith that anything's really different. Lucy is only one person, a proverbial drop in the bucket. If I take her up on the 4-H thing, it'll probably cause more upheaval and trouble for her than it's worth."

"We have to start somewhere," Chloe pointed out.

He came back around the bar to give her a gentle kiss. "*We.* I like the sound of that."

"Me, too."

He cupped her chin in his hand to study her face. "You're pale, and you have circles under your eyes. Jeremy's busy outside with Mom, and I need to put in a couple of hours at the keyboard. Why don't you take advantage of the lull to lie down for a while?"

"I just got up," Chloe protested, even though she actually did feel weary. Last night had taken more out of her than she cared to admit. At unexpected moments, she would get flashes of what had happened, and panic would claw at her insides. "If I sleep now, I'll be awake half the night."

A mischievous twinkle entered his eyes. "You may be awake half the night, anyway. Rest while you have the chance." He kissed her again, this time deeply and in a way that promised more to come. Chloe was dizzy and tingling clear to her toes when he finally came up for air. "Just as I thought. You taste like second helpings."

After he left the kitchen, Chloe followed his advice and returned to the room where she'd slept last night. She sank gratefully onto the daybed and closed her eyes, telling herself that she'd lie down for just a while. Within seconds, she was out like a light.

Chloe awakened to fading sunlight. Feeling heat beside her, she turned and snuggled close, only to wrinkle her nose and crack open one eye when bad breath blasted her in the face. She was peering into a yawning mouth. Long whiskers pricked her cheek.

"Methuselah?"

She started awake. The old cougar, lying on his back with his legs sprawled, arched his spine and wriggled, begging for a belly scratch. With a quick glance around, Chloe oriented herself, recalling that she'd lain down for a nap. She'd clearly been more exhausted than she thought. Judging by the angle of the sun coming in the window, she'd been asleep for several hours.

Unable to ignore the cougar's implicit request for petting, she sat cross-legged and spent a moment scratching the huge cat's belly. "It would seem I'm having a love affair with more than one male in this house," she said with a smile. "You're not nearly as sexy as your competition."

Methuselah yawned. When Chloe left off petting him, he rolled toward her, planted his remaining front paw on her shoulder, and gave her a goofy, pleading look. "Two more rubs. That's it," Chloe said, thinking as she delivered on the promise that this could happen only at Ben Longtree's house. "I've been lazing around in here long enough. It must be almost dinnertime."

Chloe stepped into the bathroom to brush her hair and wash the sleep from her eyes before she went to the front part of the house. She found Jeremy sitting on the living room rug, staring raptly at the oak television armoire, which Chloe had never seen open. She stepped into the room, gave the big-screen TV an admiring glance, and then bent to smooth her son's hair.

"*Scooby Doo?* Wow. How do you rate?"

Jeremy glanced up. "Ben said he had work to do. I wanted to go with him, but he says it's too far. So he rented me a movie on satellite."

"That was sweet of him."

"It's an all-day one. I can watch it again for free!"

Without taking his eyes off the television, Jeremy fished around in a bowl perched on his lap. Chloe saw that someone had fixed him a healthy array of movie snacks: apple slices, slivers of cheese, chunks of granola, and raisins.

"Yum," Chloe said. "Did Ben give you that?"

"Mm-hmm. This is a good part of the show, Mom."

Chloe knew how to take a hint. Grinning, she left the child to his movie. She found Nan sitting in her rocker in the family room. This evening, instead of crocheting, she was intent on putting together a jigsaw puzzle.

"Sorry I conked for so long. I hope Jeremy didn't take up too much of your time this afternoon, learning to crochet."

"All I have is time." Nan's busy hands went still, and she sat back in her chair. "I haven't had a child around in years. It was fun."

Chloe moved toward the love seat, planning to chat with Nan until it was time to start supper. Halfway there, she glimpsed movement through the window and looked out to see Ben walking up the tree-studded hill behind the house. He carried a cooler, a large water jug, a black satchel, and what appeared to be a sack of grain over one shoulder. It looked to her as if he was following a well-beaten trail.

"My goodness. Ben's taking enough stuff with him." Chloe stepped to the window to gaze after him. "What kind of work is he off to do?"

From behind her, Nan said, "Perhaps you should follow him and find out."

Chloe sent her a questioning look.

"You know him as Ben Longtree," the older woman said. "But that isn't who he really is."

Chloe's skin chilled. "What do you mean?"

Nan stared blankly at the puzzle for a moment.

"Just what I said. That isn't who he really is. Not all that there is, anyway."

Chloe searched Nan's face, wondering if she was having one of her spells. "I'm sorry?"

"My son is a quarter Shoshone," she said softly, "a direct descendent of Lion Claw, a great medicine man and chief."

Chloe had never heard of Lion Claw.

"Sometimes," Nan went on, "when it comes to a man's heart, one fourth of something equals a whole, and one half amounts to nothing."

"I don't understand."

"I know. It took me years to understand. When my son was a very small boy, his paternal grandfather, a full-blooded Shoshone, gave him a Shoshone name. It is the way of the Shoshone people to give children names that reflect their destiny, and Ben's Shoshone name is He Who Walks With Mountain Lions." She glanced pointedly at Methuselah, who had come in from the bedroom to lie on his pallet in front of the hearth. "Everything isn't always as it seems, Chloe. Ben's father, Hap, was half Shoshone, but for reasons I won't get into, he denied his blood in his early twenties and spent the rest of his life angry and bitter, trying to deny his birthright. Ben was a glaring reminder to him that a man can never escape the blood that flows in his veins."

She ran her fingertips over the loose puzzle pieces. "Life is like this, made up of so many little parts. Some of us can fit them together just right, and the picture comes out perfect. Others of us fumble about, trying to make sense of the jumble, and we never quite succeed."

Chloe had felt that way a few times herself, and she understood exactly what Nan meant. "All we can do is our best."

"Sometimes our best isn't good enough. I know you've looked at me and wondered at my weakness for staying with Ben's father, who by all accounts was a terrible man. What you don't know, Chloe, is that my Hap was once like Ben—as beautiful within as he was without."

Chloe moved from the window. "What happened to change him, Nan?"

"A miracle gone awry. A young man's yearning to help someone he loved that backfired in a terrible way. Hap was sensitive, just as Ben is, but he lacked Ben's strength. He tried to escape what to him was unbearable by drinking, and the drink turned him mean." The expression in Nan's eyes when she met Chloe's gaze was filled with sadness. "Occasionally, in a sober moment, he would look at me, and I'd see the old Hap, peeking out at me like a frightened child who'd lost his way. That was why I couldn't go, Chloe. I had to stay, just in case he finally found his way back to me. I put up with his anger—and with his drunkenness—and with his women, not because I was weak, but because I loved the man under all the ugliness. I thought he was worth saving."

Chloe understood. For the five months she'd remained with Roger, she'd stayed for essentially the same reason, reluctant to abandon the man he'd once been.

"I think you love my Ben. Am I right?"

Chloe nodded.

"Loving him as you do, if something terrible happened that broke his heart, and he started drinking, would you be able to walk away, knowing he might one day stop drinking and be your Ben again?"

Chloe recalled how she'd agonized over getting a divorce. She'd loved Roger, but she'd eventually come to accept that the man she'd loved was gone and would never return. "I don't know," she said honestly. "I just don't know."

"I couldn't leave Hap. I know now that it was a mistake." Nan lifted her shoulders, her eyes sparkling with tears. "I should have divorced him, if not for my own sake, for my children. Instead I tried to be both a loyal wife and a good mother. The two should go hand in hand, but sometimes life's twists and turns force a woman to choose one way instead of the other. When I reached that crossroad, I tried to walk both ways. It was the worse mistake of my life."

"Ben understands." Recalling their conversation on the deck, Chloe added, "A large part of him wishes you'd left, but another part of him understands why you couldn't, Nan."

"My son is an old soul. He's sensitive, but in him, it's never been a weakness as it was in his father. He was born with a knowing in his heart. Do you understand what I'm saying?"

Chloe didn't understand, not at all, but she very much wished she could. She went to kneel by Nan's chair. "My Ben walks a different path," Nan continued. "He always has. The way has not been easy, and for a time, he left and followed in his father's footsteps, forsaking the things his grandfather taught him, trying to be something he wasn't." Her smile was a glow that moved slowly over her face. "Now he has come home again to walk the way of his ancestors, the way his grandfather taught him, the way he was meant to walk. Ben is what he is, and he can't change. His Shoshone grandfather understood that. Even though I'm Irish to my marrow, I came to understand that. But Ben's father never did. He wanted better for his son, never understanding that for Ben, there is nothing else."

Chloe touched a hand to Nan's knee. "Tell me, Nan. About Ben? What is it that I'm missing?"

"As his mother," she whispered, "I love Ben simply for being Ben. The question is, can you?"

She looked deeply into Chloe's eyes. Chloe didn't see insanity in Nan Longtree's gaze, but more a torment that ran so deep it couldn't be expressed with words.

"You've felt it," she said. "Deep down, I think you know, but you've refused to see and haven't accepted."

"But I have," Chloe argued. She glanced at Methuselah. "He has a gift with animals. It's no big deal to me. I've accepted all the creatures, even come to love them. How can you say I haven't?"

Nan shook her head. "You've accepted only what you've chosen to see. But what of those things you've refused to see? What of the puppy, hovering at the edge of darkness, that Ben brought back to the light? What of the little boy with asthma who no longer struggles to breathe?"

A chill moved up Chloe's spine. "What are you saying?"

"What of the woman who came here with fear and bad memories in her eyes?" Nan asked. "At what precise moment did the fear go away, Chloe? Do you remember?"

"It was a gradual thing. I just—" Chloe broke off and swallowed. "The afternoon we went to the beaver dam," she whispered tautly. "On the way back, he . . ." Her voice trailed away. She threw Ben's mother a frightened look. "What're you saying?"

"Nothing. Some things can't be explained with words. You just have to take a leap of faith and believe. But in order to do that, first you must see." She squeezed Chloe's hand. "Before this goes farther, you must do that, Chloe." She gestured at the window. "Go," she whispered. "Follow the path he walks and see where it leads you. Learn the truth now. If it is more than you are prepared to accept, then leave this place. If you linger and go later, you'll take his heart with you."

Chloe grabbed a lightweight jacket from the hall tree and jerked it on as she set out to follow Ben. The jacket, she realized, was his, a black nylon windbreaker with elastic at the cuffs. The airy cloth hung in puffy folds to her hips, several sizes too large for her, just as she was coming to suspect the man might be. Ben, the descendent of a chief, only one quarter Shoshone by blood, but pure Indian at heart, a man cloaked in mystery, a man surrounded by magic. She'd felt it each time he touched her, been filled with it when he entered her, and afterwards, she'd floated back to earth, safe in his arms.

Chloe wanted to think she knew Ben, and in many ways, perhaps she did, but he was a man with many layers, and those layers ran deep.

The footpath was clearly defined and easy to follow. As she walked, she placed her feet in Ben's tracks, noting his much larger footprints. She thought back to the first time she'd seen him. She'd sensed it then— an intangible aura of separateness. She remembered the wintry chill of his blue eyes, which had seemed to sear her skin.

After an arduous climb, Chloe came to the barbed wire fence that marked the perimeter of Longtree land. She struggled to slip through the wire, snagged the leg of her jeans, and spent a moment floundering like a hooked fish. *Blast it!*

When she was successfully through the fence, Chloe picked up Ben's trail again, which zigzagged now, as if he feared he might be followed. She walked—and walked. As her muscles tired and her breathing became labored, she wondered more than once where on earth he was going. Still, she kept walking, determined to find him. Ben had meant to tell her something last night. Her run-in with Bobby Lee had veered him off course. After his mother's strange warnings, Chloe couldn't help but feel that it was time for them to talk.

Finally, Chloe came upon a cave in the side of a rock cliff. Light flickered within. She slowed her footsteps, her heart pounding with excitement and a measure of trepidation. She could see shadows dancing inside—eerie, elongated shapes that made her recall Lucy's absurd story about Ben's being a witch. What on earth was he doing that he had to conceal his activities in a remote hiding place like this?

For an instant, Chloe considered leaving. Maybe, she thought, there were some things she was better off not knowing. But then she remembered Ben's arms around her last night—the incredible gentleness of his touch—and she kept walking. No matter what secrets he might have, she knew one thing with absolute certainty: there was no evil in him.

As she drew nearer, Chloe could see him moving about inside the cave. He was caring for animals, she realized. Lantern light bathed the interior of the cave, which explained the eerie light and shadows. The enclosure was lined with cages. From where Chloe stood, she could see a badger inside one pen, what looked like a coyote lying in another. Another very large cage appeared to be empty.

Seeing Ben work with animals didn't strike Chloe as strange. She did wonder why he felt such a need for so much secrecy, however. She'd known about his wild animals from day one, and she'd surely proved to him over time that she could be trusted to keep her mouth shut.

Lengthening her strides, Chloe was about to call out when a deafening roar off to her left startled her half out of her wits. She whirled to see a huge black bear coming toward her at a dead run. The graceless animal plowed through brush and over piles of deadfall as if they weren't there.

Chloe froze. For the life of her, she couldn't make her feet move. When she tried to scream, all that came out was a squeak. There was no question in her mind that the huge beast meant to attack her. She watched in helpless horror as the distance narrowed between them. It seemed to her that the very earth vibrated with the bear's lunging advance.

From the corner of her eye she saw Ben dash from the cave. She tried to warn him away, as afraid for him as she was for herself, but her vocal cords wouldn't work.

He moved swiftly into the clearing, putting himself between Chloe and the bear. Stretching his arms high, he cried, "*Kiss,* stop! *Suvate,* it is finished!"

The bear skidded to a stop and swung its massive head, its mouth yawning and streaming lathery saliva as it let loose with another roar that vibrated the air.

"*Ka, kiss,*" Ben said, more softly this time. Then, more softly yet, he said, "*Ka,* no! *Kiss,* stop, Old One. *Habbe we-ich-ket, eh?* A death wish, yes? They kill rogue bears."

The bear rolled back onto its haunches. Its beady eyes, small for its broad head, remained fixed on Chloe, and it took a violet swing at the earth with one lethal front paw, sending dirt and pine needles flying. With only five feet separating her from the bear, Chloe's legs went watery, and for a moment, she feared she might pass out.

Ben approached the huge animal. "*Toquet,* it is well."

Chloe really did almost faint when Ben slipped an arm around the bear's neck. The top of the animal's head hit him midchest, giving measure to its mammoth proportions.

"*Keemah,* come," he said. "*Meadro,* let's go."

The bear grunted and dropped back to all fours to amble behind Ben into the cave. Ben opened the large cage and motioned the omnivore inside. When the door was secured, he crouched, reached through the wire, and said, "Sleep. It is good, yes? Sleep, Old One."

Chloe had to sit down before she fell down. She turned in search of a log or a rock—anyplace where she might sit and put her head between her knees. Instead of a log, she saw a cougar. *Methuselah,* she thought. But then she remembered that Ben's old cougar was back at the house, napping before the hearth. That no sooner registered in Chloe's fear-numbed brain than two cougar cubs emerged from the bushes, swatting at each other and tumbling in playful abandon as they raced over to the larger cat. The adult feline rolled onto her side to expose her belly, and the two babies settled in to nurse. The mother cat's green eyes half closed, and she began to purr, content to lie in a puddle of fading sunlight as her cubs suckled.

"Chloe?"

She couldn't drag her gaze from the cougar. She was dreaming, she decided stupidly. That was the only explanation. This couldn't really be happening. She was just having a weird dream.

"I'm sorry the bear gave you such a scare. When I come up to doctor the animals, I like to let Old One out for a little exercise. If not for the infection that set in, a .22 bullet would barely have slowed him down. With the antibiotics, he feels pretty good. If kept penned up, he gets stir crazy. If I'd known you were coming, I would have kept him caged. After being shot, he's a little jumpy, and for now, at least, the cave is his home. He's feeling territorial and protective of his roommates."

Chloe felt a hysterical laugh welling in her throat. She gulped it down. "He could rip that wire open with one slap of his claws. He's wild, isn't he, Ben?"

"Yes, he's wild," he admitted hollowly. "I, um— suppose that strikes you as really strange."

Oh, no. She met people every day who consorted with wild bears.

"I'm weird that way. The animals—they just come. They always have." The tendons that delineated each side of his throat became more pronounced. He looked off into the trees. "I intended to tell you everything last night." He swung his hand. "I swear to God I did. But you were so upset after the thing with Bobby Lee, I decided I should wait a couple of days."

He passed a hand over his eyes. "I guess maybe I was almost glad for the excuse to put it off. I knew there was a big possibility that you'd make tracks after I talked to you."

She couldn't think what to say. He clearly believed she would leave him now. That made no sense to her. She'd long since accepted that he had an incredible gift with animals. Granted, she hadn't realized that the gift extended to full-grown and very wild bears. But having come to know him as she now did, it didn't require a far stretch of imagination for her to accept that.

Go, Nan had told her. *Follow the path he walks, and see where it leads you. Learn the truth now. If it is more than you are prepared to accept, then leave this place. If you linger and go later, you'll take his heart with you.*

The warning had come too late, Chloe realized. She already held his heart in her hands. She saw his love for her in every fleeting expression that crossed his dark face, in the fear that shifted like shadows behind the pain in his eyes.

He hooked his thumbs over the leather belt that he'd recently begun wearing because of her son. Bending his dark head, which he'd had shorn for the same reason, he dug at the earth with his boot heel. Watching him, Chloe's insides twisted and ached, for this was not the same man she'd fallen in love with. Slowly but surely, he'd altered himself, trying to make himself pleasing to her and acceptably normal—so he could fit into her world.

In that moment, it hit Chloe like a fist in her solar plexus that he now looked more like a white man with a good tan than the descendent of a great Shoshone chief. He'd stripped away everything that made him special. Even worse, she'd watched him do it, and God forgive her, she'd been secretly glad. She hadn't wanted her son to mimic an eccentric and become a laughingstock at school.

Tears stung Chloe's eyes, and regret sliced her middle like glass. What had she done to him? And, oh, God, how could she have been so stupid? The sash he no longer wore and the moccasins he'd retired to his closet hadn't been mere articles of clothing to him. They'd been his identity, and she'd let him toss them away. She hadn't understood when he'd failed to leap for joy when he'd been asked to be the 4-H vet. Now she understood all too well. The kids in the stock program were raising animals for auction and eventual slaughter. Taking such a position would go against everything he believed.

Looking at him now, she yearned to have the old Ben back. He didn't need to be accepted in her world. Half the time, she wasn't very fond of it herself. There'd never be a finer man than Ben Longtree for her son to emulate. If Jeremy grew to adulthood, holding fast to the values and convictions that Ben believed in so strongly, he would become an extraordinary individual, a son to make any mother proud.

"I think we need to have a long talk, Ben," she said carefully.

He dug at the dirt again. "I know." He smiled sadly. "I'm just not sure how to start." The tendons along his throat convulsed as he swallowed.

"Have you dreaded talking to me that much?"

"I think *dread* is the wrong word." He thought about it a moment and shrugged. "I was married once. I don't think I've mentioned that. When my ex-wife, Sherry, found out about my gift, she wanted nothing more to do with me. What's to say you won't feel the same way?"

"Oh, Ben." She took a step toward him. "I'm not Sherry. I promise you I won't feel the same way."

He held up a hand. "Don't, please." The words were so faint she almost didn't catch them. "Now that you're here—now that you've seen this much—I've got to tell you the rest, and I'd rather you kept your distance until you've heard me out."

She noticed blood on his forearm. "Were you doing surgery? If I've interrupted, finish up, and I'll wait."

"I was just changing a bandage. A rabbit took a bullet in her haunch. She was lying outside the cave yesterday when I got here. I dug out the slug. Today I cleaned the wound and rewrapped it. In one so small, it's a serious injury. She'll be lame for the rest of her life."

Chloe knotted her hands and took a bracing breath.

A part of her felt silly for even thinking it, but she had to say the words anyway. "Why don't you just heal her?"

He shot her a wary look. "I'm trying."

"No, not with medicine and veterinary skills. Why don't you heal her the way you did me?" She splayed a hand over the upper swell of her left breast. "I would have had a scar. The gouge from Bobby Lee's fingernail was really deep. You took it away with a brush of your knuckles."

His eyes deepened to a stormy blue. For a moment, he just stared at her. Then in a gravelly voice, he asked, "How long have you known?"

Chapter Twenty-three

Chloe could have given Ben the simple answer, that his mother had told her in a roundabout way. But she realized now that she'd begun to suspect long before that. It had just seemed easier and more rational to believe the believable, that Rowdy had miraculously recovered on his own, that her breast had never actually been gouged and the blood on her clothing had come from Bobby Lee's nose, and that her son's breathing problems had gone away simply because he was finally recovering emotionally.

"Oh, Ben," she said shakily. "You're so good at making all the rest of us face our demons. Why can't you face your own?"

His jaw muscle started to throb. Chloe was beyond caring if she made him angry.

"You talked to my son about the essence of a man emerging from its chrysalis. You forgot to tell him that some men hide inside their cocoons all their lives because they're afraid no one will accept them for who and what they really are."

"It's not quite that simple for me."

She was beginning to realize that nothing had ever been simple for this man.

"If I lose you over this, Chloe, I don't think—"

"You aren't going to lose me, not over this or anything else."

"You don't comprehend the magnitude of it." He swung a hand. "What you've seen so far is only the tip of the iceberg."

"Then perhaps it's time to show me the rest, Ben, so I can judge for myself."

Shuffling his feet like a weary old man, he moved past her to sit on a fallen log. Patting the surface, he invited her to join him. Chloe went over to take a seat. He braced his arms on his knees, letting his hands dangle between them, his gaze fixed on the woods.

"To understand me, really understand me, you need to hear it all, I think—from the time I was a kid until now. If I try to start later, it'll be like plucking memories from a bag, and none of it will make sense."

Chloe swallowed to steady her voice. She glanced cautiously at the cougar lying a few feet away, still not quite able to believe it hadn't harmed them. "I've got time to listen."

He angled her a look. "Remember my telling you about my father shooting Bandit?"

"Yes."

"I was twelve then and just beginning to realize the true extent of my power. I had experimented with it a few times—on wounded birds and other small animals. It was pretty heady stuff for a kid that age, being able to heal injuries. I started to think I could fix almost anything with just a touch of my hands." He closed his eyes for a moment. "My father shot Bandit in the head with a high-powered hunting rifle at close range."

Chloe's stomach lurched, but she kept her mouth shut and said nothing.

"Except for my mother and grandfather, I loved

that dog better than I'd ever loved anything, Chloe. He was my faithful friend and confidant. Whenever I was sad, which was most of the time back then because of my father, he was always there for me. When Dad shot him, I didn't think, I just reacted, and I laid my hands on the wound."

Chloe's heart had started to race. "You could heal so serious an injury? A hunting rifle does extensive damage, doesn't it?"

"Extensive, yes. And yes, I healed it." His face had drained of color. "But that was all I could do, heal the torn flesh and tissue, and stop the bleeding. I couldn't replace what had been"—his mouth twisted—"blown away."

"God have mercy."

"That was the catch, don't you see? We can't play God. Afterwards, Bandit was still breathing, but he shouldn't have been. In a way, he was very like Roger, alive but only an empty shell. One side of his head was—just *gone*."

Chloe hugged her waist and rocked forward over her knees, imagining the horror of it. "Oh, Ben, what an awful thing for a child to go through." As she said that, she dimly accepted. All of it. As incredible as it was, she believed every word he was saying.

"I know you think my father was a drunk and flew into rages for no reason. I'll never justify what he did to me—or say it was right—but there was more to it than you know. The power is passed down through the males of the Longtree family. Not all of them have had it, but my grandfather did, and so did my father, who passed it down to me.

"When my dad was young, about twenty years old, his mother got a cancerous brain tumor. My grandfather warned him that some things were best left up to God, but my father couldn't bear to watch her slip away from them, suffering such terrible pain. Toward the end, not even morphine made her comfortable. One afternoon when my grandfather was gone from the house, he healed her."

Chloe knew what was coming next, and for the first time, she felt a measure of pity for Hap Longtree. "Oh, Ben, no. Cancer eats away tissue."

"Exactly. My father healed his mother of the cancer, but he couldn't replace what it had destroyed. She didn't die until I was sixteen years old. He'd turned her into little more than a vegetable. He had to live with what he'd done to her. The agony of it made him turn his back on everything Shoshone from that moment on, and he despised his gift as an evil thing. When he knew for certain that I'd been born with it, too, he did his damnedest to drive it out of me. He hated my rapport with the wild animals. He punished me if he so much as suspected that I was using my gift to heal them. You're right about me hiding inside a chrysalis, Chloe. I learned at a very young age to be secretive and sneak around, using my gift only when I was certain no one might find out. Hiding that side of myself became second nature to me."

Chloe could finally see why. "I understand now. I'm sorry for taunting you that way. I'm so sorry."

"Thank you for that," he said softly, "but you still don't understand. Not really. It was a horrible situation for everyone—my mother, my sister, and me. And in a way, horrible for my father, too, I think. Sometimes love turns into something ugly and injurious and sick. In his determination to spare me the same kind of suffering that he had endured, my father was cruel and unreasonable and sometimes downright vicious. Now that I'm older, I honestly believe he thought he was doing it for my own good—that someday I'd thank him."

He sighed and rubbed the back of his neck. "Anyway, that afternoon after I laid hands on Bandit, he handed me the rifle and said, 'You made the mess; you clean it up.' And he left me to finish him off."

Chloe splayed a hand at her waist, battling back nausea. "He made you shoot your own dog?"

Ben nodded. "It was the hardest thing I'd ever done, but I loved Bandit too much to leave him the way he was.

"After I buried Bandit, I stood over his grave and vowed to him that I'd never use the power again. My father had finally won. I understood in a way I'd never comprehended before that miracles could backfire in horrific ways. From that day forward, I turned my back on my gift, and I never deliberately allowed myself to use it again. Until I met you and Jeremy."

He took a deep breath and slowly exhaled. "You've seen how the animals come to me. Even after I denied my power, they continued to come to the yard if they were hurt, trusting in me to help them. And often they came just to say hello, I guess, drawn to me by something I've never quite understood. My father feared that I might waver in my determination not to use my power again, and in his usual, twisted way, he decided I couldn't be tempted if the animals grew afraid and stopped coming. Of a morning, he'd stand on the back porch and pick them off with a rifle. Sometimes he was still a little drunk from the night before and he'd miss his mark, wounding them instead of killing them. When that happened, I'd wait until he left or wasn't paying me any mind, and I'd go into the woods and try to find his latest victim. It was frustrating and heartbreaking business. I wouldn't use my power, so all I could do was try to help them in more conventional ways. I had no medical knowledge, so I lost more battles than I won."

Finally the pieces of the puzzle began to fall into place for Chloe. "So that's what led you to become a vet."

"Yes." He smiled and shrugged. "I was born to be a healer, Chloe. It's in my bones, I think. Losing more animals than I saved haunted me, and by the time I was fourteen, I dreamed of going to college where I could learn veterinary medicine. The day I turned eighteen, I left the ridge and swore I'd never come back. If life hadn't thrown me so many curveballs, I probably never would have."

Chloe smoothed her hands over her denim-sheathed thighs. "Is that where you met Sherry? At college?"

"Yeah. She was studying to become a vet, too." A distant look came into his eyes again. "She was as dedicated as I was. We got along well and had a lot in common. She was bright and analytical, always hungry to understand the why of everything. To her, the world was a scientific puzzle, and there were no questions that couldn't be answered, no mysteries that couldn't be explained. I guess you could say she didn't have much poetry in her heart." He smiled slightly. "I remember once, we saw a gorgeous sunset, and instead of simply admiring it, the way most people would, she started spouting facts about atmospheric conditions, the angle of the sun, and the reflective properties of cloud masses."

Chloe couldn't imagine Ben being happy with someone like that. As though he heard her thought, he said, "At the time, I thought she was exactly what I needed in my life for balance, a dedicated biologist who rationalized everything. I had cut myself off from the mysticism that my grandfather had drilled into my head, and I was determined never to use my power again. For that reason, I didn't see any point in mentioning it to Sherry. In my mind, it was part of my past, something that would never enter into our relationship.

"I wanted to be normal and live a normal life. Now that I'm older, I realize that most young people have those feelings. For obvious reasons, they were stronger in me. I saw Sherry as my counterweight, someone who would keep me on the straight and narrow, with my feet planted in reality and my mind pondering facts, not wondrous mysteries. She was my guarantee, of sorts, that I'd never be tempted to use my power again. If I'd told her that I could heal with my hands, she would have laughed and told me to find a good shrink."

"Were you happy with her?"

"For a time," he replied. "We graduated together, interned together. We had big dreams of opening our own clinic, and eventually, when we'd saved enough money, we did exactly that. We shared a grand passion." He flicked her a sidelong glance. "Not the kind you're thinking. We were both passionate about veterinary medicine. We celebrated our successes together and comforted each other after the failures. We were happy, if not madly in love, and I thought we'd stay that way. We were even trying to have a child."

"What happened?"

"Me. I'm what happened. We'd had our own clinic for just over three years. We were raking in money, remodeling the kennels and drawing up plans to add on. Life was great, and then in one afternoon, everything went to hell. We had these regulars—a nice old couple named Foster with a Yorkie they worshiped. Every time the dog twitched a whisker wrong, they rushed him in for an exam. I grew really fond of them. They were such nice old people, and still so much in love, always patting each other and holding hands. I used to watch them together and wish Sherry and I could be that way."

He passed a hand over his eyes. "The day everything started going wrong, old Mr. Foster keeled over with a massive coronary. He and his wife were out working in their yard. Tootles, the Yorkie, was with them. When the old man went down, Mrs. Foster called an ambulance, and when the paramedics got there, they didn't think to close the yard gate behind them. Tootles got loose, ran out in the street, and was hit by a passing motorist."

"Oh, *no*."

"When Mrs. Foster brought the dog to us, she was hysterical. Her husband was dead, and Tootles was barely hanging on. Both Sherry and I went right to work, hoping to save him, but when we saw the X rays, we knew there was no hope. The little guy was busted up really bad, inside and out, and we suspected internal injuries. It fell to me to tell Mrs. Foster. Another emergency came in. Sherry left the room, and there I was, facing this poor old lady and trying to think how I was going to tell her that Tootles should be put to sleep."

Chloe braced for what she sensed was coming next.

"I didn't intend to do it," he said softly. "I was standing there with my hand on the dog. You know? I wanted to be anyplace but there. She was crying and begging me to save her pet, saying he was all she had left. And somehow, without consciously releasing the power, it just—happened. Tootles sat up and gave his head a shake, acting like his old self. Mrs. Foster was overjoyed. Right about then, Sherry walked back in. She insisted on X-raying the dog again. I tried to talk her out of it, but she was hell-bent on it. She kept saying, 'This is impossible. You saw the damage.' "

Chloe's mouth had gone as dry as cotton. She was sitting beside a man who could mend broken bones with a touch of his hand? It seemed incredible. And yet she believed. How could she not?

"When Sherry compared the second set of pictures with the first, she kept telling me, 'This isn't possible, Ben. Just *look* at this. It isn't possible.' But the dog was fine." He fell quiet for a moment. "She knew, I think. Even before I talked to her later, I think she knew. There'd been incidents—injured dogs that showed up at the clinic, as if they knew they'd get help there—and raging bulls or frantic horses that immediately grew passive when I approached. Sometimes I caught her looking at me oddly. I'm fairly sure she suspected something. She just refused to believe what her mind was telling her.

"That night when I tried to explain, she was furious that I'd never told her, and she called me a freak," he went on in a rough voice. "Said I belonged in a sideshow. The marriage went downhill from there. She refused to let me touch her, and almost immediately, she started making an inordinate number of professional calls at a horse ranch in the area. Looking back on it now, I think maybe she was attracted to the rancher before the Tootles incident, but she hadn't acted on it. I knew what was happening when she started seeing so much of him, but I turned a blind eye, thinking she might come around if I just gave her some time. It didn't happen."

"I'm sorry, Ben. All I can say is, her loss is my gain."

He turned to study her. "You can still say that, after everything I've just told you? In a very real way, I am a freak, Chloe. Even worse, I may pass it on to my sons. Doesn't that alarm you?"

Chloe chose her words carefully. "You're not a

freak, Ben. You're one of God's special ones. There have been other documented cases of people with healing power. It's a miraculous thing—something extraordinary and wondrous. You speak of it as though it's some kind of curse."

"For me, it has been," he said simply. "For as long as I can remember, having it has made my life hell. Other kids sensed something strange about me." He swung his arm. "I was born and raised here, and I never had a single close friend while I was growing up. Then, when I tried to deny what was inside me, it came out anyway, destroying my adult life.

"Sherry couldn't handle the unexplainable. If it couldn't be analyzed and neatly proved with scientific fact, she refused to acknowledge it as a reality. God didn't exist. Ghosts didn't exist. And there was no such thing as miracles. My gift didn't fit in with her view of the world. I think it terrified her. If she accepted that, believed in that, then what came next? Maybe there really *was* a God, and maybe it really *did* rain frogs sometimes, and maybe, just maybe, she had everything all wrong."

Chloe shifted on the log and braced her hands on the bark. "Some people are like that. If you shove a truth under their noses that doesn't jive with their beliefs, they grow angry and hostile instead of adjusting their thinking."

"That was Sherry, angry and hostile. To make a very long story short, a month after Mr. Foster died, I found a note by the office phone. It was in Sherry's handwriting. An appointment of some kind. I don't know what made me do it, but I dialed the phone number. It was to a local clinic where they primarily performed abortions. I confronted Sherry. She admitted that she was pregnant, and then she told me she was getting rid of it. It couldn't possibly be her lover's, she said. She was three months along. She didn't want to have my child. What if it was a boy? It might turn out like me."

"Oh, Ben."

"I tried to let it go," he said raggedly. "But I knew when she planned to have it done, and the knowing haunted me. The afternoon of the appointment, I drove to the clinic and waited for her to show up. I had to take one last stab at talking her out of it. She arrived with her cowboy. When she saw me, she tried to walk right by me. I grabbed her arm, asking her to reconsider, saying it was a life that she was about to end, our child's life. She said, 'No, it's just tainted tissue, and I don't want it in my body.' We began arguing heatedly. I guess the cowboy was afraid I might strike her. He tapped my shoulder, and when I turned, he sucker punched me. I was already mad. That cinched it. I didn't think. I just swung. I must have caught him off balance because the blow knocked him off his feet. When he fell, he struck his head on a parking curb."

Silence fell between them—an awful, pain-filled silence. She wished she knew the right words to say, but her thoughts remained impossibly tangled. At the forefront of her mind, she kept wondering how Ben must have felt.

"I don't know what came over me, and I've regretted it ever since. I bore him no animosity. He hadn't caused the disintegration of my marriage. But he was dead, Chloe, and no amount of regret could bring him back. I was arrested for manslaughter, and the judge refused to set bail. Sherry left town—went home to her folks, I think. The clinic was left unmanned. By the time I finally got released, I had legal expenses out the yang, and when I tried to reopen the clinic, none of my staff would come back. It was just as well. I got only one client in the month I was open."

"Mrs. Foster?"

He turned a tortured gaze on her. "She remained loyal to the end. Other people wanted nothing to do with a murderer. By the end of the trial, I was bankrupt. And even though I'd been exonerated, the local people still wanted no part of me. It was right about then that my dad got killed. When I came back for the funeral and saw how bad off my mom was, I assumed the responsibility of her care. I had nothing to go back to, and my sister Karen had a job and family over in Medford. It was easier for me to move home."

Chloe stared at the ground, absorbing all that he'd just told her. This man had been so badly hurt—not only by Sherry, but also by his father and countless other people over the years. Was it any wonder that he'd been secretive with her, always holding back and afraid to reveal too much?

A dozen things came to mind that she might say, but in the end, only four words came from her lips. "I love you, Ben."

When he turned to look at her, she added, "Unlike Sherry, I do believe in the unseen, and as impossible as it may sound, I honestly think it may rain frogs sometimes. I also believe in God." She waited a beat to lend emphasis to what she said next. "And I believe in you."

His eyes went bright with unshed tears. Instead of averting his face to hide them, he hooked a hand over the back of her neck and hauled her against him. As his arms closed around her, Chloe could feel him shaking. As always that wonderful feeling that came only from Ben moved through her.

"Are you sure, Chloe? Please, be sure. If I let myself hope, and you change your mind later, it'll half kill me."

She wrapped her arms around his neck and clung to him with all her might. "I'm sure, Ben. I've never been so sure of anything."

"You may feel differently once it all sinks in. You see the cougar and her cubs? Around me, that's an ordinary occurrence. From one moment to the next, you'll never know what animal may wander into the yard."

Recalling the bear's aborted attack, she leaned back to study his face. "Will any of the animals hurt me or Jeremy?"

"No. My mom has come nose-to-nose with every kind of ill-tempered animal imaginable over the years. They'll know you and Jeremy are my family. They'll accept you and trust you, just like the fawn did Jeremy that afternoon."

"That bear didn't trust me."

He gave a laugh. "He'd never seen you before, and you were approaching his den. If I turn him loose now, he won't bother you. He may even amble over for petting."

"I think I'll pass on that experience, at least for today. Tomorrow, maybe."

He pressed his face against her hair. "What if I get you pregnant, and you find out it's a boy? How will you feel about that, Chloe? More important, won't it worry you, knowing what he'll have to go through?"

She kissed him beneath his ear and whispered, "It'll be different for our sons, Ben. They'll have a father who loves them. You can raise them to be proud of who and what they are."

He turned his head to find her mouth. The kiss was deep and long, melting Chloe's bones and making her head spin. Somehow they slipped off the log, locked in each other's arms. As always happened when he touched her, she felt a lovely glow growing within her, and all rational thought was chased from her mind. *Ben.* Oh, how she loved him. As for his gift, there were certain invaluable perks, not the least of which were the jolts of pleasure that ignited her nerve endings with every brush of his hands over her skin and every feather-light touch of his lips.

Later, much later, when he rose over her, Chloe surfaced enough to say, "I want it all, Ben—a wedding ring and vows and a life with you. How do you feel about that?"

"Like I've died and gone to heaven," he whispered.

And then he proceeded to take her to heaven with him.

Afterwards, lying in Ben's arms, Chloe noticed that the sun was setting and the sky was washed with lovely hues of lavender and rose. She shifted onto her back, using the bend of his strong arm to pillow her head. "Look," she whispered. "Isn't that fabulous?"

He joined her in admiring the view. After a moment, he said, "It's particularly fabulous, seeing it with you."

Chloe felt exactly the same way and was disappointed when he stirred and sat up. Reaching for his shirt, he treated her to a mesmerizing display of rippling chest and arm muscles. "You know what a beautiful sunset means, don't you? It'll be dark soon. I'd better finish up in the cave."

Sighing, Chloe stood to dress, laughing when he swatted her bottom to rid it of pine needles. Oddly, she hadn't noticed any discomfort while they'd been making love. When she was with Ben, the rest of the world moved away, and nothing registered in her mind but him.

When they were both decent again, she helped him finish cleaning cages and medicating the animals. All Old One did was grunt when Chloe opened his cage door.

"If you're afraid of him, I can change his water and feed him," Ben offered.

Chloe looked into the bear's beady eyes. "Nope. You said he won't hurt me, and I believe you." Her hands shook as she filled Old One's dish and gave him fresh water. When she started to shut the cage, she remembered how the small animals seemed to need attention almost as much as they did nourishment. She touched a fingertip to the bear's sloped nose. "Guess what you're getting for Christmas, big guy—a bar of Dial soap."

Ben chuckled. "Bears do stink. My ancestors used to rub bear fat in their hair to keep it from getting tangled. My grandfather told me you could smell them coming for a mile."

She wrinkled her nose. "You'll have to keep tangles out of your hair some other way."

"Wearing it short, tangles aren't a problem."

Chloe gave the bear a final pat and closed the cage door. "Yes, well, it'll be long again soon. And tonight while you're asleep, I'm burning that belt and those boots."

He shot her a questioning look.

"My son is old enough to start making his own choices," she informed him. "If he chooses to wear a headband and moccasins because you do, I won't discourage him."

"He'll get teased."

"If it bothers him, he can dress like the other kids. If it doesn't, more power to him."

Ben crouched by the rabbit's cage again. "I was almost four before I realized I was weird."

"Special," she corrected.

"Weird, special—same thing. Until then I thought all kids could walk out into the trees and pet deer or cougars."

Chloe paused in her task. "You were petting cougars at four?" She pressed a hand to her lower abdomen. "Oh, my."

Ben noticed the gesture. "There's always a chance our sons may not have it. Or that we'll have daughters."

"Would you stop referring to your gift as if it's a terrible flaw? And why would I wish a son of ours wouldn't have it?"

"It's not a gift."

"It *is* a gift." Chloe joined him by the rabbit's cage. "You're no longer a twelve-year-old, making emotional decisions, Ben. You're a vet, for heaven's sake. You can surely tell by looking at a wound how serious it is."

"Of course."

"And pretty much know if you have it in your power to fix it. This little bunny, for instance. Did the bullet destroy so much of her hip that you can't heal her?"

"Chloe, I—"

"Just answer me. Can you, or can you not, heal her hip?"

"Probably." At her narrow look, he quickly revised that to, "Most likely."

"Then why don't you do it?"

"Because. It's playing God. I have no right."

"God Himself gave you the gift. I think that gives you the right." She curled a hand over his shoulder. "God doesn't make mistakes. He's given you something incredible—something most of us can't even fathom. You can *heal*, Ben. What does it matter if you can't heal everything? If we're born incapable of running in the Olympics does that mean God doesn't want us to walk?"

"If I screw up, Chloe, I'll have to kill her. I'd rather just let her live her life."

"And live it lame?" She shook her head. "When you have the power to make her complete? There's a learning curve with any talent or gift. Do you think Michelangelo was born great? Of course not. He probably did dozens of awful paintings. Did that make him quit? No, because he realized he had an extraordinary gift, and he just kept working until he perfected it."

"This is different."

"Yes. He replicated life. You're working with the real thing." Chloe drifted her hand over the rabbit's soft fur. "Whether you try to heal her or not, worst-case scenario, she'll be lame. If left to heal this way, she's going to be lame for sure. Why not see what you can do? Nothing lost, nothing gained."

Ben stared solemnly at the tiny rabbit. Chloe could tell he was tempted. He loved the animals so much. What a torment it must be for him, she thought, to see them suffer when he knew he might be able to help them.

"Do I have this right?" Chloe mused aloud. "This rabbit came to you, thinking you could help her?"

He nodded.

Chloe let that hang there for a moment. Then she said, "You really shouldn't disappoint a lady. We get so testy when a man doesn't deliver."

Ben's mouth twitched. He rubbed his palms over his knees, a picture of indecision. He reminded Chloe of someone trying to work up the courage to jump off the high dive. His hands trembled as he laid them over the tiny rabbit. Chloe saw the bunny's pom-pom tail wiggle. Then her nose twitched. Ben sat back on his heel.

"Well?" Chloe said. "Aren't you going to do it?"

"I already did."

Chloe looked back at the rabbit. It just lay there, looking dazed. "Well. Hmm. Maybe you're rusty."

"I'm not rusty. She's drugged." He reached down to remove the blood-soaked dressing, revealing a swath of shaved, pink skin. "I can't replace the fur. It'll just have to grow back."

Chloe stared hard at the shaved place. There was no sign of a wound. "Dear God, it worked."

Ben tossed back his dark head and barked with laughter. "Of course it worked." Then he grabbed her up into his arms. She felt the wetness of his tears trickling down the side of her neck. His big body was taut, and with each breath, he shuddered as if a dozen emotions, too long suppressed, were being released. It hurt, knowing that he wept. He was a strong man, and she knew that the tears didn't come easily. Each time she felt him shudder, she ached for him.

All Chloe knew to do was hold on to Ben with all her might. She couldn't understand him completely, but she looked forward to a lifetime of trying. After several wonderful minutes of just holding each other, she pushed to her feet and went to the badger's cage. "What his problem?"

"He was shot in the leg. He'll be ready to go in another week or so."

"Can't you let him go now?"

Ben scratched beside his nose. "I could, I guess. But I—"

"Then do it." Chloe opened the cage. "Come on, Ben. Fix him."

He walked over, searched her upturned gaze, and grinned. Kneeling beside her, he laid a hand over the badger's bandaged leg. The badger got an odd look on his face. When Ben removed the bandage, the surprised animal sprang to his feet and walked in circles, as if to test his healed limb.

Next came the fawn, then two raccoons. Chloe had never had so much fun. She was seeing miracles happen. When they came to the coyote's cage, Ben shook his head. "This one's tricky, Chloe. There's a bullet lodged next to his spine. He's partially paralyzed. There could be permanent nerve damage."

"Oh, no." She reached inside the cage to touch the animal's shaggy fur. "Poor baby. If he's got nerve damage, you can't help him, can you?"

"No." Ben crouched beside her. "I can't replace what's gone. I learned that long ago. I'm hoping his body will eventually form hard tissue around the slug, preventing it from pressing on the spine. It depends where the lead is lodged. I don't have an X-ray machine to see. I can only guess—and hope."

Chloe saw the sadness in his expression. She laid her hand on his arm. "Hey," she whispered. "You win some, and you lose some in any endeavor. Stay focused on the successes. When you're powerless to heal with your gift, all you can do is fall back on your medical knowledge and do the best you can. Either way, this coyote is lucky to have you in his corner."

Some of the pain left his eyes. Finally he nodded. "That's true. He'd already be dead if I hadn't found him. At least this way, he's got a chance."

"My money's on you," Chloe said. "I'll bet he walks again."

"I hope so."

The next cage held yet another animal that Ben couldn't completely heal, a small rabbit with a missing front foot. "The bullet blew off his toes, and gangrene set in," he explained. "When I found him, he was so far gone that surgery was the only option. I can heal the stump, but I can't replace what's missing. I don't know how well he'll be able to navigate."

"I think he'll do okay," Chloe assured him. "They push off with their hind legs. It may take him a while to perfect his balance, but he'll get there."

Ben hesitated. "If he's slow, he'll be easy prey."

Chloe swallowed and nodded. "Yes, but what happens to him after you've done all you can is out of your hands, Ben. It's that way with all of them, isn't it? Even whole and healthy, they may meet with a bad end once they leave your care."

He nodded and laid his hand over the rabbit's mangled leg. Moments later, Chloe laughed joyously when the rabbit hopped away, managing quite nicely with only three sound feet. "There, you see? He's going to be fine."

As the healed animals filed, one after another, from the cave, Chloe went outside to watch them disappear into the woods. It was almost dark, that blue-gray time of evening right before all trace of sunlight blinked out. Perhaps that was it. She only knew that Ben had a bluish, electrical aura around him when he emerged from the cave behind Old One, much like the glow she'd seen hovering around him that very first night.

She hugged her waist and stared at him, not in fear, but in awe. "The night you came by my house to tell me about Rowdy, you'd healed him only a while before, hadn't you?"

He nodded.

"It does something. There's a nimbus of light around you."

He looked down at himself, then at her. "I was afraid you'd notice it last night when we were making love." He slapped at his jeans, as if the aura could be brushed away. "I don't know what causes it, just that it happens when I use my power." He looked a little sheepish. "I can't seem to stop myself with you. It happens whenever I touch you, whether I want it to or not."

Chloe grinned. "I've noticed. It happened the very first time we met. In the feed store, remember, when you caught me from falling? It wasn't as pronounced as it is now, but I felt it."

"Really?" He frowned thoughtfully, and then he grinned. "When I was very small, my grandfather used to tell me that one day I'd meet the woman who was to be my destiny. Maybe something within me recognized you long before I began to accept it with my mind."

"Maybe so."

She walked toward him. When she drew close, he caught her up in his arms. The contact sent those wonderful little jolts through her, and Chloe joyously embraced the possibility that it would always be this way. It was a lovely thought.

Later that night, after Chloe had tucked Jeremy into bed, and Nan, too, had turned in, Chloe and Ben sat together on the deck to gaze at the starlit sky. Hands linked, they were both slightly tipsy from two glasses of wine.

"Problem," he whispered. "I don't think Jeremy's old enough to handle the truth about me, Chloe."

She smiled dreamily. "How old were you, four? He's old enough. If you're worried that he'll tell someone, don't be. He's very good at keeping secrets. He's never breathed a word to anyone about Methuselah."

Ben sighed. "I just thought—I don't know. It seems a lot to explain to a child."

"Actually, Ben, it's a lot to explain to an adult. Jeremy still believes in Santa Claus."

"Point taken." He hauled in a deep breath and slowly exhaled. "I can heal the animals in front of him, then?"

"Yes. Just explain to him that it's a special gift, and he can tell no one."

"I feel like I've been let out of jail. Free, Chloe. I can't describe how wonderful it feels, and I have you to thank for it."

"You are, without question, the most incredible man I've ever known." She slipped him a teasing look. In the lamplight that came from inside, his face looked too beautiful to be real. "I want to make love again while you're still shimmering."

He chuckled. "The next time I feel a shimmer coming on, I'll let you know."

"You're shimmering right now."

He drew her hand to his mouth and sent tingles shooting clear up her arm.

"Come with me," he whispered. "Let me make you feel that way everywhere."

"Everywhere?"

"Yeah, absolutely everywhere."

Chloe jumped up from her chair. Standing, Ben laughed, swept her up into his arms, and carried her off into the woods. En route, he introduced her to an owl. Chloe had never studied an owl in the wild. She laughed when the bird blinked its eerie golden eyes and said, "Who-who, who-who?"

"Chloe-Chloe," she replied. "Ben-Ben."

He jostled her in his arms and kept walking until he found a grassy spot beneath a towering Ponderosa pine, where he proceeded to make good on his promise to make her tingle everywhere. Occasionally Chloe surfaced enough from the mindless pleasure to dimly notice her surroundings. She wasn't surprised to see an antlered buck standing over them, its horns gleaming like silver branches in the moonlight. Later, she was equally unsurprised to glimpse a raccoon sitting beside them, watching the goings-on with curious, beady eyes, as if he were about to take notes.

It was magical, and afterwards, all parts of Chloe were still humming when Ben gathered her into his arms. "How do you do that?" she asked.

"Do what?"

"Make certain parts of me vibrate that way?"

"I have no idea, but I'm glad you like it." He reared up on an elbow, bent his dark head, and took her bare nipple into his mouth. The shock took Chloe's breath. "Like that, you mean?"

"No, not exactly. Try it again."

He leaned down to send another thrill coursing through her.

"That still isn't exactly it."

He laughed and treated her to a long, slow draw that curled her toes. "Like that?"

"You're getting there," she whispered, and didn't protest when he tried again.

Chloe gave herself up to the magic of it all, trusting him, surrendering all that she was to him, needing him in a way she had never dreamed she might need anyone.

"God, Chloe, I love you," he whispered as he plunged into her. "I love you so much."

Chapter Twenty-four

The following morning at ten, Hattie called to ask if Chloe could come into the shop and finish making out the weekly supply order. It had to be ready by noon, when the driver stopped in to deliver last week's order, and Hattie's husband, Bill, was sick. Hattie wanted to go home, check his blood sugar, and confer with his physician by telephone. The sub who was replacing Chloe had never ordered merchandise.

"I can come in and work the rest of the day if you like," Chloe assured her boss. "I'm feeling much better, and it's really not a problem."

"No," Hattie said firmly. "After what happened, you need this time off. I just need an hour, dear, and I feel bad enough asking you for that."

"I'll drive you," Ben said when Chloe got off the phone.

Chloe pulled off her apron and pushed at her hair. "Ben, this is silly. You can't drive me back and forth every time I go to town."

"I'll drive you," he said stubbornly.

"But, Ben, I—"

He cut her short with a blast of his blue eyes. "You are not—I repeat, *not*—going anywhere alone while that bastard is still running loose."

"He may be running loose for fifty years!" she pointed out.

"Then I'll let you drive half the time to keep up your driving skills."

Chloe giggled at the absurd picture of Ben, gray and palsied, still driving her everywhere because of Bobby Lee Schuck. He smiled, too. "Humor me," he whispered.

"Why do I get this feeling you're going to be an autocratic husband?"

He bent to steal a quick kiss. "I'm Shoshone. What do you expect, a pussycat?" He deepened the kiss, making her head spin. Between nibbles, he said, "The only lip I want from you is this kind."

Chloe placed a hand on his shoulder. "You're dreaming. You'll either learn your place, or we'll quarrel ceaselessly. As for today, a compromise is in order. If you insist on driving me to town, you can make the trip worthwhile by taking me and Jeremy out for lunch when I'm done at the shop."

"Deal."

While Chloe dashed off to change into something more presentable, Ben made a sandwich and sliced some fruit for his mother's midday meal. By the time Chloe emerged, he was ready to go.

While Chloe made out the order at the shop, Ben and Jeremy worked in the back room, straightening and dusting shelves. Chloe managed to finish filling out the order for pickup at noon, and Hattie, beaming with happiness, returned at fifteen minutes past.

"His blood sugar is perfect," she told Chloe. "The long-acting insulin is working marvelously. I think he just ate something that disagreed with him."

Chloe was relieved to hear it.

"Out of here!" Hattie said, waving Chloe away. "Spend the rest of the day with—" She saw Ben coming from the back, and her eyes warmed with approval. "I was going to say with your son, but it would seem you now have another handsome fellow in your life."

"Yes, another handsome fellow," Chloe agreed.

"You've made a wise choice. You won't find a better man than Ben Longtree." The older woman stepped around the counter to hug Jeremy and pat Ben's arm. "Out of here, all of you. It's a beautiful, sunny day. Go find something fun to do."

Ben took them to lunch at the pizza parlor, which served wonderful deli sandwiches. Fascinated by the host of video games in the billiard room, Jeremy sat with them only long enough to grab quick bites of food and beg for more quarters.

"This is amazingly good," Chloe said as she sank her teeth into her vegetarian sub. "You really don't miss meat once you give it up."

Ben gave her a lazy look that transmitted unspoken messages. "You don't have to become a vegetarian to make me happy, Chloe. You have other, very pleasing features."

"Do I?" She grinned. "Like what?"

Ben was about to reply when they heard the screech of brakes outside. Chloe's heart caught, and she hurried over to the window to look out. "Oh, no," she told Ben when she saw a black-and-white border collie lying in a heap at the edge of the road. "Someone's dog has been run over."

Chloe could almost feel the tension that radiated from Ben standing behind her. She gave Jeremy a handful of quarters to keep him entertained, and then she and Ben went to see how badly the animal was hurt. They heard the dog's cries of pain long before they reached the crowd that had gathered around it.

"My poor Sylvester," a woman cried. "The clasp on

his leash broke, and he shot right out in front of that truck, after a cat!"

"I'm sorry, lady," a man said. "I tried to miss him. It happened so fast."

Ben and Chloe pushed through the milling bodies to see a plump, middle-aged woman standing some three feet from the dog. Every time the woman started to approach, she was forced back by a flurry of snapping teeth.

Chloe saw Ben start forward. She grabbed his arm. There were too many people watching. He didn't dare help the animal.

"Does anyone have a gun?" some man asked.

In a place like Jack Pine, that was like asking a deer if it had fleas. Practically everyone in town had a rifle rack in his truck. "My seven magnum should do the job," a burly onlooker replied.

"No!" the woman cried. "I'll take him to the vet. If he can't be helped, I'll have him put down there."

"Lady, he's in agony," the first man said. "We can't pick him up and take him to the vet. He'll bite one of us."

Ben gave Chloe a long look. She searched his beautiful eyes, and knew without his saying a word that he couldn't stand there and do nothing. Given that she'd argued so passionately in favor of using his gift, Chloe refrained from discouraging him now. She loosened her hold on his arm and let him step forward. Even with his black hair cut short, he looked purely Shoshone now that he was once again wearing the headband, sash, and canvas moccasins.

En route to the dog, he touched the weeping woman's shoulder. "I'm a vet," he told her. "Let me see what I can do."

Chloe knew what Ben could do. Her fear was that he might forget himself and do too much before watchful eyes. She pushed forward, making a show of grappling with her purse. "Thank God I have some of that anesthesia stuff!"

Ben threw her a bewildered look. Taking care to keep her hand curled over the canister, Chloe plucked one of Jeremy's asthma inhalers from her purse and handed it to Ben. "It only seems smart to be prepared for an emergency. You don't always have your bag with you."

The confusion cleared from Ben's eyes. His lips twitched as he took the canister Chloe held out to him. "Smart thinking. A dose of this will put him out like a light."

"Stand back, everyone." Chloe turned to face the crowd, positioning herself to give Ben all the privacy she possibly could. "Mr. Longtree is a vet. The situation is under control."

Ben spoke softly to the dog. Just the sound of his voice seemed to calm the animal. He was about to crouch down when a man in the crowd yelled, "Take your spells and incantations back up to your ridge, Longtree! We want no part of your sorcery here in Jack Pine. We're all God-fearing folks."

Outrage filled Chloe. Before she considered the possible consequences, she cried, "Do you see any charms or magic wands? Ben Longtree isn't a sorcerer. He's just a very caring man who has a wonderful way with animals."

The dog quieted as Ben crouched beside it. Chloe saw people's gazes shift curiously from her to the man behind her. She turned to see Ben lightly running his hand down the dog's body. It appeared to her that he'd forgotten all about the canister in his other hand.

"Hurry, Ben," she cried. "Give him a dose of that stuff to ease his pain!"

Ben glanced up with a frown. Then he did as she asked, emitting one blast of mist near the dog's nose. Chloe just hoped asthma medication wouldn't cause an adverse reaction in a canine.

Almost instantly, all the tension slipped from the dog's body. To the unknowing observer, it appeared that the medicinal mist had sedated the poor animal. Only Chloe and Ben knew differently. Ben handed Chloe the canister, and she quickly dropped it back in her purse.

"Stand back!" a deep voice commanded.

Chloe jerked around to see Bobby Lee Schuck, in full deputy regalia, shouldering his way through the crowd, his police-issue revolver in his hand.

"Get out of the way, Longtree!" he ordered.

"No!" the grief-stricken dog owner cried. She threw herself in front of Bobby Lee. "This man's a vet. He may be able to do something."

"The dog's back is broken, lady." Bobby Lee shoved the woman aside. "You're not thinking straight!"

"No, no!" the woman shrieked, stepping back into the line of fire. "Don't you dare pull that trigger."

Bobby Lee grabbed her arm and flung her roughly out of his way. The poor woman tripped and would have fallen but for the quick actions of a man who caught her to his chest. The deputy never spared the woman another glance. He was focused on Ben and the dog, his blue eyes gleaming with an unholy light.

Ben pushed slowly to his feet, placing himself in front of the injured animal. "I think the dog may have a busted hip, Bobby Lee. The injury can be surgically repaired."

"Get out of my way, you lunatic!"

"No, I'm sorry. I won't let you shoot an animal when it's not necessary."

"I'm the law here. Get out of the goddamned way, I said."

Ben just stood there. Bobby Lee aimed the gun at him. Chloe's heart almost stopped. The hatred in Bobby Lee's eyes chilled her.

Ben smiled coldly. "Go ahead. Do it. Some twenty people are watching. They'll rack your ass and send you to prison. The way I see it, Jack Pine will be better off with you deleted from the picture."

Bobby Lee trembled with rage. Chloe saw his hand tighten around the gun, and for an awful moment, she feared he might shoot. "You have no right to interfere with an officer of the law!"

Another man from the crowd stepped forward and moved to stand shoulder-to-shoulder with Ben. "If the poor dog can be saved, I'll be damned if I'll stand aside and watch it be shot."

Another person stepped forward. Then another. Chloe almost clapped and hooted when she saw Lucy Gant join the ranks. The wiry feed-store clerk leveled a finger at the deputy. "Go have yourself a cup of coffee and cool off, Bobby Lee. Ben Longtree's a vet, and he's got a license to practice. If he says this dog can be saved, you're the one interfering where you've got no right. Law and medicine are two different bivouacs."

"Shut up, Lucy!"

"I will not shut up," the small woman shot back. "And you'll mind your mouth, young man. Wearing that badge gives you no right to speak to me that way. I used to wipe your snotty nose."

Faced with a half-dozen people bent on protecting the dog, Bobby Lee wheeled away, cursing with every step. Ben turned back to the injured animal. Curling a gentle hand over the dog's hindquarters, he went perfectly still. Chloe glimpsed a faint shimmer of blue light.

"I don't think anything's actually broken," Ben said over his shoulder. He manipulated the dog's hind legs. Then he flashed a smile at the animal's owner. "His hip is just out of socket, ma'am."

The woman pressed a hand over her heart and moved closer. "Oh, Mr. Longtree, do you really think that's all it is? He was screaming so horribly!"

"You ever had your hip out of socket?"

"No."

"Well, it's extremely painful. You'd scream, too. Thanks to Chloe's having that ether in her purse, he's feeling nothing now." Ben ran his hand over the dog's hip again. "He'll be out of pain for only a few more minutes. Do I have your permission to put his hip back in before he comes around?"

"Right here, you mean?"

Ben nodded. "There's really nothing to it."

"Oh, yes, please try."

Ben curled a hand over the dog's lower spine, grabbed its left rear leg, and appeared to be relocating the animal's hip. "There. He should be as good as new when he wakes up." He leaned around to lift the dog's eyelids. "And just in the nick of time."

The dog lifted its head and blinked.

"Oh, Sylvester," the woman said with a sob of happiness. "Are you all better, dear heart?"

The border collie sprang to its feet with a furious wag of its tail. Instead of rushing to its owner, the animal went to Ben.

"Oh, would you just look?" the woman cried. "He knows you helped him, Dr. Longtree, and he's saying thank you!"

*   *   *

"I'm bored," Ben whispered in Chloe's ear after Jeremy went down for his afternoon nap. "You've swept into my life like a windstorm. I've got no patients left to worry over. My house is clean. The laundry's all done. What the hell is a man supposed to do with his time?"

Chloe batted her lashes, assuming an innocent expression. "Jeez, I don't know. I'm too short to dust the top of that case clock. I guess you could do that."

"No way. Let my ancestors rest in peace."

She giggled as he caught her earlobe between his teeth and growled. "What have you got in mind to cure my problem?"

Chloe glanced around his arm to make sure Nan was focused on her crocheting. "Hmm," she whispered. "I suppose I could take you to the bedroom and give you a body massage. Did I mention I took classes for a while to become a massage therapist?"

"No, you never mentioned that. Come to think of it, I do have a crick."

"In your neck?"

He shook his head.

"Your shoulder?"

His mouth twitched. "Guess again."

"Hmm. Maybe it's my turn to make you tingle," she murmured.

"You're on."

Ben was hauling Chloe behind him up the hall when the doorbell rang. He threw her a worried look. "Uh-oh. Now what?" He smoothed a hand over his hair. "I'll get it. You hide Methuselah. Okay?"

Chloe nodded, went in search of the cat, and found him napping on her bed. She smiled, gave the cougar a loving pat, and stepped back out into the hall, closing the door behind her.

En route to the entryway, she heard Ben say, "What the hell for?"

"I'm sorry, Ben. I know it seems like a strange request."

Chloe recognized Frank Bower's voice. She moved to stand beside Ben in the open doorway. "Chloe," the deputy said by way of greeting.

"Hello, Frank." Chloe's first thought was that Bobby Lee had finally managed to get a search warrant. "What brings you here?"

"You'll remember I told you that Jimmy Suitor went missing, and a hiker found his bloody hat?" At Ben's nod, he went on, "We've been combing the area up behind this place with dogs, and now they're wanting to cross over onto Longtree land. There's a section up there"—he swung a hand to indicate the woods behind him—"where the barbed wire is down. The hounds are baying like they've treed a coon. I was just asking Ben for permission to bring the dogs in to search his property."

Ben considered the request. Finally, he said, "I've got wild creatures that hang around up here, Frank. I allow no hunting, and they feel safe here. I don't want a pack of dogs running loose."

Diablo brushed against Chloe's leg. She rested a hand on the wolf's regal head to let him know everything was okay.

"We'll keep the dogs on leads," Frank assured Ben. "They won't go chasing any of the animals."

Ben nodded. "All right, then. Bring them on."

Frank tipped his hat. "Thanks, Ben. You're welcome to come along, if you like. It is your land."

Ben glanced at Chloe. "I think I'll do that."

Chloe kept a hold on Diablo's collar as Ben left the house. "No, sweetie," she told the wolf. "Somehow I don't think you'd mix very well with a pack of hounds."

Nan came into the entry hall; her eyes were wide with concern. "What's happening?"

Not wishing to alarm the older woman, Chloe pasted on a smile, closed the door, and patted Nan's arm. "Nothing to worry over. A hiker is lost. Some searchers just asked Ben's permission to come onto your land to have a look around."

Chloe had a bad feeling. She couldn't say why. After comforting Nan, she stared out the glass beside the front door. Though the sound was faint, she could hear the frenetic baying of the hounds. Frank was absolutely right; the dogs sounded as if they were hot on the trail of something.

Ben was surprised that a section of his barbed wire fence was down. He had checked the property line just that spring, and all the wire had been taut. Now it lay in a limp heap between two posts. The strands had been snipped.

Disturbed, he turned to follow the searchers into the woods. Sheriff Lang, who'd never made a secret of his dislike for Ben, kept sending him suspicious looks. The dogs strained at their leashes and barked with a whining shrillness. Ben had no idea what might have happened to Jimmy Suitor, and he wanted the young man to be found. He just hoped it wasn't on his land.

About a hundred yards onto Ben's property, they reached the crest of Cinnamon Ridge and started down a steep slope on the east side. Midway in the descent, the hounds came to a dense thicket of manzanita and began circling and sniffing at the earth. The men crouched in a circle around the spot. Beneath bits of rock, pine needles, and branches, the soil had been disturbed. Ben rubbed a pinch of dirt between his fingers. He guessed that the earth had indeed been turned, but not recently, maybe a month or more ago.

The sheriff radioed two deputies parked on a forestry road above the ridge to bring down some shovels. He gave Ben a burning look. "It would appear that we've found Jimmy," he said grimly.

Ben couldn't think what to say. He stared dumbly at the earth, greatly fearing that the sheriff might be right. Dogs didn't behave this way unless they were onto a strong scent.

Twenty minutes later, Ben stood solemnly to one side while three men worked to unearth Jimmy Suitor's remains. Ben felt numb. Something kept tugging at his memory. Finally he glanced downhill, and there, about fifty feet below the thicket, was the log deck that marked his mother's turnaround point when she went for walks. He remembered the morning Nan had come racing back to the house claiming to have seen a man burying a body. *Dear God.* Maybe she actually had.

The diggers finally exposed the decomposing remains of what had once been a healthy young man. Ben stared at the grisly sight in horror. He blinked when the sheriff began reading him his rights.

"Wait a minute," he interrupted. "Wait just a damned minute. You can't believe I had anything—"

"You have the right to remain silent," Lang began again.

Ben couldn't focus on the words. *Dear God.* He was being arrested for the murder of Jimmy Suitor.

"What happened?" the sheriff asked as he slipped the card inscribed with the Miranda rule back into his wallet. "Did Jimmy come onto your land to do a little poaching? It's a serious offense, Ben, but it's not punishable by death. That boy didn't deserve to be bludgeoned."

"I didn't do this. What are you saying, Lang? You've got no proof. I own a large amount of land. Anyone could have buried that body here. What makes you so cocksure it was me?"

Lang drew Ben's arms behind him and cuffed his wrists. "Tell it to your attorney, son."

"You damn well know I will."

Ben craned his neck to look back at the makeshift grave as he was led away. Who had killed Jimmy Suitor, and why? Ben only knew that he was innocent.

Chloe listened in shocked silence as Sheriff Lang informed Nan of her son's arrest. White as a sheet, Nan stood in the open doorway, shaking her head and whispering, "No."

"I'm sorry, Nan," Sheriff Lang said gruffly. He glanced at Chloe. "She shouldn't be left alone. Are you going to be around, or should I notify her daughter?"

Nan cupped a hand over her eyes and began sobbing softly. "This is a mistake, a terrible mistake."

"I'll be available to stay with Mrs. Longtree," Chloe said, "but I'm sure Ben's sister will want to be notified. It might be better if you do that. She doesn't know me, and Nan may be—indisposed."

The sheriff nodded. He patted Nan's frail shoulder. "I'm sorry about this, Nan. Please try to understand, I'm only doing my job."

As the sheriff turned to leave, Chloe followed him out onto the porch. She drew the door shut behind her. "May I speak with Ben for a moment, Sheriff?"

Lang sighed. "I can't let you do that, Chloe. It's against procedure."

Anger burned through her. "What? Do you think

I'm an accomplice or something? I only want to tell him I love him and that I know he's innocent."

"I'm sure he knows that."

Chloe grabbed his shirtsleeve. "Sheriff Lang, please."

The officer scrubbed a hand over his mouth. "Damn it, Chloe. Oh, all right."

Chloe hurried out to the county car, a white Crown Victoria with a county sheriff insignia emblazoned over the doors. Ben sat in the backseat behind a security screen.

"Two minutes," the sheriff told her as he opened the door.

Chloe crouched down, touching a hand to Ben's shoulder. He looked at her with his heart in his eyes. "I swear to you, Chloe, I didn't do it."

"I know, I know. How can you believe I might think you did?"

She leaned in to kiss him. He tugged against the restraints, clearly frustrated that he couldn't embrace her. Chloe put everything she had into the kiss, trying to show him how very much she loved him.

When she drew away, he held her gaze. "Get that scared look off your face," he said. "I'll call my lawyer. He'll have me out before Lang knows what hit him. They have nothing concrete on me. They can question me, but they can't hold me, not legally. As for making anything stick, not a chance. I'm not guilty, and they can't possibly prove I am."

Chloe couldn't help but worry. Ben's reputation in Jack Pine wasn't the best, and the distrust was bound to work against him. "Isn't your lawyer in another town?"

He gave her that slow, lopsided grin that had made her heart skip beats ever since she'd first gotten to know him. "He has a long reach," he whispered.

"Trust me, I'll be home before the day is out. He'll make some phone calls, rattle a few cages, and before you know it, this will all be over."

Sheriff Lang stepped forward. "Time's up, Chloe."

Tears filled Chloe's eyes as she backed away. She was still standing there, long after the vehicle vanished from sight.

Chloe had her hands full when she went back inside the house. Jeremy was awake and crying. Diablo and Methuselah looked at her pathetically, clearly understanding on some level that their master had been taken away. Nan sat at the kitchen table, rocking back and forth, her voice a monotonous chant as she wailed, "I told him. I told him I saw a man burying a body. Why didn't he listen? Why didn't he listen?"

A chill washed over Chloe. She remembered that morning so clearly now. Nan had come home, frantic with fear, saying she'd seen a man burying a dead body, but neither Ben nor Chloe had believed her.

Chloe believed her now. She sat across from Nan and started bombarding her with questions. "The man you saw, Nan, the one burying the body. What did he look like?"

Nan's eyes became unfocused. Chloe realized that the older woman had lost connection with reality. She waited a moment, but when Nan didn't resurface, she finally rose to prepare Jeremy's lunch—anything to keep her hands busy.

"He was tall and dark," Nan suddenly said, as if Chloe had just asked the question.

Chloe swung around to stare at her. "Tall and dark. What else, Nan? Do you remember anything else?"

"He was wearing a ball cap with the bill turned down to shadow his face. And sunglasses. He was wearing sunglasses like Hap used to wear."

"Did you know him?" Chloe asked.

"No," Nan whispered, shaking her head. "At that distance, I couldn't see his face very clearly. During my marriage, I never went to town much, so maybe I've never seen him." Mouth trembling, she fixed Chloe with a pleading look. "My Ben, they've taken my Ben. Oh, God, Chloe. Even if I tell the police what I saw, they aren't going to believe me. Who's going to believe a crazy woman?"

"Oh, Nan, you're not crazy," Chloe soothed.

Nan buried her face in her hands. "I *hate* being like this. You think I don't realize, but I do sometimes. The other morning I couldn't remember my granddaughter's name. I love her so, and for the life of me I couldn't remember her name."

Chloe could barely comprehend how awful that must be for her. She sat back down at the table and tried to think of something to make the other woman feel better. Inspiration finally struck.

"Your illness brought Ben back home," Chloe pointed out. She stared out the window for a moment. "Not just to the ridge, though I know he loves it, but home to who he really is, Nan. If not for your illness, he might still be out there somewhere, denying his heritage and his gift, with no hope of ever finding himself and true happiness."

A hopeful light entered Nan's eyes and she smiled through her tears. "That's true, I guess. He did come back to take care of me."

Chloe gave the older woman's hands a squeeze. "And because he did, he and I met. When you stand back and really look at all those puzzle pieces you call life, sometimes there's a beautiful picture that you can't see when you're standing close. A meaning to it all, as if everything that happens, even illness, may be part of God's plan."

"I never thought of it like that."

Chloe forced a smile, praying that Nan could remain lucid long enough to give her the information she needed. "And it's not true that no one will listen to you. I'm listening. I'm sorry I didn't take you seriously before, but I definitely am now. Is there anything else you can remember about that morning? Anything at all? The slightest detail may help clear Ben of the murder."

"I saw that man carrying the body down the hill and digging the grave."

"Is there anything else you saw?" Chloe asked. "Think very carefully."

Nan stared blankly at the table. Then she cried, "*Yes!* That man—the killer? Right before he dragged the body down the slope, I saw him bury a pack of some kind. Isn't it possible he was burying evidence? The murder weapon, maybe?"

Chloe pushed to her feet and started to pace. "Could you lead me to the spot, do you think? Not to where he buried the body, but to the first hole."

Nan nodded. "What are you thinking about doing?"

Chloe stopped midstep. "Going on an excavation detail. Where does Ben keep the shovel?"

Nan directed Chloe to the garage, then hovered in the doorway, wringing her hands as Chloe searched through the garden tools to get what she needed. "We can't go up there now," Chloe said over her shoulder. "They'll be investigating the crime scene." She locked her hands over the handle of the shovel. "We'll have to wait until they leave. Then we'll sneak up there."

"Isn't it against the law to mess with a crime scene?"

Chloe met Nan's gaze and grinned. "I think so. Do you have a couple of flashlights?"

*   *   *

Refreshed by a two-hour nap taken with Jeremy early that evening, Chloe was ready to go as soon as the summer dusk gave way to darkness. It was only twenty minutes before ten, but it seemed much later as they struck off down the steep driveway, Jeremy walking Methuselah on a leash, and Diablo trailing through the woods around them. Knowing that the wolf was checking for danger made Chloe feel safer. Venturing out into a forest at night would have been spooky under any circumstances. Knowing that they were about to visit the scene of a murder made it even spookier.

Their flashlight beams bobbed on the road in front of them, striking a marked contrast to the darkness all around. Jeremy pressed closer to Chloe. "Mommy, do you b'lieve in ghosts?"

"No, Jeremy, of course not," Chloe said bravely. "Not in bad ghosts, anyway. If they exist, they're just the spirits of people, like us. They wouldn't want to hurt us."

Jeremy seemed reassured. Chloe's hands were sweating so badly, she could barely keep a grip on the shovel. She tapped the tool blade on the earth with every other step, feeling a little like Moses walking with a staff across the desert.

"How far is it, Nan?" she asked, hoping that the older woman didn't trail off mentally as she was so often given to doing.

"About a quarter mile from the house. We'll be there shortly."

Nan angled to the right, taking a rutted dirt road that intersected the graveled driveway. They passed through an impossibly dark stretch where the forest canopy above them blocked out all trace of moonlight.

"This is where the trees are. Remember, I told you how I hid behind the log deck until the man wasn't watching, and then ran to reach the trees where I hoped he wouldn't see me?"

Chloe did remember, and she cursed herself again for not taking Nan seriously. Soon they reached a large clearing. Somehow, even though the area was bathed in faint moonlight, it seemed more ominous than the darkness they'd left behind. Deadfall gleamed silver in the moon-spun shadows, and huge clumps of manzanita in varying shapes and sizes dotted the landscape. Little wonder that Ben had seen no sign of turned earth from the road. There could be a dozen graves on that slope, and no one would spot them.

Chloe shivered, wishing she'd thought to wear a heavier jacket. The night air in such mountainous terrain was chilly.

"Are you warm, Jeremy?"

"Yup," the child whispered. "I'm shaking 'cause I'm kind of scared."

Chloe winced. She could only hope Jeremy wasn't permanently traumatized by his memory of this night. "Don't be scared, sweetie. Diablo's here." She glanced around, but in the darkness, she saw no sign of the wolf. "He's watching out for us. Nothing will harm us with him standing guard."

"There's the log deck," Nan said softly. "One of Hap's harebrained ideas, selling timber. He cut the trees, decked them to dry, and then left them to rot."

Chloe played her light over the pile of old logs. Much farther up the incline, her flashlight beam glanced off the bright yellow crime-scene tape that the sheriff had used to mark the area. "Oh, Nan," Chloe whispered, "you saw Jimmy Suitor's killer. You actually *saw* his killer."

"Of course, I saw his killer. I told you that, didn't I?"

Nan, wearing jeans and sneakers, made fast work

of passing under the tape. Chloe held up the plastic for Jeremy and Methuselah to pass through, then ducked under to follow.

Flashlight bobbing, she hurried to catch up. "Can you remember where you saw him filling in the first hole?"

"Up there someplace," Nan whispered, pointing with her light. "You know, an awful thought just occurred to me."

Chloe's heart leaped. *"What?"* she asked.

"Where's the killer? He isn't in jail. They arrested the wrong man."

Chloe laughed softly—the sound slightly frantic. She gulped, took a deep breath. "Let's not think about that. I doubt he's out here."

"You're right. Only a damned fool would do something this crazy."

Chloe laughed again. The humor eased some of her tension. "Two damned fools. Let's go."

Nan zigzagged back and forth once she had ascended partway up the slope. She examined the earth closely with her flashlight. "It was right up here somewhere," she said several times. "I know it was. I may forget lots of things, but I remember that, plain as can be."

All Chloe saw was bushes, pine needles, and dirt.

"He probably tried to cover the turned earth so it wouldn't be noticeable," Nan mused aloud. "Tap with your toe, Chloe. When you feel softness, give it a hard look. My guess is he strewed pine needles and brush over the spot."

Chloe was busily tapping a section of ground with her shoe when Nan said, "Here! Turned earth. This is right about where I first saw him. This has to be the spot."

Jeremy and Nan stood aside while Chloe put her

back into the digging. The hole grew deep, and Chloe was about to give up when the blade of the shovel finally struck something soft. She tossed away the shovel and went to her knees to carefully brush away the remaining dirt with her hands.

Nan, shining her light into the hole, identified the unearthed object first. "A backpack."

Excitement coursed through Chloe. She carefully unearthed the pack, reminding herself that it might not contain evidence that would clear Ben.

"Why," Nan wondered aloud, "did the killer dig a separate hole for the boy's backpack? I was hoping he'd buried the murder weapon."

Chloe soon discovered the answer to that question. Beneath the backpack was a billy club. Even after being buried for a month, the weapon was still covered with blood and strands of hair. Chloe shuddered so violently when she saw the gory leavings that she almost fell in the hole.

"There you are, Nan. Your murder weapon." She sat back and braced her grimy hands on her thighs. "I don't think we should touch it. We may destroy fingerprints." She reached for her cell phone, which she'd clipped over the waistband of her jeans. "I'll call the sheriff, and we'll wait for someone who knows what he's doing."

"I don't think so," a deep voice said.

Chloe's heart leaped. She knew that voice. The last couple of nights, it had been haunting her dreams.

"Put the phone down," Bobby Lee said. "Try to dial out, and I'll shoot you."

Nan swung her light toward the voice. The beam played over Bobby Lee, who was standing about ten feet uphill from them. Legs braced apart for balance on the slope, he held a rifle angled across the front of his body.

"Shine that light in my face, you old bitch, and I'll nail you right between the eyes. I'm a crack shot. Don't think I can't."

Nan lowered the light so only a faint glow shone over Bobby Lee's dark features. He was smiling. That frightened Chloe more than anything else; the relaxed, amused way he was smiling. She knew in that instant that Ben had been right. Bobby Lee had been shooting the animals. Jimmy Suitor must have made the fatal mistake of coming upon Bobby Lee in the woods.

"You really should have let it be, Chloe," he said matter-of-factly. He glanced at Nan. "I knew you'd seen me that morning, old woman. You being nuts, I hoped no one would believe you, so I let you go. My mistake. Luckily, I got to thinking tonight that you might've seen me burying the club, so I came up to keep an eye on things, just in case. I figured right. Lo and behold, you show up with a shovel." He gestured with the rifle barrel. "Nan, you and the kid, step back. Chloe, put the pack back where it was and get to work. You've got a hole to fill."

"And after? What're you going to do with us, Bobby Lee?"

"I guess there'll be another shooting incident, only this time I'll make the shots fatal. It'll raise a few eyebrows when the casualties are human, of course. No matter. The gun isn't registered. It can't be traced back to me."

Chloe knew Bobby Lee would kill Jeremy without hesitation. She'd seen the madness in his eyes the other night, and she saw it again now.

The rogue deputy looked at Nan and smirked. "You're not half as pretty as my mother was. I never could figure out why my father chose to stay with you when he could have had a beautiful woman like Honey Schuck warming his bed. The booze, I guess.

He was so drunk most of the time, he didn't care about much of anything, including me. He gave my mother five hundred dollars to get an abortion. Did you know about that?"

Nan's quickly indrawn breath was the only sign she gave of her shock.

"That's right. I'm Hap Longtree's son," Bobby Lee went on. "Almost a year older than your precious Ben. By Shoshone law, my mother was Hap's number one wife, and I was the firstborn son. By white men's law, I should have gotten everything. This should be my land, not Ben's. Instead, what did I get? Jack shit, that's what, while Ben got everything, including our father's name."

"So that's why you've always hated him." Chloe moved to put Jeremy behind her. "Not because of anything Ben ever did, but because of what his father did."

"*My* father, goddamn you. *My* father! And you bet your sweet ass that's why I hate him. I spent my whole life trying to make Hap see that I was the better son. I was the one who excelled at sports, the one who got the girls, the one elected student body president. Ben was nothing but an animal-loving weirdo. The only thing he ever outdid me in was grades, and that was only because I was working so hard to shine at other things.

"And what did I get for my trouble? Nothing. My father never acknowledged me. I ran into him on a sidewalk once. He looked dead at me and kept walking like I was so much dirt. Ben was the only one he gave a shit about. Never me."

"And that's Ben's fault?" Chloe saw a flash of silver in the darkness behind Bobby Lee. *Diablo,* she thought. She'd forgotten about the wolf. "It seems to me your anger is directed at the wrong person. Ben had no control over what his father did."

"Ben Longtree took *everything* from me. *Everything!* Now it's my turn to take everything from him. This is perfect. Every damned thing he holds dear, gone with a few pops of a rifle. Even his goddamned cougar. Seeing his face when he finds out—that'll be the best moment of my life."

Chloe saw the flash of silver again. She tensed, praying Bobby Lee wouldn't hear anything behind him. To distract him, she asked, "How does Jimmy Suitor fit into the picture?"

Bobby Lee's feet shifted on the slope. He dug in with a heel to keep from sliding. "Jimmy was a lazy slacker. He got it into his head that he could make a cool ten grand if he came up with information leading to the arrest and conviction of the person shooting the animals. What the hell, right? He liked to camp out, and it beat working. He knew most of the shooting incidents occurred near here, so he stayed in the area, hoping to see something. Unfortunately for him, he was successful in that endeavor."

"So you killed him?"

"I wasn't about to have him destroy my career for ten grand so he could lay around for six months, living off the proceeds. I took care of the problem."

"By bashing his head in with a billy club."

"I should have used a tree limb, but I always kept the club under the driver's seat when I wasn't in uniform, and it was handy. Burying him here was the perfect setup. There were already rumors that Ben had killed two hunters. I knew they'd arrest him on the spot if Jimmy's body was found on his land, and I could make sure the charges stuck by planting evidence to rack him."

Chloe saw Diablo closing in. The wolf slunk low to the ground, his eyes gleaming with feral intent.

"Why the club, though? It could implicate you."

"Trust me. I covered my ass. And I think our little game of twenty questions is over. You're stalling. Put the backpack in the hole, and start filling it in. As enjoyable as this has been, I can't stand around talking all night."

"That billy club can be traced back to you," Chloe pointed out. "You might be smarter to hide it elsewhere."

"They'll never search for it," he said cockily. "They've got their body, and they've got their killer. Besides me, you three are the only ones who'll ever know they've arrested the wrong man, and you won't be doing much talking."

Chloe hated to step away from Jeremy, but she had no choice. She tossed the pack back into the hole. Then, positioning herself to watch Bobby Lee and the wolf creeping up behind him, she began shoveling dirt. When she saw Diablo tense to spring, she tensed as well.

Without so much as a growl of warning, the wolf came up off the ground in a powerful leap. Chloe flung herself sideways, tackling Jeremy to shield him with her body.

"Down, Nan!" she shrieked.

"Arghh!" Bobby Lee cried.

Knocked off balance by the wolf's attack, he fell face-first in the dirt and skidded several feet down the slope with the wolf riding his shoulders. His silence broken, Diablo emitted vicious snarls as he savaged the back of the deputy's neck. The rifle, still gripped loosely in Bobby Lee's hand, struck a rock and went flying.

The instant Chloe saw the gun slide out of Bobby

Lee's reach, she was on her feet. Running, running. The rifle. She had to get to the rifle. She felt as if she were pushing against a headwind. It was like one of those awful nightmares where she tried frantically to hurry and moved like a slug.

When she finally reached the gun, she grabbed it, threw the butt to her shoulder, and flipped off the safety. "Diablo, stop!" she cried. "Diablo, stop!"

To her horror, she saw that the wolf was now at Bobby Lee's throat. Bobby Lee screamed—a horrible, terrified scream—as he pushed frantically at the dog. Chloe didn't care if the deputy died, but she did care about what might happen to Ben's wolf if it killed a man.

"Diablo!" Chloe cried. She remembered the Shoshone words she'd heard Ben use. "*Kiss*, stop! *Suvate*, it's finished."

The words worked like magic. With a low whine, Diablo aborted the attack and backed away. Bobby Lee just lay on his back, head pointed downhill, incredulous gaze fixed on Chloe. She could see blood at his throat, but she didn't believe he was seriously injured.

"Arms above your head," she yelled. "One false move, Bobby Lee, just one, and you're a dead man."

He stretched his arms up. Chloe kept the weapon trained on his face, where she knew she could take a fatal shot. It was her only option. A .22-caliber bullet might not do enough damage to stop him, otherwise.

"Diablo, help me watch him," Chloe added, not entirely sure the wolf would understand, but praying he did. Never taking her eyes from Bobby Lee, she said, "Nan?"

"I'm here."

Relief made Chloe's legs feel weak. With Nan, one never knew. Stress, Chloe had noticed, seemed to worsen the older woman's dementia. "Get my cell phone. Call the sheriff's department." Chloe gave Nan the number. "Tell the dispatcher to get two cars out here, on the double. They have a murderer to come fetch."

Chapter Twenty-five

It seemed like forever before the first sheriff's vehicle arrived. Chloe had sent Nan off into the trees with her son and Methuselah, just in case anything went wrong, and she stood guard over Bobby Lee alone, with only Diablo to lend assistance if the supine man tried something. The wolf positioned himself beside her, his eerie golden eyes fixed on the man, his shoulder pressed against her hip. The contact, Chloe knew, was Diablo's way of reassuring her.

Remembering her terror of the wolf the first time she'd seen him, Chloe could only wonder at herself now. The creature's absolute love for Ben and anyone connected to him had saved their lives tonight.

When the county vehicles turned onto the rutted road leading to the log deck, Diablo moved to stand on the uphill side of Bobby Lee again. Chloe understood. The wolf was positioning himself to defend her, just in case another enemy had arrived. He wanted the advantages of height and gravity.

The police lights sent out spiraling flashes of red, yellow, and blue over the clearing, lending everything a surreal brightness that made Chloe feel dizzy. Diablo snarled when the deputy climbed from the car and started up the slope. Afraid that the wolf might attack,

Chloe searched her numb brain for the word Ben used to tell him all was well.

"Toquet," she said softly.

The wolf sat and stopped growling.

"He going to jump me?" Frank Bower asked.

"No, it's safe."

Frank came up the incline. "For God's sake, Chloe, don't accidentally pull that trigger. You're shaking like a leaf." He reached for the gun. "Come on, honey. I'll take it from here."

Chloe tightened her grip on the weapon and kept it aimed at Bobby Lee's face. She'd had quite enough of trusting the law to take care of her. "No, Frank. You cuff him first."

"I'm not even sure what he's done yet. The dispatcher said something about him being the one who killed Jimmy. That's just plain crazy, Chloe. I know you have reason to dislike Bobby Lee, but he's no killer."

"I'll tell you what's crazy, and that's letting a snake like him be free to spread his poison while you've got a man like Ben locked up. In that hole there, you'll find the weapon used to bash in Suitor's brains. It's Bobby Lee's billy club."

"Don't listen to her, Frank," Bobby Lee whined. "She's crazy about Ben Longtree. She'll say or do anything to save his neck. I didn't kill Jimmy. Use your head, man. Remember that day I came up here with the ODF and W boys? I left the club here accidentally. Forgot all about it until tonight. She planted it, trying to cast the blame on me. You'll find Longtree's prints on it."

"Liar!" Chloe cried. "He tried to kill us! All that stopped him was Ben's wolf."

"Us, who?" Frank asked, scanning the clearing for other people.

"My son and Nan are off in the trees. I sent them away for fear Bobby Lee might try something. Would you please get the cuffs on him? He's dangerous."

"Well, hell." Frank stomped over to the hole and shone his light inside. "All I see is a pack."

"It's in there, Frank. Just take my word for it. I'm so tired of holding this gun, I'm about to drop it. Or accidentally pull the trigger." She smiled sweetly at Bobby Lee. "That'd be fun. Poor, hysterical, *terrified* woman puts a .22 slug dead center between a man's eyes. I'd never spend a night in jail."

That got Frank moving. He rolled Bobby Lee over and cuffed him as he read him his rights. "If you're wrong about this, Chloe, my ass is grass. You don't arrest another deputy without damned good reason." He swung away from the prisoner. "Now, would you lower that darned gun before someone gets hurt?"

All the starch left Chloe's body. She not only lowered the gun but almost dropped it as well. It wasn't a heavy rifle, but aiming it steadily for so long had made her muscles quiver and ache. "The club is there in the hole, just as I said," she assured Frank. "Be careful as you lift the pack not to damage the evidence."

"I guess I know how to do my job, Ms. Evans."

"I'm sorry. From where I've been standing, that hasn't always been glaringly apparent to me."

"That isn't nice."

"I'm not feeling strongly inclined to be nice right now."

Frank pulled his flashlight again and went to kneel next to the fresh mound of dirt. He carefully lifted the pack. Then he swore. "Well, hell, Bobby Lee. That's your billy club, sure as rain. I recognize that gouge on the handle. Why'd you have it in for Jimmy?"

"He didn't," Chloe explained. "Jimmy just got in his way."

The sheriff's vehicle arrived just then in a flurry of dust that rose in the multihued play of lights. Lang strode wearily up the hill, looked in the hole, and asked Bobby Lee the same question Frank had just asked him. Bobby Lee wasn't talking, and Chloe was saving her breath for a more important exchange.

The sheriff bagged the murder weapon and tagged it. Then he handed it off to Frank and approached Chloe. "You and yours all right?"

Fury—pure, unadulterated fury—restored Chloe's flagging energy. She slapped the rifle at the sheriff's chest, almost knocking him back a step. He caught the weapon in his left hand, shoved up the brim of his hat, and gave her a wondering look.

"All right?" she echoed, her voice trembling. "I very seldom get my Irish up, Sheriff Lang, but it's definitely up now."

"I see," he said warily. "Well, I guess I can understand that. You've been through a difficult ordeal."

"A difficult ordeal? That doesn't quite say it. Let's get this conversation off to a good start, shall we? I've got your dick in a crimping iron, and I'm about to turn on the heat."

He blinked. "What?"

"You heard me. You're not dealing with a local girl. I'm big city, and I'm big city pissed off."

He rubbed his jaw. "I think you're beside yourself."

"You've got that right. And all I can say to you is, watch out."

"I don't see what you're mad at me about. I'm not responsible."

"Oh, yes, you are. And you have the *nerve* to ask me if I'm all right and if those I love are all right? Ben Longtree is in jail for a murder he didn't commit!

And why? Not because you found one thread of evidence to pin the crime on him, but because he dares to be different, and you, along with most of the people in this town, distrust anyone who's different. News bulletin: Different isn't necessarily bad."

"I've taken care of that mistake, Chloe."

"Not fast enough to suit me. And you'd better see to it he gets chauffeured home the same way he left, only in the front seat this time."

"I don't usually make people hoof it when they're released from jail. Trust me on that."

"I don't trust you on much of anything."

The sheriff passed a hand over his eyes. "Calm down, Chloe."

"Not likely. In answer to your question, I'm fine, Nan's fine, and so is my son, but it is in no way your doing."

"That's not quite fair."

"Oh, yes, it is. If you'd done your job when you should have done your job, Bobby Lee Schuck would have been behind bars, and this might never have happened. He threatened to kill my little boy the other night. Tonight he almost made good on the promise. The only reason—the one and only reason—I'm standing here telling you about it instead of being stuffed into a body bag is because that wonderful wolf over there came to our rescue and saved our lives. Hell of a note, isn't it? Here you are, an *elected* official, being paid *handsomely* to do a job, and a dog has to do it for you."

"I'm really sorry about that, Chloe."

"About what? That a dog did your job?"

"No, about Bobby Lee being loose. I have to do things by the book."

"Really?" Chloe darted a burning glance at Bobby Lee. "Your book almost got my baby killed." She crossed her arms against the chill of the night breeze that swept down the slope. "You know how I see this, Sheriff Lang? I think you owe me a couple of big ones."

"How's that?"

"Let's start with the fact that I was forced to quit a very good job with excellent benefits and a chance for advancement because one of your deputies tried to rape me."

"Well, now, Chloe. That wasn't really my fault."

"He was on your payroll. He threatened me with my job and tried to force himself on me. When I told you what had happened, you chose to ignore me. In the big city where I hail from, women call that sexual harassment. It leaves a real bad taste in our mouths. And you know what else it does? It really, *really* pisses us off."

"I'm real sorry it happened, Chloe."

"Then," Chloe went on, gaining momentum, "he staged an attempted burglary, gained access to my home, threatened to bash my child's brains in, and would have raped me if I hadn't smashed him over the head with a champagne bottle."

The sheriff winced.

"And what happened when I reported it? Nothing. He never even missed a shift." Chloe nodded. "No two ways around it, you owe me."

"Are you threatening to go the news media with this?"

"Of course not. I'd never do such an underhanded, low-down, totally reprehensible thing to a fine fellow like you. All I'm asking is that you straighten this entire mess up and make things right."

He pursed his lips. "How?"

"By getting Ben Longtree his permits, not just to

cage and treat sick or injured animals, but to turn this hundred sixty acres into a wildlife sanctuary."

Lang swept off his hat and slapped it against his leg. "Hang on, now, Chloe. You gotta know I can't do any such thing. I'm county, not state. I've got nothing to do with those permits and stuff."

"This incident tonight proves beyond a shadow of a doubt, that the good-old-boy system is alive and well in Paulina County. If you'd been doing your job by the *book*, Bobby Lee Schuck would have at least been suspended until you could investigate further. I watch enough cop shows to know that much. Your careless disregard and your refusal to take action were mistakes that could have had tragic consequences for me and everyone I love."

"You are threatening me."

"No, I'm just thinking about turning that crimping iron on."

While he thought about it, Chloe turned the heat up to warm. "Did you know that, on an average, more women vote than men?"

"Shit."

She hadn't been sure of that statistic until he paled at the reminder. "And do you know what gets women steamed faster than anything else? *Men*, taking advantage of some poor, defenseless single mother and putting her in jeopardy when all she's trying to do is the most basic of things—put a roof over her child's head. We don't have any mercy for lawmen who play the game rotten, bending the rules to suit themselves."

He winced. "Sweetheart, you can have your job back."

"I don't want the flipping job back, and don't call me sweetheart."

"What do you want, then?"

"I want you to see to it that Ben gets those permits, which should have been issued to him in the first place. I think Bobby Lee made a few phone calls to see that his applications were denied. I'm asking you to recognize that injustice and fix it. A word dropped here, a recommendation dropped there, and you would be absolutely amazed at how quickly permits are issued."

"How long do I have?"

"A week sounds fair."

"A *week?* I can't get permits issued in a week. Be reasonable."

"I tried reasonable, and that bastard almost put a bullet between my little boy's eyes. A week. If you don't deliver, my story about what *really* happened at your backwoods sheriff's department will be in every newspaper between here and New York City."

Ben had never felt so proud of anyone in all his life as he was of Chloe in that moment. Standing slightly downhill from her and the sheriff, he grinned like a fool as he listened to her give the lawman a piece of her mind. He grinned even more broadly when she went to work on Lang to get wildlife permits issued, posthaste.

Over the last few days, he'd remembered more than once his grandfather's prediction that one day he would meet the woman who was to be his destiny. Now he knew for certain that the old man's words had been prophetic. How fitting that He Who Walks With Mountain Lions should join hands with a vibrant, red-haired little lioness with so much spirit and heart. Watching her, he knew he would always be able to count on her, no matter what, and that she'd not only be there to guard his back when necessary, but also to fight his battles when he was powerless to fight them himself.

That was a good feeling—an absolutely beautiful feeling. He felt like the luckiest man alive. "Chloe?"

She broke off from her rant to look down the slope. Ben wasn't sure if it was incredulity at seeing him that momentarily paralyzed her, or if she was having trouble making him out in the shadows, but for a moment, she just stood there gazing at him with wide, beautiful eyes that reflected the lights flashing behind him. Her hair was a glorious mane of reddish gold that shimmered around her face.

Slowly a smile curved her sweet mouth. "Ben?" She laughed and came running down the hill. After the third step, she launched herself the remainder of the way, trusting him to catch her in his arms. "Ben!" she said again, laughing and crying at once as he hugged her close. "You're home? I thought you were still in jail. How did you—? I don't understand. We were only just now getting this mess unsnarled."

He tightened his arms and lifted her off her feet to swing her in a broad circle. "I told you I'd be home before the day was out. It's not yet midnight. I always keep my promises."

"But how—?"

"My attorney did his job. I told you they had nothing concrete to hold me on. I had just been released and was about to call a cab when Mom phoned in. I hitched a ride with the sheriff since he was coming out here anyway."

He claimed her mouth in a deep kiss. She clung to him so sweetly, her slender body trembling, whether with delayed reaction to the tussle with Bobby Lee or sheer joy, he wasn't sure. He knew only that he held his whole world in his arms. Three years ago when he'd returned to the ridge, he'd believed he had finally come home. Now he understood that home wasn't a place but more a feeling, and the only time he really felt it was when he held this woman in his arms.

"Oh, Ben, I love you," she whispered breathlessly. "I love you so much."

"I know," he replied.

And the wonder of it was, he really did.

Epilogue

Chloe turned the vegetarian shish kebabs on the outside grill. In about ten minutes, the meal would be ready to eat, and Ben was still in his office writing. As much as she loved his beautiful stories—and as grateful as she was for the money he made writing them—this was her day, and she wanted him out there to celebrate with her. She was now officially the new owner of the Christmas Village.

The business would never produce an income that came anywhere close to equaling her husband's, but it was Chloe's, and she loved it. Soon her parents would move to Jack Pine, and they would work in the shop part-time, freeing up Chloe to be the most important of all things, a devoted mother.

"Ben!" she yelled.

Nan turned from the patio table, where she'd just unloaded an armful of condiments. "He said he's almost finished the chapter and will be out in two shakes."

"And we both know what that means. He won't appear for two hours. *Ben!*"

Nan laughed. "You need to put an intercom in his

office. Easier on your vocal cords. Should I bring out the side dishes, do you think? I hate for the salad to wilt while we're waiting for him to surface."

Chloe sighed and shook her head. "Just leave them, I guess. As soon as the kebabs are done, I'll go ferret him out."

Nan sat on one of the lawn chairs to resume reading her novel. Watching her, Chloe tried to recall the last time her mother-in-law had lost contact with reality, and she was pleased to realize that it had been over a month ago, and then only for a short time.

Six months before, Chloe and Ben had noticed a marked improvement of her symptoms, a change that seemed to stem from her constant interaction with Jeremy, who'd become the apple of her eye. The difference in her behavior had prompted them to take her to a specialist in Portland, who, after a series of tests, informed them that Nan's illness had been misdiagnosed. Her dementia had been emotional in origin, the result of living in an abusive situation for over thirty years.

Now that Nan was off all the unnecessary medications and taking only one tablet a day, a sister drug to Prozac, she was a different person. She still loved to crochet, but she did so only late in the evening after Jeremy was in bed. During the early hours, she was far too busy playing with Chloe's son, whom she proudly called her grandson, or baking, which she was once again able to do now that her mind didn't wander so badly. In addition to the change in medication, once a week, she went with Ben to see a counselor, where the two of them were able, at long last, to really talk about the past and put it behind them. Secretly, Chloe believed the sessions were as good for Ben as they were for his mom. Hap Longtree, God have mercy on his tortured soul, was finally being laid to rest.

Nan suddenly glanced up from her book to stare at something in the yard. "Oh, my."

Chloe turned from the grill to look, and for an awful moment, her heart jumped so erratically she feared she was having a heart attack. A young male cougar lay on the lawn, happily taking up half the baby afghan that Chloe had spread over the grass for their daughter, Chelsea. The four-month-old baby was lying on her tummy, gurgling happily, her chubby fist locked over one of the huge cat's ears. While Chloe watched, Chelsea decided to have a taste. The cougar merely cocked its head to accommodate her.

"Oh, dear," Chloe finally found the presence of mind to say.

Nan pushed slowly up from her chair. "This happened with Ben when he was about this age." She flashed Chloe a radiant smile.

Chloe set the barbecue fork aside and went to stand beside her mother-in-law. "I thought only the boys inherited it."

Nan raised her eyebrows. "Apparently not." After a moment, she added, "For several generations, there has been only a handful of girls born into the family. If it has skipped over some of the boys, isn't it possible it could have skipped over a few girls as well?"

Chloe watched her daughter before she nodded. Until now, she'd never really thought that deeply about it, but Nan's theory made perfect sense. Why would a gift, passed down genetically, go only to the males?

Just then Ben stepped out onto the desk. "Surprise!" he yelled.

Chloe almost jumped out of her skin. She whirled

to find her husband and Jeremy standing behind her, looking like helium balloon hawkers at a fair. An array of bright-colored balloons floated above their heads, each emblazoned with, CONGRATULATIONS!

At Chloe's blank look, Jeremy said, "Dad wasn't really working, Mom. We were blowing up balloons. He bought a tank to do it. It's a surprise party!"

Chloe was definitely surprised.

"We got champagne and everything! We're celebrating your special day."

At just that moment, Ben spotted the cougar. He lost his grip on the balloons, and they all shot skyward. Chelsea giggled with delight, her big blue eyes widening as she tried to follow their flight. The huge cat turned to nuzzle her plump little arm, clearly bewildered by the odd noises coming out of her.

"I'll be damned," Ben said softly. He stepped off the deck and went to crouch beside the blanket. After studying his daughter for a moment, he glanced back at Chloe. "I wish Grandfather were here to see this. He always told me it was only the boys who inherited the power."

Nan returned to her chair. Chloe went out onto the lawn to stand beside her husband. Together, they gazed incredulously at Chelsea. "Maybe Isaiah does see," Chloe said softly. At Ben's wondering look, she smiled and crouched down. "I like to think he's up there somewhere, watching. He left so much of himself behind, first in you and now in Chelsea. Surely a part of his spirit lingers to watch over his family."

"I don't know if this is a good idea. The cat probably has fleas." Ben lifted their daughter from the blanket and set her on his knee. Fixing the baby with a scolding look, he said, "And here I thought my biggest worry was going to be when I should let you start wearing lipstick."

Chelsea cooed and batted at her father's strong chin. Ben caught her pudgy fingers between his teeth, which made her coo again. When he left off playing, he looked at Chloe with his heart shining in his eyes. "I guess we have two things to celebrate today—your buying the business and our daughter being blessed with a very special gift."

It didn't escape Chloe's notice that Ben could now refer to his power as a blessing. Yet another thing to celebrate on this beautiful summer day.

Together they stood and returned to the deck, where Jeremy waited with more party balloons. The next two hours passed quickly. After many toasts with the champagne, they enjoyed a family meal alfresco, and then Ben and Chloe tidied up the mess together while Nan held the baby and read *Bandit* to Jeremy.

When the last dish had been rinsed and put in the dishwasher, Chloe sighed and stepped into Ben's arms. He nuzzled her neck and kissed her deeply.

"Come for a walk with me," he whispered.

Chloe glanced worriedly toward the deck. Chloe had never left Nan alone with the baby.

"They'll be fine," he assured her. "We won't go far."

Relenting, Chloe let him usher her from the house. After leaving Nan in charge, they took off into the woods at a leisurely pace, their hands loosely clasped. As they passed the baby afghan still lying in the yard, Chloe saw that the cougar had left.

"I wonder where he went," she said.

Ben smiled and scanned the woods. "Not far, if my

guess is right. He'll probably come back to see her often. That was the way of it with me, anyway."

Chloe took a deep breath of the evening air. The crisp coolness that always descended as the sun went down felt marvelous after the heat of the day. "I love it here," she whispered. "It's strange, in a way, because it's not what I imagined for myself back when I was a girl. I always thought I'd live in the suburbs. Now I can't imagine being anywhere else. I got my heart's desire without ever knowing it was what I wanted."

"I always knew what I wanted."

Chloe glanced up at him. "And what was that?"

He stopped, turned her to stand with her back to him, and hugged her waist. "You," he whispered. "And everything you've brought into my life. Just look, Chloe."

Chloe relaxed against him and did as he said. Below them, she could see patches of the house through the trees. Off to the right stood Ben's newly constructed hospital, where he could now administer to wild creatures without fear of being fined or, even worse, arrested. He had all the necessary permits, and the sign above the log gate at the front of the property read, CINNAMON RIDGE WILDLIFE REFUGE. It seemed fitting, given the fact that Chloe could see several deer grazing at the edge of the back lawn.

"It's wonderful, isn't it?" she whispered.

"You're what's wonderful. You've enriched my life in so many ways, I can't begin to name them."

Chloe turned in his arms. "You've enriched mine, as well. I think we're pretty much even."

He bent to kiss her. The instant their lips touched, Chloe's pulse quickened. When he slipped his hands under her top to feel her bare skin, her nerve endings leaped to life and thrummed with pleasure. It was a feeling she'd come to realize she would never take for granted. There was magic in his hands, and the wonder of that would never dim.

When he swept her up in his embrace and carried her deeper into the woods, she didn't ask where he was taking her. As long as she was in Ben's arms, she was right where she belonged.

For a preview of Catherine Anderson's
next contemporary romance,
coming in December 2003,
read on. . . .

A drumroll reverberated through the bar, punctuating the end of the last band number. The lead country singer hooted into the microphone, the sound of his voice seeming to bounce off the walls. After tipping his Stetson to a pretty lady in red on the dance floor, he smiled and lightly strummed his guitar, leading into the next song, "She'll Leave You with a Smile." The music throbbed in the air, bearing testimony to the state-of-the-art acoustics that made Chaps the most popular country-and-western nightclub in Crystal Falls, Oregon.

Tapping the toe of his boot in time to the base

guitar, Hank Coulter balanced a quarter on his thumb, took careful aim at the empty beer mug at the center of the table, and let fly. Flashing in the spiraling lights, the coin flipped end over end in a high arc, struck the edge of the glass, and bounced away. The other men sitting with Hank laughed, and someone shoved a full mug of beer toward him.

"Chug it down, partner!"

Everyone at the table took up the chant, yelling, "Chug, chug, chug!"

Determined to shake off his bad mood, the result of a quarrel with his older brother Jake that afternoon, Hank laughed and started to drink. The rule of the game was to consume all the beer without coming up for a breath. Foam touched his nose as he gulped. When he slapped the empty mug back down on the table, his buddies cheered. Hank wiped his mouth with his shirtsleeve. Eric Stone, seated to his left, refilled the mug.

"Go again," he ordered, yelling to be heard over the loud music. "Pray for better aim this time, partner, or you'll be drunk off your ass before the pumpkin hour. What's that make now, three?"

"Five," Hank corrected. "And getting drunk won't cut it. I've got plans for later tonight."

"Don't we all?" Eric nudged back his tan Stetson to survey the bar, his brown eyes dancing as he took inventory of the babes. "I've got dibs on that cute little brunette over there."

Hank had noticed the brunette himself and toyed with the thought of hitting on her later. She had a saucy smile and a way of swinging her hips as she danced that warmed a man's blood. "Go for it." Hank winked at his friend. "Maybe you'll get lucky."

Taking the coin that Pete slid toward him, Hank took aim at the glass again. For the life of him, he couldn't recall how he'd gotten talked into tossing quarters. He came to Chaps on weekend nights to have a few laughs, throw back a few beers, and hopefully end the evening with an accommodating female. Getting drunk off his ass at so early an hour was not part of his plan, but now that the competition had commenced, he couldn't very well beg off.

Once again, the quarter missed its mark, this time ricocheting off the glass and rolling out onto the dance floor. Joe Michaels guffawed and dug in his pocket for more change while Hank swilled the contents of the mug.

Seated at a nearby table, Carly Adams watched the cowboy. His hair was the same rich color of the fudge her friend Bess had made the other night. As he leaned his head back to swallow, his throat worked, and his larynx bobbed. Watching the play of muscle drove home to Carly how differently men were made. Her own throat felt soft when she touched it, no muscles in evidence unless she strained to tighten them.

Carly had no idea how old he might be. In his late twenties, possibly, or maybe even older. Accurately judging someone's age took practice, and she'd had precious little opportunity to hone that skill. No matter. Finally, at long last, she could actually *look* at a guy. Little wonder her friends in high school had spent so much time whispering and giggling about boys. Everywhere Carly was soft and full, he was hard and flat, and every place she was smooth, he had interesting bulges.

Carly wasn't sure why she found this particular man so fascinating. Unlike the other cowboys in the bar, most of whom were decked out in flashy, western-style clothing, he wore a plain, wash-worn shirt, a pair of old jeans, and sturdy, no-nonsense boots with badly scuffed toes. Maybe he stood out in the crowd because he wore no hat—or maybe he was just so handsome that he drew the female eye. She honestly couldn't say if he was attractive by societal standards. She only knew she found him intriguing.

Even at a distance of several feet, his deep, rumbling laughter was infectious, and he had a wonderful, lazy way of grinning that made her want to smile. Fortunately for him, the new coin changed his luck, and he got the quarter into the glass with his next toss. Looking relieved to be off the hook, he rocked back on his chair to watch as the next player took his turn.

Carly wanted to study everything about him, and she was glad of this time alone so she could do so without feeling embarrassed. Her friend Bess would tease her, she knew. *Hey, Carly, it's just a guy,* she would say. *Don't stare. People will think something's wrong with you.* News flash. It was difficult for Carly *not* to stare when she was seeing so many things for the first time. Bess tried to understand, but no one who'd been sighted since birth could really grasp what it was like to suddenly have the lights come on after twenty-eight years.

Carly decided that she especially liked the way the man's shoulders and chest filled out his shirt. Every time he moved, muscle rippled and bunched under the cloth. She even liked the way he held himself, his dark head cocked to one side, his attention fixed on the game. His posture was relaxed, his arms elbowed out, his thumbs tucked over a wide leather belt that rode low at his narrow hips. Each time his chair tipped back, a large silver belt buckle flashed at his waist.

He was gorgeous, she decided. In her opinion, anyway, and that was all that really counted. A lovely tingling sensation spread through her as she watched him.

A woman with bright red hair approached his table. Her large green eyes were heavily lined with makeup. When she spoke, the cowboy glanced up, then grinned and pushed to his feet. Before escorting the woman onto the dance floor, he grabbed a dark-colored Stetson from the table and settled it on his head.

Carly couldn't take her eyes off him as he guided the redhead to the center of the dance floor. When he was at a distance, she had trouble keeping him in focus. One moment, she could make out his features, the next he was a blur. When the music started, the pair began dancing, their feet executing the steps so quickly that Carly couldn't follow them. The cowboy swung the woman with an easy strength and polished precision, shifting his hold on her hand so she could duck under his arm. Occasionally, the redhead sidled away to cut circles around him, her boots tapping out a fast tattoo, her denim-sheathed hips and legs moving with seductive grace, her long hair cascading down her back.

A sharp pang of envy moved through Carly. When her eyes healed enough for her to wear makeup, it would take months of practice before she mastered the art of putting it on, and she'd probably never get the hang of styling her curly blond hair. Tonight, Bess had helped Carly get ready, dispensing with her usual ponytail and lending her an outfit to wear, but Carly despaired that she'd ever be able to manage as nicely by herself.

The dance number suddenly ended. The cessation of noise jerked Carly back to the moment. The cowboy caught the redhead in the circle of his arm to lead her off the floor. At the edge of the jostling crowd of dancers, a short lady with dark hair clasped his arm and went up on her tiptoes to whisper something in his ear. He smiled, bent to kiss the redhead's cheek, and returned to the center of the floor with the other woman.

The man's popularity with the ladies answered one of Carly's questions; he must be very good-looking. While waiting for the next number to begin, he chatted with his new partner, listening intently when she spoke, smiling or laughing when she said something amusing.

Suddenly, as though he sensed Carly watching him, he glanced up. Carly was so embarrassed to be caught staring that she wanted to die. Her face went prickly and hot. *Oh, God.* She anxiously scanned the dancers, looking for her friend Bess, who had been line dancing for almost an hour. It was impossible to find her in the milling throng.

Carly stiffened when she saw the dark-haired cowboy walking toward her. Heart pounding, she glanced quickly away, fixing her gaze on her glass of beer, which she'd been nursing all evening. He would move right past her, she assured herself. He'd seen someone he knew at one of the tables behind her. That was all.

From the corner of her eye, she saw him stop beside her chair. At a distance, he hadn't seemed quite so tall. She looked up—and found herself staring into the most beautiful eyes imaginable. They were a deep, clear color that put her in mind of a picture she'd seen a few days ago of a tropical lagoon.

His wide, firm mouth tipped into a grin that deepened the creases in his lean cheeks and flashed strong, white teeth. The burnished cast of his skin emphasized the chiseled sharpness of his features. As straight and sharp as a knife blade, his nose jutted from between thick, dark eyebrows.

"Hi," he said.

Only that, just one simple word. *Hi.* But the deep timbre of his voice made Carly's pulse grow erratic. "Hi," she managed to reply.

A twinkle warmed his eyes. "May I have this dance?" he asked, extending an upturned palm to her.

Carly couldn't think what to say. Finally her brain clicked into gear. "Oh, no—I can't. Really. I'm sorry."

He hooked his thumbs over his belt and glanced over his shoulder. "You here with someone?"

"A friend. She's line dancing."

The corners of his mouth twitched. "Girlfriends don't count. I meant a guy."

"Oh." Carly felt stupid. "I, um—no, I'm not with a guy."

He extended his hand to her again. "Well, then? Come polish my belt buckle for a while."

Carly dropped her gaze to the silver oval at his waist. "Pardon me?"

He chuckled, turned a chair out from the table, and straddled it to sit down. Nudging back his hat, he gave her a slow once-over, ending with a long look at her white running shoes. "Is this, by any chance, your first time at a country-western bar?"

"Yes." Carly decided he was a little drunk. Considering the quantity of beer she'd seen him consume, she supposed that was to be expected. "My friend Bess loves to line dance. I came along to watch."

"That explains the language barrier, I guess. Sort of like visiting a foreign country, isn't it."

Carly nodded. "It's interesting. I've always been told that men are supposed to remove their hats inside a building. Here, everyone wears them."

He feigned an expression of horror. "Take off our hats? Bite your tongue. Cowboys can't dance without their Stetsons. They'd feel half dressed and lose their balance. Most of us only take them off when we sleep, and even then, we hang them on the bedpost, in case of emergency."

Carly laughed. She liked this man, she decided. He wasn't afraid to poke fun at himself.

"When a cowboy asks you to polish his belt buckle, it's just another way of asking you to dance," he explained. "Same goes if he invites you to rub bellies with him for a while."

Carly's cheeks went warm. "I see."

He arched a dark eyebrow. "So, what d'ya say?"

"I can't." She threw a panicked glance at the dancers. All her life, she had prided herself on never being afraid to try new things, but she wasn't ready for the Texas two-step. "I don't know how. It looks complicated, and I was born with two left feet."

"Country-western dancing isn't as complicated as it looks." He lifted his hands, the gesture implying that her lack of experience wasn't a stumbling block. "Not to worry. I know enough about boot scootin' for both of us."

Before Carly could guess what he meant to do, he grasped her wrist, swung off the chair, and drew her to her feet. Hooking an arm around her waist, he steered her through the dancers to the center of the floor. When he turned her to face him, he winked and grinned. "Don't be so nervous. Everyone out here had to learn how at one time or another. It's really not all that different from regular dancing."

Carly had never danced in her life, regular or otherwise. People were bouncing around everywhere she looked, ladies twirling under the uplifted arms of their partners and executing fancy footwork. Her body broke out in a clammy sweat.

"I really, *really* can't do this."

He took her right hand and slipped his other arm

around her waist. "Sure you can. Stop watching everyone else and concentrate on me." He smiled when she looked up at him. "There's a girl." He started to move, a slow, swaying motion that wasn't difficult to follow. "We'll keep it simple."

"Simple's good," she agreed breathlessly.

He ran his gaze slowly over her face. "Damn, you're beautiful. I suppose you hear that from men all the time."

No one had ever told her that. Carly stared up at him, feeling as if she'd somehow fallen asleep and slipped into a lovely dream. He thought she was beautiful? Even if he was lying, she wanted to believe him—just for this little while.

He swung her in a wide arc, and she stepped on his boot. "Oh, I'm *sorry!* Did I hurt your toes?"

He laughed and tightened his arm around her waist. "Don't worry about it, darlin'. I walk on 'em all the time. Let's try it again, the other direction this time." He dipped to the left, pressing his thigh against her right leg to make her step back. "There, you see? Easy as pie." He trailed his gaze over her face again. "Where have you been hiding all my life? When I spotted you awhile ago, my heart damned near stopped beating. You looked like an angel, sitting there."

An angel? Carly knew better, but it was a lovely compliment, anyway. "I just moved to the area."

"Ah. That explains why I haven't seen you before. Where you from?"

"Portland."

"Uh-oh, a city gal. No wonder we speak a different language. Right turn," he inserted, cuing her with his body before executing the swing. Then, "You've got the most gorgeous blue eyes I've ever seen. I swear, they were shining at me like beacons from clear across the room. Tinted contacts, right? No eyes that blue can be natural."

While pursuing her bachelor degree, Carly had heard men in college-campus bars say things like this to her friends. Pickup lines, nothing more. He was hitting on her. And, oh, God, it felt wonderful. All her adult life, she'd sat on the sidelines, listening to life happening all around her and wishing that someone would notice *her*. Now, at long last, someone finally had. Even better, he was handsome and charming. She felt like a princess in one of the fairy tales her mother had read to her years ago.

"Nope, no contacts," she assured him with a tinkling laugh. She fluttered her lashes. "These are the real McCoy."

"You're kidding. Damn. Is this my lucky night, or what? You're the most beautiful woman in the place."

Carly knew he was only telling her what he thought she wanted to hear. And he was right. It *was* what she wanted to hear. *My turn.* A reckless, dizzying excitement coursed through her. Just this once, she wouldn't analyze or question. She had waited a lifetime for this moment, and she meant to enjoy every delicious millisecond.